EXIT
STRATEGY

I0654372

OMAR SHABKA

BERKELEY HOUSE PRESS LTD.

Published by Berkeley House Press Ltd.
London, United Kingdom

ISBN: 978-0-9929103-1-0

WWW.GETEXITSTRATEGY.COM

@GETEXITSTRATEGY

FB.COM/GETEXITSTRATEGY

ABOUT THE AUTHOR

Omar Shabka moved with his wife and infant son from Washington, DC, to London, in 1996, to chase the dotcom dream. He started out building online communities in a leaky basement in Fulham and has been working in the cloud ever since.

Exit Strategy is his first novel.

in   UK.LINKEDIN.COM/IN/OMARSHABKA/

t   @OHSHABKA

f   FB.COM/OSHABKA

DEDICATION

To Gwen & Zak

ACKNOWLEDGMENTS

Wife and child, life and home.
Parents, who showed me the world.
Brother, who is always there.
Charlie the cat, who wakes me at dawn.

The ESBC. Ten years, still kicking.
The Chairman, who is always up for a tea break.
Maria White for patience and perseverance.
The Santa Maria Book Club for a night to remember, and
our hosts, whose generosity knows no bounds.
Friends who voted, read, and supported.

Alabama 3, for such fine music.

The GET collective, for ideas, effort and safety checks.

And a big thanks in advance to everyone who adds to the
GET Exit Strategy metafiction mix.

Apologies to anyone I missed.

CHAPTER 1

A light rain shimmered red, white and blue in the flashing lights of the emergency services, whorling with the smoke and steam rising from the burned-out flat. A small crowd had gathered just beyond the police cordon, attention fixed on the blackened third floor windows, a fine mist settling on their upturned faces.

"They found a body ... young woman," said one bystander. "Murdered," said another. "A struggle ... police asking questions."

A young man hung back from the crowd, tears and rain streaking his face. From the blur of despair, his subconscious heard his name, triggering base instincts of fear and flight. Shoving his hands deep in his pockets, he jerked his anorak hood tight to hide his face, turned and walked away, miles and miles, until he was alone on a dark country lane.

By now, the rain was coming down hard. He took shelter under a railroad trellis. Climbing the steep, gravelly embankment, hands and feet scrabbling for purchase, he found a ledge beneath the Victorian ironwork, hidden, dry, alone. He curled up and gave free rein to his despair, letting it erupt in a deluge of tears, his animal wailing echoing eerily in the pitch black arch.

Hours passed. The rain stopped. With forced effort, he unwound his lanky frame, climbed down from his hiding place and began the long journey home, his feet guiding him blindly until he stood once again outside the soot-streaked windows of his flat.

The emergency services, the crowd, were gone, leaving only a deathly silence. He slipped his key in the lock. The loud click made his heart skip. Inside, he navigated the creaky staircase to the third floor, Flat 3G.

The hallway reeked of damp, charred destruction. The door was still warm to touch. Quietly as he could, he pushed it open and ducked through the police tape. The frame was splintered at the latch but not the deadbolt. He threw it, locking himself in.

He cast the faint beam of his penlight around the flat, felt a spasm of grief as it passed over the chalk outline on the kitchen floor. *Michelle* ... His throat clenched, choking back the pain, the scream only in his head. Turning away from the ghostly outline, his feet squished on the soot-soaked carpet as he made his way down the hallway to the bedroom. Her closet. He held her sweater to his face, breathed deep, desperate for one last scent, one last living memory of her. But she was gone. Only the acrid taste of death remained.

Flashing lights brought him to his senses. He noticed the holdall in his hand, half full. He edged over and peered out the broken window. Two policemen climbing out of a patrol car, heavy Maglites aimed at the front door, approaching, slowly, carefully. Murder, he remembered. They were looking for him.

He turned, the holdall nearly knocking over a small table. The chess board, the game they had been playing only hours earlier. She had beaten him. Again. No one else could. He picked up her White Queen, swung it gently, knocking down his King. Checkmate.

He pocketed the Queen and ran back to the bedroom, the sound of heavy boots pounding a sense of urgency. His computer was charred, useless, a melted mass of plastic. The metal box of floppy disks looked more hopeful. He stuffed it into his holdall and climbed out the window just as he heard wood cracking, the door being rammed open.

Down the fire escape, he hit the ground running, never stopped, never looked back.

CHAPTER 2

Once servants' quarters, the fifth floor of Berkeley House was now the heart of Daniel Logan's empire. Offices to the north, penthouse apartment to the south, it was Bauhaus clean, cocktail high-tech, the art modern, furniture linear and brutal. This was in stark contrast to the lower floors where a meticulous restoration had transformed the Georgian mansion into an exclusive members club that catered to London's corporate elite.

Logan adjusted his tie and shot his cuffs, studying himself in the full-length mirror. He flicked an invisible speck of dust from his lapel and patted his thinning light blond hair, swept back, slick, with detached approval. The cultivated look of manicured success hung well on him.

With a practiced turn of the wrist, he checked his Patek Philippe, examined himself once more in the mirror, then left the bedroom.

With time to spare, he made an espresso and indulged in a moment of solitude on the veranda, taking in the clear skies across Mayfair's rooftops, Green Park, Buckingham Palace. Below, Berkeley Square was still waking, a discordant orchestra warming up, each instrument intent on its own tune—the electric whine of the milk float, the throaty tock

4

tock of a taxi, hydraulic groans of a refuse lorry—every city its own urban symphony.

Logan turned his gaze inward to the Jackson Pollock displayed on a distant wall, pride of place. He thumbed his smartphone and the wall transformed, opaque to transparent, offering a clear view through to his office. He pressed another button. Through the next wall, he could see Adam Lazarenko seated at the conference table, preparing his morning briefing.

A third button slid the wall open. Logan stepped through and the wall slid silently back into place behind him. On this side, the Pollock was replaced by a Rauschenberg. He willed himself to appreciate their beauty—the two paintings, the nanotech smart glass technology, courtesy of one of his Cambridge University start-ups—but it all fell flat, anodyne, abstract.

He had been like this for months. With a sigh, he sat down, put his feet up on his desk and watched Adam Lazarenko through the one-way wall. People were starting to notice, none more so than Lazarenko. Natasha too. Cold was one thing, vacuum another—weakness. He needed to shake this, whatever it was.

At precisely 7:30 a.m., he entered the main room of his office. Like his apartment, it was a vast open space, minimalist yet expensive. To the left were two lounge areas separated by a wide expanse of bleached ash floor. Lazarenko was seated to the right at the long, mahogany conference table polished to a mirror shine. He glanced up, nodded acknowledgement and led with their headline project.

"T-Mobile's a done deal. They signed last night. You were right. It is Orange. Deutsche likes the idea of merging with another national carrier. A marriage of equals. Vodafone upped the ante, but ..."

"When's the announcement? Today?" asked Logan.

"Yes." Lazarenko thumbed the remote.

On the center screen, the clock ticked off the seconds. It gave an odd sense of vertigo when the camera zoomed down on a private corner in the Africa Room. Three sharply cut Germans, Hugo Boss, short, clipped hair, Italian shoes, enjoying cognac and cigars. Lazarenko thumbed the volume, filling the room with their familiar voices.

Logan listened, leaving the translated transcript untouched on the table. A few minutes in, he stifled a yawn, caught the puzzled look on Lazarenko's face, and responded with a menacing glare. Lazarenko's lanky frame tensed with fear, twitching, eyes darting nervously here there everywhere. Anywhere but Logan's.

No, I thought not. sighed Logan. Signaling 'Pause,' he dialed on the Polycom.

"Dump Rio Tinto just before closing bell."

"Yes, Mr. ...," the reply was cut short as Logan hung up.

With an impatient wave, he signaled 'Play'.

The vignette rolled on, seconds counting to minutes. Lazarenko was right—the project had played out, time to exit. Easy money—six months, £3-4 million, low risk. Too easy—predictable, no challenge, no satisfaction, boring.

Logan forced a smile as he leaned back, trying in vain to squeeze even a hint of sweetness from his victory. But he felt nothing, only cold, clinical appreciation, like when he looked at the Pollock.

With a heavy sigh, he activated his holographic keyboard. Tap, tap, tapping a muffled tattoo on the polished mahogany tabletop, his fingers fired electronic tracers into the ether, setting in motion a complex chain of events, executing the end game. Around the world, across the telecoms ecosystem, from gold mines to ringtones, rumors were milled, memos leaked, legislators lobbied (one blackmailed), stocks traded long and short—dozens of financial transactions, none large enough to draw attention, all seemingly unrelated. Collectively, they would add several figures to Logan's already substantial net worth.

He hit ENTER, his last instruction a post-dated Sell order for Nokia. Their beleaguered share price would bask momentarily in the reflected sunshine of T-Mobile's announcement, aided by rumors of an exclusive deal for their next generation smartphone, a fabricated report leaked to a respected industry blog, the source seemingly unimpeachable.

"What's next?" he asked, yawning, not attempting to mask his boredom.

Once upon a time, Logan had been motivated by money, the early millions marking distance from a lifetime—generations—of poverty. With five million in the bank, he came to London, bought Berkeley House, and the zeroes started flooding in.

The club was a goldmine, its discreet ambience shrouded in an invisible web of light, binary pulses down gossamer strands of fiber optic, sensors sifting the air, trapping shards of information, insights, secrets. From the panopticon of his office, Logan saw all, heard all, and recorded all in high-def digital format.

He had spent years cultivating his public profile, polishing the veneer of respectability, easing his way into the Establishment. His portfolio reflected his social aspirations—a boutique investment bank, a small law firm, a property development concern, an impressive collection of Cambridge start-ups, a clutch of pet charities, Berkeley House. He had all the trappings, too ... private helicopter to a Georgian pile in Shropshire, chateau and vineyard in the Dordogne, chauffeured Bentley, Savile Row suits, an enviable wine cellar.

The real scale of his fortune lay in the murky depths of offshore accounts and shell companies, its mass growing silently, steadily, fed by the many, many secrets of Berkeley House. He was never greedy. No need. A little here, a little there. Berkeley House offered an endless supply of fresh opportunities and he had a wide repertoire of strategies for exploiting them, all now well-worn, the wins virtually guaranteed. His projects no longer offered any real sense of victory, just money, money, more money. His game was rigged, and he had grown bored with it.

He had tried 'doing Good,' a bit of *pro bono* for the soul. But that fell flat, too, leaving him with nothing but scorn and disdain for the hapless and helpless. In frustration, he had lashed out the last time, destroying the very man whose business he had just rescued, losing £3 million in the process. The money did not matter. The ennui he could not escape.

Lazarenko continued with the briefing, working his way screen by screen across the video wall—a bank merger, a large outsourcing company closing in on a £100m NHS contract, financial irregularities at a FTSE 100 company, and so on. All told, Logan had a dozen or so projects active at any one time, each worth £2-5 million, mostly tax-free.

Of the current lot, only XTracta, the FTSE 100 with the cooked books, gratified. And that was only fleeting, a minor act of revenge on a man he had once crossed swords with. A leak, a scandal, disgrace. But it was an assassination, not a duel, and there was no challenge in that.

Lazarenko's voice droned through the agenda, Logan absently scanning the daily log, sifting for new threads, patterns, intrigues—*God forbid something challenging*. The thrill was gone.

"What's this?" Logan pointed at the page.

Reading upside down then thumbing his own screen, Lazarenko replied, "Richard Ashton and Gary Tate."

"I can read," said Logan. "What I want to know is why they were here so long. Ashton arrives at 5:00 pm, Tate at 5:45. They don't leave until midnight. Not their usual pattern." Logan knew every member of his private club intimately—their names, faces, professions, habits, birthdays, predilections, weaknesses.

Lazarenko was caught off guard but recovered quickly, bringing up the main camera hidden in the ornate rosette directly above the nook where the two men were sitting. It was not on his shortlist of new prospects. He hoped he had not missed the blindingly obvious.

Referencing the arrivals log, he cued the video with practiced ease to the moment when two subjects were settling into over-stuffed leather sofas and ordering drinks.

"Who's the guest?" Logan's tone was abrupt.

Lazarenko referred to the arrivals log, "Mark Haddad."

"I've heard that name before," said Logan, his voice softening to a whisper as he leaned forward, elbows resting on the polished table, sensing intrigue. He waved a hand impatiently, *more volume!*

They listened to minutes of banal conversation, the idle banter of old friends catching up. Logan watched the screen intently, transfixed, senses tingling.

"... You want to quit your job" ... "Yes" ... "About time ... "You don't know the half of it." ... "What'd they do this time?" ... "Shafted Duncan. Stole his idea. Screwed his company ... PaySense ... Max Greenberg's an asshole ..."

Lazarenko felt Logan's smile before he saw it. He had no idea why, but the conversation clearly interested him.

"Open a new file." Logan's instruction was spoken so quietly Lazarenko almost missed it. "Have the brief on my desk by noon."

Lazarenko nodded and made to continue with the agenda, but Logan waved it off. "Leave it. Focus on this. PaySense and this fellow, Haddad. I want to know everything about them. And I want a full transcript."

"But ..."

"Yes, of course," interrupted Logan. The transcript would take time. "Have that on my desk by tomorrow morning. The background report today, by noon." Meeting over.

Alone, Logan reset the video to the beginning. Reading the timestamp, he called up different cameras, tracking Rick Ashton and Mark Haddad back to the moment they arrived at Berkeley House. He found the frame he was looking for, a full profile of Haddad. He dragged the image to the side and expanded it to fill a 2x2 grid of screens, the face staring back at him larger than life.

Over the years, he had learned to trust his instincts, nurtured an uncanny ability to get inside the minds of his opponents. That was always his starting point, not the game itself—he played people not games. This time, he had no idea what the game would be, only that there was one to be had.

Haddad seemed affable enough, though beneath the easy smile, Logan sensed a sharp intelligence. Conjecture, to be sure, an assumption based purely on a few minutes of video footage, a frozen frame. But he sensed something deeper, more complex, at play in the mind of the man he was studying.

He stared at the frozen image, minutes ticking by, the silence interrupted only by an occasional whispered comment to the empty room. They were about the same height, 6' 2", but the resemblance ended there. Northern European vs. Mediterranean. Where Logan's hair was blonde, thin, receding, Haddad's was enviably thick, black, long, just shy of a ponytail. His clothes hung well on his muscular frame, off the rack but well chosen. The style was not to Logan's taste— he did not even own a pair of jeans. But Haddad took care, something else they had in common.

Glancing at his watch, Logan called his secretary on the Polycom.

"Yes, Daniel," replied Natasha Kurkova, her words dripping with suggestion.

"Hold my calls. I don't want to be disturbed until my 12 o'clock with Adam."

"Of course."

Logan hung up, ignoring the disappointed pout on the other end of the line. He strolled into the kitchen and prepared another espresso, all the while focusing on Haddad. Back at the table, he settled in, remote in hand, cued the video tape to Mon 07 Sept 16:52, and spoke to the room, "Max Greenberg, my old *friend*."

CHAPTER 3

Mark Haddad was back, fresh from two weeks in Greece recreating, recharging, reprioritizing. Monday morning, he gave up his sandals and rejoined the daily commute into central London, like a trail horse, millions more like him, plodding their well-worn paths, door to train to door. This time he found the routine cathartic, a perfect prelude to the day ahead, to all future days, droning along at work on autopilot.

He had taken a lot of baggage, pent-up rage, on holiday. It had started building in the pressurized confines of the air cabin soon after takeoff. He spent the first few days venting, sweating it out on the beach volleyball court, swimming, running, digging a great big hole for the kids to play in. Sport had always been his therapy, intense, physical, focused, immersive, mental.

Before Greece—more precisely, up to the Thursday before he flew out—he had been facing a dilemma; a nice one, to be fair. On the one hand, he was locked in to Adware. After five long years, his golden handcuffs were shining bright with the promise of an IPO just around the corner. Running the numbers, Mark's stock options looked like they would net a solid seven figures after taxes. Sterling. On the other hand, he had Dynamo, a skunk works project he had kicked off two years earlier with a couple of mates. They had finished writing the code just hours before he left for Greece and it was now ready for market. Therein lay the quandary.

Rather, it would have been if he had not hit Print late on his last day at the office: some last-minute work, a proposal to read on the plane. He had stuffed the thick wad of papers in his bag without a second glance, another tick on his long pre-flight to-do list.

Then, on Sunday, the plane at cruising altitude, the kids absorbed in their seatback videos, Susan a fashion mag, Mark fished out the proposal. As he flipped through it, he realized he had accidentally picked up another document from the printer, the company share register, marked Classified.

Curious, he began flipping through it, anger, shock, disbelief mounting with every turn of the page. He ordered a Bloody Mary, went back to the beginning and started over. The company share capital had been restructured, rendering his stock options—all staff options—worthless, his handcuffs fashioned of Fool's Gold.

He had said nothing to Susan. Let her enjoy her holiday. She had sensed his tension but did not press. She knew he would bring it up when he was ready, not before.

From Waterloo Station, Mark hopped on the Tube to Tottenham Court Road, the office a short walk from there. The first thing was a catch-up with his team. His deputy, Marie Atherton, had run a tight ship while he was away, closing two deals against the odds during the August doldrums. Next was email. A slash and burn through 969 emails filled his time until lunch with Peter Palmer.

It was a warm, sunny day, so they ate al fresco at Gordon's Wine Bar. Syncopated riffs of an afternoon jazz quartet drifted on the breeze from neighboring Victoria Embankment Gardens.

"So? Good holiday?" asked Peter.

Mark skipped the chit chat, dove right in about his worthless stock options, the changes to the share register.

"You seem to be taking it in stride," said Peter.

"On the plus side, now there's nothing holding me back, nothing to lose. Full steam ahead with Dynamo! I'm ready to hand in my notice as soon as we raise the money."

After his initial anger passed, he had found it easy to shift focus, align his priorities with Dynamo, and plan to exit Adware sooner rather than later. There was nothing left to hang around for. "I should've seen it coming. It's exactly the kind of thing Max would do. So now I know. Besides, we'll make a hell of a lot more money with Dynamo. Sure, after busting my ass for the past five years, it would've been nice to get a windfall but, hey. Move on."

"So where do we start?"

"Where we left off."

Mark arrived back at the office just in time for the afternoon highlight, the weekly management meeting. Warmed by the sun beaming in through the window and the chilled bottle of white Rioja he'd had at lunch with Peter, he found it easy to drift off when they got to the management accounts, did not tune back in until Max Greenberg, Adware's Chairman, began describing a partnership deal he was working on.

"... So when I was in New York, I pitched it to American Mutual Bank. They have got 65% of the US online market. They were all over it. They love my idea!" Max was excited, in sales mode, a full court press, winning the room (mostly) with his infectious energy. He stepped up to the whiteboard to diagram the business model, talking fast and smooth all the while. "In today's numbers, we clear £2.5 million a year," he summed up with a satisfied grin and a slash of marker. "Easy money. All margin."

Before the holidays, Mark would have reacted differently, bitten his tongue, suppressed his moral outrage and internalized the guilt by association, all for the sake of job preservation, the promise of a seven-figure exit. Now that he knew his options were worthless, all his reservations vanished. He had nothing to lose. And he was bullish about Dynamo.

In a misguided moment of absolute clarity, Mark decided to speak out. "For the record ..." He paused, looked at Fiona Clarke, who was taking minutes, then waved at the whiteboard, "That is PaySense's business model. Duncan Brown is my friend. I introduced him to Adware *in good faith*. What you're telling us now, Max, is that you've breached the NDA and stolen his business model. Or is there something I'm missing?" Making no effort hide the sarcasm in his voice, he added, "Because if I am, I'd love to hear it." Mark looked again at Fiona, "I'd like my objections noted for the record, please, Fi."

The room fell silent, stunned by the open challenge.

Max barely missed a beat, "I didn't steal his idea, I've been talking about this for years!" He gestured at the whiteboard and began re-explaining.

As Max droned on, Mark sat back and shook his head, a look of utter contempt on his face. "Bullshit, Max!" he finally burst out, "That is *exactly* PaySense's model. All you've done is taken their name out and put in AMB!"

"That's ridiculous!" snapped Max.

"Damned right it's ridiculous!" countered Mark. "It's also criminal. I'm no lawyer, but last I heard, stealing is a crime." He looked around the room, savoring the tension, no one meeting his eyes. "If you go along with this, you are *all* complicit ..." The sharpness of his tone, the lingering silence as his eyes made their way around the room, made everyone edgy. When he got to the secretary, he said, "Fiona, please, for the record. PaySense is going to sue. You can count on it." He let out a perturbed laugh, added, "So much for your IPO."

"*Our* IPO. You've got skin in the game, too, Mark," cautioned Max, adopting a conciliatory tone. "C'mon, let's be reasonable. You know as well as I do that PaySense will never survive. They're a tiny start-up in the land of giants. They've got no backing. As soon as the banks got wind of the idea they'd do the same thing."

"And that's your justification?" asked Mark.

"We can't risk such an important part of our operation with an unfunded start-up," reasoned Max.

"But that doesn't give you the right to steal their idea. It's simple. If you don't want the exposure, you walk away. But you don't steal their idea and take it to their competitor."

"You're over-reacting," said Max.

Mark snorted in disgust and let it go. No point. In fact, he was starting to regret having opened his mouth in the first place: not a battle he needed to fight right now. He let the meeting run for a few more minutes before excusing himself, "Sorry, I've got to go." How true those words. "Late for a meeting across town. So, if you'll excuse me ..."

"Who with?"

Mark ignored Max's trailing question as he shut the boardroom door behind him and made his way to his own office to collect his laptop and coat. Max watched him through the glass wall as he left the building, phone to ear.

A few minutes later, Max stepped out of the meeting to make his own call. He never came back.

0100010001001001010101011001

"It's not your fault, Mark. You did warn me he was a snake." Duncan was being kind, but even over the phone the quiver in his voice betrayed anxiety.

Anything I can do to help, just shout. I mean it, Duncan."

"How about a drink this evening? The Plough, say 9ish?"

"Sounds good. Again, mate, I really am sorry."

"Not your fault. You're not the first person to warn me about Max. But it *was* ultimately my call."

"Yeah, but you trusted Adware because of me ..."

"Still my call. Seriously, don't beat yourself up about it. But if there's anything you can get your hands on ..."

"Consider it done."

"Cool. See you at nine."

0110110101100010101110100

Mark lost himself in the crowd, wandering aimlessly around central London, thinking, cooling, weighing options. At 3:40 pm, still early, he turned up Bolton Street toward Curzon Street, idly window shopping his way to Berkeley Square, the tourists thinning mercifully the farther he moved away from Piccadilly.

It was one of his favorite neighborhoods, clean Georgian lines, elegant simplicity, wedged between gaudy baroque bookends. Still early, he parked on a bench in Berkeley Square, burning time as he waited for Rick Ashton's meeting to end.

An hour ago, life had been simple—put the day job on autopilot, focus on fundraising, launch Dynamo. Job done, exit sorted. But now? His little outburst had complicated things. Sure as spam, a shitstorm was brewing at Adware, trouble he did not need. He would have been better off keeping his mouth shut and helping Duncan build his case on the quiet.

But it was all out in the open now. Of course they would suspect him, probably already did. He could picture the scene back at the office—Max, Nigel, and Russell huddled behind closed doors plotting and conspiring. He knew enough HR law to know they did not have him on gross misconduct. Not yet, at least. But he *would* help Duncan, give him whatever evidence he could, testify if asked. After being screwed on his share options, he would gladly do so without hesitation.

In the meantime, he had needlessly put himself in a precarious situation. Fundraising could take months. He needed a Plan B should his position at Adware become untenable. He needed to start looking for another job. Which is why he had called Rick Ashton. His old friend was a head-hunter, one of the partners in the boutique firm of Ashton Tate.

Mark glanced at his watch. 4:15. He got up from the bench, left the park, crossed the street to No. 9, and pressed the burnished brass buzzer for Ashton Tate Executive Search. The firm's offices were housed on the 3rd floor of an 18th century mansion block long since converted into offices.

There was a growing trend in Mayfair for restoring these historic buildings to their residential grandeur, but the W1 postcode still remained a firm favorite amongst London's venture capitalists, head-hunters, investment bankers and other boutique professional services. The shops were boutique too—Cartier, De Beers, Marc Jacobs, Stella McCartney—haute couture and expensive baubles dressing many a ground floor window, lending to the quiet atmosphere of leisured wealth that so appealed to Mayfair's denizens, residential and commercial alike.

A smooth Home Counties voice crackled brightly over the tinny tannoy, "Good afternoon, Ashton Tate. Can I help you?"

"Hi Sophie. It's Mark Haddad. I'm here to see Rick."

"Oh, hello, Mark. Do come up." Sophie's voice was replaced by the purr of the door buzzer.

A ping signaled the arrival of the lift. Mark stepped into the tiny space and rode up to the third floor, the doors opening directly onto the offices of Ashton Tate.

Sophie greeted him with the familiarity of old acquaintance, a friendly peck on each cheek, chit chat, offer of coffee. Mark took a seat on the sofa and idly flipped through the latest issue of *New Media Age*. A few minutes later, she returned with a perfectly prepared espresso, a lemon rind and small biscuit artfully balanced on the saucer.

"What's this?" said Gary Tate as he rounded the corner. "Here to see Rick, not me? You're my client, Mark," he added with mock indignation.

Gary was Rick's partner, mid-thirties, good-looking, intelligent, cocky, charming, the consummate bachelor. He had clipped blond hair, a strong, chiseled jaw and light blue eyes that radiated intensity. He was slim but worked out and had the svelte, proportioned build of an all-rounder.

"Gary," laughed Mark, drawing out the last syllable as he stood up to give him a firm, two-handed shake. "Keeping well, I hope."

"No complaints. Feeling the crunch like everyone else. But all in all, not too bad. So? Are you hiring?" replied Gary, wringing his hands with comical greed.

"Just a social visit," said Mark.

"Hmm," replied Gary, still fishing. "Referral?"

Before Mark could answer, Rick Ashton appeared, escorting a well-dressed urban warrior. He shook the man's hand and saw him off before turning back to Mark, a warm greeting, a big bear hug for his old friend.

They had been roommates freshman year at Franklin & Marshall College, close friends ever since. By chance, a lot of the old crew now lived in London—Mark and Susan, Rick, Stephanie (well, sort of ... she was now tax-exiled to Monaco, offices in London), John and Tess. Grad school, jobs, globetrotting, yet somehow, years on, they had all landed here, married (mostly), kids, settled in their American emigration.

"You've got first dibs on the guy I just interviewed! He's sharp, hungry, definitely varsity player. He'd be a great addition to your team," offered Rick.

"I'm not hiring," replied Mark, his eyes locked on Rick's with unspoken meaning.

"Give me a sec to wrap up. We'll go to my Club. We can talk there." Rick turned back down the hall, Gary in his wake. He returned two minutes later, alone. "Gary will be done in an hour or so. Mind if he joins us?"

"Sure. I just want a bit of time alone first," replied Mark

barely containing a smile. Gary sensed something was up and wanted in.

Rick glanced at Sophie who nodded. She would pass the message.

011000010110011001101001

Berkeley House was a magnificent old mansion occupying half the north side of the eponymous square. Built in 1792, it was once the home of a successful merchant banker whose family had long since squandered his legacy. Centuries on, the stately building had settled comfortably into its latest incarnation as an exclusive private members' club. For all its history, grandeur, gravitas, Berkeley House was just part of the furniture within London's elite business circles. That was exactly how its current owner liked it.

The liveried doorman greeted Rick by name, "Mr. Ashton, good evening, sir," and ushered them in.

Rick swiped his ID card at the concierge's desk and led Mark up the sweeping marble staircase to the first floor. The Africa Room was muffled in ancient leather-bound editions, hushed tones, and thickly padded carpet. Rick made his way to his favorite corner, where a tall period reading table and an antique floor-standing globe defined an arc of privacy around two over-stuffed chesterfields and a low coffee table.

011000110111010001101001

Logan had been through the footage once already, pausing, rewinding, a plan taking shape in his mind. Two in, ten out, an £8 million profit. Textbook. In his current funk, he might have walked away, too easy. But hearing the name Max Greenberg gave it an added zest he found irresistible.

Max. The memories, not so much buried as forgotten, came flooding back—the school playground, the taunts, the bullying, the abuse. Logan's desire for *something* infused them with more poignancy than they deserved, whetting his appetite for revenge. He googled a recent photo of Max and displayed it alongside the still image of Mark Haddad, chuckling, thoroughly enjoying himself for the first time in a very long while. He pressed 'play' once more and let the scene play on.

Ashton orders martinis and a bowl of nuts. He opens the humidor (one at every table), enjoying the ceremony, trimming, rolling, slowly flaming a Montecristo to life. "Cuban cigars. One of the reasons I love living in London."

Mark laughs, lights his own.

"So, what's up?" asks Rick, straight to the point. "Wild guess ... you want to quit your job." They had been here before.

"Yes," replies Mark nodding his head, leaning back, a long, slow draw on his cigar, smoke rings. "I'm serious this time."

"About time. Max is an asshole ..."

Upstairs, watching from his penthouse, Logan contrived a memory, 'embellished' perhaps the better word. The bully's eyes burning vicious. The smirks as his minions circled, taunting Logan with their shrill pre-pubescent voices. Max egging them on, doling out the chocolates, feeding their puerile savagery ... the frenzy, the pummeling, the pounding, the kicking. He used it to build his own rage, turn it into a lust for revenge.

"He's been screwing you for years."

"You don't know the half of it," replied Mark.

"What'd he do this time?"

"Two things. First, my options. Worthless. I found out just before I went to Greece. Then, today, I find out he's screwing Duncan, stealing his business model, pitching it as a joint venture to a big American bank."

"Your mate? The guy who's doing that online banking

thing?"

Mark nodded. "PaySense."

"So are you serious this time? Or are you just PMSing again?"

Mark chuckled, but when he looked up, his green eyes were filled with resolve. "Deadly serious. Besides, after what I did this afternoon, I wouldn't be surprised to walk in tomorrow morning and find myself sacked."

"For what?" There was more than a hint of doubt in Rick's voice.

"Well, at the management meeting, I did sort of accuse Max of stealing Duncan's idea."

Rick's brow furrowed with concern. "Tell me *exactly* what you said."

Mark recounted the salient bits.

"They can't fire you for that," pronounced Rick. "But for chrissake, Mark, what were you thinking?!"

"I know, I know. It was dumb ..."

"That's an understatement. For starters, my job is infinitely easier if your C.V. says 'to present'. It's like dating—girls always want the guys who're taken. Trust me. I know. I deal with it every day."

Mark was not quite sure whether Rick was talking about dating or job hunting. Probably both.

"Let's go back over the details, word by word. Tell me *exactly* what was said."

"What are you getting at?"

"If they suspect you for a whistleblower ..."

"I thought there were laws protecting whistleblowers?"

"There are, but it's never that simple. You have to tread carefully, Mark. Right or wrong, something like that can ruin your reputation, drag your name right through the mud."

"I said *PaySense* would probably sue." The word 'whistleblower' was echoing guiltily in his head. What he did not add was that he had also promised to help Duncan any way he could.

21

"Well, from now on, you need to be a lot more careful." Rick fixed him with a stern expression. "The first thing you need to do is go back tomorrow and make nice. Got it? You may despise the bastard, but you can't show it!"

Mark was about to bring the conversation round to Plan A—Dynamo—when Gary arrived. Rick gave him the headlines—why Mark was pissed off, looking for a new job. He was not aware there were missing pieces. Mark saw what was happening but felt powerless to stop it—he was not close enough with Gary to feel comfortable talking about Dynamo.

"Are you thinking what I'm thinking?" asked Gary, latching onto the misperceptions.

Rick smiled, "If you're thinking what I'm thinking."

"You first."

Turning to Mark, Rick said, "Want to do some damage on your way out?"

"Go on," said Mark, intrigued.

"Take your team with you," continued Rick. "Leave Adware dead in the water."

Gary tag-teamed with, "Not only that, it ups your market value—the whole team's. We could get a bidding war. Think about it, you're the Dream Team! And not because I placed them all with you. You've made Webdex how many years running? Four?"

"This'll be the fifth."

"And," said Rick, "If you *really* want to hurt them, take your services to the competition."

"Who's your biggest competitor?" asked Gary.

"ABC. They're a big American player. Haven't really set up shop in Europe yet."

"Perfect!" replied Gary with a wicked glint in his eye.

Mark had to admit, the idea had its appeal. But, he reminded himself, a new job was Plan B. And he did not want to jerk his team around. Plan A was to raise money for Dynamo. Finding a new job was just a backstop, insurance. But he did not want to talk about that with Gary. Which made for a frustrating conversation, them pressing, him resisting without meaningful explanation. More than once he caught Rick's questioning look: *'what aren't you telling me?'* That would have to wait until they could speak privately.

Mark left at 8:00 pm, another engagement, did not say who with, 'whistleblower' still echoing in his mind. He said to Rick, "We need to talk. I need to explain ..."

"Hey, don't worry about it," cut in Rick, misinterpreting. "We'll handle it however you want. Scout's honor. You're the client."

Mark read the disconnect but parked it for the night. "Dinner tomorrow? On me." He turned to Gary and added, "Sorry, mate, just some personal stuff."

"Sure," replied Rick.

When Mark was gone, Gary asked, "Think you can bring him round?"

"Hard to say. There's something he's not telling me."

"You've heard the rumors," said Gary, half statement, half question.

"What rumors?"

"Adware's gearing up for an IPO. They're wrapping up the bridge round now, floating on NASDAQ in the spring. Maybe that's why he's holding back. If his options are vested, he wouldn't want to throw a spanner in the works ..."

"Quite the opposite. We talked about it. They screwed all their staff, Mark included ... restructured the company share capital, staff options are pretty much worthless. No rumor: he has the documents. No, it's something else. I think he was about to tell me when you walked in."

"Yeah, go on, blame me," laughed Gary.

"Either case, I'll find out at dinner tomorrow. Just don't you show up." Rick laughed and signaled the waitress for another round.

0110111101101110000101110

There were four more hours of footage. Logan left it for the transcript. He had what he needed. PaySense and Adware. He would have to keep an eye on Ashton Tate too—the Dream Team idea could be a problem. He had no interest in derailing Adware's exit strategy. To the contrary: he wanted it to be a resounding success. Once he had a slice of the pie.

The intercom buzzed. 11:58 am. Lazarenko had arrived.

CHAPTER 4

The Plough's garden was crowded with people enjoying the warm evening air. Mark spotted Duncan. As he sat down, he tossed a flash drive to his friend. "D'you use Outlook?"

Smooth catch, one-handed. "I do," smiled Duncan. Turning the stick over, he eyed Adware's logo printed on the side and laughed, "Thanks," catching the irony too.

"You know I'm a pack rat. I save everything ..." Mark's words, the pause laden with teasing innuendo.

"So ...?"

"So there's an email thread on there. Started just before I went to Greece, right after your first meeting with Max. There's one email in particular, dated August 20th, 4:37... while I was in Greece ... I'm sure you'll find it ..." Mark smiled, left his words hanging.

"C'mon! What's it say?"

"It's a long thread. The next person who replied trimmed it. So it only surfaced the one time, in the original message— August 20th, 4:37. I'm pretty sure he did not mean to hit Reply All." Mark was enjoying teasing his friend.

"Who? What'd he say?" asked Duncan eagerly, leaning forward in his chair.

"Max," said Mark, "He was replying to Thornton, our

Finance Director. I'm just paraphrasing, but he said he'd just had a long call with someone at AMB ... can't remember the name ... said he'd explained the model to them and was sure he could get a better deal than PaySense was offering. Asked him to draw up a term sheet."

Duncan laughed. "You're kidding? That's gold dust." Then his brow furrowed. "But how do I prove it's not a fake? The email ..."

Mark's face spread with a wicked grin. "Max signed it ... with his PGP key."

"Why'd he do that?" asked Duncan.

Created in 1991, PGP (Pretty Good Privacy) had become the de facto standard for digital signatures and encryption. But it took effort—you had to sign each email, could not just hit Send—so most people only used it if they needed to.

Mark shrugged. "It's his latest obsession. Frankly, it's annoying. He signs everything. It's his way of making everyone in the office install it. Half the time, he even encrypts his emails—no PGP, no read."

"So anyone can verify the signature and that the contents are unaltered?" asked Duncan.

"Any *original* recipient," explained Mark, "which I was."

"Mark, you just made my day."

They toasted, downed their pints, and left The Plough, heading down Well End. The narrow lane, crooked, cobbled, empty, unlit, belonged in a country village, not a London suburb.

"So what about you?" asked Duncan tentatively, wondering if Mark had changed his mind about leaving his job.

"Like I said earlier ... I'm outta there. I've had it. Wheels are already in motion."

Duncan shot Mark a quizzical look.

"You know I've been working on Dynamo ..."

"I had a feeling," chuckled Duncan. "Is it ready?"

"v1.0," said Mark with a grin. "Checked it in the morning before I left for Greece."

"No kidding! That's brilliant news!" blurted Duncan.

"Well it's a little complicated. This evidence ... can you keep it under wraps for a while?"

Duncan nodded understanding. He had been trying to raise venture capital for his own startup for more than a year. "I don't think I'll need to produce it till later, anyway. Either way, I'll let you know before anything happens."

"And in the meantime, I'll be going full guns with fundraising, hopefully sooner rather than later." It was a sensitive subject, so he stopped there.

"I assume Susan knows?"

"Actually, no, not about any of it. Didn't have the heart to tell her when we were in Greece. Then today, this shit, I haven't been home yet, came straight to meet you." Mark glanced at his watch, realizing he had forgotten to let Susan know he would be out late. Too late now. "Speaking of, I'd better go."

He turned and started down the last short stretch to his house.

Duncan called after him, a whispered shout that echoed down the quiet suburban street, "Drinks later in the week?" He mimed 'call me,' adding "Otherwise, I'll see you at John's on Saturday!"

Mark nodded, waved goodbye and headed down the hill. The downstairs lights were on, Susan still up, probably waiting for him, dinner cold. He slowed to take a moment to collect his thoughts.

A call or a text to say he would be late would have been enough. He had not done either. So as soon as he opened the door, he led with an apology, a hug and a kiss. With a weary sigh, the weight of the world on his shoulders, a bit of melodrama to melt her frost, he filled her in. "I didn't want to bring this up in Greece, but ..."

The duplicity of it pissed her off, though she was not crying over the stock options. She had seen enough start-ups to know that shares and options were paper thin until they became cash in the bank.

When he got to the part about meeting Rick, she jumped to her own conclusion, taking the conversation with her. She was happy Mark was looking for a new job, excited for him, confident Rick would find him a better position, better pay, better people, better prospects, a real career move.

It was not any one thing, but after 20 years of marriage Mark knew that this was not the time to bring up Dynamo. Besides, it was late, a school night. Time for bed.

CHAPTER 5

Mark did not talk to Susan in the morning, leastways not about Dynamo. He was itching to—it was all he could think about, what he had dreamed about. But a school day morning was definitely *not* the right time. So he kept quiet about it and let the morning fill instead with the blissful banalities of suburban life—getting the kids dressed, fed and watered, teeth brushed, bags packed, smatterings of neighborhood gossip, schedules aligned...

7:45 am brought an illusory calm, T minus 15—everyone ready but too early to leave. Tempting, but too big a topic for a 15-minute window. It had lain dormant for two years, one more day would not make a difference.

He poured a fresh cup of coffee and escaped into the garden. In the warm sun, his swirling thoughts began to settle into a semblance of a plan as he watched Susan through the kitchen window. At 42, she could still hold her own against much younger women, long dark hair framing mesmeric ice blue eyes, her elfin face suggesting eternal youth. She felt his eyes, looked up, her smile turning into a sultry pout. She ran her fingers seductively through her hair and looked over her shoulder—no children—fingertips caressing her neck, sliding along the curve of her breast, lingering, tickling, teasing.

For the first time this morning, Mark had something other than Dynamo on his mind as he watched her walk toward him.

"Where are the kids?" she asked.

"Don't know," he replied, shuddering as she touched him, her tongue slowly licking her lips.

"Why don't you catch a later train?" He felt her hot breath as she leaned in and whispered.

"Mummy! Can we go now? I want to see Cindy before school! She's got a new Nintendo DS!" Their daughter, Layla, was standing in the kitchen door, hand on hip, a determined look on her face, her mother's daughter.

Mark laughed, "Wish I could, but I have a meeting at half nine."

"You're quitting, aren't you? What does it matter? Aren't I worth missing one boring meeting for?" She let her words linger as she turned and walked toward Layla with a sultry look back.

Mark let temptation fade before following Susan inside. As she shuffled the kids out the door, she turned, pulled him into a deep hug, and whispered, "I love you, babe." Stroking his hair, she added, "And I know you've made the right decision. I'm behind you 100%." She leaned back and held his eyes, bonding her words to her heart. "Rick will land you a much better job. You deserve it."

He gave Susan a lingering kiss goodbye as she dashed after Layla, Ben already far ahead.

Back in the kitchen, Mark considered his situation. After five reasonably comfortable, low-stress years, Susan had no intention of giving up the security and stability of their current lives to chase yet another one of his web dreams. Not again. Not unless he raised some serious money. Two years ago, when Dynamo was just an idea, she had put on a brave face, tried to hide her apprehension, her relief, when he and Peter had tried and failed to raise investment capital.

They had not talked about it since. Not that Mark was hiding anything—she knew what he, Jason and Peter were up to. It was simply a non-subject. But Susan was not a fool—she had to realize it was just a matter of time before they finished writing the software and it came up once again. It struck him that she had probably already connected the dots and was waiting for him to bring it up.

Realizing the time, he snapped out of his reverie, grabbed his bag and dashed out the door—the day job. *Can't neglect that.* As he hurried along the back streets, his brain shifted into planning mode. The daily walk to and from the train was prime headspace, private time to sort out his thoughts.

He had three things to juggle—Dynamo, job hunting, and Adware. Top priority was to defuse things at the office, get the day job back on autopilot. Two birds, one stone—less focus on work, less pressure for Plan B. He found a seat (lucky, someone off-boarding at Barnes) and shamelessly slid in, ignoring the reproachful glare of the person he beat to it. He fired up his tablet, a list already building in his mind.

By the time the train pulled into Waterloo Station, the list ran to three pages. The other commuters filed off, shuffling and queuing at the barriers. Mark stayed, scribbling notes, almost missing the conductor's whistle, escaping just before the doors closed for the return journey West.

He set off on foot, taking his usual route over Hungerford Bridge to Embankment, up St. Martin's Lane, then a diagonal through Chinatown to Soho. On the bridge, he made a conscious call to break step, stopping midway to gaze out over the tidal waters. He fished out his tablet and scribbled some more, drag and drop—ordering, prioritizing, a plan starting to take shape.

At 9:15, his phone chimed a reminder. He sighed—the meeting he had missed getting laid for. He could not remember who it was with and at this point did not really care. But he had to go through the motions, keep Adware on an even keel until he had his exit sorted.

It was Nathan Campbell's third meeting with Urban Nomad—early days, but he was already closing for the kill. Mark watched his young star work the room, playing old jokes to fresh ears, reading body language, watching the buying signals. Nathan was the youngest and newest member of the team, but already looking the veteran.

Urban Nomad was a trendy, up-market fashion brand that breathed zeitgeist. Nathan had already sold the young founders (26 and 28)—that much was obvious from their body language.

Today's meeting was for the money men, Newton Capital, a private equity firm looking for a big return on its latest investment. They were part of a trend of brand spotters—find something hot, fresh, build it, sell it. They had a solid track record. In the bigger picture, they were the client, not Urban Nomad.

Digital media was core to Newton's brand building strategy—ecommerce, social networks, blogs, interactive engagement, online advertising. Which is where Adware came in. Mark was there to lend gravitas, credibility, to Adware's proposition, show Newton that they were in seasoned hands. It was a strategic account—win it, deliver results and Urban Nomad would be just the first of many from Newton Capital.

Mark had arrived late, so Nathan had given him a hurried 90-second briefing, key facts, figures. Added to what he already knew about the brand and its private equity backers, he would sprinkle this into his opening remarks, demonstrate that visibility of this important account went right to the top, board level ... very excited, blah, blah, blah.

Mark sized up the audience. 26 & 28 had not clocked that they were not calling the shots anymore. With Newton's investment, Urban Nomad was no longer just an avant garde fashion label, it was a real business with an exit strategy. Newton Capital would build the Urban Nomad brand, then, in two or three years, sell it on to one of the major fashion houses, turning their £20 million investment into a £200 million return. Their track record was impressive.

To his own detached ears, Mark's words sounded empty, but with only six minutes gone, he could see they had found their mark with the men from Newton Capital. The room was relaxed, the body language positive.

He handed the meeting over to Nathan, who launched into his pitch. From there, things quickly spiraled out of control. 26 & 28 seemed to think it was their pitch, interrupting, derailing Nathan's presentation. Mark watched the Lead Investor's growing impatience, a parent's frustration with a spoiled, petulant child.

When 26 & 28 both jumped up and raced to the presentation board, Mark finally decided enough was enough. He stood up, cleared his throat loudly, turning all heads to the opposite end of the room. He glanced once at Nathan then locked eyes with the Lead investor: "Trust me." Turning his attention to 26 & 28, he said, "You guys have already seen Nathan's presentation."

They nodded.

"Then why don't I give you a tour of the office?" It was not a question. As he ushered the young designers out the door, he caught the Lead's eye once more, "I'll bring the boys back in an hour or so."

The Lead returned the smiled with a nod of gratitude, mutual understanding.

The tour lasted all of five minutes. After all, what is there to show in an open-plan office? Pods of desks clustered into departments? *Ooh.* Meeting rooms? *Ahh.* The kitchen? *Oh.* The foosball table? *Cool! I want one of those!* How about a cigarette? *And Starbucks! Loo break first, please!*

26 & 28 returned from the washroom bouncing off the walls, sniffing, rubbing their noses. Not even midday. *Sad,* thought Mark, *Charlie's going to blow through their millions for them.*

Outside, he chatted idly with his charges as he led them

down Dean Street to a café, then on to a shop that stocked the Urban Nomad label. They revealed themselves and basked in the celebrity of it, *He's Urban! I'm Nomad!*

At 11:00 am, Mark brought Urban and Nomad back to the office. Nathan was just wrapping up. As they walked in, he gave Mark a subtle nod—it had gone well. Mark ushered his charges into the room then excused himself momentarily.

He returned a few minutes later, a leather portfolio tucked casually under his arm. "I've ordered some coffee and pastries," he said. "Why don't we move over here ..." He indicated the lounge area. "Anyone need a comfort break?"

Urban and Nomad shot their hands up like schoolchildren and scurried off. Mark watched the Lead Investor watching them and wondered whether he knew about Charlie, suspected he did. Nathan took his cue and offered the five minute tour to the other two money men. That left Mark alone with the Lead.

"They're a bundle of energy, those two," said Mark with a hint of humor, a casual probe as he sat down.

"Yes, I've got my hands full," replied Lead.

Mark opened the leather portfolio and set it on the coffee table. "This is our standard contract." It was turned to the signature page. "I trust Nathan's explained the cost structure. It's really quite transparent." Mark held Lead's eyes. "I think this can be a great partnership." He fished out his Mont Blanc pen, uncapped it, set it down on the signature page, and leaned back in silence.

After what seemed like an eternity, Lead broke the spell with a deep, rolling laugh. He picked up the pen, scribbled a few lines, then signed with a flourish. "Subject to legal review," he said, voicing the words.

"Of course. Lawyers need to earn their crust," joked Mark. "Thank you. We won't let you down."

"No, I suspect you won't," smiled Lead as they shook

hands, sealing the deal. "I do like your style, Mark. I look forward to working with you. Are you free for lunch next week?"

"That would be nice." Mark scanned his calendar on his smartphone. "How about Tuesday?"

"Perfect. I'll email you." Lead then turned to the others, who had just returned, and said, "Gentlemen, I'm pleased to say we have a new digital partner."

Smiles, hurrahs, looks of surprise, handshakes, promises to be best of friends, to be excellent to each other, blah, blah, blah.

01000110011011110111011100010

Back in his own office, Mark shut the door and ruminated. He usually got a buzz out of closing a sale. This time, he had felt nothing. Even using the pen close—ballsy, something he had never tried before—had offered only bland, abstract appreciation. He saw it as a clear sign that mentally he had moved on.

Through the window, he watched Nathan sharing the win with the rest of the sales team. Mark loved their camaraderie, the chemistry between them. Gary had called it the Dream Team. He was right and it would be hard for Mark to say goodbye.

Now he was torn. He had been planning to share what he had discovered about the stock options, but after yesterday's conflag over PaySense, he was not sure he could. Still, he owed them. "Well," he said to himself, "the sooner you get your funding, the sooner you can come clean with them."

He picked up his phone. "Lunch?" he asked when the call was answered.

"A bit short notice," jibed Peter, "But yeah, I can fit it in."

"Good. Gordon's again? Say 1:00 pm?"

"Sounds good."

Thumbing through his contacts, Mark made one more

call, to Jason Hunter. "Good morning, Jason!" he said cheerily after eight rings. Kiddie Coders. Up all night, sleep all day.

"Mark, is that you?" answered a groggy northern accent. Glug, glug, belch—warm cola. Jason's voice cleared, his words accelerating, as the fug clearing and the caffeine coursed through his system. "I added some new libraries. Been at it for three days straight ... You back from Greece?" He did not wait for an answer, "This is very cool. The more we build these libraries, the easier it gets to develop apps. You know how long it'd take me to build something like Facebook?"

"Are you up for lunch?" interrupted Mark. "I'm buying."

"Make it breakfast. I could really go for a full English."

Mark thought for a moment, "How about Balan's?" He made a mental note to text Pete with the change in venue.

"Okay, I'll find it. Soho, you said?"

Mark laughed and shook his head in mock resignation. For someone with a genius IQ, Jason could be a total space cadet. "It's on your street. Out the door, turn right, two doors down from your flat. Can't miss it. Big sign."

"Oh, that place. Yeah, we've been there before."

"See you in an hour."

"So, what's up?" Jason started to ask but the line was already dead. He lumbered out of bed, rising to his full 6'3", a gentle giant with a bit of a stutter. He crossed his studio flat, dark, curtains drawn, a sea of pizza boxes and empty cola bottles, dirty socks and bike parts, books, papers everywhere.

He detoured en route to the bathroom, drawn like a moth to the green glow of his terminal. His fingers settled gently, natively on the keyboard, firing by reflex, command consoles opening, eyes fixed on the MRTG graphs scrolling by, a real-time load test he had left running overnight. "20,000 concurrents and it's still only running at 25%! Sweet!" he said, upping the simulation to 30K concurrents.

Remembering the promise of a full English, he killed the

urge to settle in for more and headed for the shower. He absently wondered what it was about before his mind was lost once more in a binary cloud.

0110101101110000011100001

Balan's was busy, but Mark managed to find a corner table that afforded them a little privacy. He waved to Peter and Jason when they arrived, wondering not for the first time why Jason always hauled around what must be at least 10 kilos of computer hardware and books in his rucksack.

"Right, Jason, I already told Peter yesterday. Your turn." He recounted the abridged version of what had happened. "So, cut to the chase ..."

"I always said Max was a wanker." He had done a brief stint at Adware and had his opinions (strong as always). Mark's story only reinforced them. "Moral turpitude," he spat, the scorn amplified by his stutter. "I hope Duncan nails them with his lawsuit. And I'd love to see the look on Max's face when you quit."

"In which case, we've got a lot of work to do." He reached into his bag and handed round sheets of paper, his tablet for himself. He had spent the past hour working on his list (the Dynamo section). "I figure we can be ready to go out to the VCs in a couple of weeks. Peter, you and I need to dust off the old business plan, run some fresh numbers, and put together a fresh deck. Jason, can you build us a demo site?"

Jason nodded. "Just tell me what you want."

"On the phone you mentioned Facebook ..."

"Easy. Give me a couple of days." He smiled and added, "but it'll just be wireframes. I'm not a graphic designer."

"I'll rope in my mate, Kevin," offered Peter. "He's freelancing ... You've met him, Mark. He owes me a favor so it shouldn't be too expensive. Speaking of, we're out of cash."

"Let's take that offline," replied Mark with a warning look. There were two subjects that tended to spark Jason into impassioned rants—money and copyright. Both were best avoided when there was work to be done. He turned to Jason and changed subject, "When can you have the demo ready?"

"Definitely by the weekend," he replied. "Do you want it transactional?"

Mark laughed. "Yes, actually. Plug PaySense's payment engine in if you have time. I just signed a partnership agreement with Duncan. I'll forward you his technical specifications. Nothing fancy, just some clever Social Commerce—the VCs will love that." Mark made a note on his tablet and pulled up his calendar. "Can we regroup on Saturday? I'm free after twelve …" The others nodded, so he fired off the invite.

"Peter, can we see Kevin … next Tuesday? I'm free after 3 …"

"Works for me. I'm emailing him now to give him a heads-up. I want him to have a crack at our branding as well. We need a logo," replied Peter.

They fell into a rhythm working through Mark's list, transforming it into a plan—dates, times, actions, critical paths. The atmosphere around the table was intense, urgency charged with the mounting reality of what they were doing. Two hours came and went. By the end, they had a working plan. Stunned silence. As if on cue, the three men began giggling like schoolgirls, each passing look triggering another hysterical outburst as they vented the last of the energy that had been firing them along. Exhausted, they fell into another stunned silence.

They had a product and they had a plan. Dynamo was real, it was happening. They were pumped up, confident, no one doubting they would raise the money and soon be launching their own company. After two years burning the midnight oil, it felt great.

"I've got to shoot off," said Peter, breaking the spell. With a huge sigh, he slid out of the booth, stood up and stretched. "Some of us have day jobs."

"Ditto."

Jason eyed their half-finished plates. "Do you mind?"

"Not at all," laughed Mark and Peter as they left, picking up the tab on the way out.

CHAPTER 6

Adam Lazarenko had been summoned for 3:00 pm. It was now nearly half past and he was still waiting. He paced the reception area, much to Natasha Petrova's annoyance. He tried to glimpse her screen as he passed her desk, but each time he drew near, she glared him away.

She knew who he was, what he did for Daniel Logan. He was a Black Hat hacker who had earned his reputation breaking into corporate computer networks. In Ukraine, as a teenager, KGB had been his master. After democracy, he had gone freelance, renting out his zombie army by the hour to the highest bidder. Logan had talent spotted them both plying their wares in the hotel lobbies of Kiev, hustling for hard currency, American dollars, brought them to London, installed them at Berkeley House.

Lazarenko's domain was the basement, Natasha's the penthouse. He had eyes and ears in the Club, but not here. It did not matter that he would soon see who Logan was meeting. For now, she knew and he did not. Balance of power. She also knew he was stewing. Three hours earlier, he had felt Logan's sharp edge, scurried away to his basement with barely a glance at Natasha's tits.

He knew his mistake. He had grown complacent. Hours

earlier, he had seen Logan change, come out of the doldrums, seen the fire rekindled. He had been glad of it, though he had failed to respond in kind, his noon report substandard, amateur—articles of incorporation, share register, annual accounts, LinkedIn profiles.

Not this time. This time, Logan would be very pleased.

Lazarenko 'owned' a growing list of venture capitalists' email systems. Most had been child's play to hack then install Trojans to copy every email, in and out. A treasure trove, terabytes of data growing daily.

PaySense was a start-up. Doh! He ran a search, lightning algorithms sifting years of porn, banalities, chain mail jokes, affairs, and smatterings of useful intelligence—confidences, itineraries, inside information. By the time he sat back down, the results were in. Sort by Sender, Size. Bingo! Lazarenko selected the most recent email, opened the attachment and hit Print. PaySense's business plan, less than two weeks old.

He resisted the urge to run back upstairs. So soon after would only remind Logan of his earlier failure. Instead, he settled in to learn everything he could about PaySense. It soon became apparent that the company did not stand a chance of getting funded, not in London. One by one, the VCs had turned it down. Internal communiqués, notes to mates, warned about the founder's abrasive nature, one even commenting that he was not photogenic—"not a poster boy for the online payment industry, old chap …" Unfair, thought Lazarenko, a slight twinge of sympathy for the misunderstood. PaySense *was* a clever idea. Shame. But not all clever ideas got funded … nor were all funded ideas clever.

Logan did not know about Lazarenko's offshore data haven (at least, Lazarenko did not think so). He used it judiciously, when he needed to impress Logan, like now or, a bit more lately, when he wanted his own inside track on a hot IPO.

He put his feet up on his desk and smiled. It was only 2:00 pm and the report was ready. He fired off a string of keyword searches, trawling the wider web for more information. PaySense. Adware. Mark Haddad. He had pegged Logan's game.

01110100011010000011110011

Eventually, the door opened and Stuart Lassiter, Managing Director of Peterman Brown, Logan's private investment bank, stepped out. Natasha nodded at Lazarenko, *You can go in now.*

Lazarenko cast about for clues. Secrecy was the norm—he could not think of a single project where Logan had spelled out his strategy. He simply made demands and issued orders, arranging the pieces in his own mind, keeping his own counsel, leaving Lazarenko to work it out for himself. He relished the challenge of piecing together the complex machinations of Logan's mind. He harbored no delusions of ever matching wits, but he had apprenticed well.

Their meetings were normally held at the boardroom table, formal, abrupt, agenda- and time-driven. But this time, Logan was sitting on a sofa, relaxed, leg crossed, foot dangling by the edge of the deep glass coffee table. He smiled, motioned Lazarenko to sit opposite. Even offered coffee. Logan was in a good mood. It was when he could be his most dangerous.

Lowering himself into the Corbusier sling chair, Lazarenko slid the report across the coffee table, its momentum on the slick surface careening it into a stack of documents, dislodging them. He caught a brief glimpse—*PayS*—before Logan straightened the pile. But that was enough. His instincts had been right—the meeting with Lassiter had also been about PaySense.

Logan spent a few minutes riffling Lazarenko's dossier. "You sent this electronically," he said, statement not question.

"Of course," replied Lazarenko, relieved. He could tell Logan was pleased with his work.

"Good … good … good …" Logan looked up. "Excellent summary. Reliable sources?"

"Extremely," replied Lazarenko with a crafty smile.

"And the business plan?" asked Logan, fiddling with his phone.

"Less than two weeks old," replied Lazarenko.

Logan stood up and paced as he spoke. His deep baritone drawl had an uncanny way of directing itself, crystal clear to targeted ears but resonating only as a low rumble to anyone else trying to listen in. All Lazarenko caught was the name on the end of the line—Lassiter. Peterman Brown was involved. That gelled with what he knew.

"Good work, Adam," said Logan after hanging up and returning to the sofa. His words, his gaze delivered a compliment laden with subtext—*That's more like it*—a stern yet unspoken rebuke for his earlier disappointment.

"Now I want you to find out everything you can about Adware. A full background—their cash position, directors, share register … everything from Companies House. Their client list, press coverage." He paused, leveled his gaze at Lazarenko. Again, the silent rebuke for past misdemeanors. "They're planning an IPO. I want to know everything about that. Rumors. Bad blood. Lawsuits. Enemies. Analysts. The VCs involved. Everything. Do you understand?"

Lazarenko nodded, a lump in his throat.

"Good. And the same for American Mutual Bank." Meeting over, Lazarenko was back in Logan's good books and in the know.

CHAPTER 7

Netscape, August 9, 1995, the IPO that kicked off the dotcom boom. Trading opened at $28, twice the book price. The five million shares on offer were 20 times over-subscribed. It broke the system. Trading could not open for two hours. When it did, the price shot up to $75 on the day, $171 by year's end.

By 1999, the dotcom boom was in full swing. Robert Durand arrived in Silicon Valley armed with a Wharton MBA, strong gaydar and a bucket load of ambition. With a bit of schmoozing, cruising and some help from Dad, he soon found himself exactly where he wanted to be, at the top end of Sand Hill Road.

Ignite Capital was one of the granddaddy venture capital firms, its name synonymous with the Internet. Its ego wall boasted a lion's share of the most spectacular IPOs in dotcomdom. Its reputation alone added zeros to the valuation of any company lucky enough to feature in its portfolio. For Durand, there was no better place to be.

Alas, things did not quite work out as planned. In the spring of 2000, at the last minute someone said "Boo." The bubble burst. Party over.

But Durand was nothing if not resilient. In the aftermath,

while other VCs licked their wounds, he rooted in the ashes, turning up truffles and green sprouts with impressive regularity. A string of shrewd deals—mostly trade sales of distressed companies—got him noticed, and it was not long before rival VCs came courting. Ignite fended them off with golden handcuffs, an offer of a full partnership—his own portfolio, profit share, front row parking for his new Ferrari 599 GTB Fiorano Coupe.

As a freshly-minted Partner at Ignite Capital, Durand set his sights higher, made bigger plays, wore more expensive suits, gave Miguel 20 bucks a day to wash the Ferrari. He was an effective leader who commanded his small army of analysts well and soon emerged as Ignite's star performer.

Ultimately, though, he was just a bottom feeder. *Mr. Distress.* The loathsome moniker was a constant reminder, the whispered tune of his reputation, the tenor of his success. No one dared say it to his face, joking or otherwise, but everyone knew it. Mr. Distress was fast cementing his place in the Silicon Valley food chain.

Durand bore the ignominy of the nickname with stoicism—like it or not, it made him a player, gave him a niche. When the markets did eventually heat up again, which he knew they would, there would be plenty of opportunity to turn it around, to establish the reputation he truly deserved. One spectacular IPO was all it would take for the moniker to be forgotten. He, though, would long remember its loudest proponents.

When Web 2.0 arrived, Durand knew Boom 2.0 would not be far behind. Google floated and the tech IPO market began to rally.

Durand stumbled upon Adware by chance, a casual conversation with another business class passenger on the flight from San Francisco to New York. It was not based in Silicon Valley, not even American. But it ticked the right boxes ... serial entrepreneur, 'Cloud Computing' (flavor of the day), advertising (flavor of the month), behavioral targeting (flavor of the year). Healthy revenues, fast-paced growth, market leadership (Europe). Durand smelled a winner. Adware would be his debut IPO and it would be spectacular.

He championed Adware through Ignite's investment committee and secured $30 million in second round funding. He flew to London business class, a staff of four analysts, back in premium cattle.

That first morning at his newest company, he left the entourage at the hotel. It was his moment. Mr. Distress, his loathsome nickname left in California, soon to be a thing of the past.

He had dressed for the part, spit-shined, hand-tooled cowboy boots, pressed Levi's, black turtleneck, tan Armani mohair blazer, his sun-bleached hair wavy and long. He oozed Silicon Valley VC. The buzz was audible as soon as he walked into the office. *He* was the buzz, and he loved it.

It was like that every time Ignite Capital came calling. But this time was different. The room was not thick with desperation for a dying company. It was alive, rippling with hopes and dreams, the whispers ripe with anticipation. 'invested $30 million! ... major Silicon Valley VC! ... IPO! NASDAQ!'

Durand had casually taken a seat in the reception area and given the room a big, warm California smile before focusing on his BlackBerry. The board was having its last meeting without him, voting to approve Ignite's investment, two seats on the board. A formality.

"Robert! Good morning. Good to see you again."

He had met Mark Haddad on his first visit to London. Fellow Americans, they had instantly hit it off.

Durand stood up with a broad smile and a firm handshake. "Mark. So good to see you too."

"So, is it too early to say 'welcome aboard'?" asked Mark with a nod toward the closed boardroom doors.

Durand laughed. He liked Mark; in another life, they might

have been friends. He was sharp. Consistently beat his targets. Good leader. Nice guy. His staff were fiercely loyal to him, and he to them. There was the rub. He would have objected to the new capital structure—the preferred shares and warrants that diluted the staff stock options pool to nothing. Durand knew this, which is why Mark had been left in the dark and why he would never have a seat at the table, not while Durand was in charge.

The boardroom door opened, signaling an end to their brief conversation. "We should catch up soon. I expect I'll be spending a lot of time in London gearing up for the IPO." Durand spoke loud enough for those nearby to overhear, smiling to himself as he saw his words ripple out across the room. He shook Mark's hand once again, full of California warmth, before stepping into the boardroom and shutting the door firmly behind him.

For the next two years, Durand and his small team at Ignite Capital worked tirelessly preparing for the IPO. They drafted the prospectus and fed the PR machine, while he hand-picked the venture capitalists to invite to the bridge round.

It was a proven route to market—find a promising company, finance its growth through one to three funding rounds, syndicate the bridge round to a cabal of other VCs, do a Roadshow to court the institutional investors, then IPO. The bridge round was essential. The cash it raised was useful, but the real value was having more people with skin in the game, more voices to hype the IPO. It was a simple formula perfected time and again by the wealthy and powerful denizens of Sand Hill Road, Menlo Park, California.

001001100110001101101111

Robert Durand was back in London for the monthly board meeting. They had started at 7:30 am, powered straight through lunch, dispatching the regular agenda in quick order.

The afternoon was set aside for the topic on everyone's mind. IPO. Word spread throughout the office. Everyone was buzzing, the place upbeat, excitement palpable.

Durand called a break at 3:30 pm. The other board members—six men and one woman—immediately reached for their devices, addicts desperate for their fix, worse than smokers. Robert's Rules banned calls and emails during board meetings. He had learned to watch for signs of withdrawal—twitching hands, cold sweats, darting eyes, lapses of concentration—and called breaks as needed, usually every couple of hours.

The room emptied, leaving Durand and Max alone. Max buzzed his PA and ordered two espressos before propping up his tablet and polishing the screen, once more failing to invite comment. Yesterday's news. Half the Valley had been sporting them for weeks, like Max, proudly displaying them as badges of übercoolness. Durand abstractly appreciated Apple's brand success, the Resurrection, Steve Jobs's godlike aura. But he could not be bothered with the toys themselves. He would never admit it, but technology actually bored him.

He handed his BlackBerry to Max and demanded, "What's this?"

Max scanned the email, his brow furrowing as his brain processed the message content. "I ... I ..."

Durand saw shock, fear, but not surprise. *The sonofabitch knows!* He took a deep breath choked back his anger and spoke in a flat, ominous tone. "Max?"

Durand listened as Max spun, trying to discern reality from half-truths. He did not like what he was hearing. When Max finished, Durand stood up, his expression stone cold. "I'll be back in a minute."

In the lobby, he passed two men. The cut of their suits, the shine of their shoes, the shape of their briefcases said 'lawyers'. Outside, he stopped, turned, and watched.

"Call from Conrad Baine. Answer or ignore?" asked his Bluetooth headset.

"Answer," replied Durand, turning down the volume as his managing partner immediately launched into a tirade.

"What the fuck is going on over there?!"

A knot twisted in Durand's stomach as he watched Max emerge and escort the two lawyers toward his office. "I'm on it, Conrad. I'm sure it's just a misunderstanding ..."

"Don't give me that sissy-ass horseshit, Bob."

Bob. Durand hated it as much as Mr. Distress. Baine knew that, derision intended. He was an old school bigot who had only accepted Ignite's first gay partner because he could not risk losing him to a competitor.

The line went dead. With a sigh, Durand stepped into a corner shop and bought a pack of cigarettes. He had not smoked in years.

He arrived back at Adware's office just as the lawyers were leaving. As their paths crossed, one caught his eye, his lip curled in a sardonic sneer. Durand looked at Max, the question on his lips, but the answer was writ large on Max's face, in fine print on the documents in his shaking hand.

Durand read them. The first thing he noticed was the law firm letterhead, *Edelman Jones*, the obligatory list of partners.

"It's bullshit," asserted Max. His phone rang. He fished it out of his pocket, glanced at the screen, about to answer.

"Don't!" snapped Durand.

"It's John Smith, from AMB."

"He can wait."

Max hesitated.

"Put the fucking phone away. Now!"

Max did not like taking orders. "I'm going to have to speak to him ..."

Durand cut him off. "Not now! I want answers first. And from now on, you don't speak to anyone without my authorization. Got it?" He stared Max down. "It's obvious this isn't just some shot out of the blue ..."

Max began to protest. Durand raised his hand, stopping him. "Shut up and listen!" His voice dropped to a threatening whisper as he got in Max's face. "I just had Conrad Baine on the phone. He is *not* a happy man. And trust me, he is not someone you want to fuck with. He's just had the CEO of AMB on the line. They're golf buddies. Remember who made the intro?" He waved the documents under Max's nose. "I've got $30 million sunk into this company and I want to know *exactly* what you've just dropped us into! Who the hell is PaySense and why are they suing us and AMB?"

0110111001101110011001100101

Daniel Logan hung up the phone and leaned back, a broad smile on his face. He had played his opening move, lawsuits hand-delivered on both sides of the Atlantic. He closed his eyes and tried to visualize the scene at Adware's offices less than two miles away, the board meeting, IPO top of the agenda. And he had just tossed a hand grenade into the room. He laughed gleefully, picturing the look on Max Greenberg's face. For the first time in months, he was enjoying himself.

He blocked Caller ID and dialed +1 650 ... Time for his next move.

CHAPTER 8

Max Greenberg eased his Rolls Royce through the sea of red and white, flash and mass propelling him forward in equal measure, the crowd parting, reforming in his wake like a school of fish, a predator in their midst. Twice he sounded the horn at fans too drunk or oblivious to sense his hulking presence.

The approach changed when he turned into the Emirates Stadium's private access road. Cordoned off. Unobstructed. VIP. It might as well have had a red carpet. Max loved that too, the attention.

He had driven the same route to every Arsenal home game for the past 10 years. Always the same. Fans gawking, pointing at 'celebrity' mere inches away, just out of reach, the great unwashed pressed against the barriers, reaching, peering, cameras flashing blindly through darkened windows, ambitious for a lucky souvenir snap of fame.

Max thumbed the remote. Benign music—Luther or some such dross—faded out, replaced by the sound of the crowd outside rising to a crescendo of speculative adoration coming from the grille-mounted mikes.

Hey! Isn't that Thierry Henry's car? ... Cheryl Cole ... I heard Jack Nicholson was coming today, he's a Gooner! ...

The passengers fell silent, absorbing the adulation as their own, each in a moment, living a childhood dream—Arsenal center forward, celebrity actor, pop diva. They were all rich and powerful, but none were famous, Max merely notorious. Giving his guests this magical moment always filled Max with a sense of his own generosity.

With a familiar nod to the security guard, he ushered the Rolls down the ramp into the quiet of the stadium's private underground garage. GREENBERG emblazoned on the tarmac, alongside the names of Arsenal luminaries—players, legends, managers, directors, owners. He pointed them out— the Ferraris, the Bentleys, pimped out Range Rovers, all bling and ridiculously low profile tires. His voice suggested familiarity, intimacy. "That's X, Y, check out Z's Humvee ..." He rattled off ownership as if they were mates.

When the lift door opened, they stepped out into the subdued opulence of the Diamond Club. Dark wood polished to a mirror shine complemented intimate expanses of white marble and hand-tooled leather. Directly ahead, through a glass wall spanning the length of the Diamond Club, his guests got their first view of the stadium. "Hallowed ground," he said with a smile. "Just like at Highbury. Fans still have their ashes scattered on the pitch."

The concierge greeted Max, fawned over him, then escorted his party to the bar where a round of G&Ts was already waiting. A generous Christmas bung made sure Max was VVIP.

Max gave his guests a moment to absorb their surroundings before leading them on a brief tour. They looked down through the glass wall, red and white worker ants filing in, ready to cheer the home side on to another victory. Or not. Man United. Big game. It was still early in the season but the pundits were billing it as a battle for the title. Continuing the tour, Max pointed out trophies, memorabilia, Arsenal legends and other famous faces mixing in the Gucci-clad crowd.

Tony Levine. Max's eyes bored in on the small, oval-shaped man. He craned his neck for a glimpse of the rest of his party.

"Trevor, mate!" said Max cheerily, pulling a large, weathered looking man into his circle. Leaning in close, he whispered his own name in the man's ear. "Guys, I'd like you to meet my mate, Trevor Starr. Arsenal legend."

"Max, good to see you again," said Starr. Like other retired players, he was on retainer, paid to socialize, regale the Diamond Club VIPs with well-worn stories of past club glories. Introductions made, he slipped into his practiced role, cocktail in hand, the tense rivalry with Man United the theme of the day.

Max excused himself and made his way across the room toward Tony Levine. His cold smile disappeared when he saw Robert Durand.

"What are you doing here? If I knew you were an Arsenal supporter, I would have invited you myself." It was almost an accusation.

"I'm a ManU fan," replied Durand deadpan. "Max, I'd like to introduce you to Daniel Logan."

Logan stood up, stepped forward, hand extended. His grip was firm, eyes cold, unreadable.

Max immediately noticed the watch, a Patek Philippe Tourbillon, rare, worth more than a million, a sign of true wealth. He had already picked out his own. *Soon!*

"Daniel is Chairman of Peterman Brown."

Max stared at him, a vague glint of recognition. Something about the eyes.

"They recently invested £2 million in PaySense," added Durand.

A cold smile traced Logan's lips as his grip tightened. "Please, do join us. Robert and I were just discussing this unfortunate situation."

"Do I know you?" asked Max probing the icy depths of Logan's pale blue eyes.

"Perhaps you've been to my Club. Berkeley House?"

Over the past two decades, Logan had changed beyond recognition. New nose (twice, Zurich then Stockholm), chin in Hong Kong, teeth in LA, ears in Rio, new name, new passport each time. The last cut was digital—hacking into Scotland Yard with a surprisingly easy BIND exploit to replace the digitized fingerprints and DNA records for Case 118764 with those of a man buried in an unmarked grave thousands of miles away in Siberia. Two days after that, Daniel Logan stepped out into the world.

"No, I've never been there," replied Max, though it was obvious he knew of it, as a man of his caliber would.

Logan pulled out an engraved silver case, handed a card to Max. "Stop by anytime. I'm usually around. Perhaps I can interest you in membership. It is rather exclusive."

Max offered his own card in exchange. Logan held it by its edges, respectfully studying it Japanese-style before carefully placing it in the case, fingerprints intact. No specific need, but he was not one to waste an opportunity.

"Please, do join us," offered Logan as he sat back down.

The lights dimmed twice, indicating lunch was about to be served.

"Perhaps another time," replied Max. "I should return to my guests. I hope you enjoy the game. Actually," he added with a wicked laugh, "I hope you don't! Arsenal all the way!"

Logan and Durand watched him swagger off, smiling, waving greetings to other tables along the way. At one point he stopped, studied the card in his hand, glanced back, then stuffed it in his pocket and continued on his way.

"How long have you known him?" asked Durand.

"A long time," replied Tony Levine. "A very long time." It was clear from his tone there was no love lost between them.

"Everyone seems to have history with Max."

"Indeed." Logan smiled. "Now, about this matter ..."

CHAPTER 9

Mark was tired. He had been up to Edinburgh and back, nine hours on the train for a two-hour meeting that could have been done by conference call. All he wanted was to go home and sleep, but Duncan had insisted. Would not say why.

He arrived at the Plough just past 9:00 pm. Duncan was sharing a table with two other mates from the neighborhood. Mark nodded at their near-empty glasses and offered, "My round ..." *Guinness* ... *Pride* ... *Bombardier*. He returned a few minutes later, four pints artfully balanced. Chit chat, football, today's topic another foreign despot trying to buy silverware.

Downing the last of his pint, Mark said, "Guys, it's been a long day. I need to get home." Duncan cut out with him.

"So what's up? You look really worried about something," said Mark as they walked down Well End.

"Can we go to my place?"

"Sure."

Duncan had converted his garage into a home office. He grabbed a couple of beers from the fridge and finally spoke. "You know I got funding ..."

"Yeah, that's great news! So why so down?"

"It happened really fast ..."

"It didn't fall through, did it?"

"No, no. Cash is in the bank."

Mark's face asked, *so why so worried?*

"I'm so sorry. I had no idea. They asked ... now that I think about ... they asked about it a lot, but I didn't think anything of it at the time ... just seemed like normal due diligence."

"What are you talking about?" asked Mark.

"My investors filed a lawsuit against Adware and American Mutual Bank today. I swear, Mark, if I had known ..."

That explained the three missed calls from Max, the terse messages he had left unanswered. "They know about the emails?"

Duncan nodded, drew a deep breath. "I showed them to the partner, Stuart Lassiter."

"Right," said Mark, pursing his lips, his mind racing.

"I'm so sorry, Mark. If I'd known ..."

Mark waved away the apology. "I gave them to you, Duncan. I told you to sue. But, yeah, a bit of warning would've been good."

"I only found out this afternoon, after they'd done it."

"They didn't tell you?"

"Not a word, not even a hint it was coming."

"Tell me exactly what happened? Do you have a copy of the lawsuit?"

Mark flipped through the document. "I want to get Warren's advice." He fished out his phone and dialed. "Hey, mate. It's Mark. Sorry to call so late," he glanced at his watch, 10:15. "I'm with Duncan. Can we pick your brains? It's kind of urgent." ... "Great. Thanks. We'll be right over."

Warren Steinberg scanned the documents, mumbling to himself, making notes on a legal pad. After a tense several minutes, he turned to Duncan. "You really should have talked to someone before signed this document. Mostly, it's boilerplate. But there is one clause," he pointed, "that gives Peterman Brown the right to unilaterally pursue any potential legal claim by or against third parties. It's unreasonable, prejudices the other shareholders and the board. You can get rid of it, but it'll take time.

"Meanwhile, it puts them in the driver's seat. My guess is they planned this from the start. Now that it's in motion, you really don't have much choice but to see it through. If you back out now, PaySense would be exposed to potential counter-suits from both Adware and AMB."

"Are you saying they invested in my company just to file a lawsuit?" asked Duncan. His face was crestfallen.

"Not necessarily the *only* reason. But definitely *a* reason."

"Why?"

"The IPO," said Mark. "Adware's about to close a bridge round and is gearing up for a spring floatation with a billion dollar valuation."

"Very crafty," said Warren.

"I don't get it," said Duncan.

"The timing's perfect," explained Warren. "Sue Adware. Force them to cut a deal fast to make it go away so they can keep their IPO on track. Basically, they're holding Adware to ransom."

"That's extortion!" replied Duncan.

"Not when it's done legally."

"But Adware doesn't have any cash," said Mark. "Wouldn't it make sense to do this *after* the bridge round closed?"

"*If* it was cash they were after," replied Warren. "But with an IPO on the horizon …"

"They want equity," finished Mark, nodding understanding. "Bloody hell!"

"So PaySense would own Adware stock?" asked Duncan.

"Well …"

"Well, what?"

"If I were them, I'd structure it so that the equity was held by Peterman Brown, not PaySense." He waved the papers still in his hands. "Cut you out. This is their lawsuit, not yours."

"So I get stuffed?"

"You still have the $2 million. But if they wanted to get nasty, they could sue you, too, for non-disclosure. Claw back the $2 million, even sue you for damages."

Duncan could not believe what he was hearing. "This is bullshit! There's no way they can sue me. I told them about it. They can't claim non-disclosure!"

"Can you prove it?" When Duncan did not reply, he added, "There is another possibility. The deal could be structured so that Adware acquires PaySense. A paper deal, straight stock swap. That's how I'd play it."

"So, after what he's done, Max ends up owning my company? No way!" Duncan was furious.

"Not Max. Adware. And you would be a shareholder. To be honest, it's probably the best end game you can hope for. Give you something to cash out when Adware IPOs."

Duncan had been played. No amount of protesting would change that. Mark and Warren had seen it before, the world full of Peterman Browns and Max Greenbergs.

After a long silence, Warren asked again, "Can you prove it?"

Mark and Duncan both nodded.

"I gave Duncan some emails," offered Mark. "Max signed one with his PGP key."

"Good. PGP is admissible, if you have the recipient's public key to validate the signature."

Mark nodded. "We do. My key."

"And Peterman Brown knows this?"

This time it was Duncan's turn to answer. He furrowed his eyebrows, leaned forward and said, "Come to think of it, they're the ones who brought it up."

"What do you mean?"

"I was going to tell them—precisely because I didn't want

to risk non-disclosure—but they brought it up first."

"How did they know?" asked Warren, scratching his head.

"Maybe they've got someone on the inside?"

"Max?" said Warren. "If he knew you were going to sue, and knew you had a strong case, what better way to control the situation than to own both sides."

"I don't know," replied Mark, his voice laced with skepticism. "Even for Max, that's pretty Machiavellian. Besides, he doesn't have £2 million to invest."

"It doesn't have to be his money. Could be a proxy? Someone he trusts?"

Max Greenberg doesn't trust anyone," laughed Mark.

"You know what I mean. He is well connected."

"Maybe," conceded Mark, his expression still doubtful.

Changing tack, Warren said, "So Peterman Brown now have these emails ..."

"No," cut in Duncan. "I showed them to Stuart Lassiter. He's the Managing Partner. But I never gave him a copy, soft or hard. And I did redact the hard copy with a black marker before I showed it to him."

"Good ... that's good," said Warren. "That's your leverage. Where are they now?"

"On a USB at my house. The redacted hard copy too. I suppose Mark probably still has copies."

Mark confirmed with a nod.

"Okay, this is what we need to do. Duncan, dash over to your house and get the USB and hard copy. I'll put it in my firm's safe in the morning. Go on! What are you waiting for?"

When Duncan was gone, Warren turned to Mark, "This can get very awkward for you."

"I realize."

"I can keep you out of it for a while by filing an injunction under the Whistleblower Act, but your name will eventually come out."

Whistleblower. Rick's words of warning echoed in Mark's mind. "I want to help Duncan. But, yeah, I need time to sort out my own exit strategy." He filled Warren in, what happened at the management meeting, Dynamo Plan A and job hunting Plan B.

"You're happy to walk away from your options? Surely if Adware's planning an IPO, it's worth sticking around."

Mark shook his head. "They restructured, shafted staff. All the money's in preference shares. By time they convert to ordinary shares, staff options will be diluted to almost nothing. After taxes, I'd be lucky to see $50K."

Warren was not surprise, only nodded at the information. "Still nothing to sneeze at."

"My shares in Dynamo will be worth a hundred times that. Besides, there's a six-month lock-in post-IPO. It's just not worth it."

"You sure?"

"Yeah." Mark nodded.

Duncan returned a few minutes later with the flash drive.

"Next steps," continued Warren. "Duncan, you need to meet with your investors and find out as much as you can. Be smart. Look like you're on-side." Warren scribbled a name and phone number on a piece of paper. "Call Dmitri first thing. He's one of my associates. I'll brief him. I want him there with you when you meet with them. Let him do the talking."

"What are your rates?" asked Duncan.

"Don't worry. I'll keep an eye on costs and I won't bill you for my time." For levity, he added, "Besides, what're you worrying about? You've got £2 million in the bank."

That settled, he turned to Mark. "I'd advise you to hire an HR lawyer. I can recommend someone. She's young, sharp, and affordable. I'll make an intro tomorrow. She can file the injunction and protect you if they come after you."

"One of yours?"

"No. I don't want any conflicts of interest. She's a sole practitioner. But she's very good and will cost you half what my firm would."

CHAPTER 10

Nigel Thornton, Adware's Finance Director, was stationed outside Mark's office when he arrived at work the next morning. Given what he had learned the night before, Mark was not surprised.

Thornton was small in stature and mind, lived for moments like these when his diminutive presence could fill the room. Gone was yesterday's synthetic laugh, the tight smile that could not hide a stern face. Today, his lips were pursed, his posture rigid and officious.

Mark drew a deep breath of tense air and slipped into a role of feigned ignorance, casting carefree good mornings and smiles as he crossed the office. "Good morning, Nigel!" he said with exaggerated cheer as he neared his own office. Before he could reply, Mark added, "Is that a new suit? Looks good on you. Ozwald Boateng? Fancy a Starbucks?" He smiled as his flippancy caught Thornton off guard. He did wonder about the suit. Thornton usually wore cheap polyester numbers.

"You're wanted in the board room," said Thornton, ignoring the conversation.

"Oh?" said Mark with exaggerated concern. "Nothing's happened to any of my staff, has it?" He looked around, as if doing a headcount.

"No …"

"Thank god! So, what is it?"

"Follow me. They're waiting." Without another word, Thornton turned and marched across the office, conscious that all eyes were on him.

Marie Atherton, Mark's second in command, cast a questioning look at him as he passed by. He shrugged ignorance. She muted the call she was on, nodded toward the boardroom, and whispered, "Max, Harry, Nigel, and Robert Durand have been in there all morning. Something happened yesterday at the board meeting. Any ideas?"

"I guess I'm about to find out," replied Mark, living the lie.

"Catch up later." Marie returned to her call.

Mark nodded, patted her shoulder reassuringly and set off for the boardroom, ignoring the eyes, the tension, that followed him, his own face a mask of bemused curiosity.

"PaySense has filed a lawsuit," said Max without preliminaries. He glared at Mark. "Against us and AMB. They're seeking £100 million in damages."

Mark remained impassive. Durand studied both men, the scene, the room dynamics. Russell and Thornton flanked Max, one edgy, the other mopish, eyes downcast, fingers fiddling. Fiona Clarke, the secretary, sat fingers poised, ready to minute the moment. The silence stretched on.

"Well?" demanded Max, "What have you got to say?"

Mark shrugged. "I told you so?"

"Fuck you!"

"Strike that last comment, please, Fiona," said Durand staring at Max. "Let's try to keep this civil."

"It was your deal!" barked Max.

"Actually it wasn't. I was very specific about that from the start. Check your email. Duncan is a friend and I did not want a conflict of interest. All I did was make the introduction. It's always been your deal, Max." Mark felt Durand's eyes on him but did not turn to meet them, his own fixed on Max.

"From this moment, you are to no longer have any contact with Duncan Brown ..."

Mark shook his head. "Sorry, Max, you have no right to ask that. He's my friend. You have no right to impose on my personal life."

"You're giving him information!" leveled Max, glaring.

"This conversation is over. If you want to make accusations, talk to my lawyer."

"Your lawyer, eh? ... So you did do it," said Max.

Mark paused, his hand on the doorknob, turned, thought better of it, shook his head, and walked out.

"That was constructive," said Durand.

"He's probably been planning this for months," said Max.

Durand studied the other executives, let the uncomfortable silence drag out. They knew. They were also afraid. Which only left one conclusion—Mark's was the version closest to the truth.

"Let me speak to him." Durand got up. "See if I can take a more reasoned approach." He cast a reproachful glance over his shoulder at Max as he left the room.

Max hurried back to his own office, drew the blinds and unlocked the bottom drawer of his desk. The dusty face of the bulky gadget was all Bakelite dials, toggle switches, and meter screens. Analog, old skool. He uncoiled the power lead and plugged it in, needles revving, whirring, lights flashing as it warmed up. Earpiece in, he flipped a switch, adjusted a dial, and tuned into the crackly conversation in mid-flow.

"... good friend. I don't want to be involved."

"I'm not asking you to be," countered Durand. "Nor am I accusing you of anything." His voice dropped confidentially. "I don't know all the facts but, fair to say, I have a pretty good idea what's going on."

Mark said nothing so Durand continued. "The whole company—shareholders, staff—should not pay the price for one man's actions. We need to work together to resolve this, Mark. I'll do whatever it takes to keep our IPO on track."

Mark studied Durand, his own face poker, giving nothing away. He had a point, but he was also being disingenuous in his concern for staff considering his hand in the company's capital restructuring. Of course, neither he nor Max knew that Mark knew about that. And this was not the time to let on.

"Perhaps you can talk to Duncan …"

"Like I said, I really don't want to be involved. From the start, I have made every effort to avoid a conflict of interest. It's not my mess …"

Durand pressed on, unperturbed, "I met with the Chairman of Peterman Brown last night," He saw a glint of recognition at the mention. "They're the VC that just invested in PaySense. They want a quick settlement too. Help me, Mark. What's their number? What'll make them happy, make this go away?"

"What about AMB? I wouldn't be surprised if they also sued Adware for dragging their name through the mud."

"Conrad Baine and Jim Bradley, AMB's CEO, are old friends. I'm sure they can reach an agreement over a round of golf. But they'll want a fall guy … this isn't the first time Max has put us in a tricky situation. Frankly, he's a liability."

"Look, Robert, I appreciate your predicament. But I really don't want to be involved. Besides, you don't need me. You said yourself, you're already engaged with Peterman Brown."

"Rest assured, when the dust settles there will be some changes around here. I'd like to know that I have my best people on board." Stick and carrot in one breath.

"I'll see what I can do," conceded Mark.

"Thanks," said Durand. "I'm flying to San Francisco tonight. Back in a week. If you hear anything … oh, and the management meeting you mentioned … Can you forward me the minutes?"

"Sure. I don't think they've been circulated yet, but yes, of course, as soon as I get them." Mark was happy to have an olive branch, keep things neutral at worst.

"Thanks, buddy. I knew I could count on you."

When the door closed, Mark fished out his phone. "Are you free for lunch? ... sounds good, I'll leave now ... see you there."

Max hurriedly unplugged the ancient analog device, managing to close and lock the drawer just before Durand tapped on the door and let himself in like he owned the place.

"Do you really think that was the best way to handle things?" asked Durand.

"Bullshit. He's helping those bastards!" countered Max.

"You don't know that, Max. Trust me, I plan to get to the bottom of this. Until then, back off. We need him. I calmed things down and I want to keep it that way. Got it?" There was a menacing glint in his eye. "He's my back channel. *My* back channel. Do you understand?"

Max snorted, nodded, humiliated. Enemies within. But this was not the time. He needed to pick his battles. "You're right. I flew off the handle. You really think he'll cooperate?"

"Look at it from his point of view. He's between a rock and a hard place. If I can convince him that it's in everyone's best interests, yes, I do. He's pragmatic, more than most."

Max had cooled down, knew better than to rise to the bait. He was more concerned about what Durand was *not* saying, not to him at least. He had asked him about the game last night but he had given little away. As for what he had actually said to Mark ... not for the first time, Max congratulated himself for having installed the bugs. *Enemies within.*

0110001101110100011111001

Once upon a time, there had been an Embassy of Texas in London, set up during the Lone Star State's brief period of independence in the 1830s. A blue plaque marks the building it once occupied on historic St. James's Street. A few blocks away, at 1 Cockspur Street, its namesake cantina occupied another landmark building, the former home of the White Star shipping line. Original photographs of the Titanic hung proudly alongside memorabilia of the Alamo, the Wild West.

By the time Rick arrived, Mark was well ensconced at the bar, two bottles of Corona in front of him, one half-finished. Rick helped himself to the other.

"You were right," said Mark without preamble. He quickly filled Rick in on what had happened in the past 24 hours.

Rick listened, drawing long drinks from his cold beer. When Mark was finished, he signaled for another round and said, "Your mate Warren's right—you need a lawyer. Who'd he recommend?"

Mark nodded. "Caroline Bassett. I spoke to her this morning."

Rick nodded approval. "I know her. She's good, tenacious. This can get ugly fast. IPOs have a way of bringing out the worst in people."

"You're not kidding. Robert's openly gunning for Max, said as much in our little 121."

"You're absolutely positive your options are worthless?" It was a valid question. Someone in Mark's role as Global Sales Director in a pre-IPO company usually had a meaningful stake, stood to make a lot of money.

"Not worthless, but massively diluted. I have the documents. All the money's in Series B & C shares. Trust me, I'm not leaving much on the table. There's nothing to keep me there."

"I've lined up three interviews for next week."

"And we've finished the business plan."

"Think you can raise the money? How much?"

"We're aiming for two mill though frankly I'd be happy with a seed round for now. Stephanie's helping. We're getting together tonight to polish the pitch. She's lined up some meetings with VCs for next week."

Stephanie Turner was another one of the old Franklin & Marshall crew who had ended up in Europe. She was a venture capitalist, one of the first to set up shop in London in the mid-90s. Her rolodex was a who's who of the European VC community, with a fair swathe of contacts in Silicon Valley as well.

"Couldn't her fund back you?"

"Wouldn't want to ask," said Mark shaking his head. "Besides, they're exclusively biotech."

"Fair enough," replied Rick. "Another round?"

"Need some food too." Mark signaled for the bartender. After a long pause, he said, "Look Rick, finding a job really is Plan B. I know I'm wasting your time."

Rick laughed off the apology, "It may be Plan B for you but not for Susan."

"Susan?" replied Mark, surprised.

"Uh, your wife," laughed Rick, "She's been on the phone to me every day this week. Finding you a new job is Plan A for her."

"Yeah, her and Liz both. She and John were over for dinner the other night. It was a full court press. They even floated Gary's Dream Team idea."

Ricked laughed.

Mark shook his head in dismay, not for the first time, regretting his recklessness at the management meeting. The situation was of his own making. And it would only get trickier with the lawsuit now in the mix. "I was hoping for a head start, a bit of time to just focus on fundraising."

"Well, it is what it is, mate," said Rick. "Either way, I'm glad you've finally, actually, decided to leave. But, the race is on." He laughed and tossed back his beer.

Dick Bailey had been watching from a table by the window, kicking himself. No ears—he had forgotten his directional mike. Not his fault. His secretary, Deidre, had been more randy than usual. His shirt was stained with sweat, from her and from rushing to Soho, late, then following Haddad on foot, fast. He finished his second beer, ignored the passing waitress and walked to the bar to order another, insinuating himself into the space next to Haddad.

Twenty years in the business had made him a good observer. This was no casual conversation. He could tell from the body language. They were friends. That was obvious too. But it was a serious discussion.

The bartender arrived with a fresh round for Mark and Rick, took their lunch order, then turned to Dick Bailey.

"Let's eat outside."

"Sounds good," said Rick.

Mark's shoulder brushed against Bailey's as he leaned down to pick up his satchel. Their eyes met as he mumbled an apology. It was only a flash, nothing given, no lasting memory, just another over-the-hill barfly.

Bailey swigged his beer and debated following them outside ... he could use a smoke. But he decided against it. A second look would leave a lasting memory. So he settled for watching from a distance, preserving his anonymity.

When they left, Haddad headed south, probably back to his office, Dick Bailey followed the other guy west. He did not know what had been said, but he could at least find out who he was.

01101111011101010101110010

Mark sat at their usual table upstairs, absently glancing up at the TV screen—Knicks vs. Lakers, on mute—sipping a bottle of Moosehead. Fiddling with his phone, he noticed the message flag, started to call voicemail, then aborted when he saw Stephanie and Peter walk through the door together.

Pleasantries done with, they placed their orders and turned to the business at hand. Stephanie went through the Dynamo business plan page by page, giving feedback on every section, from marketing and technology to the financial projections. She had seen an earlier version a couple of years ago when Dynamo was just an idea. She had warned them at the time that ideas did not get funded, not in London, but they had insisted on giving it a shot, so she had made a few introductions.

"You know I've always liked the concept," explained Stephanie, "and, personally, I had no doubts you'd deliver." She paused. "I did say then you'd need a beta version." Subtext, "I told you so."

Point taken.

"And now you do." Stephanie smiled.

"It's not beta," said Mark. "It's production-ready. Version 1.0."

"That's a change I'd like to suggest," replied Stephanie. "Start with a beta release, get people using it, giving feedback. It'll help create a buzz. Warm up the audience. A beta release gives the community a sense of ownership. Google does it every time they come out with a new app. The early adopters become your advocates. VCs are big on that too."

Mark smiled and nodded, remembering the shared sense of mission at his first dotcom start-up, Digiterra, the way the developer community had grown around it. Some had been angry when it went tits up, but most had been sad when Mark made his final posting to the forums, "Goodbye, World," before powering down the servers and closing Digiterra's doors for the last time.

"What about scalability?"

Mark reached into his bag and pulled out a handful of graphs. "We've load-tested a complex, transactional application—an ecommerce site. Running on a single web server, commodity kit, we simulated 25,000 concurrent users and it barely hiccupped. I'm telling you, Stephanie, this is seriously efficient code. It's a whole new way of thinking, embedding taxonomical constructs within the language itself."

Stephanie looked at the familiar green format of the

graphs and laughed, "I've still got to send Tobi a postcard." The graphs had been output using MRTG, a widely adopted old skool sys admin tool used to graph just about anything, from router traffic to coffee machines.

Who's Tobi?" asked Peter.

"The guy who wrote MRTG. It's postcardware," explained Mark.

"Like beerware," said Peter, drawing a chuckle and a reminiscent smile all round. Back in the days of bulletin boards and dial-up modems, people used to write software and share it freely, asking only for a beer or a postcard in return, a token of appreciation from those who found it useful.

"My next question," continued Stephanie, "is about licensing. We don't have anything to worry about here, do we?"

Peter exchanged a look with Mark before offering, "No, Jason's on board. He just took some convincing."

011100110111010001101111

It had been touch and go the previous Saturday.

Jason was a fanatical open sourcer, adamantly opposed to any form of proprietary software licensing.

Mark and Peter were more pragmatic. Open source worked well as a software development model but not necessarily as a commercial model. They had spent weeks formulating their own license, one they believed struck a balance between commercial and technical needs.

Jason had been quick to react at first mention of it, his defense of mainstream open source license models well-practiced, well-worn. Once Mark calmed him down and got him to actually read the license, his skepticism eroded. It was still open source but with a commercially sensible twist. "Kinda cool that we have our own license," he said, as he turned over the last page. "DPL ... Dynamo Public License ...

I like the sound of that."

011100100110100101100101

Mark pulled out a copy of the license from his bag and handed it to Stephanie. "We're going to open source Dynamo, under our own license ... DPL. Peter and I wrote the first draft, but we've had an intellectual property lawyer go through it as well." He summarized the key points as Stephanie thumbed through the document.

"Good," said Stephanie. "You still control the source code. What about patents? From what you've described, it seems there could be a few of them. Everybody loves patents these days."

"There are," replied Peter with a smile.

"Good. Email me a list, anything unique—constructs, processes, algorithms. I'll run it by a friend who's a patent lawyer with one of the big DC firms. The US is always the best place to file first." Changing subject, "So when do I get to see the demo?"

They consulted their calendars. Stephanie, who was based in Monaco, would be back in London the following week. They agreed a date.

"Why don't you stay at our place? I'll cut out early from work and give you a complete walk through. We can even build a new site. Simple wireframes. Grey screens only. But it'll give you an idea how easy it is to develop with Dynamo. Programming for the masses," he added with a smile. "Does that work?"

Peter and Stephanie both nodded. Stephanie held up her beer, a toast. "Guys, I gotta say, I am really impressed. You've put in the sweat equity. I never had any doubts, but now that you've done it, I'm confident we can get you funded."

"Really?"

"Absolutely. I'm always straight with you. If I didn't think it'd fly, I'd tell you. But do you really need two million dollars? This is the first round ... two mill's more than just seed money."

"We've already been through seed funding. Now we have a product and are ready to go to market. What we need at this stage in the business is two years' operating cash to focus on sales, revenue growth and market share." That was the pitch, but for Stephanie he added, "Neither of us can go through that again."

He did not need to say what 'that' was. Stephanie understood. They'd been friends a long time. Mark's last start-up survived the dotcom crash in early 2000, but 9/11 made it a one-two punch. He knew now—knew then, really—that he should have thrown in the towel. But he had fought on for five more long years. By the time Digiterra finally went into administration, his marriage, friendships, finances were battered and broken. He had spent the rest of the decade recovering.

"Just playing devil's advocate. You know what VCs are like. They'll squeeze, and your salaries will be the first thing they go after."

"Actually, we'll both be taking substantial pay cuts. About 30%," said Peter. "Compared to what it would cost to hire in senior management with our experience, what's in the budget is a bargain."

"Good. Don't excuse it. Don't be apologetic. Simple matter of fact."

Peter nodded.

"And you both need to go full time?"

"If we plan to hit our targets, yes."

"You don't have any proof-of-concept clients or revenue streams yet. Is that correct?" said Stephanie, deadpan.

"You've got to be kidding!"

"Like I said, I'm playing devil's advocate. Every VC will ask that. Guaranteed. We're not called vulture capitalists for nothing. We don't give a shit about you ... just our own slice of the pie. We'll squeeze you any way we can. But as long as you anticipate it, you can deal with it. Focus on the plan. It's all in there. You're targeting key verticals, proven markets. Talk up your Rolodex, your track record, drop a couple of names, teasers. And keep reminding them, you only need a tiny sliver of market share to hit your Year 1 targets.

Mark nodded. "I've got a dozen prospects I can hit Day One …"

"Pick two and build compelling business cases around them. Build prototype sites for them. Use them to demo to the VCs. Can you do that? Talk as if they're already in the pipeline."

"They will be," said Mark. "I'm prospecting now, off the record, of course …"

"Isn't that in breach of your contract with Adware?"

"They're not in my Adware pipeline. My proposition will be non-competitive. And my contract does allow me to hold non-exec board seats in other companies."

Stephanie smiled. "Okay. But be careful. Not even a hint of impropriety."

"Of course."

"We should schedule a dry run. We can do it at my office next week. I'll bring in my partners to give you a bigger audience."

"More of a grilling you mean," laughed Peter.

"I wouldn't be doing you any favors if it wasn't." Stephanie paused, added, "I think Angel Investors will be the best route. Most were entrepreneurs themselves so they tend to be more sympathetic. Two mill's a bit rich for them, but I might be able to syndicate it. Let me make some calls."

Stephanie glanced at her watch and began wrapping up. "Next steps. Mark, you're going to send me your list of innovations and I'll kick off the patent filings. I'll also line up some pitch meetings, say, two weeks' time? We've got the demo lined up for next week—I'll bring my partners and you're going to mock up some prospect prototypes for that. Am I missing anything?"

Mark and Peter exchanged a look. Peter reached into his bag and pulled out a manila envelope, set it on the table in front of Stephanie.

Stephanie pulled out the contents and studied them, eyes shifting back and forth between them, Mark and Peter.

Before she could speak, Mark explained, "Those are founder's shares. We'd like to offer them to you in exchange for *your* sweat equity."

"Guys, you don't need to pay me. I'm happy to help."

"Well, we'd actually like you to do a bit more than that," cut in Peter. "We'd like you to front the whole fundraising exercise."

"Why? You guys will be fine on your own. I'm happy to make intros and offer advice. You don't need to pay me."

"We've both got to fly below the radar," explained Mark. "If my name's out there, Max will hear about it. He knows everyone. And that's a complication I don't need right now. As it is, this whole PaySense business is getting ugly, but that's another subject. Peter's in a similar situation. Until we actually have cash in the bank, we both need to keep a low profile."

"I see," said Stephanie. "You've thought this through."

Mark and Peter both nodded.

"I'll have to clear it with my partners," said Stephanie. Then her eyes widened as she saw the numbers. "Whoa, guys! This is a big stake!"

"We'd also like you to sit on the board, as a non-exec," said Peter.

Mark added, "You know this world, Stephanie. And you know me. Boardroom politics is the last thing I'm interested in. And it's the sharp end. I need you to watch my back—our backs—so we can focus on the business. Like you said," he finished light heartedly, "you're not called vulture capitalists for nothing!"

There was a long silence as Stephanie stared at the share certificate, weighing her thoughts. When she finally spoke, her tone was serious. "Guys, I can't accept this ..."

"But ..."

Stephanie held up her hand, "Let me finish. I can't accept it without some conditions." Mark and Peter looked at each other. "As you know, Pi Capital invests exclusively in biotech, but I do still see plenty of business plans for other kinds of tech start-ups. Once in a while, I like the story and make a small personal investment."

Peter and Mark sensed where this was going. Stephanie acknowledged it with a smile. "Honestly guys, I decided last week when I read the plan," she pointed at the share certificate, "long before you pulled this out. I was going to ask if I could get in on the action with a £50K investment of my own."

"Wow."

"So that's my condition." She reached into her bag and pulled out the check, already written, and placed it on the table facing Mark and Peter. "We ..." pause for effect, "We are going to need operating capital for the next few months. Lawyers, travel, wining and dining. It adds up, but £50K should cover it, plus Jason goes full time as of now, building up the library, kicking off the beta community."

"Are you sure about this?"

Stephanie pushed the check across to her old friend. "Yes, I've given it a lot of thought. And these shares are far more than I would've expected for it."

Mark raised his beer in cheer. "Welcome aboard, partner."

CHAPTER 11

"What do you mean, 'they've dropped out'? They can't do that!" shouted Max, banging his fist on the table.

He was one a conference call with Robert Durand and Ignite Capital's managing partner, Conrad Baine, in Menlo Park, California. Baine waved Durand silent, his own voice a deep, gravelly Texas drawl, "Let's not play the fool, Max. Of course they can. They signed a term sheet. That's it. Read the clauses. *Material omission.* They've got every right to walk away. Hell, by all rights they could sue."

"What material omission?" snapped Max, before his words trailed off. He had been about to point out chronology, that PaySense's legal actions had started *after* the term sheet was signed, but it was a hollow argument and he knew it.

The crisis had been mounting for two weeks. Since filing the lawsuits, PaySense had been running an unrelenting smear campaign, not a day passing without at least one headline story.

In credit-crunched America, the target was American Mutual—"Big bank screws little guy." In the UK, it was Max. Not Adware, Max. The brash upstart from North London had long been a favorite target for the press. A litany of past misdemeanors always dredged up. He was not short of enemies willing and eager to fan the flames.

Until now, Max had refused to take the PaySense threat seriously. He had ranted and raged as if indignation alone could quell the mounting crisis. But his blustering had had the opposite effect. For Ignite, it lent credence to the allegations. For the press, it was a rich source of colorful quotes, Max his own worst enemy. Adware's PR firm had been working in overdrive for the past two weeks doing damage control.

With Midas withdrawing from the bridge round, Max could no longer deny that he had a very real crisis on his hands. As soon as word got out, the rest of the syndicate would collapse. Adware's IPO—his IPO—was effectively stalled. And his company was rapidly burning through its dwindling cash.

"I'll call Tom Brown at AMB. This lawsuit is bullshit!" said Max. "We need to join forces."

"You will do no such thing. I've already spoken to Jim Bradley." Baine's tone allowed no dissent. "I'll handle AMB." He did not need to add that Bradley, AMB's CEO, was his golf buddy and one of the few people he counted as a friend.

Max could not understand the inertia, doing nothing, letting PaySense take pot shots, not firing back. "We've got to do something! PaySense is nobody! They can't afford a lawsuit!"

"Wrong, Max," said Durand, not hiding his exasperation. "You keep forgetting Peterman Brown's investment. They've got a £2 million war chest." He let the words linger before adding, "The problem is, you don't."

"'You' not 'we'," heard Max, seething. Durand was hanging him out to dry. "That's why *we* need to close this round."

"That's no longer possible, not now, not with this hanging over our heads," said Baine. "The bridge round is meant to underwrite an IPO, not fight an expensive and damaging lawsuit. If I was Midas, I'd be doing the same thing, sit on the sidelines, watch how things play out. Trust me. They will not budge."

"Then I'll talk to Peterman Brown. Settle out of court. We can't let it derail our IPO. We're too close. There's too much at stake."

"Are you suggesting there's some basis to these allegations?" Baine glared at the conference phone.

"Of course not," said Max. "Like Robert said, they're opportunists. Filing a lawsuit just before an IPO? That's exactly what Yahoo did to Google in 2004. They settled ten days before the IPO for shares that must be worth well north of a billion today. It's obvious, isn't it? They're trying to hold us to ransom. Robert? You met the guy ..." There was a hint of accusation in his tone as he recalled the scene at the Diamond Club. He flicked through his rolodex, found the card and stared at it. "Daniel Logan. All I'm suggesting, Conrad," continued Max, adding a dash of moral indignation, "is that we throw them a bone, make it go away. Without prejudice. We're talking a billion dollar IPO. I'm willing to kick in some of my shares. For the £2 million they sunk into PaySense, I'm sure they'd be happy with a £10 million slice of the pie."

Hearing this only confirmed Baine's belief that there was substance to the claims. He scribbled on his notepad and pushed it in front of Durand.

"I met Stuart Lassiter in New York yesterday," said Durand. "He's the managing partner at Peterman Brown."

"And?" Max was trying to sound nonchalant, in the loop.

"He said they have proof."

"What proof?" snapped Max, standing up, almost knocking his chair over. He paced like a caged animal, shoulders hunched, anger seething from his pores.

"He wasn't specific," replied Durand, "although he was awfully confident."

Max ignored the insinuation. "So why did he tell *you* this?"

"We've been negotiating."

Max wondered what other loops he had been cut out of. "What progress on that front?"

"Of course, I denied any wrongdoing and insisted they substantiate their claims before I would consider their terms."

"And? ..."

"And nothing. They're stalling.

"Why?" Max realized it was a rhetorical question as soon as he asked it.

"Let's cut to the chase," said Baine, the voice of authority. "Given these developments, I see no option but to suspend Adware's bridge round. Midas have agreed to withhold their withdrawal from the syndicate if we do that, give us time to sort things out."

"We've got too much at stake," pleaded Max.

"I don't need you to remind me what's at stake, Max," snapped Baine. "I've sunk $30 million of my money into your company. But their offer is non-negotiable. Either we suspend or they pull the plug. I need not remind you, Max, that *our* reputation is at stake." It was clear he meant Ignite Capital, not Adware.

"There is no basis to any of this," insisted Max.

"We'll see."

Durand let the finality of Baine's words sink in with a long silence before offering the lifeline, his tone conciliatory, "I've made the case with our Investment Board. They've agreed to a short-term capital injection, a loan."

"How much?" Max's reply came quick. Money was on the table.

"Half a million. Sterling. Another half at my discretion."

"But we've got immediate cash flow problems," protested Max.

"Yes, I'm aware. And we're going to have to tighten our belts, make some cuts. I'll be taking over finances for the interim. Unless, of course, you have any objections."

Max did but was in no position to voice them. They all

knew Adware was almost out of cash.

"Robert's flying over tonight," said Baine. "He'll take the lead on managing this situation." With a sneer, he added, "He's become quite adept at handling this sort of thing, haven't you, Robert?"

Mr. Distress. Durand seethed at the barb but said nothing.

"Adware's burning north of £250K a month, with £150K in short-term liabilities and less than £600K in the bank," said Durand. "That gives us less than two months of working capital. I've already started going through the books. We can slice £80K off monthly outgoings immediately. I've also instructed Nigel to identify further cost cuttings."

Max tried to hide his fury. Durand had been talking to his finance director without his knowledge. "We can't lay off people. That would send the wrong message."

"I agree," replied Durand. "We can lose a few here and there but we don't want mass layoffs, nothing to spook the markets. As you say, Adware can't look weak. But there are savings we can and must make across the business. We'll discuss it tomorrow. Please clear your calendar. I'll see you in the morning."

Baine terminated the call, letting the silence fill his office. "You stay there until this is resolved," he said, the subtext loud and clear, "And don't come back if you fail."

It was not just the money, Durand's partnership at Ignite Capital, his reputation, his place on Sand Hill Road, were all at stake. Fail and Baine would destroy him with homophobic, bigoted glee.

0111001101000000001100110

Daniel Logan leaned back and crossed his legs. Stuart Lassiter, Managing Director of Peterman Brown, sat opposite, accompanied by Seth Edelman, managing partner at Edelman Jones, Logan's private law firm.

Lassiter summarized his attendance at the Global Invest

Conference, who he had talked to, what he had said, seeds he had sown. Logan nodded approval. Lassiter had done as instructed.

"Derrick Schmidt?" mused Logan when he heard the name.

"Yes," replied Lassiter, "he's ..."

"I know who he is," said Logan. "Continue."

Derrick Schmidt was a Silicon Valley legend, a serial entrepreneur who, over the past 30 years, had launched more successful IT companies than anyone could count. His presence at GI could mean only one thing—his latest venture, ABC, was expanding into Europe. Potential ally, potential threat.

"Arrange a meeting with Schmidt. I'm sure he'll be in London soon. In fact, he may already be here." Logan offered no further explanation, just a wry smile. Turning to Edelman, he asked, "And the lawsuit?"

A nervous look passed between Edelman and Lassiter. "There's a problem," said Edelman, avoiding Logan's eye as he gave a quick summary.

Logan listened in palpable silence.

"I know they exist. I've seen them."

Logan had too, watching from his penthouse. He also knew the source, Mark Haddad, but that too was privileged information.

"Why don't I lean on Brown, threaten to withdraw funding?" offered Lassiter.

Logan shook his head, "No. We're not pulling out of PaySense."

Lassiter nodded, mumbling, "I wasn't suggesting we actually ..."

A look from Logan cut him off. "PaySense is a goldmine. I don't want any problems with Duncan Brown." He paused, rubbing his chin. "Leave it with me. I'll get the emails for you." Logan glanced at his watch, signaling the end of the meeting.

Taking their cue, Lassiter and Edelman gathered their papers and saw themselves out.

Edelman whispered, "He took it better than I thought."

"I *will* talk to Duncan."

"Careful, mate. You heard what he said. He doesn't want anything upsetting the apple cart."

"Yes, loud and clear. But I'm sure Duncan is just peeved about being kept out of the loop, the way this whole thing has gone ahead without him. I'll fall on my sword, say it was my fault, being in Boston, forgot to brief him before I left. That sort of thing."

"Well, be careful."

"Of course," said Lassiter. "Trust me, I know how to handle prima donna entrepreneurs."

"Alright," replied Edelman, still not convinced.

"What do you think Daniel meant, 'he'll take care of it'?"

Long pause. Drawn breath. "Don't know, old chap, and don't *want* to know." replied Edelman.

Both men had worked for Logan long enough to know that he played by his own rules. Sometimes it was best not to ask questions. The lift doors closed.

Adam Lazarenko had heard enough to not be surprised by the instructions he was then given.

CHAPTER 12

Neither dog nor alarm posed a problem. In fact, the one nullified the other, a household pet not real security.

Finding a WIPS—wireless intrusion prevention system— at the first site was a surprise. It was the kind of device one would install at a high-security facility like a bank or government agency, not a private residence. The man had spent two nights probing the WIPS, port scanning it, trying to hack in with his usual bag of tricks. It was state-of-the-art, industrial-strength, professional kit, expertly configured. There was no way past the front door, not without stronger measures. And those could trigger alarms.

Safer to get physical, they had agreed. Daytime, plain sight, no one home. The man pushed the dustman's trolley down the narrow, overgrown alley, thankful of the overalls and mask as he caught the stench of animal shit, piss and rotting vegetation. He stopped just past No. 23 and got to work hacking, raking and bagging weeds and detritus.

Cover established, he cast one last look toward the street before springing silently up and over the fence. Landing crouching tiger, he checked the neighboring windows. Curtains drawn, no lights, no movement. He edged toward the house and called the dog (knew his name since yesterday).

Rex barked, came running, stopped dead at the raw steak.

Five minutes later, Vladimir picked up the limp canine, eased and followed him through the dog flap. He scampered down the hallway on all fours, eyes taking in the motion sensors—on when he moved, off when he stopped—but no alarm triggered. Still, he crawled the rest of the way to the front door.

He stopped, looked up at the control panel. B was lit, the word 'Perimeter' penciled in next to it. He smiled and stood up, one eye on the nearest motion sensor. Good. One less thing to deal with.

He walked back to the slumbering Rex, carried him into the living room and gently laid him in his bed. He stroked the retriever lovingly, admiring his shiny, golden coat, then set about his business.

There were two parts to the job—surveillance and data retrieval. After finding the WIPS, he took no chances, scanned for counter-measures first before planting hidden microphones around the house. Next, he set about copying hard drives, checking drawers for flash drives. When he was finished, he then retraced his steps, looking into every room for more computers. Kid's room, dining room. He copied those hard drives too.

Within minutes he was back in his guise as municipal worker, on his way to the next target site. The Haddad house would be much easier.

011000100010111001100011

Adam Lazarenko's report to Daniel Logan highlighted the presence of a WIPS at Duncan Brown's house, the hard drive's impenetrable 2048-bit encryption. The flash drives and two other hard drives had nothing useful either.

Perhaps they had overlooked something, offered Lazarenko, an external hard drive maybe, hidden somewhere in the house. "We could look again."

Logan shook his head. No point. Even if they did find another device, he suspected it would be heavily encrypted. Brown was obviously serious about data security, as he should be. PaySense was a pioneer in the highly targeted world of online credit card payments. Logan felt begrudging respect. Not for the first time, he thought there might be real value in this PaySense investment, beyond just being a vehicle for extortion.

They had had more success penetrating Haddad's home network but found no trace of the emails there either.

"How do you want me to proceed?" asked Lazarenko.

"Prepare a Lazer drive."

"Yes, of course," replied Lazarenko with a smile. Lazer was his baby, a highly specialized computer virus. Where other viruses sought to replicate and spread, Lazarenko specialized in precision targeting.

"I'll provide final parameters tomorrow."

Lazarenko knew when he was dismissed, and was glad to escape unscathed. Not his fault. The operation had gone to plan. But still, Messenger had been a dangerous occupation through the ages.

Alone, Logan considered his next move. He could target Brown once more, intervene personally, reason with him. But he had seen what happened the last time Lassiter had tried that. The relationship between PaySense's founder and its investors had soured and they were barely on speaking terms.

He had an idea, made a call. "Tony," he said, no preamble, "I'm launching a new venture. I'd like you and Arthur on the board." He explained a little more, ending the conversation with an appointment for Thursday morning.

"Seth," he said when his second call was answered. "I need an off-the-shelf company, operational by Thursday. With an office. Seed it with a quarter million from Peterman Brown, but at arm's length. An offshore entity. Channel Isles will do."

"Area of business?"

"IT Services," replied Logan vaguely.

"I'll have something set up by the end of the day," replied Edelman. He suspected it had something to do with PaySense, but knew better than to ask.

Logan leaned back and surveyed the battlefield. Things were *not* going to plan. He needed those emails. Each day that passed without him producing the smoking gun weakened his position, emboldened his adversary. He had been stalling, and Durand was now threatening counter-suits, clearly sensing a bluff. But it was not. The evidence was there. Logan just needed to get his hands on it. If it cost another quarter million, so be it. If anything, the new twist might add some piquancy to the project.

CHAPTER 13

Tony Levine stared at the resume in front of him. There was nothing wrong with it. On the contrary. On paper, Mark Haddad was the perfect candidate. More to the point, he was the only candidate.

Over the years, he and Arthur Barker had sat on the boards of a number of Logan's companies. But this was different—sudden, only a single candidate for CEO. Levine could not shake his nervous feeling.

He glanced at Lord Barker, wondering if his long-time friend shared his concerns. He dare not ask, not here. He knew Adam Lazarenko had been round to install the 'security system' at BizTech's new offices at 126 Kingsway, Holborn. Euphemism—he knew the place was bugged, like all Logan's companies, including his private fleet of black cabs. Oddly, it had never occurred to Barker to suspect that Berkeley House was, too.

Levine had no problem with the practice. Over the years it had proven a treasure trove of useful information. It was also commonplace, everyone did it. A personal point of pride for Levine was his own talent for playing to the cameras, using them to seed disinformation, foil his adversaries. He knew better than to try that with Logan. He had never met anyone who could so easily spot a lie. Conscious of the cameras, he tried to appear relaxed, natural, as he chewed things over.

Yes, of course, he thought, furrowing his generous, pepper grey eyebrows. No IP. No Cambridge boffins. Only a quarter million? Logan liked round numbers, never brought less than seven figures to the table. BizTech was a stalking horse. That's when Levine saw the connection—Adware. It was no coincidence.

The conference phone beeped, red lights pulsing. Lord Barker leaned across the table and pressed the big grey Answer button. "Yes?" he said in a deep baritone.

"Mark Haddad is here for his 3:30 interview," replied a silky feminine voice.

"Two minutes," instructed Barker before hanging up and turning to Levine with a smile. "Well, old chum, here we go again. Odd this, only one candidate. But Logan's chosen well. As usual." His tone was condescending, as if he were talking about the hired help.

Levine glared admonishment, a warning.

Lord Barker snorted. Disdain was the prerogative of class. Perversely, it had gave him a certain power over people, none more so than the likes of Daniel Logan, barrow boys made good who craved but would never have what was his by birthright.

Levine arranged the documents in front of him and idly toyed with the flash drive Lazarenko had given him. Another odd thing. The instructions had been very specific.

Precisely two minutes later, the secretary knocked and ushered Mark Haddad into the boardroom. Barker devoured her long, slender legs and ample breasts as she took coffee orders. Levine focused on Haddad.

Like most people, he was taller than Levine. Athletic, well-proportioned, natural confidence. He was smartly dressed, neatly pressed, a designer blazer, fine Italian loafers and a form-fitting black mock. No collar. No tie. Levine tried to mask his immediate dislike of the man.

All three beamed artificial smiles as they shook hands, exchanged pleasantries. When the secretary left, Lord Barker's eyes followed her until the door closed.

"Charming, isn't she?" he said, directing a lascivious grin at Mark, who nodded non-committally and also caught the look that flashed on Levine's face—jealousy.

Mark was not sure why he had agreed to the interview. He had already invested more than enough time in the job search and had three offers on the table. At this point, he was more concerned with stalling for time as he pursued Plan A, an investor for Dynamo.

At first, he had not been interested. But their keenness won him round, especially after they let slip to Rick that there were no other candidates. All things considered, he supposed, if he did end up doing Plan B, as a day job, this sounded as close to running his own show as it could get—CEO of a well-funded start-up. Not a bad thought.

But he was already underwhelmed, wondering if he had made the right call in agreeing to the interview. In either case, he was here. Go through the motions, hear what they have to say.

Levine opened with a leading statement, "I understand you've been job hunting for some time."

"Only a few weeks, actually," replied Mark, parrying smoothly. "It's a very," he searched for the word, "robust ... job market. I already have several offers."

Mark acknowledged the sounds of mild surprise, comments about the credit crunch, with a shrug. He took a sip of water and leaned back in the deep leather chair and crossed his legs, body language saying 'buyer' not 'seller'. "So, tell me a little more about BizTech. I couldn't find anything online, just a holding page." He did not add that he had not found anything at Companies House either.

Levine laughed nervously and explained, "Yes, of course. We're a new start-up, all still quite hush-hush. As you can see, we're just setting up." The office was a construction zone, wires dangling, fresh paint on the walls, tarps and ladders everywhere.

Barker picked up the thread, "BizTech is a new digital advertising company. We recognize the growth potential in this sector and believe we can bring a number of USPs to market. I'll be blunt, Mark. We will be in direct competition with Adware. Do you have a problem with that?"

Mark studied Barker. Levine had introduced him with his full title, Lord Barker of Godalming. *Figures, always a lord on the board.* He'd had his own once, Lord Rothcoe. Mark had fired him after two exasperating years. Useless. That is, until he was on the outside pissing in. No fond memories there.

It was obvious Lord Barker knew nothing about the Internet. He probably did not even use email. All he brought to the table was connections to other lords on other boards.

"Of course not," replied Mark. "Though I suspect they would want to enforce my gardening leave."

Lord Barker changed gear. "Do you think Adware will make the Webdex 100 again this year?"

"I guess we'll find out in a few weeks," smiled Mark.

"I'd like to understand more about your reasons for leaving Adware. From where I'm sitting, it doesn't make much sense," pressed Levine. "A little birdie tells me an IPO is in the offing. You're obviously an important part of their operation ..." He left his sentence hanging in pregnant silence.

Mark faced this line of questioning in most interviews and had developed a boilerplate response, although it was a bit of a porky. "I've been with Adware for five years. My options have vested and I'm looking for a new challenge."

"Still, to walk away now, with an IPO just around the corner?"

Mark's tone was sharper than he had intended. "I thought

we were here to discuss BizTech?"

Barker glared at Levine, warning him to back off before returning his chummy attentions to Mark. "I'm sure BizTech can offer you a lot of challenges, all quite exciting, really. New company, disruptive technology, shake things up a bit, opportunity to get in on the ground floor, build a great company." He smiled warmly.

"How ground floor? How far along is your development program?"

The nervous look that passed between Barker and Levine, answered Mark's question, BizTech was still just an idea. The thought triggered a pang of resentment. No one had been willing to fund Dynamo when it was just an idea, yet these two clowns had backing.

"We haven't started yet. Which is why we're interested in you. Your technical background."

Mark interrupted, "I'm sorry. I must have misunderstood. I thought we were talking about the CEO role. I'm really not interested in a technical role."

"No, of course not," replied Barker smoothly. "CEO. That's correct. But your technical background will still be invaluable. Your first objective, of course, will be to get our R&D program underway, hire a technical director, choose the platform ..."

Mark suddenly found himself interested. *'Choose the platform. ... Dynamo! What else?'* He could use BizTech to launch his own company—without investors. *Plan C!* He almost laughed out loud. Dynamo could be profitable from Day One.

It took a moment for Mark to realize the room had fallen silent. Barker and Levine were looking at him expectantly, waiting for a response. Like a kid caught daydreaming in class, he had no idea what the question had been.

He ad libbed. "Interesting. How quickly do you plan to launch?"

Barker smiled, sensing that he had piqued Haddad's

interest, that he had moved the meeting beyond the obvious personality clash between him and Levine. "That would be your decision, of course, as CEO. But time is of the essence." Pause. Smile. "The board has agreed an incentive scheme—for you and your team—to make us operational sooner rather than later."

Mark stifled a smile. This was getting better. "Your target?."

"One year," said Barker.

"And the incentive?"

"It's all in here," replied Levine, taking the opportunity to hand over the flash drive as instructed. He slid it across the smooth mahogany table. It stopped at arm's length but Mark made no effort to reach for it, only acknowledging it with a nod. He did not want to come across as over-eager.

"And if I delivered sooner, say six months?" With Dynamo, he was confident he could do it in three.

Barker studied Mark carefully, sensing it was not a frivolous question. "Well then," he laughed, "you'd be a miracle worker ... St. Mark ... ha ha ha. ..." He paused, lending due gravity to his next words. "I'm sure the board would show its appreciation. But we mustn't cut corners. It must be enterprise-ready."

"Of course," replied Mark, with an understanding smile. "But there are ways to fast-track the R&D—using existing tools, open source software, agile development—"

"Oh, I see," replied Barker, sagely rubbing his chin. "It would be your decision, of course."

Levine's eyes narrowed, thinking he now understood why there was only a single candidate. "You're, ah, your experience at Adware would of course be invaluable," he began, choosing his words. "I realize your role is sales, but your ... erm ... your technical experience, your knowledge of the Adware platform, if you see my meaning. You must know it inside out. I can see how that ... erm ... *knowledge* of their source code would be helpful."

The way Levine emphasized the word 'knowledge'—sort of a nudge nudge, wink wink thing—was a bit slimy. Then again, Mark was probably giving him too much credit. He let it pass.

Levine pointed to the flash drive. "Do consider our proposition. I think you'll be suitably impressed by the business plan. And the offer. As Arthur's already explained, BizTech is well funded. You'll have all the resources—and incentives—you need."

"What's the salary?" asked Mark, as he reached across the table and picked up the flash drive, twirling it in his fingers.

"Base is 25% on top of what you're currently earning. Choose your best month this year. And, of course, performance bonuses. Not just for delivering the software, but for hitting revenue targets as well."

Mark ran a quick tally. He had closed three deals in March, grossing just over £25K. That'd bring their offer in at over £300K a year. Plan C just kept getting better! CEO role. Great salary. Dynamo's first client. No need for venture capital. He kept a poker face while also stifling the little voice in his head that said it was too good to be true. Swallowing the quiver in his voice, he tapped the flash drive. "I'll give it serious consideration. It's an interesting proposition."

Barker smiled. "And of course there's a very generous share scheme. Obviously, we want to compensate you for what you will be giving up by leaving Adware. But I won't spoil the surprise. See for yourself." He leaned back with a magnanimous smile and added the final touch, "Mark, join BizTech and I promise you will be a very rich man inside three years."

"Shall we meet again on Monday? That would give you the weekend to consider our offer."

Mark thumbed through his calendar and offered, "3 o'clock?" He was glad the interview was over. His brain was churning and he wanted to give free rein to his thoughts, talk to someone he trusted. If he could make this work ...

0110111101101101001011111

"Job hunting," repeated Dick Bailey. "He met with Rick Ashton again on Monday—the head-hunter. And today I followed him to a meeting on Kingsway. Company called BizTech. Looked like another interview."

It was the fourth time Dick had reported Mark going to what appeared to be interviews. There were probably others.

"Any meetings with Duncan Brown?"

Dick's client had never said why he wanted Mark Haddad followed. But he was a private investigator. It was his business to figure these things out. And it did not take a genius. He read the papers, used Google.

"They've met a couple more times." Fishing some photos out of his briefcase, he added, "They seem to be friends. Live in the same neighborhood."

The client studied them. He still had no proof, but his instinct told him he was right—Mark was helping Duncan, feeding him information. "They're doing something more than just having drinks," he insisted. "I hired you to get me proof!"

"These things take time, Mr. Smith," replied Dick. "Corporate espionage. In my experience, they're careful. Not like husbands having affairs." He paused then added, "Do you want me to … ah …?"

"What?"

"Best you don't know, Sir."

"Do whatever it takes. Just get it done."

Five minutes later, Dick Bailey climbed out of the limo and watched it drive off, his briefcase a little heavier with a fresh installment of cash. Men who rode around in limos had deep pockets, and for whatever reason preferred to pay in cash. This was exactly the kind of case Dick loved. Handled right, he could string it out for months.

CHAPTER 14

Stephanie emerged from l'Escalier de la Costa. Below, to her left, lay Port Hercule in all its opulence. To her right, nestled in the steep gorge was l'Eglise Sainte Devote, shrine to Monaco's patron saint. Above and behind the modest chapel, the gorge's sheer cliff was riddled with terraces, bridges, and tunnels, in the foreground the ruins of an ancient Roman aqueduct. Stephanie paused for a moment to appreciate the contrasting views from one of her favorite spots in her new hometown. Heading toward the Port, she crossed Boulevard Grimaldi at the first turn of the Monaco circuit, smiling at the bronze sculpture of William Grover-Williams, winner of the first Grand Prix, in his Bugatti. For a devoted Formula One fan, there was no place more evocative of the history of motor sport than this famous turn.

Heading east alongside the quai, she took in the mega-yachts, each grander, sleeker, more flamboyant than the last. From the lobby of the Port Palace Hotel, she took the glass lift to the rooftop Mandarine Restaurant. As she stepped onto the terrace, she took a moment to appreciate the sweeping vista across the harbor to the Rock of Monaco. The terrace basked in urbane minimalism, over-sized cream-colored sunshades keeping the Carrara marble tiles cool beneath the feet of its well-heeled guests.

"Stephanie!" bellowed a deep voice from the far end of the terrace. Sam Leonard was a barrel-chested man, late-fifties, sporting a white linen shirt, his open collar displaying a thick spray of white hair, unashamedly hinting at the large belly below. In one hand, he had a trademark Churchill cigar that he waved in the air as he talked.

He came over, embraced Stephanie, kissed her on the cheeks, and wrapped his arm around her shoulder, fingers heavy with gold rings, a diamond-encrusted Rolex President dangling from his wrist. "So how's my favorite venture capitalist doing? You look great!" Without waiting for a reply, he swept his arm taking in the table and said, "Girls, say hi to Stephanie!" He laughed loudly as he held out a seat for her.

Sam's entourage was legendary, a bevy of beautiful women more glamorous than the glitterati, impossible to ignore. Sam loved the attention, thrived on it without apology. He was who he was, and he lived it larger than life. But the girls were not just eye candy. They were his employees, and each held a clutch of degrees from the world's elite universities, with specializations ranging from finance to physics.

Sam had built his first business on his own, turning a rickety street stall in London's Portobello Market into an international fashion powerhouse. Much of his subsequent success could be attributed to his entourage. As bright as they were beautiful, his girls would charm and disarm, then close the deal on his terms. Everyone he transacted with knew the score, but few could resist, man or woman, gay or straight.

His penchant for beautiful women was also what had drawn him to Pi Capital, to Stephanie Turner. He was an incorrigible flirt and she was very attractive. In most men, Stephanie found this irritating, but Sam was an exception. He never crossed the line and she never felt threatened. He flirted incessantly, could not help himself, but over the years they had grown quite fond of each other. He made her laugh, and she made them money.

"I got your note about Genex," said Sam, referring to one of the many companies in which he had invested on Stephanie's advice. Pending shareholder approval, Genex was about to be acquired by its largest competitor, earning its investors a very healthy return. "Happy to give you the proxy for my vote. Just let me know when the cash hits the bank! Need plenty of it for the casinos, don't we girls?" Sam Leonard roared with laughter. He was in a particularly ebullient mood today.

"So, tell me more about this sideline deal, Dynamo. I read the plan. What I'd like to understand is what is it to you? Why are you working it outside of Pi Capital?"

No small talk. Dead giveaway. Sam was interested. Stephanie had known the man for years, met him when she was raising Pi Capital's first fund. It was now on its fifth fund, and Sam Leonard had a stake in all of them.

"As you know, Pi Capital only invests in biotech. But I do sometimes come across something I like that doesn't fit our portfolio, and I decide to take a personal stake. To be completely transparent, I should add that one of the founders is a close friend. But you should also know me well enough to know that I wouldn't be backing it if I didn't think it was a winner. Also, I do have a seat on the board." What she did not say—what Sam already knew—was that she *never* sat on the boards of companies she invested in, only held observer status. Which meant this was special.

"Tell me more."

"Better yet, how about a live demo? I'm telling you, Sam, even you could program with Dynamo." Stephanie flashed a cheeky grin.

"Me? Program? You're having a laugh!" bellowed Sam. But a live demo did mean it was not vaporware, which piqued his interest further, although he tried to hide it. "Tell me what it is first. How are we going to make money?" Stephanie knew that Sam and his analysts had already been through the prospectus with a fine-toothed comb.

"Let's do the demo first," said Stephanie, keeping control of the agenda. "I promise not to get too technical. Then we can talk numbers." Without waiting for a reply, she pulled out her laptop and launched a web browser.

"Cynthia. Come join us," said Sam, waving her over.

Cynthia was Sam's think buddy, his closest advisor. Armed with an MBA and a law degree from Harvard, at age 26, she had joined McKinsey, a leading management consulting firm, straight out of university. By 29, she had become the youngest partner in their history. Two years later, after she sold his first company for him for a cool $150 million, Sam poached her. They had been together since.

She was a vision as she stood up and glided across from the far end of the table, her long, lustrous hair dancing in the breeze, the sun radiating from her gold lamé dress, making it seem as if she had risen from the glistening sea behind her. Across the restaurant terrace, conversation dropped to a murmur as people stopped and stared. Stephanie had experienced the effect before, could only describe it as bewitching. Then, just as effortlessly, Cynthia released the idle rich from her spell and turned her full attentions to Stephanie.

The two women greeted each other with genuine affection. They had formed a relationship over the years, one Stephanie was still trying to get her head around. They kiss-kissed and exchanged pleasantries. Cynthia stepped back to admire Stephanie's dress, a demure Chanel number, commenting on the way it showed off her legs. Stephanie indulged the flattery with a gracious smile. They were both playing their parts with intent, but that did not stop either from enjoying it.

As they sat down, Cynthia opened her small Dior clutch and put on a pair of dark rimmed glasses, transforming from catwalk model to business executive. As always, Stephanie felt pity for the men who fell under her spell. Even after so many years working together, she was still not entirely inured to it herself.

Stephanie matched Cynthia's change of pace and turned to the business of describing Dynamo, a software development platform that could be used to build virtually any kind of interactive website. Stephanie kept the demo short, steering it by Sam's reaction and Cynthia's questions. First, she showed them three example sites to demonstrate Dynamo's breadth of application—a web shop, a social network and a content portal. Then, she logged into an empty sandbox site and asked them what they wanted to build.

With a straight face, Cynthia said, "A lingerie shop."

Sam laughed. Stephanie grinned. She opened a browser window and searched for some copy/paste images and content. Within minutes, she had assembled a rudimentary, yet fully operational, lingerie shop.

"See, Sam. Even you could build a site with Dynamo. If we had inventory, we could take orders right now. It really is that easy. And the library of widgets will just keep growing."

Stephanie closed her laptop. Time to talk numbers. "The main revenue stream at launch will be software licensing. It's a freemium model. The basic service is free, but we charge an annual subscription for premium licenses. Charities and non-profits are exempt. There are a lot more revenue streams we plan to bring online—cloud hosting, professional services, transaction fees from online payments, and so on. It's all in the business plan, forecast out to three years." She paused, added with a twinkle, "There are a few we left out. Don't want to give away to much just yet."

"The prospectus says it's open source ..." said Sam with feigned distaste.

The last thing Stephanie wanted was to get sidetracked into a debate on open source vs. proprietary software licensing. Besides, she knew Sam was playing devil's advocate. His portfolio already included investments in a number of open source companies, including Red Hat, Debian, Magento. But it was also a gift of an opening.

"Yes, it is," replied Stephanie, "And we've written our

own license. The Dynamo Public License. DPL for short. It's much more commercially sensible than the existing open source licenses, so we expect wider adoption by the open source community." With complete sincerity, she added, "Whether or not you invest in Dynamo, Sam, I'd really appreciate your feedback on DPL. I believe it's as revolutionary as Dynamo." Stephanie held out a flash drive.

Sam nodded toward Cynthia. From the way his eyes followed the exchange, Stephanie knew she had piqued Sam's curiosity and that he would be reading the documents as soon as the meeting was over. She was on a roll, could feel it. "We also have several patents pending. That's being handled by Russell Fitzsimmons from Smith & Jones in Washington, DC. The filing documents are also on the flash drive."

"Smith & Jones? Expensive," said Sam.

Stephanie smiled, said nothing, let the silence hang like a piñata waiting for Sam to break it. Russell was an old friend doing a favor, but Sam did not need to know that.

"Two million in two tranches. One now, the next in six months. For that, I want 51% of the company. And I chair the board, with two votes." Stephanie caught Cynthia's double take. Sam had meant to play coy, drive a hard bargain, but in his excitement he had shown his hand, gone off-script. He *never* tabled an offer at the first meeting.

It was a good sign, but Stephanie did not react. Her strategy was working better than planned. Sam loved disruptive technologies, and disruption was part of Dynamo's DNA. It was why Stephanie had kept DPL, their software license, out of the original prospectus, to surprise him with it in person. The tactic had worked—caused an unforced error.

Stephanie did not budge. She reiterated what was in the prospectus. "We're raising two million dollars for a 10% stake. One seat on the board. This is a billion dollar play, Sam. At 10%, two million buys you a $100 million return on your investment."

"If you're so confident it'll hit a billion, then you should be happy with my offer. Your guys split half of that."

Stephanie gave him a withering look that said, "C'mon, Sam. You're going to have to do better than that." She packed up her laptop.

"Twenty-five percent and two seats, two votes. You keep the Chair," countered Sam.

The way he said it, the way Cynthia glared at him, spoke volumes. He had gone straight to their best offer. At least it had been. Now, it was, in effect, their opening bid!

Stephanie stifled a smile. "I'll take it back to the guys, see what they say." Her voice conveyed doubt. "We do have other interested parties."

"You've got my offer and my sat phone. Come back to me," said Sam, folding his hand for the day. He raised his voice for the rest of the table, "C'mon, girls. Time to set sail."

Cynthia's eyes locked on Stephanie as she stood up. "It was lovely seeing you again. We really should have a drink soon."

Cynthia held out a business card. "In case you don't have my number." Stephanie took it, felt a spark as their fingers touched.

"Call me," Cynthia purred, her words laden with innuendo. "I'll be back in Monaco next week."

When they were gone, Stephanie stood up and leaned against the balustrade, her heart racing as she took in the view across the harbor. The meeting had gone far better than expected.

A moment later, she saw Sam's party emerge on the street below and cross the Corniche, Cynthia playfully skipping along the quai, laughing her way up the gangway. She waved at Stephanie and blew her a kiss, as the gin palace cast off and eased its way toward the open sea.

010001110100010101010100

While Stephanie watched *Eliza's Revenge* clear port and

head for open waters, Mark stood outside Jason's building in Soho making the final edits to an email. It was simple. Plan A (get Dynamo funded) + Plan B (find a new job) = Plan C (CEO of BizTech). En route from Holborn, he had spoken to Susan and Rick. Both had been skeptical, pointed out the obvious conflict of interest. Mark was undeterred.

He hit 'Send' and pressed the buzzer to Flat 4G. The door buzzed back and he made his way down the dark, narrow hallway. His hand found the light switch (a timer) and he took the stairs two at a time, racing darkness to the top floor.

Jason's door was ajar. He had made an effort to tidy up, empty pizza boxes and soda cans stacked unevenly next to the overflowing trash can, dirty dishes piled in the sink. The place was still a tip. Peter was already there, pacing, not quite sure where to park himself.

Mark got straight to the point, laid out Plan C exactly as he'd described it in the email he had sent to Stephanie, Susan and Rick.

"I like it," said Jason.

"You're being naive," said in Peter. "Nice idea, but there's no way they'll go for it."

"Why not? They get what they want," countered Mark.

"What they want is you as their CEO, not some guy breezing in, selling them some software then pissing off. They want you to build *their* business, not yours."

"But don't you see? That's the beauty of it. I—we—would be doing both."

"Don't get me wrong. I see where you're coming from. All things being equal, I can see your logic. But look at it from their perspective. You can't serve two masters."

"We're meeting again on Monday. I'll play it straight. What have we got to lose? If they don't go for it, I walk away, no harm done."

Peter was still not convinced. "There's an obvious conflict of interest."

"I don't see it that way. The two companies' objectives are

perfectly aligned." Mark counted off on his fingers. "BizTech gets a fast-track go-to-market solution. Dynamo gets license revenue. The more I drive BizTech's sales, the more revenue Dynamo earns. It's a win-win. Everybody's happy."

"Why not just sell them licenses?" offered Jason, who had been half listening, his eyes and hands darting continuously to his keyboard.

"Maybe. But I'd have to pitch to the guy they bring in as CEO. The thing is, if we can pull this off, we won't need VC funding. Think about it. Dynamo can be profitable from Day One. Nothing to lose by trying."

"How long would you need to stay at BizTech?"

Mark smiled, sensed that Peter was warming to the idea. "Don't know yet. We can agree a fixed term or a revenue target. I figure a year, 18 months, two years max."

"Most CEOs are *on* a year's notice," laughed Peter. "You'd effectively be handing in your notice as soon as you joined. What then?"

"Dream Team," said Jason over his shoulder, eyes fixed on the rows of green letters scrolling up his computer screen.

"What?" asked Mark.

"Dream Team," replied Jason as if it was obvious.

"Care to explain?" said Peter, his tone tetchy—Jason had a way of winding him up.

Jason swiveled his chair round and said, "Peter's right. You're only joining them for the short term. If you want them to go for Plan C, you need to future-proof it."

"I still don't get what you're saying…"

"I do. He's saying 'build in a succession plan'. Take your team, Marie as Sales Director, CEO in waiting." He laughed. "This gets better and better!"

"Not so good for Adware, though," cautioned Mark.

"Screw them! Screw Max. He deserves it!" For all his blustering, Jason did not really wish ill on anyone, not even Max. But as long as they remained abstract, cruel thoughts could fill him with wicked glee, almost as if it was just a video game.

"It does make sense," said Peter, in a reasonable tone. "More incentive for these guys to go for it."

"I'm not sure I'm comfortable with it." Now it was Mark who was getting cold feet.

"What? Don't think Marie can step up?"

"No, that's not it. She'd be a natural. I have complete confidence in her. But as pissed as I am with Max and Adware, I'm not out to screw them. It's bad enough that I'd be joining the competition, but take my team with me? That'd be harsh. I'd rather just walk away."

"Well, for what it's worth, I'm with Jason on this." It was not often that they agreed on something. "From BizTech's perspective, it makes Plan C very compelling. They get a fast-track platform, a CEO and a shit-hot sales team, and they hurt the competition big time. If I was BizTech, I'd be all over it, before the IPO, cause maximum damage. Who knows, on the back of the lawsuit, it could completely derail them."

"That's hardcore," said Mark, growing uneasy with the direction the conversation was going. "I can't do that."

Peter ignored the comment, his mind working the PR angles. "You could package the whole proposition, press releases, timing—announce it at Webdex! Wow! That'd really hurt."

"Guys, guys, c'mon. I'm just trying to get out, not burn the place down," said Mark. He had to admit, all the pieces did fit. But it was not in his nature to be vindictive.

"Another plus," said Peter, "You could help your mate, Duncan. Launch BizTech with PaySense as its payment gateway. Give them the idea Duncan proposed to Adware. Jason's already done the integration."

Jason nodded.

Peter could see that Mark was still reticent so he added, "Look, mate, they've screwed you, screwed your team, screwed everyone. Even your mate! You don't owe them anything. Besides, as soon as you leave, how much do you want to bet your team will leave, too? That'll happen regardless. Why not take advantage of it?"

"Yeah, maybe."

Sensing that he had pushed it far enough, Peter changed subject. "So, what about these forecasts you mentioned? What is BizTech's growth plan?" he asked, glancing at his watch, reminding them that time was pressing.

Mark fished out the flash drive and tossed it to Jason. "Everything's on there—the offer, employment contract, company prospectus, budget forecasts, share options ..." he grimaced at the last two words.

Peter noticed and smiled to himself. *Give it time. I'll bring you round.*

Jason fumbled the drive a few times before getting a grip on it. He spun round in his chair and slotted it home in his PC.

"Got anything to drink?" asked Peter.

His back turned, Jason waved over his shoulder and mumbled, "Fridge."

Peter went foraging but came back empty handed. "Just cola. Let's go down to the coffee shop."

As they made for the door, neither Peter nor Mark noticed how engrossed Jason had become, leaning into his computer screen, no longer listening. Nor did they think anything of his furious tap-tapping on the keyboard. It was just the way he was.

"Yeah. I could use some fresh air," replied Mark. After years off them, he had been having the odd cigarette recently, and was now starting to crave them, plan them. It was a slippery slope. "Back in a minute," he called over his shoulder as the door shut. Jason was immersed and only grunted in reply.

Five minutes later, Mark and Peter stood outside the building, waiting. They had pressed the buzzer a few times.

No answer. Finally, Mark held it down, impatiently jiggling a staccato rhythm.

"You gotta see this!" said Jason, his excited voice bursting out from the intercom, scratchy and hollow.

"Let us in, Jason. We've been standing here for ages."

"Oh yeah. Sorry." He buzzed them in.

They raced the timer, taking the stairs two at a time. When they reached the top floor landing, Jason's door was open, his burly form hulking over his keyboard. In an agitated whisper he said, "You gotta check this out. That flash drive? Something weird about it."

CHAPTER 15

Fine English pub fayre accompanied by several expensive bottles of Bordeaux, 2004 Clos de Marquis, Saint-Julien. It'd been a thoroughly (mostly) pleasant affair, a bit of a celebration, Max's party numbering ten rather than the usual two to four.

The bridge loan from Ignite had been agreed. He had driven a hard bargain, but they had finally caved in and agreed to the full million. Sterling. Cash in the bank this morning, with a further half million on tap, Max was feeling flush and bullish.

The PaySense issue was still unresolved, but Max was sure they would soon put it behind them and get on with the IPO. Durand was here—not at The Ivy, thank God—but in London. Max did not trust him, but it was in their shared interest to get the matter resolved, so he was giving him space to get on with it.

The waiter arrived with the bill. Max did not give it a glance as he flashed his Platinum Amex. He keyed in his pin and handed the terminal back to the waiter, rejoining the conversation.

"Sir, there seems to be a problem," said the waiter. "Excuse me one moment."

A few minutes later, the maître d' whispered a quiet word to Max and ushered him to the privacy of his station.

"I am sorry, Mr. Greenberg. There seems to be a problem with your credit card."

"Must've put in the wrong pin …"

"I'm afraid not, sir. The pin was correct. I'm afraid the card's been cancelled. The error code instructs me to destroy it …"

Max glared at him.

"But of course, as a long-standing patron, I am sure we can reach an accommodation. Clearly there's been a mistake. If you have another credit card …?"

Max was livid. The indignation, the embarrassment—he never paid for lunch, the company card the endless well of his generosity. He brushed the incident off with a laugh, but as soon as he was back at the office, he went on the warpath.

He found Robert Durand in Nigel Thornton's office doing what they had been doing for the past week—number crunching. Max slapped the bill down on the desk. "Nigel, reimburse this by bank transfer. Today."

"What is it?" asked Thornton, although his eyes had already seen enough to know. Like everyone else, he had long lived in fear of Max, bullied, browbeaten, jumping when told. Not this time. He scrunched his face into a heavy frown, lower lip extruding, and slowly shook his head, forcing back a gloating smile with a tut tut tut.

He slid the receipt over to Durand, who raised his eyebrows when he saw the amount, over £1,000. "Your lunch bill?"

"My credit card didn't work, did it? The maître d' said it had been canceled. Wanted to cut it up there and then. Do you know how embarrassing that was?" He let his pent-up rage boil over, his face turning red from the effort.

"Your lunch bill," repeated Durand, deadpan.

"I was entertaining clients."

"At £145 a bottle."

Silence.

"How dare you cancel my credit card! I'm Chairman of this company! My company!"

Thornton was enjoying this immensely but was not foolish enough to wander into the middle of it.

"No, Max, it's not your company," replied Durand, his voice even. He had been expecting the showdown, pegged the timing perfectly, just past lunch. "You are a shareholder, one of many. And as Chairman, you have a fiduciary responsibility to all shareholders. We've already discussed this. You know the company needs to make cutbacks, zero the gap between revenue and expenses. We cannot have £1,000 lunch bills."

"I was entertaining clients," repeated Max, his posture aggressive, threatening.

It was the cue Durand had been waiting for. "Last year, your expenses ran to nearly a quarter million pounds. That's just discretionary expenses—restaurant bills, entertainment, the Rolls."

"How dare you!"

But Durand was undeterred. "Then there are your travel expenses. First class, five star hotels, Michelin dining. This has got to stop, Max. It simply isn't tenable."

"So you cancel my card without even telling me? Do you want to embarrass me, embarrass the company?"

"You've already topped last year," continued Durand, "and there's still a full quarter to go." Durand's tone carried a hint of incredulity.

"So you cancel my card without even telling me?" persisted Max.

"I rather hoped you would have grasped the situation and exercised discretion yourself. Clearly you haven't. This week alone ..." he fished out a list of expenses, "Lunch at The Ivy twice, dinner at L'atelier de Joel Rubochon twice, £300 bar bill at the Dorchester, £600 cash for a strip club ..." He stood up, on a roll, reciting from memory, not the piece of paper he was waving. "More than £10,000 and it's only

Thursday!"

"I want this reimbursed by bank transfer today," demanded Max.

"No, Max, I will not authorize it. You buy your own lunch from now on."

"You won't authorize it?" Max squared up to the shorter man, but Durand refused to be intimidated. He had the upper hand and he knew it.

"That's right."

"Nigel, give me the checkbook. I'll write it myself."

"You're no longer an authorized signatory on the company bank account."

"You have no right …"

"Ah, but I do, Max. We've been quite clear about this from the beginning. It's stipulated in the terms of our loan."

"This is bullshit," protested Max, still refusing to accept what he was hearing.

Durand chose his moment to deliver the coup de grace. "The Bentley …" He let his words hang, watched the color drain from Max's face. For months it had been all Max could talk about. Production of the Continental GTC was massively over-subscribed and he had pulled a lot of strings to get on the list. The £100,000 deposit had come from company coffers and the car was due for delivery in a few weeks. Durand chose his next words carefully, architecting the outcome he wanted. "We've had an offer of £300K for our place on the list. The company can make a tidy profit."

"You can't do that."

"I realize how important the car is to you, Max. So I spoke to Conrad. It wasn't easy, but he'll let you have it for £200K."

"You're going to sell me *my* car?" Max was incredulous.

Durand held his silence for the longest time. "Conrad already has an offer for 100K more. This is a one-time offer."

Max whipped out his personal checkbook and Mont Blanc pen, signed a check, threw it on the desk, and stormed out without another word.

It was war. They both could see that. Max thought he had won with the last word, but the first battle went to Durand. It had not taken long for him to see that Max's personal finances were as over-extended as the company's. He had been spending like a billionaire since the first whiff of the IPO. There was the super-yacht on order, half a million deposit, £2 million balance due on delivery. A major house renovation, already well north of its original £2 million budget. Now, his lavish lifestyle was no longer being subsidized. And Durand was just getting started. With a smile, he returned his attention to Thornton, "So, where were we?"

CHAPTER 16

The business card served as a VIP pass. Yes Sir, no Sir, of course Sir. The concierge tripped over his words as he led Max up the grand staircase and ushered him into the bar.

From his penthouse, Daniel Logan ruminated while he watched his surprise visitor on the video screen. He had just been on the phone with Robert Durand, who had made his position clear—no negotiations until Logan produced the evidence.

That had left Logan in a foul mood, angry with himself as much as anyone for his schoolboy error. The emails existed. Lassiter had seen them. He had described the 'garbage text'

The problem was, Logan still did not have them in his possession. Brown refused to hand them over. Searching his and Haddad's house had turned up nothing either. Third time lucky. He was sure of success this time. The Lazer virus had never failed before.

Back to Max.

He wondered why he was downstairs, at his Club. Instincts told him he was not here as an emissary of Robert Durand, that he was acting unilaterally. Interesting.

"Max Greenberg! Welcome to Berkeley House!" said

Logan, greeting his guest after keeping him waiting ten minutes. "I hope my people have been taking good care of you." He glanced at the bartender with an approving nod. "Let's sit over there, shall we?" Without waiting for a reply, he led Max to a discreet corner by the tall window.

"So to what do I owe this pleasure?" asked Logan, ignoring the elephant. "Are you thinking of joining Berkeley House?"

"How do you know Tony Levine?" demanded Max.

"Yes, I gathered you share some history," chuckled Logan.

"How do you know him?" persisted Max, leaning forward, jaw jutting aggressively.

Still the bully, thought Logan, bemused, not intimidated. "He's on the board of one or two of my companies. Very well connected. I'm considering him for my Adware seat."

The flash of surprise on Max's face confirmed what Logan already suspected—Durand was keeping him out of the loop. Divide and conquer.

Max recovered well. "The reason I ask is that he just interviewed my Sales Director."

"Really?" feigned Logan. "Are you sure? Perhaps—"

"Yes, I am sure," cut in Max. "It's a new company. BizTech. Offices in Holborn."

Pulling out his phone, Logan made a point of noting the name, asking Max to spell it. "I'll speak to him." With a look brimming with false sincerity, he added, "Adware's strength is its sales. I'll make sure Tony understands that."

"I'm not following." Max really was out of the loop.

"You must be aware that we're negotiating a merger."

"Yes, of course," said Max. He clearly was not, which Logan would later confirm by playback, studying his facial reactions in slow motion.

"Well then, *su casa es mi casa*—your IPO is my IPO. Neither of us wants to see that undermined, now, do we? Rest assured, I will look into this matter. And I thank you for bringing it to my attention. What's his name, your Sales

Director?"

A lot of thoughts swirled in Max's head, central amongst them being that he was sitting with a man with whom he could do business. Sure, Logan was suing him, but he could appreciate the play. Given the opportunity he would have done the same thing, had done similar in the past. A fellow predator. But as an ally, he sensed Logan could be a real asset. He smiled warmly, accepting the aura of partnership Logan had woven. "Mark Haddad. H-A-Double D-A-D."

"Excellent. Consider it done," replied Logan, putting his phone away with a flourish just as the waiter arrived. "Perfect timing! I trust our business is concluded." He waited for a nod from Max before offering, "Then let me tempt you with what Berkeley House has to offer."

They toasted with vodka, blini and caviar. A half dozen test tube-shaped glasses floated in a bucket of ice water, a bottle of premium vodka at the center. On Logan's side, they were filled with water. They finished the round of six and Logan refilled from the bottle, Max too far gone to notice how he poured his own into the ice water, how his cupped hand raised empty shots to Max's full ones.

"So, tell me, how do you know Tony Levine?"

"I brought him on board as a director at one of my companies. You should be careful," Max's words were beginning to slur. "Don't trust him."

"Oh, really," replied Logan.

"It's in the past," said Max. "We were all much younger. I'm sure he's a perfectly decent fellow."

Logan did not press. He had heard Levine's version, read Lazarenko's report, probably knew more about their shared past than either man could remember.

"So how did you get started in all this? The web, I mean?" Logan was just making conversation, studying his adversary.

"I was in Cambridge, back in the 90s" replied Max. 'In' not 'at', misleading but short of a lie. He wondered where this story was going.

"I knew this computer geek. Showed him Jerry's Guide to the World Wide Web—remember that?"

Logan laughed disingenuously, "Yes, yes, I do." Jerry's Guide grew up to be Yahoo.

He also remembered the conversation, as vividly as if it had happened yesterday. He was the computer geek Max was talking about.

It had been mid-afternoon, between lectures, dark skies, a storm brewing. Max had tracked him down to the cafeteria. He had been hounding Logan for weeks, refusing to take 'no' for an answer. The conversation had become heated, Max dropping all pretense of friendship, resorting to his trademark playground bully tactics. Someone had called security.

"I explained to him that what Jerry was doing wasn't scalable. That the web was going to explode and a directory wasn't going to be able to keep up. What we needed was search, an intelligent agent." He laughed aloud. "IA. Get it?"

The blood drained from Logan's face. "An ... an intelligent agent?" he stammered.

Max attributed his new friend's sickly pallor to the multiple shots of vodka they had just consumed. "Yeah. IA. Reverse of AI—Artificial Intelligence. Get it?"

Logan reeled as long-buried memories, images, voices, emotions came pouring out. After 20 years, he finally saw the truth. It was obvious, always had been, but at the time, he had been too wracked by guilt to see it, had been running from it ever since, blinded, never looking back.

For two decades, he had been living a lie, living with the guilt, living a life a without Michelle, a life without life. All because of the man sitting opposite him.

"You alright?" Max repeated the question, a look of concern on his face. His words finally penetrated Logan's consciousness, drawing him back to the here (the man shaking his arm) and now (the past, the present, his life, all changed).

Logan needed to be alone. "My apologies, I do not feel

well. I must go. But please, do stay, enjoy yourself. On the house." Standing up, he offered, "I'll also arrange a complimentary membership. I'll inform the desk. They'll have a card for you when you leave."

It was an abrupt departure but Max did not think much of it, figured Logan could not handle his vodka. His eyes roamed the well-appointed room, recognized a few faces. And the waitresses! He poured another shot, helped himself to a cigar and decided he could come to enjoy his new membership at Berkeley House.

It took all of Logan's self-control to maintain his composure as he left the bar, made his way to the private lift, past Natasha's desk, to the privacy of his office then through to the sanctuary of his apartment.

Cold sweat, heart pounding madly, lungs gasping for air. He lurched for the bathroom, retched violently, over and over. Then, dry heaves, each empty spasm more painful than the last, his face flushed with blood, sweat and tears, eyes bulging, vessels threatening to burst.

Slowly, slowly, he regained control, gulping water, choking back the retching dry heaves, steadying his breathing. He crawled to his bed and climbed in, fully clothed. One hand reached out gingerly for the remote control, killed the lights, drew the blinds, plunged the room into pitch darkness.

He curled into a damp, sweating, shivering ball, his mind's eye trying to corral the memories, the demons unleashed from their long-buried box, unable to do anything but submit to their hypnotic miasma. In time, he fell asleep, whimpering, crying, anguished. That was when the nightmares started.

When Logan woke, it was dark. The White Queen was in his hand. Unfolding his naked body, he gingerly climbed out of bed, followed the trail of clothes, saw the open safe, stared at the Queen, his bloodied hand. He had been gripping the sharp-edged marble figurine so tightly it had broken skin.

He made his way to the kitchen, gulped water and washed the clotted blood from his hands.

He sat at the conference table and poised his fingers above the holographic keyboard, fired up a web browser, Adware's homepage. He breathed deeply as he randomly chose a client from the roster—a home electronics retailer—it did not matter.

Placing the cursor in the search box, he drew a deep breath and typed 'Kc1 Rc2# 0-1'. The moment of truth. Enter. The site instantly spat back a 404 error page. No matches found.

Logan did not understand. Every bone in his body told him he was right. He had programmed the Easter Egg so deeply in the source code that it had to be there, would have been nigh on impossible to remove without completely rewriting the search algorithms.

Then he spotted his mistake, a double space. He retyped. "Kc1 Rc2# 0-1." Double, triple checked it, drew another deep breath and pressed 'Enter'.

Michelle's photo instantly appear on screen. Logan let out an anguished wail that threatened to pierce the soundproofed walls. His hand reached for the nearest object, a heavy crystal ashtray. He hurled it at the screen wall with all his strength and collapsed at the table, eyes filled with tears.

After a while, he got up and walked toward the screens, his bare feet cut and bleeding on broken glass. He reached out and touched Michelle's face, caressed it, kissed her cold dead lips. His hand squeezed the bloodied Queen tighter, tighter, fresh blood dripping from his clenched fist as he whispered her name over and over.

CHAPTER 17

Mark waved goodbye as Susan pulled away from the curb. It was an unseasonably warm October morning and she and the kids were setting off to spend half term at their place in West Wittering, on the south coast.

They had fallen in love with the eccentric village years ago, when the Franklin & Marshall crew, fresh off the boat from America, had rented a house there in the off-season for Thanksgiving. A couple of years on, Mark chanced upon a sweet deal, a local farmer wanting to offload an awkward tract of land that was costing him money and headache.

What Mark had noticed was the plumbed water and power, a derelict shed—precedence for a structure. Years on, the Haddads still had not broken ground. Their planning application for a modern design was being fought every step of the way by local conservationists, fishermen, farmers, and retired colonels.

After two years of frustrating roadblocks, Mark found a pair of surplus US Army mobile officers' quarters on eBay. Like the land, he had bought them for a song. By dead of night, he and the boys had hauled them down from Lincolnshire and installed them behind the copse of trees at the crest of the hill. It had been a military operation, done by dawn, no one the wiser.

It was nearly a year before a neighbor to notice that a camouflaged M.A.S.H. compound had sprung up in their idyllic backwater. By then it was too late, nothing doing. Unless, of course, they approved the paperwork for a permanent fixture. The difference now was that the Haddads were happy to wait, however long it took. They had withdrawn all concessions and resubmitted the original design.

Mark shut the door and returned to the kitchen for another cup of coffee, enjoying the rare solitude of an empty house. He stepped into the garden, basking in the unseasonably warm weather. After a few minutes, he made a call.

"Yeah. Nice and quiet round here too." John Harding's family was with Mark's, en route to the coast. "Still on for a jam session?"

"Definitely."

"The guys will be here around noon."

"Cool. Mind if I come earlier? There's something I want to bounce off you."

"Sure, no problem."

"How about 11?"

"Perfect. See you then."

Two hours later, John leaned back, deep in thought. Mark had just outlined Plan C.

"The only downside I can see is Max—he'll go nuts. Frankly, BizTech should be all over it—you'd be doing exactly what an incoming CEO should be doing—beating the shit out of the competition." He laughed. "Webdex is coming up in a couple of weeks. If you time it right ..."

"I can't believe I'm even thinking like this," said Mark.

"You work your ass off for five years. Then they go and screw your stock options like that? Trust me, no one will think less of you for it. Besides, like you said, you'd be doing right by Duncan and your team. It gets my vote. As long as you're ready to make an enemy of Max."

"Yeah, there's that too," replied Mark, as he tallied the score: three for—Jason, Peter, John, three against—Susan, Stephanie, Rick.

"What about the job itself?"

"What do you mean?"

"If they say 'no' ..."

"No big deal. I just keep fundraising. Landing a job would still be Plan B. Besides, Rick's got other opportunities lined up."

"In which case, there is no downside."

010001010101111100001101001

With the combined effects of a mild hangover and an empty house, Mark slept in late Sunday morning. The band had jammed through the afternoon, cold beer flowing steadily, keeping them chilled in the late summer heat. The evening had brought more home-alone dads, families away for the half term break. They had fired up the grill for a boys' night in, chatting, drinking, more jamming. Mark was fast asleep by the time his head hit the pillow at 3:00 am.

The muffled, persistent ringing of his phone finally roused him from his stupor. He fumbled for it, found it in his jeans pocket, still dressed from the night before, answered, groggy, voice thick with hangover. "Hello."

"I didn't wake you up, did I?" There was a smirk in Jason's voice, a rare opportunity to turn the tables.

Mark glanced at his watch. It was past noon. "Yeah, late night," he replied as he swung his legs out of bed and made his way downstairs for coffee.

"I've been trying to call you for hours." The oddness of the statement did not immediately register in Mark's still foggy brain. Jason was most definitely *not* a morning person. "There's something you've got to see."

"Slow down. I haven't even had coffee yet." Mark could hear the excitement in his friend's voice. "What? What is it?"

"I have to show you."

"Give me a clue? Got some new libraries?"

"No, it's about that flash drive you left here the other day."

"Oh, yeah, I meant to ask if you'd cleaned the virus off it. I need to review the docs before my meeting tomorrow."

"That's what I want to talk to you about. Something really weird. Can you come over?" There was urgency in his voice.

"I don't understand. Please don't tell me you accidentally erase the files."

"No," replied Jason, "That's not it. But not on the phone. When can you get here?"

Not on the phone? And I thought I was the paranoid one! "Okay, okay. This better be good. Give me an hour," replied Mark.

An hour later, Mark slipped into a lucky parking spot on Dean Street, just around the corner from Jason's flat.

"This better be good," he said when Jason opened the door. He was still nursing his hangover.

Jason tossed the flash drive to Mark, the one Tony Levine had given him. "It's got a virus."

Mark turned it over in his hand. "I *know* that. What? Couldn't you clean it?"

"It's not a normal virus," replied Jason. Mark stared in silent disbelief as Jason explained what he had found.

"Let me get this straight. You're telling me this device has a virus written specifically to target me? C'mon, that's ridiculous!"

"No, it's true. My mate Ivan works at Inoculatus, the antivirus lab. He said your name is actually hard-coded into it. Trust me, Ivan is über badass. He knows his shit. Besides, I never mentioned your name. He did."

"He probably saw it on the documents," countered Mark, still skeptical. "Or maybe the virus did …"

"Part of it's a root kit," continued Jason undeterred, "designed to gain total access to your PC. Are you sure you didn't jack it into your laptop?"

Mark thought about it for minute, then said, "No, I came straight here. I didn't even have my laptop with me."

"Good. Because if you had, that would have been it, total control. And there's no way you'd have known. No mainstream antivirus software will recognize it. It's boutique, not mass production."

"So what's it supposed to do?" asked Mark irritably, "this super-virus?"

"Corporate espionage. Steal data. This is where it gets interesting. It's got very specific instructions." Jason paused for dramatic effect. "Ivan is a majorly elite hacker. He was a Black Hat before he joined Inoculatus. He says he's never seen anything like it. Only a few people could have written it. It's very clever. First, if you type on the keyboard or jiggle the mouse it stops—opposite of a key stroke logger. That's why he calls it Hermit, like a hermit crab."

"C'mon! You're winding me up!"

"Trust me. I'm not. Let me finish. When the computer's idle, it opens a UDP port and starts shoveling data through."

"What data?" asked Mark nervously.

"Email, just email. Oh, and your PGP key ring. My guess is that they wanted to forge your credentials."

"Are you absolutely certain about this?"

"Ivan's not easy to impress. He's a legend ... for years, he ran a massive zombie army, millions of compromised PCs, never got busted. If he says only a handful of people could've written it, I believe him. Most viruses are designed to spread. This one's not. It's a laser-guided smart bomb. It goes in, does its job, then self-destructs, doesn't leave a trace. Somebody out there thinks your email account and PGP key ring are worth something ..."

Mark sunk back into the sofa, speechless. A long time passed before he finally asked, "You think Tony Levine gave me the flash drive knowing what was on it?"

Jason scratched his head, shook it. "No, the way you described him, the guy's a Luddite, doesn't know bits from bytes. But whoever gave it to him ..."

"Can you trace the IP address it opens the connection to?"

"Forget it. Too many hops, never the same route twice. I'm telling you, the guy who wrote it is a major badass hacker. But he did make one mistake," added Jason with a glint and a smile. "He assumed it'd only be loaded on a Windoze box, not a heavily fortified Linux machine like mine."

After a long pause to digest all this, Mark said, "There goes Plan C, just as I was warming to it."

"It could just be coincidence."

"No. From what you describe, I'm being targeted. The friggin' virus has my name on it! I knew there was something shady about those two. But you're right—no way they're savvy enough to be behind it. So the question is, who is?"

"What are you going to do?"

"Focus on what we've been doing, fundraising. Dynamo. Full steam ahead. But I do need to figure out who's behind this. If it's organized cybercrime, could be nasty." Swirling images of the Russian mafia sent a shiver of shock through him. "The only person I can think of who wants my email and PGP key is the VC backing PaySense."

"What for?"

"Evidence, which they've seen but don't have."

"If it is them, Duncan is already in bed with them."

"He wouldn't do something like this," said Mark rising to his friend's defense.

"That's not what I mean. What I'm saying is, you have to warn him," replied Jason.

CHAPTER 18

Stephanie called from Monaco. Good news. She had met with the Angel, Sam Leonard. "He's very hot. Wants to meet you. I think we can close him."

"I'm there. Just tell me when," offered Mark.

Stephanie chuckled. "Week after next will do. He just left for New York. Put it in your calendar. Mid-week ideally. Wednesday/Thursday. Make it a long weekend. We'll have some fun."

"This is brilliant, Stephanie, really. Just what I needed. Some *good* news."

"Why? What's up?" Stephanie had known Mark long enough to catch the subtext.

"Plan C."

"I wanted to talk to you about that ..."

"Yeah, I know, I know. Don't say it. 'I told you so'. But it's something else ... Have you got a sec?"

Halfway through his story, she cut Mark off, "This is serious."

"You're not kidding."

"More than you know." Even that was more than Stephanie had wanted to say on an open line. She let it sink in, her own thoughts casting downstairs to the whiteboard, the spider's web diagram of companies and people she had been building. "We need to talk, but not *now*," emphasis, 'not on the phone'. "I'm flying in this evening." It was a spur of the moment decision.

"Cool. You can crash at my place. Family's away …"

"I know. Mine's with them. Remember?" said Stephanie. "I'll call you when I land."

"Happy to pick you up at the airport," said Mark.

"No worries. I'll catch a cab."

"Okay," replied Mark.

"One more thing …" Stephanie left a long silence. "Walls …" She was speaking in subtext, hoping Mark picked up on it.

'*have ears*'. He did. Stephanie's paranoia was legend. Mark played along. Fluent spontaneity they had developed as merry pranksters at university. "Vanilla ice cream. Of course, I'll stock up. Forget you can't buy it there." Subtext, '*Understood*'.

"Don't forget the Flakes," laughed Stephanie. '*Copy that*'. "Now, I really do have to go."

Mark hung up, pumped. Only a month in and they had a hot prospect, an Angel too, better than a VC, and he was interested in the whole tranche. With a bit of luck, Dynamo could be in business in a matter of weeks. No more Adware. No more job hunting. None of this crazy shit. Just Dynamo. He had, however, taken Stephanie's warning to heart, the little voice inside agreeing that a bit of paranoia would not be misspent. It struck him that Stephanie's flight to London had been spontaneous—she usually shared her schedule in advance so they could meet up. He was puzzling that when his phone vibrated, email from Stephanie. An encrypted email.

He read it twice, then twice more. He then followed the instructions.

"What are you doing right now?" he asked when Duncan answered.

"Just about to mow the lawn."

"Up for a bike ride?"

"Sure. When?"

"Now. I'll be there in 5 minutes."

They cut through the Common, down the wooded trail to Bog Gate. Rather than following the outer circuit, Mark led them into the middle, toward Isabella Plantation, until he found a secluded spot.

"Why are we stopping?"

"We need to talk."

Several hours later, Stephanie's flight landed. Instead of going straight to Mark's house, she drove to her office in the West End, picked up a briefcase, then headed back west. She parked at Petersham Gate and hiked up to King Henry's Mound.

"You're sure you weren't followed?" she asked, no preliminaries.

"Positive. We did three laps of the park, different route each time."

It was dusk, the park closed to cars, bikers and hikers down to a trickle. Mark noticed the briefcase. "You carried that up the hill?"

Stephanie reached in and pulled out a paddle-shaped object. "It's not that heavy."

She made small talk as she scanned them, their bikes, their phones. They were clean. "So, you two seem to have landed yourselves in it."

"How did you know?" asked Mark. He had been chewing on the question for hours. Stephanie's email had simply said: "BizTech is connected to PaySense. Tread carefully."

"They're both backed by Peterman Brown. I didn't think much of it, not until you called. Tell me about this flash drive."

"We've decided the easiest thing is to just give them the emails. Make it go away," said Duncan.

"Not so fast. Tell me about the flash drive first."

Mark started from the beginning, the interview with Tony Levine and Lord Barker, how he had come up with Plan C. As he spoke, he realized he was still trying to convince Stephanie it was a good idea.

When he got to Jason, Ivan and the virus, Stephanie started asking questions. Then, when they arrived at the here and now, she said, "How about we head down to that pub where I parked? I don't know about you two, but I am famished."

They cut through the woods and down the hill, took a table in the garden of the Dysart Arms, ordered food and drink. Stephanie made sure the conversation stayed off-topic while they ate.

When they left, they split up, Mark and Duncan traveling by bike, Stephanie by car. They rendezvoused at Mark's house then went to Duncan's, found bugs in both, nine in total. Stephanie took it in stride, though she was glad to see the others were sufficiently spooked. It would focus their attention. She hand-signaled until they understood, they would leave the bugs in situ. They then drove in Stephanie's rental car to her office in Mayfair. Once she had settled them in around the conference room, she said, "We're safe here. We can talk."

Her words punctured Mark and Duncan's stunned silence since finding the bugs.

"I always thought you were just paranoid," said Mark, trying to make light of it all.

"Now you know why. You've probably been in countless bugged meeting rooms, and just didn't realize it."

"Elevators, taxis," said Mark.

Stephanie smiled. "What have I always told you?"

"Never talk in a cab that was called by the company you're visiting," recited Mark. "I don't. Ever."

"Good. Now what's the first rule of counter-surveillance?"

"Don't let on that we know," answered Duncan. His first reaction had been to rip the bugs out. Stephanie had to restrain him, explained why later, on the drive over. It was the first lesson in her crash course in counter-surveillance.

"So what do I do about tomorrow?" asked Mark. "This interview ..."

"Keep it. But you have to act natural. You can't let on that you know *anything*."

"Can't give the game away."

"Exactly," said Stephanie with an approving nod. "I like the idea of saying you lost the flash drive. That should remove any doubts about why the virus didn't activate. Where is it, by the way?"

"The drive ... I left it with Jason."

"Good. Because they were in your house, which means they probably searched it. If they didn't see it, they'll have no reason to doubt you." She let that sink in.

"From now on, you have to think about everything. Even the smallest detail is important. Both of you. We need to know who we're dealing with. Now, I want you to think back on every single time you discussed this. Where, when and with whom. Here." She handed them each a tablet. "Write it down. We need to work out *exactly* what they do and don't know. Mark, start with our call earlier. I want you to remember everything about it, every word we said, what happened immediately before and after, then work backwards. Duncan, start with your first meeting with Peterman Brown."

Stephanie stood up. "I'll put on a pot of coffee. We're in for a long night." She left the room, then popped her head back in, "Sit apart, work alone. That way, we have two versions of the truth to work with."

Minutes later, when she returned the room was as silent as a library. Mark and Duncan murmured thanks, then lapsed back into quiet concentration, styluses tapping on touch screens.

Stephanie busied herself at the far end of the conference table with a bunch of electronics.

They reached end point at around the same time.

"Okay, first thing," said Stephanie. She handed Mark and Duncan new mobile phones and chargers. "Secure communications. I've programmed each of our numbers into these handsets. From now on, we use them for all operational voice, email, text communications. For everything else, continue to use your normal phone, including calls to each other, but always assume someone is listening. And remember—no changes in pattern."

"Is this really necessary?" asked Duncan. "Why not just give them what they want and walk away?"

"You can't just walk away. Mark maybe, but not Duncan. They've got £2 million invested in your company. And they've thrown a lot more at it—BizTech as a front company, this super-virus, the bugs, the surveillance. We need to know what their end game is. Once we know that, then we can plan yours."

Duncan had a grim look on his face but nodded, point accepted.

"Trust me, I've done this before. First thing is to understand what we're dealing with."

Mark and Duncan familiarized themselves with their new smartphones while Stephanie wheeled out the whiteboard. She picked up a tablet and began tapping away. The overhead projector whirred to life, rotated 90°, and adjusted focus on the whiteboard. The screens from Mark and Duncan's tablets appeared onto the whiteboard side by side.

"Mark, let's start with you."

"That is so cool!"

Stephanie's smile said, "just wait."

Mark leaned over for a closer look at the app she was using to control it. "Homemade?"

"A prototype."

"One of the companies you're invested in?" asked

Duncan.

"My own little side project," said Stephanie.

She stood at the whiteboard, the two narratives displayed side by side, drawing shapes, lines, connections, moving things, adding notes, zooming in out. She did not sit for an hour.

"That is really cool. I assume you're going to productize it."

"Already filed the patents. Code's pretty much done. I just need a UI designer." The user interface was a bit rough around the edges. "And some funding." She smiled. "Now, back to this email. Duncan, are you absolutely certain you redacted all attribution on the copy you showed to Stuart Lassiter?"

"I checked it three times. I'm sure. I can get it from Warren if you want to check it yourself."

"Warren … he's the lawyer you gave them to for safekeeping?"

"Correct," replied Duncan. "All hard and soft copies. He's a partner at one of the big City law firms. He has a safe in his office."

"And you trust him?"

"Absolutely."

"No disrespect, I'm sure his firm's security is tight, but I'd feel more comfortable if you kept it here. Do you mind?"

Mark and Duncan both shrugged, "of course not."

"In which case, Duncan, please call him first thing tomorrow. Use that phone." Stephanie nodded at the encrypted handset she had given him earlier. "Call him at work on his landline."

"Are you sure that'll be safe?" asked Duncan. "Not this phone … his …"

Stephanie laughed but was also pleased. Too much paranoia was better than not enough. "Don't worry, big City law firm—his end will be secure, trust me. Bear in mind, though, that their conversations are also recorded, so try to say as little as possible, be cryptic where you can."

Duncan turned the phone over in his hand. It looked like any other mass-market smartphone.

"What if I'm being followed?"

"Someone else will meet him. Can you think of somewhere near his office that you could suggest without actually mentioning it by name?"

Duncan shook his head. They tended to meet up in the neighborhood.

"Okay, don't worry about it. We'll come up with somewhere later."

"You said 'someone else'?" said Mark.

"People I know. Now, these phones. It's critical you keep them hidden. Use your own phone like normal, even for calls to each other. Only use these if it's operational and safe. Remember, it's all about patterns. If the people following you are good—and we have to assume they are—then they will know your patterns, spot any changes in behavior. And we don't want that. They're covert. We have to be doubly so."

Mark and Duncan looked at each other, still a bit dazed, still trying to absorb it all.

CHAPTER 19

Daniel Logan tapped an impatient tattoo on the polished mahogany table. He was in a foul mood, had been since Friday. "You're late."

It was 12:02 pm. Lazarenko said nothing, sat down, haggard, deep shadows under blood-streaked eyes, face pasty, gaunt. He had not slept in four days. He was desperate for a coffee but too scared to ask, dared not help himself.

He slid the flash drive across the table. "There it is."

"Summarize."

Lazarenko knew better than to bullshit Logan on technical details. He offered his explanation, fielded a barrage of detailed questions and gratefully accepted the wave of dismissal.

When the door shut behind him, he breathed a massive sigh of relief. Natasha was on edge too. They exchanged a glance. None of the usual banter or peek-a-boobing, just the sympathy of confederates in fear, eyebrows asking questions, answering. Neither of them knew why Logan had been like this for the past four days.

Natasha handed Lazarenko an espresso. She had never done that before. Biscotti on the saucer, beneath it a slip of paper, only a corner peeking out. "You look like you haven't slept in days."

Lazarenko palmed the biscotti into his pocket before knocking back the coffee in a single shot. "Da. I go shower now. More work to do."

Lazarenko did just that as soon as he got downstairs. Like Logan, he lived at work. His setup was nowhere as nice, but it suited his needs.

With the shower steaming, he fished the biscotti out of his jacket pocket, munched on it and read Natasha's note.

A rendezvous. 3:00 pm. Good timing. Logan would be preoccupied with the Haddad interview. It also gave Lazarenko a couple of hours to dig, maybe figure out what had triggered the change in Logan. Would be nice to impress Natasha. He pressed the piece of paper to his nose, inhaled her scent, then chewed it slowly, savoring it as he stepped into the steaming shower, thinking of her.

01110100010100110111010100

"Sorry, no, I haven't." Mark gave a sheepish grin, "Awfully embarrassing. I lost it, must've dropped it on the way home. In either case, as I said, I really don't think this is right for me at this stage in my career. I thought it only fair to tell you face to face."

There was a long, awkward silence. Levine and Barker could feel Logan watching. Like Natasha and Lazarenko, they had sensed the change in him over the past few days, feared him all the more for it. Failure was not an option.

"Let's not be too hasty," replied Levine. "We spoke to our Chairman, told him what you'd asked—if there were incentives for delivering sooner."

"Yes, you seemed quite confident, very encouraging," added Lord Barker with a knowing smile. "He was very intrigued."

"So we've added a bonus pool of options. Sliding scale.

Up to 10% more at your discretion. For you *and* your staff, if you deliver a working platform in under a year. And ..." Here was the kicker. Logan had told them Mark was fiercely loyal to his staff. "We'd like to know what it would take to bring your people from Adware with you. Quite the dream team from what I gather ..."

"Generous terms for them as well," add Lord Barker, in flow with his partner.

"We've put it all on a new USB memory stick," said Levine as he slid the flash drive across the table. "Eight gigabit. Worth keeping." Levine tried to make the casual last words sound enticing.

Mark had to keep himself from laughing, remembering what Jason had said. Bytes not bits. He dropped the flash drive into his jacket pocket. "Thank you. I have to say, it is compelling." He hammed a smile, "Tell you what, I'll give it some more consideration. Perhaps we can meet again next week."

Logan smiled. The simplest explanation after all—Haddad had simply lost the first flash drive, nothing more sinister than that. And, fortuitous as it turned out—with the revised payload he had upped the stakes. Consumed with manic bloodlust, Logan had failed to notice the brief flash of suspicion in Haddad's eye as he pocketed the second flash drive.

01110010011000010111010

Mark felt like everyone was watching him. *Assume they are.* Stephanie's words echoed in his head as he boarded the Central Line to Bond Street. From there, he switched to the Jubilee, northbound to Baker Street, Circle to Hammersmith. The last leg was a bus, the 33.

Whenever it felt OTT, all he had to do was remind himself of what they had found—the virus, bug infestations in his and

Duncan's houses, the patterns and connections they had mapped on the whiteboard. Still, the new flash drive weighed heavily in his pocket, his heart racing every time he thought about it, thought about them, watching.

He eyeballed everyone, looking for familiar faces from hop to hop. A fat guy at Baker Street, sure he had seen him before.

A few kids, an OAP, a mother with pram and toddler got off at his stop. Last, the fat guy, who stayed under the awning, pretending to study the map.

Mark crossed the street and went into the corner store. The man was still there when he came out. Mark crossed back over and started walking. At the corner, he turned into the wind to light a cigarette, have a casual glance behind. The fat guy stopped walking, gazed in a shop window.

Mark's heart was pounding when he stepped into the house and closed the door. Stephanie was there, finger to lips, making small talk. She passed the paddle over Mark, his jacket, his bag. Mark was clean. She nodded. Still, they whispered.

"I'm being followed! And they gave me another flash drive! Quite insistent. It would've been awkward for me not to accept it."

Stephanie barely reacted, simply digested the information. "You told them you'd lost the first."

"Yeah. Also said I wasn't interested."

"Did they believe you?"

"I think so."

"Good. They sweetened the offer?"

Mark nodded. "Big time. How'd you know?"

"Makes sense," said Stephanie, "They got nothing the first time. Either you lost the thing or never plugged it in. Game theory, model all possible scenarios, plan for all eventualities."

"Or I discovered it."

"Possible. But hackers are usually too arrogant to accept that possibility."

Mark did not disagree. He had worked with enough programmers to know that myopia correlated with arrogance. "Fair point. It still seems so ... unreal."

Stephanie nodded toward the living room. "Now, let's play to the mikes and get out of here."

They walked in, raising their voices to normal conversation level. "So, how'd it go? You had that job interview today, didn't you?"

"Yeah, I tried to turn them down."

"Tried?"

"They upped the offer."

"They must really want you."

"My team, too," said Mark. Something niggled but he could not quite put his finger on it.

"So you're still thinking about it?"

"Well, it does have a lot going for it. CEO, run my own show. But Susan really wants me to go corporate. I don't know, it's just not my style. Can you picture me at IBM?"

Stephanie laughed. "Suit and tie brigade? Not you, mate. But don't drag my name into it! Anyhow, enough shop talk. How about a spin round the park before the sun goes down?"

"Best suggestion I've heard all day. Give me two minutes to get changed." The niggle persisted. Something they had said. He could not quite put his finger on it.

CHAPTER 20

"Something's wrong with the equipment!" shouted Daniel Logan.

"It's half term. Their families are away," explained Lazarenko, not for the first time. Logan glared at him, eyes burning, vicious, deadly.

Lazarenko lived in fear, always had. But this was on a different scale. Gone was the stone cold predator, the brutal logic, the dispassion, the purity of purpose—what had drawn Lazarenko to Logan in the first place.

Since last week, the day Max Greenberg had come to the club, Logan had changed. He had become erratic, mercurial, capricious, unpredictable. Irrational, even crazed. He had taken to summoning Lazarenko several times a day, demanding updates when there were none, always foul-tempered.

Nothing. From the bugs, only long deafening silences punctuated by banal domesticity, music, TV, the occasional conversation. Two eavesdropped phone calls confirmed why Lazer was offline—Haddad still had not used the flash drive.

Normally, Logan would have been patient, bided his time. Projects took months, sometimes a year or longer. Sometimes they went dormant for long stretches. Patience, his greatest ally, seemed to have abandoned him.

Lazarenko and Natasha both could see he was consumed by this project. Nothing else mattered. He rarely left his office, no sex, even canceled his biweekly trip to the Dordogne to join his family. This had put their world in chaos. Neither dared voice it, but both thought Logan had snapped, was having a breakdown.

On Monday, he had met secretly with Natasha, shared intelligence. Not everything—Lazarenko kept schtum about the trigger event, the Max Greenberg Moment, as he had come to think of it.

01100101011001110101111001

Lazarenko had assigned the task of tailing Haddad to Vladimir Valachenko. The first thing he had to report was that someone else was following Haddad. *Interesting,* thought Lazarenko. He ordered Valachenko to call in a second team to shadow the shadow. He wanted to know who and why.

The first part was easy. The man was a lone wolf, no backup team. When Haddad returned home on Tuesday evening, the man dropped off, caught the night bus to Hammersmith. From there, he took the Tube to Edgware Road and entered a rundown walk-up. Moments later, the lights turned on in a second floor window.

Less than a half hour passed before the man exited the building and took public transport to Highgate, where he let himself into a nondescript council flat. The name on the postbox was 'Bailey, Richard'. Sergei Petrov broke off from his unit and returned to Edgware Road, arriving just past midnight.

Save for a smattering of Arabs drinking tea, smoking hookah pipes and conspiring al fresco, the street was steeped in quiet shadows. With practiced ease, Petrov slipped unnoticed into the doorway, made quick work of the lock, and let himself into the building Bailey had visited earlier.

Second floor. He smiled. "Richard Bailey, Private Investigator" stenciled on the door. He was tempted to go further, but Valachenko's instructions had been clear, and life had taught him the hard way—do what you are told, no more, no less.

00101100100110101101001

Logan flipped through the report. Thorough, but not enough. He studied the photographs of Richard Bailey. An overweight, slovenly man, a gumshoe who had seen better days, clearly Max's man. It would explain how he knew Haddad had interviewed at BizTech. But he still wanted confirmation, and to know why Max was having him followed. He authorized the break-in.

He read the report line by line. Half term. Family away. House guest for one night. Train Tuesday morning to Chalk Farm. Sales call. Work. Innocuous. Logan ordered full background reports on the two new players. It was an obvious waste of effort, but Lazarenko said nothing, knew better.

Logan read on. Haddad met two men for lunch. Soho. Walked there fast, lost the gumshoe on the way. Logan studied the photographs. The odd man out was the younger one, a sloppily dressed twenty-something techie geek. They were relaxed, obviously knew each other well. On the surface, a casual lunch with friends. But their tablets and phones were out, some sort of serious discussion. He selected one photo and handed it to Lazarenko without looking up, "Background on these two."

Lazarenko nodded, hiding his exasperation. Four more so far today, more than twenty Subjects all told. Logan was demanding profiles of everyone Haddad met, even the guy in the corner store. Full teams carrying out 24/7 surveillance on Haddad, Duncan and Bailey. Already, they had more than 30 people in the field! Now Logan wanted a team on Max

Greenberg as well. Lazarenko's resources were being stretched. And he was being run ragged.

Logan read on, the pages quivering in his hand, not a lot, but enough for Lazarenko to notice. 2:30 pm, back to Adware's office. Clocked out at 5:00 pm. Met a man at a bar in Mayfair. Logan recognized him, had an idea. *Richard Ashton!* He called the Club's manager. "Richard Ashton has just won the monthly draw. Courier an invitation to him immediately. An evening on the house, with friends. Full Monty. Drinks, dinner, a private snooker room."

"But sir, we've just had a winner ..."

"Just do as I say!" snapped Logan, "Valid for this Friday only."

Lazarenko knew immediately what Logan had in mind, suspicions confirmed moments later by Logan's call to Natasha. Lazarenko did not have a problem with it, but the decision was impulsive, reckless, very unlike Logan. And that did worry Lazarenko.

011110000111001001100101

Rick Ashton was sitting in his office, feet up on the desk, when the secretary buzzed him. "There's a courier here. Says you have to sign for it in person."

Rick and Gary looked at each other quizzically before getting up and making their way to reception.

"What is it?" asked Gary, peering over his shoulder. Expensive card stock, gold foil, the Berkeley House crest, hand calligraphy.

Rick turned away with a mischievous smile. "Wouldn't you like to know."

"Gone on," said Gary.

"I've won a complimentary evening for four at Berkeley House," announced Rick with a smile.

"Sweet," said Gary, "I assume I'm invited."

"Boys' night out with Mark and John?" he offered.

"They're home alone this week. Timing's perfect." He handed the invitation to Gary, "I suppose there's room for one more."

"Cool. Private snooker room," said Gary studying the invitation as they walked back to Rick's office to RSVP.

CHAPTER 21

The taxi pulled up at Berkeley House just after 6:00 pm. The doorman attentively ushered Mark and John into the Club's marbled foyer. The concierge checked their names against the guest list and logged them in. Upstairs, silent alerts flashed.

"Finally!" said Daniel Logan. An image of Haddad and Harding appeared on his screen. He tapped it twice, once on each face, enunciating their names in turn, "Haddad ... Harding." His network of cameras began to automatically track them. It would display their location anywhere in the Club on voice command.

Click. Click. Click. One by one, the top row of screens on his video wall came to life as the cameras followed Haddad and Harding up the stairs. Logan caught the appreciative exchange, smiled with them, his eyes following their escort, stiletto heels, toned slender legs, the graceful sway of her skirt. She glanced back demurely and Logan found his own heart racing. He touched her face on the screen, spoke the words "New Girl." *I'll look into you later.* The stirring in his groin told him he had his mojo back. The stasis had been killing him.

New Girl ushered them across the lounge to a corner nook where Ashton and Tate were already settled. Logan pressed a button. A 3x3 square of screens filled 360°, an overhead view in the middle. Every table in Berkeley House was wired the same, audio-miked in surround sound. He turned up the volume.

"Can we get a round of martinis?" asked Rick as they settled into the over-stuffed leather chesterfields.

Logan fired off an instruction to Lazarenko, "Profile John Harding."

The camaraderie, the laughter, the easy banter downstairs spoke of friendship and trust, things Logan knew nothing about. Watching alone in his penthouse, he was hit by a sudden sense of regret, tears for the man he had once been.

Twenty years ago, he had run, run away from everything—Michelle's death, her memory, his guilt, his past. It was not until he was on board the night ferry to Holland that he had dared pause to reflect. Standing alone on the stern deck, he had stared into the abyss, contemplating throwing himself overboard. Then he saw a great white stalking the dark waters below. *Carcharodon carcharias.* Pure, ruthless, fearsome, fearless, void of emotion or feeling. Like him, the great white was lost, in unfamiliar waters. Yet it was the ultimate predator. It would adapt and thrive, its survival never in question. His was.

The great white rose out of the water as if to strike, cold, killer eyes locked on his, then dived and disappeared into the inky depths of the North Sea. He knew then what he had to do, what he had to become to survive.

"Michelle," he whispered her name over and over. His soul mate, his one true love. Free of the guilt of her death, he cried fresh tears of sadness, as if she had only died yesterday. Then came anger and rage, a thirst for revenge.

"Focus!" he shouted at himself, willing back the cold control he had mastered these past two decades. His eyes searched out words on the page, read them, forcing them from his lips like so many Hail Marys. "Roommates ... Franklin & Marshall ... Class of '86," the dossier a litany of

143

penance.

Downstairs, the scene played on with a spirit of bonhomie.

"Gorgeous," pronounced Gary as he watched the waitress walk away. "They all are."

Logan had first noticed the value of surveillance and attractive staff in Las Vegas, where legions of scantily clad waitresses worked the casino floors, especially attentive to the high rollers. He had immediately adopted both practices when he opened Berkeley House. In keeping with the club's ambience, the sexuality was more understated, tailored uniforms demure rather than revealing. He also made sure his floor staff were warm and charming, intimate with the guests yet never crossing the bounds of probity. In this way, Berkeley House trumped Vegas with its enticingly addictive atmosphere.

The gender balance was still sharply skewed, but in recent years the number of male staff had been rising steadily to accommodate the Club's growing membership of powerful businesswomen and all preferences in between. It was no surprise that members rarely brought their spouses to Berkeley House.

"Oh, I nearly forgot," said Rick, "I talked to my mate at the *Times* this afternoon. He let slip that Adware's going to scoop first place at Webdex in two weeks." He raised another toast to Mark. "Well done."

"Hopefully, I'll have resigned by then."

"It's your award. You deserve to collect it."

"I'm with Gary," said Rick. "Plus it puts you in the spotlight. Webdex is the perfect place to go public about Dynamo. It'd be perfect timing if you managed to close your funding round first."

"If you don't," added Gary, "no worries, the place will be packed with VCs. Just don't forget to bring plenty of your new business cards!" Gary raised another toast, glasses clinking.

Mark had been hoping to relax, forget for a while, but the whole subject made him edgy. His house was bugged. He was being followed. He had been given flash drives with personalized viruses. He had been jumping at shadows all week. Understandably. The worst part was being in limbo, not knowing what he was up against. At night, alone in the dark, he would stare at one of the bugs, sometimes for hours, trying to make sense of it, tiptoe around his own kitchen. At least Susan and the kids were away in Wittering. He hoped it would all play out before they came home.

"Enough shop talk, boys. We're here to party. I don't often get a hall pass." Mark knocked back his martini and signaled the waitress for another round.

Logan had heard enough to make him curious. Dynamo, he guessed, was a start-up. He recalled the report of the lunch meeting a few days earlier, Haddad and two other men, one a young techy geek, connected the dots. It also explained why he had not jacked in the second flash drive . He speed dialed Lazarenko, "Find out what Dynamo is. I also want to know what VCs Haddad is talking to."

They were on their third round of martinis when the hostess came to say their table was ready in the Grill Room. There, they shared a chateaubriand, baked to perfection, the rich flavors of the foie gras and black truffles fusing with the succulent beef tenderloin. This was complemented with roast potatoes and fresh spinach, topped off with a 1998 Chateau Margaux.

Berkeley House's wine cellars were renowned, but Rick had always restricted himself to the more affordable vintages. So when the sommelier casually rested his finger near the bottom of the wine list and quietly said, "Compliments of the house, sir," he gladly accepted. He felt positively spoiled when the sommelier arrived with a second bottle of the delicious premier cru, unasked.

After dinner, the party moved to the Club's main bar. Rick and Gary ordered champagne. Mark and John opted for beer. They had been drinking steadily since the afternoon and even after the filling meal, were starting to feel the effects. And it had only just gone nine. A tilt of the head, a nod back and the two of them went out onto the terrace for some fresh air.

"I see why Rick likes this place so much. They really lay it on, don't they?"

"Well," replied Mark as he leaned on the railing and looked out on the clear night sky, "I don't think it's always this indulgent, but yeah ..." He let his words drift off as they both enjoyed the gentle, warm breeze.

"I have to fill Rick in on what's going on," whispered Mark.

John nodded. "Sooner rather than later. I'm sure we're safe here, but ..."

They returned to the table to find Rick and Gary deep in conversation with four attractive women, the waiter dutifully filling their glasses from a fresh magnum of Veuve Cliquot.

With a glint in his eye, Gary said, "Poor girls. Their feet were killing them and there weren't any other free seats." He was right. The bar was packed. "I hope you don't mind."

John cast a furtive glance at Mark, but his friend laughed it off, his eyes saying, 'Why not?' as he settled himself into the deep sofa. John took the armchair next to him.

Rick was deep in conversation with one of the girls and barely acknowledged his friends' return. Mark smiled as he watched him, clearly smitten with the raven-haired beauty he was chatting up. Gary took charge and made introductions.

Seated opposite Mark, Katerina and Anna were both blonde, Katerina's long hair flowing freely down bare shoulders, Anna's clipped short, accenting her long, graceful neck. Mark's eyes were irresistibly drawn to her endless, tanned legs and short sequined skirt. Elena was seated next to him, her attentions focused on Gary, the air heady with the delicate flowery scent of her perfume. When she laughed, her auburn hair danced across Mark's shoulder, tickling, electric. Rick and Yasmin were lost in each other. Katerina and Anna were chatting happily amongst themselves, taking no notice of the two married men.

John was clearly uncomfortable. Mark leaned over with a chuckle and said, "The whole bar seems to be watching us."

"Yeah," replied John nervously. "I hope there's no one I know." After a moment's pause, he added, "Look, I should cut out."

"No way," said Mark. "We've got a snooker table in a half hour. Besides, no harm done." He added with a wink, "Just relax, let the boys enjoy themselves."

A few minutes later, the four pairs were drawn together when the waitress arrived with a large tray of oysters on the half shell, caviar on ice and thin glass tubes of vodka floating in a bucket of ice water. Mark was full from dinner but could not resist a taste of his two favorite delicacies. The oysters prompted clichés and innuendo from Gary as he and Elena chased theirs with shots of vodka.

Shortly after, the maître d' came over to announce that the snooker room was ready.

"Would you like to join us?" offered Rick.

The girls nodded in unison. When he realized what had just happened, John shot a nervous glance at Mark, who brushed it off with a shrug of his shoulders as if to say, "What can we do? Let the bachelors have their fun."

Logan watched as the party made its way across the bar, led by Rick and Yasmin. Next were Gary and Elena, his arm around her waist, heads together in whispered conversation. Katerina and Anna followed, with Mark and John bringing up the rear.

"I don't like where this is going," said John. "Why did Rick have to invite them? I thought this was a boys' night out."

"Lighten up, John," ribbed Mark. "Rick and Gary are in heaven. Let them enjoy it. I mean, how often does a foursome of beautiful women drop in your lap?" Seeing the look of consternation on John's face, he quickly added, "You know what I mean." He glanced at his watch. "Look. It's half nine. We play a couple of games, then we cut out, leave the bachelors to have their fun."

"Alright," replied John, only slightly mollified.

The maître d' ushered them into the elevator, which was altogether too small, their bodies pressed close. As he closed the door, he told the operator to take them to the 2nd floor and hurried down the stairs to arrive ahead of them.

As the elevator crawled down two floors, Gary and Elena nestled into a corner, inseparable, oblivious to the rest of the party. Rick and Yasmin looked like they would be happy to stay in the lift forever. John, meanwhile, stared resolutely ahead at the whorl patterns on the elevator wall, lips pursed, body tense.

That left Mark facing Katerina and Anna, who were whispering and giggling, bodies pressed close. Anna locked her emerald green eyes on Mark's then leaned in, slowly, sensually brushing her lips across Katerina's. Her friend responded hungrily, long fingers gently caressing Anna's sequined hip as they kissed. Mark was left spellbound. Much as he tried, he could not stop watching. Nor, he had to admit, did he want to.

When the doors finally opened, they spilled out of the elevator and the maître d' led them to the private snooker room. Mark broke off, following the sign to the restroom, calling over his shoulder, "I'll catch up in a minute."

He rounded the corner and stopped, leaning against the wall to take a few deep breaths. He had been married to Susan for 18 years, happily monogamous for longer. Like most, he'd had his share of temptations. Like some, he had always resisted. But the elevator, Katerina and Anna, had been one of the most erotic things he had ever experienced.

He would need all his willpower to make it through the night.

John's right. Go home now! He splashed cold water on his face, looked in the mirror and knew he would not. How far could he go? Could he control it? He tried to rationalize, *Just a bit of drunken flirting. What have you had? Three, maybe four martinis, wine, beer, champagne.* He breathed a deep sigh and left the restroom. Somehow he took a wrong turn and found himself wandering down a long hallway.

The echo of clicking heels caught his attention. He looked up, saw a man rounding a corner. It looked like Tony Levine. He hurried after him, but by the time he reached the landing, the man was nowhere to be seen. *Tony Levine.* That was when he remembered what had been eluding him since Monday. Levine had used the words 'Dream Team'. Coincidence?

"Check it out!" beamed Gary as Mark joined him in the snooker room. "This is great!" He pointed at the reproduction Wurlitzer jukebox in the corner. "Great playlist." His arm swept round to take in other appointments. "Stocked bar. Sofas. Massive plasma screen. And, we can smoke." He ended his tour by opening the humidor with a flourish.

He tossed a cue to Mark. "But first, it's your shot. I broke. Mate, we are in for a glorious night!" He stretched the long word, punctuating it with a wink and a lustful grin as his arm slipped around Elena's waist. She nuzzled in and whispered playfully in his ear.

That left Mark alone with Anna and the snooker table, too close for comfort. He tried to focus on his shot, but was distracted by her presence, the heat of her body pressing against his, the intoxicating scent of her skin, the electric touch of her hand resting gently on his back as she leaned in for a look down the length of his cue. "Will you teach me?" she asked.

Mark's heart was racing. He panned the room, took in Rick and Yasmin by the jukebox, John and Katerina at the bar. He drew a deep breath, and scratched.

Logan watched the evening unfold from his penthouse, everything to plan, the script simple, human nature so predictable. Haddad and Harding had unwittingly gifted the opening when they stepped out for a cigarette, leaving the bachelors alone. Easy targets—no marital inhibitions, no significant others, no reason to suspect or resist the attentions of the four beautiful women he had dropped in their laps. By the time Haddad and Harding rejoined the party, it was already too late, Ashton and Tate ensnared in Yasmin and Elena's web of charms. Anna and Katerina, meanwhile, were playing their roles to perfection, now ignoring the two married men, flirting with each other, making themselves irresistible, eye candy.

'Professionals,' thought Logan with a satisfied smile. For the first time in days, he felt back in control, a bit of his old, cold self. The scene in the elevator, Haddad's sudden dash to the restroom, his remonstrations as he stared at himself in the mirror—Logan knew with all certainty his resistance would break down. Not so with Harding. He would leave. No matter. He was superfluous. If anything, his early departure would add an intriguing dimension. *Which of the three remaining couples will become a threesome?* he wondered with lustful anticipation.

The atmosphere quickly heated up as the party settled into the cosseted intimacy of the snooker room. As soon as the doors were closed, the sexual energy flowed freely from the already-paired couples, flooding the dimly lit room with erotic undercurrents. Logan felt himself becoming aroused, as he watched the scene of his making unfold. He called for Natasha.

She had been his mistress for more than ten years. Like him, she was now in her forties, but his desire had only grown over time, fed by her wicked appetites.

His eyes shifted back and forth between her and the screens as she let herself in and crossed the room toward him, her stride slow, sultry. Her long blonde hair was pulled back in a severe twist, exposing the length of her graceful, ivory neck, pale blue eyes locked on him, head tipped forward as she peered lustfully over the top of her glasses.

Logan's eyes slid down her pinstriped Prada suit. Its narrow satin lapels were tailored to accent her ample décolletage. Her long fingers slowly opened the top button, offering tantalizing glimpses of her breasts swelling with each breath. The narrow skirt emphasized her hourglass figure, hips swaying sensually with her catwalk stride. As she drew nearer, Logan's view was filled with black silk stockings, the short skirt offering teasing hints of suspenders, the bare flesh of her thighs, red patent leather stilettos.

She stood in front of him, legs parted, height and sensuality dominating her supplicant. He resisted the urge to drop to his knees, kiss her feet, lick her painted toes. Like a goddess, she gazed down on him, her wry smile laced with wicked temptation, eyes demanding submission.

Logan was a control freak. He managed everyone and everything in his life to the atom, including Natasha. When she was at her desk. In private moments like this, he relinquished control, craved her domination (not the S&M kind, though she did on occasion offer thrilling samplings). Of course he was the master. That was never in question. But when it came to sex, her insatiable appetites fed desires he never knew he had, filling their liaisons with endless surprise.

He lowered his eyes. Submission. She loved that moment, reveled in its power, especially now after more than a week of abstinence. She turned abruptly and walked toward the video screens, licking her lips as she studied her girls. With a dismissive wave, she ordered, "Champagne."

Logan felt the flush of thrill. He rose obediently and did as he was told.

"You want to fuck my girls don't you, you naughty boy?" She laughed. "I think Katerina will be free tonight." She held out her hand for the remote control and deftly filled the four middle screens with a frontal view of Katerina and John standing at the bar. "He's nervous. He'll leave soon. Go home to his little wife and children." Her barbed words took in Logan's own wife, Catherine, a subtle reminder that she could never feed his carnal needs the way Natasha did. "Then what will we do with my Katerina?" she studied Logan and laughed again. "Oh, I see." Her hand reached out and rubbed his hard cock as she spun around and planted herself in front of him. "You want to watch her join one of the others, don't you?"

Logan nodded, thrilled into submission.

She licked her full red lips and groaned, her eyes locked on his, searching for the answer, "Hmmm, which one? Yasmin? No? Anna?" She pouted. "No? Elena? Oh, I see," she cooed mischievously. "You want to watch Katerina and Elena ... with him." She turned and flicked to another camera, Gary and Elena. She gasped, "Yes, I'd like to fuck him too. He's young. Strong." Her voice dropped to a teasing whisper as her hand stroked harder. "I bet he's huge. You want to fuck him? Want him to fuck you? Is that what you want?" She smiled as he exploded with a shudder, the sticky moistness seeping through his trousers.

It took all his concentration but Mark potted three in a row. When he missed his next shot, he quickly left the table and headed to the bar, ostensibly to rescue John, although he also needed to distance himself from Anna.

His position behind the bar offered the illusion of control, the polished wood a physical barrier between himself and a room rife with temptation.

"So who wants a drink?" he called out too loudly as he reached into the fridge for a couple of beers. "John, beer?" Without waiting for a reply, he popped the tops off and handed one over.

Anna sidled up to the bar and set her empty glass down expectantly. "Katerina, too," she said before launching into small talk. "So how long have you lived in London?"

Drawing the other two into the conversation, he answered, "John and I moved here about the same time. What was it? Ten years ago?"

"Twelve, actually," replied John, welcoming the support.

His eyes pleaded with Mark, who set the refilled champagne flute in front of Anna. She grabbed his hand before he could pull away, fingers gently twirled his wedding band. "Married?"

Mark's throat felt dry as he uttered, "Yes."

"Good," purred Anna. "No complications." She walked slowly back to the snooker table, knowing Mark was watching. "It's my turn," she called over her shoulder, "Come to teach me."

"Let's get some music on first," he replied, turning to Katerina and saying, "Can you help Anna choose?"

Katerina obliged, letting her fingers caress John's back as she walked away.

"I gotta go," said John flatly.

"Yeah, it's pretty intense," replied Mark, unable to take his eyes off Anna and Katerina dancing together.

Gary appeared at the bar and announced with a smile, "Okay, boys. I just booked a room upstairs for the night. There're two more available."

"Jesus, Gary! We're both married!" blurted John loudly. "This is too much. I've gotta go!" He turned and left without saying another word.

The girls looked up in surprise, then shrugged their shoulders in unison. Anna drew Katerina toward her in a hug and slid her hands down her sequined skirt. Katerina responded by pressing herself into her friend, whispering in her ear.

"Look, Gary. I'm having a great time, but this is as far as

it's gonna go. You and Rick do whatever you want. But I'm with John on this." He held up his ring finger. But he still did not leave, still could not take his eyes off Anna as she seduced Katerina.

An hour later, Mark did finally decide to leave. It was a snap decision.

"Where are you going?" pouted Anna before he reached the door.

"It's been a fantastic night, but I have to go home." He sheepishly added, "It's a school night and I've got a long day tomorrow."

"You can't leave me all alone," pleaded Anna. It was true. Katerina had joined Gary and Elena on one of the sofas. Rick and Yasmin were on the other. That left Mark and her. He had tried to keep the sexual tension to foreplay, but she had relentlessly pushed the boundaries to the point where either he would break or leave. He had chosen the latter.

Mark lamely replied, "These guys are all staying."

Anna suddenly threw her glass across the room and stormed out, slamming the door in her wake. Stunned silence filled the room. Mark looked at the others, his hands held out in shock and surprise.

Mark went after her but she had already disappeared. He went to the end of the hallway and looked in all directions, down the stairwell. Then he noticed the elevator dial going down. He took the stairs two at a time. It had been a fun evening and he did not want it to end on a bad note. He had kept reminding them both. Hadn't he?

As he rounded the corner on the first floor landing, he ran straight into the lead VC from Newton Capital, who put his arm over Mark's shoulder and guided him into one of Berkeley House's vast parlors.

Mark finally managed to get a word in. "Look, I'd love to chat, but I have to go. Someone's waiting for me. Really. I've gotta run." Mark shrugged off the arm draped over his shoulder and almost ran down the stairs to the lobby. Anna was nowhere to be seen.

He asked the doorman who nodded, pointed outside.

Mark stepped out onto the dark street and looked both ways. The Club was in the middle of the block, pavement stretching 100 feet in either direction, empty both ways. She could not have gone far.

Then he heard a scream coming from the square. It was dark, the footpaths unlit and it took a moment for his eyes to adjust. Down the left fork, he saw a silhouette, heard crying. He hurried over, head scanning left and right for danger. As he drew nearer, he called Anna's name. She looked up and, after a moment's hesitation, ran into his arms.

He cradled and comforted her, asking, "What happened? I came looking for you."

Gingerly, she pushed herself away from him, exposing her torn dress and stockings, her mud-stained hands.

"Oh my god! Were you mugged?"

Anna's face twisted in agony, tears streaming down her face. Mark wrapped his arms around her again and held her, soothing her. After a long few minutes, he gently eased her back, took off his blazer and put it over her shoulders before cradling her again.

A few minutes later, she asked for a cigarette. He led her to a bench where he sat them down and lit two, passing one to her. They smoked in silence, Mark's free arm wrapped protectively around Anna's shoulder. He felt her strength returning, shivers fading, pulse rate slowing, breathing steadying. Mark's eyes kept shifting around the perimeter. He had a strange feeling they were being watched.

"Let's go inside. We can take care of you there."

"No, I can't go back. Look at me …" Anna was on the verge of tears again.

"Don't cry. We can go somewhere else. Do you want me to take you home?"

Anna nodded, eyes desperate.

They got up and walked away from the Club, exiting on the other side of the park onto the empty street. A black cab rounded the corner, its yellow light a welcome glow. Mark stepped between the parked cars and flagged it down. As he helped Anna in, he asked her the address, relayed it to the driver and jumped in after her.

"Do you want to call someone? Maybe Elena or Yasmin? We should probably call the police."

"No. Please. No police. I'll be okay." A quizzical look came over her face as she muttered, "My purse! They took my purse!" A look of terror filled her eyes as it dawned on her. "They have my keys and my address." She started to panic, "I can't go home. Driver, driver stop!"

The driver looked in the rearview mirror, but Mark waved him to carry on. "It's alright," he said to Anna, "I'll call a locksmith. I'll wait with you until they arrive. You'll be safe. I promise."

Reassured, Anna collapsed into the seat and tugged at Mark's arm, pulling him back toward her. Tucking her feet up, she nestled into his chest and seemed to fall asleep as he gently stroked her hair.

With his free hand, he pulled out his phone, thumbed open the 192 app and typed 'Locksmith' and 'Primrose Hill'. Posh neighborhood, he thought. He called the first listing that advertised 24-hour service.

That done, he leaned his head back and closed his eyes, soon succumbing to the rhythmic lull of the moving taxi, the alcohol washing away the adrenaline that had been surging through his bloodstream.

It took a moment to separate dream from reality as he felt the wet warmth of Anna's tongue licking him, sucking him, long fingers rhythmically squeezing and massaging.

"No! Stop, Anna! Stop! Please! Don't ..."

He groaned involuntarily as she swallowed him, for a moment losing himself to the sensation before regaining control. He gently but forcefully pull Anna off.

She looked at him with a pained, frightened expression before burying her face in his shoulder, muttering over and over, "Please don't leave me. I'm scared. I can't be alone tonight."

Mark caught the cabbie's lustful gaze in the rearview mirror. "Just turn the mirror, will you?"

He stroked Anna's hair, feeling a confusing mix of guilt and desire. He rationalized his own innocence, but knew he had been playing dangerously close to the edge all evening. He should have left long ago with John.

Still, he felt guilty, somehow responsible for the mugging. If he had not led Anna on all evening, if he had not let her run off, this would never have happened.

With one hand, he reached down, fumbling to close his zipper, button and belt. Anna slid her hand down squeezing his still-hard cock as she breathed heavily in his ear, her tongue and hot breath caressing his neck.

Mark noticed the driver still watching and barked, "Turn the mirror!"

The driver, a heavy set Londoner in his late 50s, laughed and touched his finger to it, barely shifting the view.

"Anna, please," he pleaded. "I know you're scared. I'll stay as long as you need. But I can't do this."

"Please, Mark. I need you. Please. Your wife is away. She does not need to know."

Mark could not remember telling her that Susan was out of town, but supposed he must have. The thought was instantly lost as Anna leaned into him, her lips finding his, her tongue hungrily opening his mouth. She straddled him with newfound strength, fingers gripping him by the hair as she pulled him into the corner of the seat, her body pressing and grinding against his.

His hand involuntarily caressed her firm body, her ass, the bare, smooth skin of her legs. Sensing the moment, she guided his other hand to her breast, squeezing it, sliding it inside her low cut dress. Her skin was warm and soft, her nipple pert, aroused. His mind screamed *Stop! Stop! Stop!* but his body, overwhelmed with carnal desire, refused to obey.

"C'mon, lovebirds. Out you go!" called the leering cabbie as he pulled over outside No. 11 Rothwell Street.

Mark looked up at the driver leering in the mirror. Anna started giggling as she skipped out of the cab and climbed the stairs to the front door landing.

"That'll be £22.80, guv."

Mark handed him two twenties and said, "Keep the change."

The driver replied, "And the videotape!" before laughing and driving off.

Mark knew he was in a jam as he looked up at Anna standing at the top of the stairs. Beautiful. And now, after what had happened in the park, her appetite had become insatiable. He had about six seconds to steel himself before reaching the landing. The invisible line had blurred long ago. Yet he knew he could not just leave. Anna would not let him and it would be dangerous. He had to wait for a locksmith, until she was safe.

As he mounted the stairs, he said, "Are you sure you don't want to call Yasmin and Elena? Or maybe someone else to come stay the night?"

"But you're here," she said, "You will look after me." She held up a key and explained, "I keep it hidden. Sometimes I forget to take mine." Anna took his hand and led him into the building, dancing her way up the two flights of stairs, her short dress flashing tantalizing glimpses.

When they reached the landing, Mark stepped forward, took the key from Anna and pushed her back protectively against the wall. He slowly edged the door open and walked into the flat, eyes scanning for signs of disturbance. Sliding sideways, he checked the closet then behind the kitchen island. His eyes took in the knife block. One missing. Glancing around, he breathed a sigh of relief when he spotted it in the sink.

He ushered Anna into the flat and put his finger to her lips, signaling for her to stay by the door. He picked up the chef's knife, hefting it to find its balance, then set off down the hallway. A minute later he returned to the living area, set the knife back in the wooden block, closed and bolted the door. He leaned back, closed his eyes and breathed a big sigh of relief.

When he opened them again, Anna had disappeared. He tiptoed down the hallway, eyes avoiding the intimate trail of clothes she had stripped off and dropped on the way to the bathroom. He heard the sound of the shower, breathed a sigh of relief and returned to the kitchen, where he made a pot of coffee and settled in to wait for the locksmith.

CHAPTER 22

Mark woke with the sun, still fully dressed, groggy, bleary eyed. He dragged himself to the bathroom, moving gingerly, head pounding with each step. Downstairs, kettle on, he reached for the Resolve and absently watched the tablets fizzling in their mesmeric dance. With a final swirl, he downed the restorative and took a cup of coffee into the garden.

For several minutes he sat still, eyes closed, letting the sun's rays, the coffee and the Resolve do their magic. As his mind cleared, memories started emerging from the fug.

The taxi. Not a dream ... the cabbie, leering, Anna pulling him down, her mouth on him, groping, hands sliding under her skirt ... Mark fell back in the chair, jaw hanging. *Shit! What did you do?*

He reached for a cigarette. As he raised it to his lips, Anna's musky scent drifted from his fingertips. Lust, guilt, arousal all hit him at once. He puffed heavily, filling his nostrils with the acrid smoke.

He stripped, gathered his clothes. Upstairs, he stripped the bed. Her scent was everywhere—her perfume, her skin, her hair, on him, in his clothes, his bedroom. Susan's bedroom. *Fuck! Fuck! Fuck! Laundry! Shower!* Mission focus.

He did not let himself think about Anna, about last night, until he was under the hot, steamy shower. Then he let the night replay. Anna's flat in Primrose Hill. He had left. The taxi. *Well* ... He had stopped her.

The fresh memories were arousing. Anna untying her robe, letting it drop, stepping toward him, naked temptation. Doorbell. The locksmith took all of five minutes, offered Mark a ride to the local minicab rank. He had cast one last, longing look down the hallway, the bedroom door ajar, beckoning him. He locked the door behind him, slipped the key underneath and left. A cowardly escape, not saying goodbye. But the right call, the safe bet.

He edged up the heat to tingle burn, closed his eyes, put his head under, and let the guilt wash away—*nothing happened!* He had blurred the line, but he had not crossed it. *Taxi didn't count ... can live with that ... no big deal.*

He was happily married, faithful for 18 years. *Still am*, he was relieved to confirm. As he saw it, marriage was an institution, not human nature. Sexual attraction, on the other hand, is hardwired into the DNA. He'd had other close calls over the years, assumed everyone did, including Susan. This just happened to be closer than most.

Showered, laundry done, hangover cured, guilt absolved, Mark set off on a punishing bike ride around Richmond park. Three loops, 27 miles.

011000010110110001101001

Across town, Rick showered too, with Yasmin, long, hot, steamy. He then went out for croissants. When he returned, he found her wearing his pale blue Oxford, nothing else, looking radiant in the sunshine on the balcony. They made love again. She left, a dinner date agreed.

He called round. No one local answered so he called Stephanie in Monaco.

"Amazing night last night. I'm in love." Rick told

161

Stephanie all about Yasmin, winning the prize, the amazing night they had had.

Something about it bothered Stephanie. She hung up and returned to her lunch guests, but could not shake the feeling that something was not right. An hour later, walking through the crooked, cobbled streets of Vieux Nice, she realized what it was. She made a couple of calls to cancel her afternoon meetings and hurried home. She had some digging to do.

CHAPTER 23

Mark arrived at Adware Monday afternoon, back from a meeting. He was just settling in when the front desk rang. "Delivery. Needs your signature." Back in his office, he sat down and opened the thin, stiff brown envelope. Right then, his mobile rang. "Mark Haddad speaking," he answered hands-free, the Bluetooth tusk dangling from his ear.

"Hello, Mark. How are you? It's Tony, Tony Levine." His voice was particularly oily this morning, immediately putting Mark on his guard. The weekend had been a welcome reprieve, quiet. He had almost but not quite managed to forget about the bugs, the virus, the lawsuit, the game he had being unwittingly sucked into.

"Good morning, Tony." He tried to sound indifferent.

"Mark, I just wanted to ..."

Levine's words faded as Mark stared at the contents of the envelope. Photographs. Him. Anna. The taxi. He flipped the envelope over. No address. He stared at his phone. *Tony Levine!* The timing could not be coincidence. *Deep breaths ... keep cool ... count to ten ...* Much as he wanted to lash out at Levine, his instincts told him it would be a bad move.

Levine's voice faded back in, "Are you there, Mark?"

Mark was now sure it had been Levine at Berkeley House

on Friday. "Yes, I'm here, Tony. Just dropped my headset." He drew silent, steadying breaths as he stuffed the photos back in the envelope, out of sight.

His other mobile phone, the encrypted one Stephanie had given him, started vibrating. He thumbed it under the table, sending the call to voicemail.

"Mark, I think there are some … ah … pretty compelling reasons for us to meet again. You've seen the … ah … you've seen how serious we are. I'm sure we can reach a mutually agreeable accommodation."

"I'm listening."

"Oh, good," said Levine with an audible sigh of relief. "We can meet then."

"Next Monday, 3:00 pm," replied Mark, not bothering to consult his diary.

"I was rather hoping to meet today."

"Not possible. I'm booked out for the rest of the week. My first opening is Monday at 3:00 pm."

"Next Monday it is, then," conceded Levine. "Our offices?"

"That's fine," replied Mark, adding a demand. "I want to meet your Chairman."

"I don't think that will be possible."

"Of course it is," snapped Mark cutting him off. "Make sure he's there." He hung up before Levine could counter, leaned back and stared at the manila envelope, his mind churning.

The other phone vibrated again, this time a text message from Stephanie. "Call me ASAP from somewhere secure."

They had discussed that before. Nowhere was totally secure, but outdoors was best. Buildings, rooms could be bugged. Restaurants, crowded places were better, but had their risks too. The best place was alone, outdoors, somewhere like a park.

He stuffed the envelope into his rucksack and hurried out of the office.

0111010001111001001001100

"Well done, old chap," said Lord Barker without enthusiasm.

"Do you think he's seen the photos?"

"No doubt. Could hear it in his voice."

"But why delay? He was quite adamant."

"Buying time, trying to assert some control over the situation while he tries to figure a way out."

"But there is no way out. We own him," replied Levine with a sneer. "The last thing he wants is another envelope arriving at home addressed to little wifey."

Unable to contain his indignation any longer, Lord Barker drew himself straight and pronounced, "I am *not at all* comfortable with this, old chap. Never was. Not cricket. So ... so vulgar." He spat the last word out with distaste.

Levine's eyes widened in alarm, flitted around the room, trying to silently warn his friend, *Bugs!* But Lord Barker did not need reminding. He knew they were there. And he knew exactly who was listening and watching—Logan and that cretin Ukrainian sidekick of his.

"Well, what's done is done. We've shown the stick," conceded Barker. "Now we must proceed as gentlemen from here on in."Lord

The reprimand stung. No one other than Arthur, Lord Barker would dare. 14th Earl of Godalming, Knight of the Garter, peer of the realm, etc., he was Logan's Mirror Mirror on the Wall.

Logan was a student of history. The Great and the Good? Misnomers both. Every title, every fortune, had its past, no different to his—blackmail, bribery, theft, piracy, murder, war. It was not so much about *being* a gentleman as being *seen* as one. It was an art Logan had long perfected, his public persona a polished veneer without blemish. Until now.

He was angry with himself. Barker was right. He had become reckless, impetuous. The reprimand was also a marker, a unspoken debt of secrecy which Barker would one day call.

Logan tried in vain to be cold and objective, something that until recently had been second nature. Logic and rationale once grasped so firmly were now just delicate, ethereal strands in a bubbling cauldron of dark emotions. His desire for revenge was overwhelming, was all that mattered now. And it was clouding his judgment.

011001100110100101100011

Left, right, straight ahead—it did not matter. Through Chinatown, Covent Garden, Holborn, the Strand, in and out of the Underground. Mark had been a quick study in Stephanie's crash course in tradecraft and soon found the process cathartic, one part of his brain driving his movement, another mulling his situation.

The manila envelope weighed heavily in his rucksack. He had let his guard down for one moment, one night, and the photographs were the price. The taxi had obviously been part of the setup, maybe the mugging too. Logically, that possibility extended to the whole evening, to Berkeley House.

That's when he made the connection, the thing that had been niggling for days. *Dream Team*. Tony Levine had used those words, trying to sound cool, hip, like the eight gigabit drive gaffe. Gary had said it first, at Berkeley House, the night he had joined Mark and Rick for drinks, the night, Mark now guessed, when all this had started.

The ferry churned water as it readied to pull out of Embankment Pier. Making a split decision, Mark jogged down the gangplank and hopped on board just as the gates were closing. No one boarded after him. If he was being followed and they were good, they would pick him up again across the river at Bankside. But it did give him a few minutes of privacy. He pulled out the encrypted phone and speed-dialed Stephanie.

"What do you know about Berkeley House?"

"Funny, I was about to ask you the same thing."

"I'm being blackmailed," said Mark, getting straight to the point. He only had a few minutes before they reached the next pier.

"Let me guess. Gorgeous Russian bird, compromising photographs."

"Ukrainian, but how did you know?"

"Rick told me,. not about the blackmail, but about your night out. Straight off, it sounded like a honey trap. What is it with men? You are all so bloody predictable."

"I didn't do anything. I swear! The photos ... they don't tell it like it was. It's not how it looks." When Stephanie said nothing, he changed subject. "Tony Levine was there."

Stephanie was standing in front of her whiteboard, her eyes studying the growing web of connections. "He's just a pawn, Mark. This goes much deeper. I've been digging. Trust me when I tell you this—you are in seriously deep shit. You have something somebody wants very, very badly. And they're not going to stop until they get it."

"What are you saying?"

"We need to meet. I have a plan. Obviously this adds another twist ..."

"I'm coming to Monaco on Thursday for the meeting with Sam Leonard."

"Before then, with everyone. And you need to talk to Susan, come clean. Harsh as it may sound, she is the least of your problems."

Sounding braver than he felt, Mark asked, "Can you come here? We could drive down to Wittering."

"Exactly what I was thinking. Have you broken ground yet?"

"The house? No. Still chasing planning permission. Why?" It seemed a strange question.

"Public records will show you own it. But it'll still be listed as undeveloped farmland."

"I see what you mean." Stephanie's paranoia was steps ahead of Mark's but he was starting to catching on. "How do we get there without being followed? Actually, my ferry's about to dock. I should kill this call until I find somewhere else safe to talk."

"Okay. My flight gets in around 7:00 pm. I'll call you when I land. Meanwhile, get everyone ready for a road trip."

"On it."

"Be careful where you talk, Mark. I mean it."

"Trust me. I don't need a reminder. At this point I'm more paranoid than you."

"You don't know the half of it. But we'll talk later."

011101000110100101101111

Mark played the ferry game on the way back, too, jumping on board at the last second, buying a few safe minutes to call John Harding and email Duncan. He got off at Millbank, Tate Britain, then walked across the bridge to Vauxhall. The MI6 headquarters loomed large in front of him. He turned into the station and jogged up the stairs to Platform 3/4.

Homeward bound, deduced Vladimir, boarding a car behind. The rest of his team was moving in parallel, by car and by bike. He called in the night shift, young mothers with strollers, Polish builders, who would blend into the leafy suburban neighborhood.

Mark was home by 6:00 pm. Stephanie was not due to land for another hour so he whipped up a sandwich and chewed things over. He had lost the fat guy hours ago, back in Chinatown, was certain of it. But he still could not shake the feeling he was being watched. He had not pinged anyone, not with absolute certainty, but he would if he saw the skinny blonde guy again.

In either case, he was home now, safe, out of sight. Sure,

the place was bugged, but at least he knew that, and some rooms were still safe. He took his sandwich into the living room, stared at the painting above the fireplace as he ate. He had been doing this a lot lately. It was oddly cathartic knowing the bugs were there, incontrovertible proof that this was all very real. It was also empowering knowing that they had been turned, were now his assets which he was using to feed disinformation to the people watching him. Double agents. Bug, human, same difference.

Mark fired off an encrypted email to Duncan. "Change of plan. Bike ride. Bring clothes. Meet at cafe by Ballet School. You go via Roehampton. I'll go the other way. Watch for tails."

Next, he called John and Rick. They were on unsecure lines so he kept his words cryptic, innocuous. From years spent playing stupid pranks at university, they had developed a code, a subtext to their words. As soon as both realized what Mark was (not) saying—that Stephanie was flying in— they knew he was arranging something more than an impromptu social gathering. Mark said 'no' when Rick asked if he could bring Yasmin. Rick did not understand why, but played along, said nothing.

011011100010111001000001

"You're clean. Mind if we shower?"

"Are you going to tell me what's going on?" John stared at the scanner in Mark's hand.

"Shower first. We've been round the park twice." Mark handed the device to John. "Scan Rick when he arrives."

"I don't know how to work this thing," said John.

"Just hold the button down. The light will turn red if it finds anything."

Rick had arrived by the time Mark and Duncan were done showering. John took Mark aside, whispering. The scanner had turned red twice, Rick's jacket pocket, now hanging in the hallway, and his shirt collar. Rick stared wild-eyed. Every time he started to speak, his friends put fingers to lips, John maintaining a casual conversation, a monologue to Rick's one word replies. Mark remained silent.

"Glass of wine?" offered John.

He led them into the kitchen and made loud sounds of pulling the cork, pouring the wine. Spillage. "So sorry. Give me your shirt. I'll give it a quick wash. You can borrow one of mine."

It took some effort for Mark to keep Rick silent until John returned.

"We can talk now. You were bugged," said Mark. He knew it was pointless asking Rick if he had been followed too—he had no idea what was going on, no reason to be jumping at shadows. Yet. Figuring he had to see to believe, he led his friend into the hallway to show him the small device planted in his jacket pocket. He also shot a close-up photo which he emailed to control@5551212.com. It was a role account Stephanie had set up for routing all inbound intelligence.

Rick did not believe them at first, thought it was some elaborate gag, a wind up. But as the depth of the story unfolded, coming from three separate voices, disbelief gave way to stoic acceptance. Being played by Yasmin hurt. He was a hopeless romantic, gutted once again to find out that the love-of-his-life was not. But it also pissed him off. He did *not* like being played. That sharpened his focus.

Mark was under no illusions any of them actually knew what they were doing—just dumb luck that he had pinged the fat guy. *Too easy,* he thought, filing it for later consideration. But they all watched *Spooks,* read spy novels, lived in a surveillance state, the UK the biggest brother of them all. The concept was not alien, just not something they had ever figured into their own lives.

Stephanie's call came at 7:30 pm. "Where are you?"

"John's. Everyone's here. We found two bugs on Rick. Both have been secured. We can talk."

"Well done. There's an 8:36 to Reading, the fast train from Paddington. Think you can make it?"

"Paddington. 8:36," repeated Mark with a question mark. John nodded.

"Assume you're being followed."

"I am. I was. Pretty sure I gave him the slip in the park. But I think there's someone else. Besides, won't it give the game away if we all suddenly go off grid?"

"I have a cover story. I'll explain later. See you in Reading."

As soon as the doors closed, Stephanie accelerated the black BMW X5, heading south. "Anyone follow you?"

"Not as far as we could tell," replied Mark, adrenaline pumping. "Rick walked to the station, took the train to Putney, then a black cab to Paddington.

"I got out at a red light a couple of blocks before Paddington. Paid the cabbie to continue on to an address in Maida Vale. Left the tracking device in the cab."

"What about the bug?" asked Stephanie.

Mark laughed, told her about the trick John had pulled with the wine. "Anyhow, we gave Rick a 10 minute head start then drove to Paddington in John's car. It's got dark windows. Duncan and I kept low in the back seat, hopped out around a corner, out of sight. Then we rode to Reading in separate carriages, front, middle and rear."

"I'm impressed," said Stephanie meaning it, taking in everyone. "Well done, guys." Her eyes kept shifting to the rear view mirrors as she turned down several side streets. Once she was sure no one was following, she pulled into an empty recreation center parking lot, killed the lights and jumped out. A minute later, she tossed an empty water bottle in the back seat floor well, explaining with a smile, "Mud on the plates. Don't need it anymore."

"This is unreal," said Rick.

Stephanie laughed. "Quite the opposite. It's all very real." She stepped on the gas and navigated back to the main roads. The others slowly relaxed, settling into the rhythm of the road. Another crash course.

They drove the last mile with parking lights only, following the wending country lane to an old, battered farm gate. The last quarter mile was off road, by moonlight. The silhouette of the X5 disappeared behind a small copse of trees. Two rows of weak fairy lights turned on to guide their approach, like an airport runway.

"Nice." Stephanie had been about to turn on her parking lights.

"Motion sensor. And solar powered. We installed them a couple of weeks ago, so we don't wake everyone up when we come in late."

It was midnight but lights were on inside one of the mobile units, the grownups sharing a late bottle of wine. The kids would all be fast asleep in the other caravan.

Stephanie went in alone, finger shushing against her lips. She made eye contact with her husband, Eric, who understood, resuming the conversation as if nothing had happened while Stephanie swept the room with the scanner. Susan and Beth looked on in silent shock.

"Good. You're clean. We can speak. I didn't think I'd find anything, but best to be safe."

A barrage of questions followed her as stepped outside. "What are you doing here? What is that thing?"

Stephanie began to explain, the paddle first, a tangible baseline for suspending disbelief. With the ground set, she moved on to Mark's situation. The narrative switching between her, Mark, and Duncan and they quickly covered everything but the honey trap. Mark had to broach that in private with Susan first.

For a while, Susan, Tess and Beth just stared, dumbstruck.

172

As the shock wore off, their questions started. Mark took it as his cue, squeezed Susan's hand and led her off into the woods, hand in hand, down the path to the kids' tree house. His heart was pounding.

"There's more."

Susan fixed her eyes on him. She had already sensed that. "Go on."

"There'll be a time for dealing with emotions but this is not it," began Mark. "Right now, we have to focus on the situation at hand. Crisis mode. Can you promise me that, no matter what you hear?"

Susan stared at her husband for the longest time. She had heard that opener countless times over the years as his company, Digiterra, lurched from one disaster to another, raining chaos on their family life. He was right. She knew from experience, there was only one way to deal with it. "Go on."

It was after 3:00 am when Mark, Stephanie, Duncan, John and Rick climbed back into the SUV and set off for London. They were talked out, exhausted. Stephanie put on some chillout music, nudged it to the back speakers and let Rick, Duncan and John drift off.

Sotto voce, she said to Mark, "I told Eric."

Flat. "I told Susan. She took the photos."

"You're still alive." Gallows humor.

Grimace.

"Eric is going to talk to her."

Another long silence.

"Are we good?"

Mark nodded, drifted into contemplative silence. He had hurt Susan. They had hurt her. Now he wanted to hurt them.

Stephanie reached over and squeezed his hand. They had been friends a long time. She knew he was completely devoted to Susan and believed his story. She hoped Susan could see through her hurt and believe him too.

CHAPTER 24

Incessant calls each more wired than the last had kept Lazarenko awake all night. At 7:00 am, he reported upstairs. Natasha's distressed look warned him of the mood inside, not that he needed it. Still, he was shocked by what he found when he let himself, Logan pacing, muttering, un-showered, shaved or changed since last night, the room filled with the loud crackle of dead radio static. He rounded immediately on Lazarenko, a wild look in his eyes.

"Update!"

Lazarenko did not have one. Nothing had happened in the past 20 minutes other than Lazarenko having a shower. He bowed his head for the inevitable torrent of abuse.

Their morning agenda was no longer standing, not since last week. For more than a decade, it had been their constant, without fail, 7:00 am, 8:00, on Sundays. With its precise format, even dialogue had been turned to shorthand, stripped bare of all but keywords, facts, decisions, instructions. Cold. Methodical. Like the boss used to be.

On paper, the template itself revealed nothing. Having experienced it daily though, Lazarenko had learned volumes. In the countless half-sentences and seeming disconnects, he had studied Logan's genius, dissected his thought patterns, reverse-engineered his logic. He quietly applied these skills now, ears blocking out the stream of meaningless invective, brain churning, focused on root cause. What made this project different?

He had found the trigger event, studied the video countless times. *Intelligent Agent*. He had watched the color drain from Logan's face at the precise moment that Max said those words, seen him change, prone ever since to emotional swings, volatile, impatient, capricious, unpredictable. He now had a permanent a crazed look in his eye. His hair was messy.

There was nothing new, nothing unusual about a subject going off grid. It happened all the time. Trackers got lost, bugs failed (all eventually fried in the laundry). Even tails were given the slip from time to time, not necessarily with intent, just lost in the hustle and bustle of urban movement.

Logan had always taken these eventualities in stride. Until now. In hindsight, failing with the Lazer virus the first time had been fortuitous. Dumb luck, nothing planned or calculated about it. But it had been the opening to up the ante by adding Adware's source code to Lazer's target list on the replacement flash drive.

Lazarenko was puzzling over that thought when a crystal ashtray flew past his head and smashed into the screen wall. The bang, the tinkle of broken glass, the thud of the ashtray crashing heavily to the floor, the sizzle and smoke of fried circuit boards left the room in a shroud of awkward silence.

Second time this week, thought Lazarenko.

As if on cue, the static on the stereo speakers was replaced by voices. Logan froze in his tracks, hands shaking, jiggling the remote.

"My head hurts," groaned Haddad at full volume.

Logan rushed to the conference table, dropped into a chair, elbows on the table, wringing his hands.

"Coffee?"

"Yeah. Got any aspirin?"

"Better. I've got Resolve. Best cure for a hangover."

Sounds of kitchen rustling, water running, kettle boiling, moans and groans of 'oh my head hurts!'

Logan reached for the remote, cranked the volume.

"I can't believe we let Peter hijack us like that," said Stephanie, playing out the story for the listening audience: on their bike ride, they had run into a friend who diverted them into a late night drinking session, first a pub then his house.

"You're not kidding. I lost count when he started on the Tequila shots."

A long silence followed, punctuated only by the slurping of coffee and muted groans of hangover. The intermittent conversation also explained the long radio silence in plausible bits and bites, the words a tonic for Logan, visibly relaxing him, restoring some semblance of normalcy.

He glared at Lazarenko. "From now on, make sure you have cyclists on both surveillance details. That's the last time they lose you on a bike ride. And get someone up here to replace that." He nodded at the cracked screen, then left the room, disappearing into his private office, slamming the door behind him. He never slammed doors.

Out in reception, Lazarenko made eye contact with Natasha. Fear of Logan had drawn them together. Now, she was his eyes and ears in the penthouse, an asset he wanted to keep sweet.

She had been surprisingly open since they had started working together. She placed great meaning in her and Logan's sexual liaisons, or the absence thereof, reading them like a pack of tarot cards. He had dismissed it at first. But after her graphical recollection of Friday night, he realized there might be something to it, insights to Logan's mind that he had otherwise never been privy to.

It had also given him a raging hard on. He had often fantasized about Natasha, almost got there once, back in Kiev. But this dominatrix thing, talk of orgies, made him lust for her even more. He could not be sure, but he also felt the intimacy of conspiracy drawing them closer, her eyes now inviting his to her breasts rather than admonishing his leer.

She slipped him a note, her touch lingering maybe a little longer than necessary. *Maybe, maybe ...*

He eagerly read the note as soon as he was back in his apartment. Logan was going out at 3:00 pm. They would meet. She would come to him.

01101110011110010110101

"You're sure he's got nothing?" demanded Conrad Baine.

"Positive," replied Robert Durand, brimming with confidence. The valley was overrunning with patent trolls and he had seen his share of intellectual property wars. It was never a question of right or wrong, only price and expediency. "It's a bluff. If they had anything, they'd have played it by now."

He had just had another meeting with Daniel Logan, attributed the other man's edginess to his having come up short yet again. If ever there was a time to table his mooted evidence, it was now. Twice, Durand had set a deadline. Twice, Logan had missed it. Twice, Durand had extended it, not once asking Logan to ease up on the media attacks. The first time, it would have been a sign of weakness. After that, it no longer suited Durand's interests. He now *wanted* the attacks to continue.

At first, Durand had aimed for a quick resolution—settle out of court, keep the IPO on track no matter the price (within reason, of course). Ten, twenty, even fifty million was nothing, all things considered. On that basis, he had accepted Logan's invitation to the Diamond Club, expected to find common ground. The timing, the venue, inviting him not Max—Logan had played it well, exactly as he would have done.

Textbook from the opening handshake, barely a mention of the war, just pleasantries and platitudes, shallow banter about the match. When the conversation did eventually turn to business, they danced around numbers and words almost apologetically, neither man forcing the issue, each just probing, testing, measuring, the prelude to a quick negotiation.

There was also at least one axe to grind. Tony Levine, their erstwhile host, had said as much after Max had barged in on them. Logan had been more circumspect, but there had been that fleeting spider-to-the-fly glint in his eye that got Durand wondering if Max's head would feature on Logan's list of demands. That was what gave him the idea for the debenture.

At the end of the evening, he had taken the proffered limousine back to his hotel, convinced his initial assessment had been correct—opportunistic blackmail, quick buck, nothing more. Logan had seemed a reasonable sort and Durand had been sure they would settle in a matter of days.

At first, he had assumed Haddad was in on it. It stood to reason—he was Duncan Brown's friend. But as things dragged out, days turning to weeks, deadlines coming and going, Durand became more and more certain it was a bluff. Haddad had given Logan nothing, did not have the balls to get in the game. 'That's exactly why you're not on the board,' thought Durand.

Meanwhile, Adware's IPO had started to unravel, years of waiting, months of planning and hard work gone to waste. That really pissed off Durand. To make things worse, Conrad Baine was now trying to muscle in, take over his IPO.

That was what this conversation was about. Plan B. His, not Baine's.

"What about Max?"

"What about him?"

"Don't play dumb," snapped Baine. "The debenture."

"He still hasn't read the fine print," replied Durand with a smug smile. It had been a bone of contention when he first suggested it. Now he had been proved right. "I told you he wouldn't. He's too busy plugging holes in the dykes on the home front."

"Dikes, yeah," chuckled Baine.

The snide, bigoted comments had long grown wearisome. Durand bit back a retort and replied, "His wife's off the payroll, so are the nanny and the maid. His PA quit last week. I followed that up by losing the headcount. No replacement. I've also slashed his expense account—no more Michelin stars and first class travel. Any expense over £100 needs my approval. The check for the Bentley cleared. The car's now his, provided he can pay off the £300K balance due next week. I know that hurt. The renovation work on his house is now well into seven-figures, bills past due, job half done. Then there's the £2 million balance due on his yacht in two weeks' time. All in all, Max is massively over-extended."

"Death by a thousand cuts." As much as Baine despised Durand, he had to admire his cunning. The debenture had been a clever play.

"If it wasn't for him, we wouldn't be in this situation in the first place." Durand's voice was stone cold. Max had always been a liability. This last in a long litany of offenses was by far the worst. Repercussions were inevitable.

"So when are you going to call the note?"

"I gave Logan a two-week extension."

"What the fuck you do that for?" barked Baine.

Durand smiled. He had researched Max's personal net worth to the penny. "Right now, he's scrambling to raise the £2 million balloon payment on his gin palace. Hit him with the debenture now and he'll have the cash to pay it off. Wait two weeks and he won't. It will be sunk in the yacht. Add in regular upkeep—say £50K a month for a boat that size—and he'll be burning north of £200K a month. That's Max, not Adware."

Baine chuckled. Durand was even craftier than he'd thought.

"Besides, I've got more to do here to position Adware for the, ah, restructuring," continued Durand. "I'm slashing operating costs, but the mounting legal and PR bills will more than make up for that. The way things are going, the company will run out of cash in …"

"Two weeks."

"Correct." Durand smiled, self-satisfied.

"Just before you call the note."

"Yes. And then we immediately go on the offensive and counter-sue PaySense, kill that off for good. The timing has to be perfect."

Baine had been pressing Durand to sue PaySense and Peterman Brown for damages, but that was a sideshow. Durand had his eye fixed firmly on the prize. The IPO would go ahead. That was all that mattered. Especially after he called the debenture and Ignite owned Adware lock, stock and barrel. The lawsuit had started as a black cloud, but Durand knew he had found the silver lining, a billion dollars' worth. At 10%, his bonus would be north of a hundred million. He'd become a legend on Sand Hill Road.

"I still say we should squeeze them."

"I know what I'm doing," replied Durand, biting his tongue on "You small-minded, bigoted prick."

0110010101100100001101001

Daniel Logan woke with a start, cold sweat, shaking, eyes wild, a scream trapped in his throat. He threw off the covers and padded to the bathroom. In the mirror, the face of a stranger. He could trace every cut of the scalpel but the scars were invisible. He splashed cold water, ran wet fingers through his hair, rubbing harder, harder, his head ready to explode, staring at the face in the mirror.

Twenty years ago, he had killed his soul to save his life, gnawed it off like a wolf, its leg caught in a trap. All because of a lie.

The truth was now tearing him apart. Long-dead emotions burst out of his cold, dead heart, released like furies, nightmare images flashing, twisting, contorting and distorting the face in the mirror.

They said he killed Michelle. He had believed them. He *had* been angry, jealous. He *had* hit her, run away in shame. When he came back to beg forgiveness, she was dead. Crushed by grief, he had never questioned his guilt.

He ran. It was all he could think to do. From England, from himself, a fugitive in every sense. In Hull, he stole a passport. It was a clumsy first effort and the picture did not even look like him. Still, it worked, got him onto the ferry and out of the country. That night, the shark stalking the inky waters had kept him from jumping, showed him what he had to do to survive, what he had to become.

For months, he cried himself to sleep each night, visualize putting his past in a box one painful memory at a time. When the nightmares finally stopped and the pain subsided, his soul was dead, his heart an impenetrable black void. He had become the predator whose cold, impenetrable eyes now stared back at him, the stranger in the mirror.

As past faded back to the present, Logan saw tears streaming down his face. He had spent twenty years forgetting. Now, he could think of nothing else. And without the lie, without the burden of guilt, he could finally mourn his loss, Michelle, his love, his life. And exact his revenge.

He left the bathroom and went out to the veranda, the stone cold, refreshing beneath his bare feet. The clock read 3:23 pm. A cool breeze caressed his naked body, heightened his senses, cleared his mind. He drew deep breaths, heart pounding as he remembered a beautiful life.

It had taken him months to work up the courage to ask Michelle out on their first date. The memory of her smile so vivid, her eyes teasing, 'what took you so long?'

The next few years had been the happiest of his life. Michelle had helped him discover an inner strength he never knew he had. She had nurtured him, pushed him to challenge himself. Together, they would expand the boundaries of theoretical physics in ways even their Nobel laureate professors could barely grasp. It was an intellectual lovefest, soul mates at every level, 'in every dimension of the space-time continuum,' they had joked.

Their offspring were papers, brilliant co-authored papers. He was quantum, she relative. Together, they would find 42, the theory of everything, big, small, quantum, string.

Those first years together had been bliss. Then Max showed up.

He had read an article about Logan's search algorithms, his use of fractal dimensions to map the universe, to bring cohesion to the world's archive of astronomical data. Max did not understand it, but he did see commercial potential—if his old schoolmate's algorithms could map space, why not cyberspace, the World Wide Web? He quit his job that day and set off for Cambridge in search of his fortune.

A 'chance' encounter at college. Michelle adored him from the start. Her lover's childhood friend was witty, charming, generous, full of bonhomie. She thought it was sweet how he slung his arm over Logan's shoulder and called him 'Danny Boy'.

He fast became a regular fixture in their lives, there at every turn. Logan was powerless to stop it. He bore the shame of the victim, the ignominy of his past in silence. His worst fear was having that exposed, being emasculated in front of Michelle. Max had zeroed in on that with a bully's instinct for weakness. He did not have to say a word. A single sharp look, the threat of exposure, was all it took to keep Logan in check as he inveigled his way into their lives.

He knew Max had not come to Cambridge by chance, that he was not a student as he was pretending—he had checked. There was a reason. He wanted something, Logan just did not know what.

Then, one afternoon, after a long lunch with Max, Michelle came home bubbling with excitement. She had an idea, a wonderful idea—'Let Max use your search engine to index the World Wide Web! It's so clever!' That night, they had their first argument. It would not be the last.

Once out in the open, Max's pursuit of Logan's software became relentless. He had cast Michelle as his champion, himself the victim, Logan the villain—cruel, mean, selfish, denying a simple kindness to his best friend, happiness for his life partner. The bitter irony of the role reversal did not escape Logan, but he could offer no reason, no basis for his steadfast refusal, not without exposing his shame. He just said, "No."

Logan began spending more time at the lab, but escape came at a cost—it left Max alone with Michelle. He knew he was being manipulated, but felt powerless to stop it. On the rare occasions when they were all three together, Michelle would spend the whole time begging and pleading with him, Max looking on, sheepish and forlorn, a wounded pup. When they were alone, they argued, the words cutting deeper each time.

They had been arguing the night Michelle died. Logan had lashed out, accused her of having an affair with Max, although he knew it was not true. She hit back. Things got nasty. He raised a hand, slapped her, ran away in shame. He had been running ever since.

Standing on the cold balcony staring down over the sleeping city, he now knew. He would need that stranger in the mirror to avenge Michelle's death, exact recompense for man he once was, the life he never had.

CHAPTER 25

Mark woke as the plane was descending on its final approach to Nice Côte d'Azur Airport. No matter how many times he visited, he always loved the approach, the plane sweeping low over lazy cerulean waves, skirting the famed Boulevard des Anglais. From the grandes dames of the Belle Époque like the Hotel Negresco to the minimalist modernism of mid-twentieth century buildings, this particular stretch of coastline encapsulated the excess and luxury that was the French Riviera. The Corniche was slowly giving in to globalization, prime spots surrendered to McChains, but from the low, airborne sea view, the golden arches weren't visible and the Côte d'Azur still evoked visions of Bardot and Picasso.

Not for the first time, Mark idly dreamed of setting up Dynamo here, in Sophia Antipolis, the technology park in the hills above Antibes. It was something he dreamed about every time he visited Stephanie.

She met him in the arrivals hall. She was wearing a billowy white cotton blouse and dark blue jeans that flattered her figure. Her sun-bleached hair was pulled back in a ponytail, her skin rich and olive with the slow, deep tan of a local.

"Life here suits you," said Mark as he greeted his old friend.

Stephanie smiled. "Suits you, too. If we can close this deal, I can think of a lot of reasons for you and Susan to relocate. Tax breaks in Sophia Antipolis for starters."

Mark said nothing. The shit he was in, he was not yet ready to think beyond getting out of it.

"They just extended the tax incentives for another 10 years," continued Stephanie.

"I need to sort out this shit first, before I can even think about that," replied Mark as they turned left, veering away from the main exit. "Where are we going?"

"How about we buzz by Sophia Antipolis then follow the coast road?"

"Opposite directions," replied Mark, confused, as Stephanie stepped up to a counter and began speaking in French. Mark looked at the sign and smiled.

"This way," said Stephanie after a brief negotiation, leading him through a door. They exited the terminal building to a private stretch of runway. "There she is," she said with pride. "A Robinson R44. Beautiful, isn't she? Cruise speed 135. Range, 350. Better than a lot of cars I've driven." She ran her fingers down the helicopter's polished dark blue body as she gave Mark a 360 tour. "We take off westbound, circle over Sophia Antipolis, then loop south out to sea, out of the flight paths, then up to Monaco."

"Sounds good."

In the cockpit, Stephanie's demeanor changed completely, easy banter replaced with short, clipped words, measured, efficient, commanding, all business. She handed Mark a headset. "Check, check. 1-2-3."

"Check," replied Mark, his voice ghostly in the cavernous silence. "Amazing. I can't hear anything except you."

"You can listen in on take-off," said Stephanie as she opened a channel with traffic control. "Just don't say anything."

When they got the nod, Stephanie revved the engine and lifted the chopper, dipped its nose, then hovered waiting.

When they got the all clear, she accelerated to 140kph, the gees forcing them back in their seats as the chopper zipped along the runway barely feet off the ground, jumbo jets whizzing perilously close overhead. They cleared land and started their climb, Stephanie maintaining a steady, clipped dialogue with traffic control.

When they cleared the main air lanes, she let out a whoop. "What a rush! Nice is the third busiest airport in France, after de Gaulle and Orly. Monaco's much smaller." With a big smile, she added, "Once you move here, you might want to join our Owner's Club. It's actually quite reasonable when you're sharing."

Mark laughed, "I'll just tag along." Reasonable for Stephanie was still well out of his price range.

Spread across nearly 6,000 acres of mesa, Sophia Antipolis was a beautifully designed science park, home to dozens of hi-tech campuses nestled in forests of coastal pine. Cranes permanently dotted the skyline, new buildings rising, each more futuristic than the last.

"Can we shoot down over Vallauris on the way back?"

"Sure. If you lived there, you could bike to work," said Stephanie with a smile.

"In case you haven't noticed, my circumstances aren't quite ... fluid."

"Not yet," said Stephanie. "But trust me, it's all in hand." She banked the helicopter into a hard turn to starboard and headed south, back toward the sea.

"Wow. That's beautiful," said Mark pointing at an old villa on the crest of a hill.

Stephanie dropped to a hover, then turned the helicopter square on to view the villa. A wide veranda stretched across its rear perspective, a sweeping staircase leading to a large coral swimming pool, terraced gardens of fruit trees and flowering vines cascading down the hillside toward the sea. The property was dilapidated, the gardens overgrown but that only added to its charm.

"Do I see a for sale sign?" said Stephanie bringing them in for a closer look. "I do! Looks like a fixer upper. Maybe the price is right. We should drive over later and take a look."

"Susan would love it," said Mark.

"How's she doing?"

They had talked that morning. Yesterday too. She had been cool but not cold. He still could not tell where she stood, where they would be when this was all over.

"Still on board."

Stephanie had talked to Eric too. And to Susan. She nodded. "Good, because we have some unfinished business to sort out. Let's head home." She banked the chopper into a sharp turn, diving low, skimming the sea as they headed east to Monaco.

Less than an hour later, they were on the ground, racing along Monaco's ancient streets, the Porsche hugging the tight corners as they climbed the steep, winding roads to his villa. Stephanie's demeanor had not changed from the chopper, concentration steely, body now tuned to car and road. In another life, she would have been an F-1 driver.

Mark braced through the hairpins and switchbacks, the 911 GT2 RS's tires gripping the tarmac, inches from the sheer cliff edge. His heart pounded, waves of adrenaline and dopamine coursing through his body. But he trusted his old friend, always a speed demon, never out of control.

She had been a motorhead as long as Mark had known her. He recalled the first time they met. Sophomore year. She had just moved into the off-campus group house next door to his. One day, he came home to find an old roadster parked out back. Its body panels were banged up, mismatched, and patched with bondo, the ragtop tattered, chrome bumpers rust-spotted and faded, but it was still the most beautiful car Mark had ever seen. He walked around to the front, a mechanic under the hood. 'Hi. Gorgeous …' His words stopped when she stood up. She was dressed in baggy overalls, hands covered in grease, a big smear across her sweaty forehead, and she was still stunning. "Jag, '67 E Type. I'm restoring her. Hi, I'm Stephanie." They shook hands and had been best friends since.

"Wow!" was all he could say when they finally arrived at her villa, hands shaking, the engine growling like a tamed beast as they waited for the iron gates to swing open.

Stephanie smiled and offered, "Sometime, I'll take you to a road where you can give her a go, get a feel for how she handles. I've never driven anything like her."

The front door opened and Rick stepped out. He methodically waved the paddle over Mark, his coat, his bags. Stephanie, meanwhile, maintained a steady, innocuous monologue, an animated description of the recent landscaping work she and Eric had done.

Rick signaled for Mark to take his jacket off then emptied the pockets, scanning each item. Digging deep, he pulled out a small wad of lint from the left outside pocket.

Finally, with a nod from Rick, Stephanie led them down a path skirting the side of the villa. Built on a hill, its ground floor rooms opened onto a wide stone patio, a stretch of lawn and the swimming pool.

"You put in a boules court?" chuckled Mark eying the level expanse of hard packed sand. "Old man's game, isn't it?" he jibed.

"Not down here. Everyone plays. A glass of Campari, bit of sunshine … perfect way to while away a lazy afternoon. Maybe we'll get a game in tomorrow."

They entered the villa through the gym, Stephanie zigzagging through the crowd of equipment. With an enigmatic smile, she opened a door and ushered them into the sauna, Rick piling in behind them. Stephanie must have done something because the back wall swung open, a door into a windowless, L-shaped room. Ahead was all business, long workbench, shelves crammed with books and electronics, a small server rack, pair of cabinets and a desk, everything meticulously organized.

The left of the L was a den, sofa, coffee table, massive flat screen, wet bar. Rick fished three beers from the fridge and tossed them round while Mark took it all in.

"Cool, huh?"

A smile slowly spread across Mark's face as he spun round taking it all in. "What's this? GCHQ? Your own little Echelon?"

"You have no idea. You think Big Brother's bad? Little Brother's worse. Private, corporate surveillance is ubiquitous."

"That bad?"

"Here," said Stephanie with a gleeful expression as she slid open a drawer of a card cabinet. It held a handful of flying insects, gossamer wings, and an oblong body. On closer inspection...

"The latest in microrobotics. I caught these bad boys a few weeks ago in London. The proverbial fly on the wall. I gave a couple to Philippe. He's hacking them so we can recycle them."

"You recycle?"

"Waste not want not," laughed Stephanie. "They're state-of-the-art, cost a few hundred quid each."

Rick examined the insect closely. "Imagine if these go into mass production. The price will drop and there'll be swarms of them. Nowhere will be safe."

"What else have you got?" asked Mark as he started peering inside the other drawers.

"To the left are trackers, bugs on the right."

"How much did all this set you back?"

"Nada," replied Stephanie with a satisfied smirk. "All that is the stuff I find and recycle." She nodded toward another, smaller cabinet. "The stuff I buy is over here."

"There's gotta be hundreds of them!"

Stephanie looked at them with a need-I-say-more expression. "No exaggeration, half the meeting rooms you walk into are wired. I collect a few a week on average." She tipped her bottle in a toast. "Anyhow, welcome to Monaco. I'm sure I don't need to ask but please, don't mention what you see here to anyone. Even the kids don't know about it. Just you guys and Eric, although I suppose I have to tell John now."

"Why'd you never say anything before?"

"I do warn you all the time. But this," she swept her arm around the room, "is strictly need to know." She gave him a moment to absorb, look around, then turned back to business. "The GPS tracker we just took off you is state-of-the-art, just like the bugs we found at your house. Expensive kit. My guess is they tagged you at the airport."

"You think they followed me here?" Mark crossed the room and had a look at the tracker through the magnifying lens. Stephanie had already cracked open the case to expose its innards.

"Maybe not straight away, but they'll show up." Stephanie's tone left no room for doubt. She sat down at her desk, painted nails driving keyboard and mouse. She fired up a bank of monitors. Mark leaned in for a closer look, CCTVs showing different parts of the house, the streets outside.

Mark pointed at one, a fisheye view of the street. "Hey, that's from across the road ..."

Stephanie smiled and nodded. "It took me months to figure out how to rig that without being seen. What's interesting is, I found another camera mounted up there, small, camouflaged, almost identical to mine, just a slightly older model."

It took a second for this to register. "Hold it, are you saying ..."

"Monaco is brimming with private surveillance. It makes sense. A lot of money lives here, money that doesn't like attention. Paranoia's built in to the rich. Has to be. Armored cars, bodyguards. It's not Big Brother, not like London, where the government is watching everything you do, but every house here has CCTV, sophisticated intrusion detection systems, armed guards … and we're not talking run-of-the-mill security. The people who live here are the super-rich. They can afford to protect their privacy."

"Yeah, I noticed. It's like when you buy something, then suddenly start seeing it everywhere …"

"Blue Car Syndrome," offered Rick.

"That's it. So suddenly I'm seeing cameras everywhere. Must've always been there, just never noticed them. Now that I know where to look …" He closed his eyes and started counting off his fingers, "Next house down, two breadboxes on the gate—that's what I call the long, white ones—four more on the top corners of the house, three mounted on the wall aiming down the street. Another in a tree at the far corner of the property …" He continued down the street, petering out after the fourth house, as surprised by his level of recall as Stephanie and Rick were.

"Well done. You missed a few but that's pretty good."

"I didn't spot that, though," said Mark pointing at the GPS tracker they had found in his jacket pocket.

"That's a lot harder. It takes practice. We brush past people all the time. There are literally hundreds of opportunities every day for someone to plant something on you, if they are so inclined. I scan myself as often as I wash my hands." Stephanie nodded toward the organizer drawers. "There's the proof." She was right. There were hundreds of them.

She turned off the monitors and stood up. "Anyhow, the alerts are all set up now. We'll know the moment your friends arrive. Shall we go upstairs and get to work? We have a lot of ground to cover."

They sat in the garden, feet up, soaking in the warm

Mediterranean sun. Stephanie had wheeled out a whiteboard that now displayed a complex web of people, entities and notes. She had been suspicious of BizTech from the moment Mark called him with his Plan C idea. It was the interviewers—Barker and Levine—names she had come across before. They were circled on the whiteboard, lines connecting them to a number of other entities. Stephanie traced her finger down the line connecting them to Edelman Jones.

"Edelman Jones is a law firm. I knew the name from somewhere, but it took me a while to figure it out. It was the Neurocom deal I did a few years back ... Pi made a killing on it ... but my point is, Edelman Jones represented ..." her finger traced connecting lines. "... Peterman Brown ... and Peterman Brown is connected to ..."

"PaySense," the boys chorused.

"Voila! A full circle. So I started digging into both firms, turned up some interesting stuff. For starters, Edelman Jones filed the paperwork to incorporate BizTech and, you guessed it, seed funding came from Peterman Brown, through an offshore vehicle. But I still couldn't figure out the connection. Then I started making lists of all their deals. Peterman Brown was easy—they have an ego page on their website."

Stephanie tapped her tablet and a new column of boxes appeared along the right-hand side of the whiteboard, lines connecting them to Peterman Brown. "This is their investment portfolio over the past five years." She tapped the screen and five of the boxes turned green. "The green ones are the deals I'm in. That's what I was looking into when you called and told me you were being blackmailed."

"I still don't see how this is connected to Berkeley House," said Rick.

"Daniel Logan," said Stephanie. "He owns all three entities—Berkeley House, Peterman Brown, and Edelman Jones." She tapped once more and a fresh collection of boxes appeared. "These are the companies he has a direct interest in. At least, the ones I've been able to dig up so far. It was a set-up. The prize, four gorgeous women dropping into your laps—god, you men are so predictable. Thinking with the wrong head—you should have seen that coming a mile away." Stephanie shook her head wearily. "Anyhow, the timing of it is what got me thinking. I made some calls, jogged a few memories, flipped back through my own diary, and suddenly a pattern emerged—every time Peterman Brown wormed its way into one of my deals, at least one meeting had occurred at Berkeley House. Five for five. I'm still looking into the rest of my portfolio, but, so far, it's the same story every time."

"What, blackmail?" asked Rick.

"No. Berkeley House. There's always a meeting at Berkeley House," said Stephanie. "Which leaves only one conclusion—Daniel Logan shares my hobby."

"Are you saying he's bugged his own club?"

"It's genius, when you think about it." Stephanie tapped the tablet and a host of colored boxes began flashing on the whiteboard, all companies Logan had an interest in. "The amount of insider information he has access to must be massive. He just sits back like a spider and waits. The member list reads like a who's who in London's high tech scene. It's a beautiful setup."

Stephanie then applied it to Mark's situation. "You met Rick there, told him about what Max had done to PaySense. A week later, out of the blue, PaySense closes £2 million in funding from Peterman Brown. Next thing you know, lawsuits are flying. It's a classic play. Basically, legal blackmail, looking for a quick out-of-court settlement—a slice of Adware shares to make it go away, keep the IPO on track. I call it the Sunnyvale Shakedown."

"Why's that?" asked Rick.

"It's where Yahoo is based. And it's pretty much what they did to Google just before their IPO. The shares they got in the settlement are now worth more than a billion dollars."

"Wow," said Rick.

"But things didn't go to plan," said Stephanie, continuing. "Mark's friend, Duncan, refused to hand over the email implicating Max and Adware. No evidence, no settlement. You with me so far?"

Mark and Rick nodded.

"The other thing they know from listening to your conversation is that Mark is job hunting. So when Duncan refuses to hand over the evidence, Logan goes to Plan B."

"The virus?" asked Rick, following her train of thought.

"Actually, I suspect an intermediary step. First, someone broke into Mark and Duncan's houses …"

"But they didn't find what they were looking for."

"Exactly," continued Stephanie. "So they planted some bugs. That's when Logan comes up with Plan B—sets up a fake company, stages the interview with Mark, and uses an offer that is too good to be true—sorry, Mark—to get the infected flash drive into your hands and into your computer."

"But that didn't work either, because Jason found the virus," said Rick. "So they tried again with a second flash drive. But that didn't work."

"Which brings us to the honey trap. Plan C."

Stephanie noticed Mark wince at the mention. She had been on the phone with Susan every day since the trip to Wittering, knew how much her friend was hurting. True, Mark had been set up, but what was it about men? They just did not think. He should never have gotten himself into that situation. Stephanie wanted him to feel some pain, to realize how he had hurt Susan, make amends, but she was also pragmatic. This was not the time.

"Has Jason come back to you about the second drive?" asked Stephanie.

"No, not yet. It's still with his buddy, Ivan."

"So now that we know all this …" said Rick.

"We use it," said Stephanie.

"Like the bugs in my house."

"Yes. As long as Logan does not realize his surveillance

has been compromised, we can use it to control the game."

"Is that what this is? A game?" asked Mark, a sardonic edge to his voice.

"That's *exactly* what it is. And I always play to win."

0110000101100111011101101111

The next morning, Mark and Stephanie set off down l'Escalier de la Costa. They reached the harbor and walked along the Quai des Etats Unis until they found the berth for *Eliza's Revenge*.

"Serious yacht," said Mark as they stepped onto the gangway. "Gotta be 60 feet at least."

"Seventy," replied Stephanie. "A Sunseeker Manhattan. Fast. 1550 horsepower. Top speed 37 knots. Range 300 nautical miles."

Mark chuckled. Land, sea or air, if it had an engine, Stephanie knew the specs.

Sam saw them, waved from the fly bridge, and hurried down to meet them at the gangway. Five minutes later, *Eliza's Revenge* left Port Hercule and made for open water, a light breeze, clear skies and calm waters ahead.

"We'll head for Juan les Pins," said Sam from the helm. "There's a little place called Tetou. Best bouillabaisse on the Riviera, in the world! Used to be Picasso's favorite haunt. It's still run by the same family. After lunch, we'll cruise back, maybe stop for a swim in the deep blue. The girls love it out there, miles from nowhere. Bikinis not required. Stephanie?" He raised his eyebrows suggestively then bellowed out one of his signature laughs.

He was not usually so crude; beneath all his machismo he was actually quite the pussycat. But Stephanie had bested him last time they met and he was trying to unsettle her. All that did was show his hand again. She knew he wanted this deal. Badly.

A few minutes later, Sam handed the controls to his

captain and led them down into the cabin. It was minimalist but luxuriously appointed in rich woods and soft, creamy leathers. Cynthia stood up to greet them.

"Mark Haddad, I'd like you to meet Cynthia Jones. She's my analyst. She tells me if a deal's good or bad. I'll be straight, Mark. I like what I see, so let's do a deal."

Five hours later, *Eliza's Revenge* drifted in the gentle waters twenty miles out to sea, engines off, Sam pacing furiously inside the cabin. "You have got to be realistic, Mark. This valuation's nuts! $100 million? Cynthia, Stephanie, tell him! It's not even a company yet!"

"That's not true. We are a registered UK company. And we have a great product and a number of patents. Frankly, $100 million's on the cheap side. We're not just talking about a killer app. It's what people will use to *build* killer apps."

Sensing negotiations had reached breaking point, Stephanie said, "How about we take a break, stretch our legs?"

There was an audible sigh of relief as everyone stood up. Out on deck, Sam poured glasses of freshly squeezed lemonade from an iced pitcher and opened the lid of his humidor, spinning it round for Mark to choose a cigar.

Holding up his phone, Mark said, "I need to check my email." He wandered off toward the forward deck, impressed by the five bar Wi-Fi signal he was getting 20 miles out at sea.

As Sam busied himself trimming and lighting a Churchill, Cynthia tapped Stephanie lightly and nodded toward the fly bridge.

Cynthia followed. They stood in silence for a while, just the wind and the gulls, the waves gently lapping against the hull, watching Mark, alone, out on the bow staring out to sea. Cynthia took Stephanie's hand and led her to the lounge area where she sat down and curled her legs under her.

"If this doesn't work out ..."

"We'll make it work."

Cynthia reached out and touched Stephanie's arm. Her fingers were delicate and coy on her sun-warmed skin, the sensation electric. Stephanie pulled away.

"Are you sure?" asked Cynthia, her words ripe with innuendo, eyes smoky, pouting, alluring.

Stephanie stood up and crossed the fly bridge to the evident safety of distance. She left her purse on the divan. She was an attractive, wealthy, powerful woman at the top of her game. People flirted with her all the time. She did not mind. In fact, it was flattering. It made her feel sexy, as long as lines were not crossed. With Cynthia, she was never quite sure where those lines were.

Stephanie counted to 30, visualizing what Cynthia was doing, not rushing her. Then she turned and said, "Mark is right—Dynamo is disruptive technology. It's a game changer. Sam has to see that."

"He does. But ..."

"I know," replied Stephanie, cutting her off, owning the objection. She reached down, took Cynthia's hand, and caressed her delicate fingers with her thumb, playing the sexual tension right back at her. "I love your color." It was a soft peach, natural, words intended to disarm. "If—*and it's only an if*—but if I can convince Mark to take $5 million for 25%, would Sam go for it?"

Cynthia gave her a questioning look. "I thought we were talking about two million?"

"Pre-money, it's the same valuation. $20 million."

"But why would he dilute so much? I've been through the numbers. They don't need that much to get to the next funding round." It was the ABCs of venture finance, a series of funding rounds that led to an IPO, the valuation, share price, and money raised increasing with each successive round. "Is there something in the forecasts I should know about?"

"No, no," said Stephanie, "That's not it. If anything ... and I think you agree ... the forecasts are conservative. Call it comfort factor. Look, I was as surprised as you were when he sprang this on me last night." Stephanie sat down on the edge of the divan. "I tried to talk some sense into him, but …" Stephanie fiddled with the strap of her purse, looking pensive, as if about to reveal a confidence. "Mark's first company, Digiterra … it didn't fail fast. He struggled for 5 years after the bubble burst. That took its toll. His wife, Susan, she's a dear, dear friend … I've known her longer than I've known him … it almost destroyed them."

Cynthia nodded understanding. "And he'd be willing to dilute another 15% to make sure that doesn't happen again."

"In a nutshell, yes," said Stephanie.

Cynthia considered what Stephanie was proposing. It was more risky, but in the long term it could pay off. Disruptive technology and a seasoned management team made for a winning formula. She also knew Sam was bullish on Dynamo's prospects. A bigger stake in the Series A round would appeal to him. And, with a surplus of cash, the execs could focus on growing the business, accelerating its growth plans.

"What about his partners?" she asked.

"I don't know Peter that well, but you've seen his resume. Same story, burned in the first crash. I think he'll be on board. Jason Hunter, their developer—he'll go with the flow."

"So, why the silly numbers? All this non-exec business? Why all this?" Cynthia's gesture took in everything that had happened since they'd weighed anchor.

"He's not thinking straight. He's got a job offer, big package, career path, lots of security. He wants to accept." Stephanie spoke with a tone of helpless disbelief as she shared the confidence. "I tried talking sense to him last night … told him he just can't do that. It's not how things work. But he was adamant. He knows hiring in a CEO will dilute his shareholding so he's trying to claw some of that back from the venture round."

"It's not tenable."

"I couldn't agree more."

There was a long silence before Cynthia said, "Five million's a lot of cash."

Stephanie stifled the smile of victory. She had her. Time to play coy. "Sam doesn't have to take all of it. I do have other interested parties who I can bring in."

Cynthia stood up. "Are you sure you can get Mark on side? Five million for 25%, plus a seat on the board? Make that two."

"Yes, I do. I know him. I can bring him round."

"Okay." Cynthia nodded toward Mark who was standing alone at the bow of the yacht. "You go speak to your man child and I'll go speak to mine. I do want this to work."

"So do I," replied Stephanie, giving Cynthia's hand a warm squeeze.

Stephanie joined Mark at the bow. "You're my best friend and I'm going to tell it to you straight. You're blowing this deal."

Silence.

"I know what you're thinking, but you're going about it all wrong. No one in their right mind is going to put £2 million into a start-up for such a tiny slice. You have *got* to see that."

Mark kept up the silent treatment.

"And this crap about being non-Exec Chairman. I told you last night it was a Bad Idea, and that's with capital letters. All it says is that you don't have faith in your own company." Her words were angry, provocative.

"Bullshit! Dynamo's brilliant!" said Mark before dropping his voice to a humble mumble, "That's not what it's about."

"Give me some credit, Mark. I've known you for more than 20 years. You think I don't know what's going on inside that pretty head of yours? Think I don't talk to Susan? I know what you guys went through with Digiterra. I was there, remember? For both of you."

Cut to a long, scripted silence.

OMAR SHABKA

Stephanie fished out a pack of cigarettes. She was one of the rare breed who could smoke out of choice, not habit. And she chose to do so around Sam and Cynthia. Mark was not so lucky. He was fast slipping back into the habit. They smoked, letting the silence draw out, standing side by side, staring out at the calm, azure waters.

"If I can raise $5 million … is that enough comfort factor for you to stick to the plan?"

"Five?" said Mark. "But we're talking two."

"Leave that to me."

"What terms?"

"Same. But obviously a bigger slice."

"25%?" said Mark, doing the math.

"That is a damned good deal. But I'll warn you right now, you cannot dump me in it again. I'm vouching for you here. My reputation's on the line."

"Okay," said Mark.

"No backing out."

Mark shook his head. "You have my word."

"Good. Now let's talk valuation."

"I thought you said 25%? That's a $20m valuation."

"Look, you really dumped me in it. I can salvage a deal but I am not a miracle worker. I need some wiggle room."

"I was just trying to …"

"I don't want to hear it Mark Haddad." Stephanie's tone was scolding, like a mother to an errant child. "Just give me your bottom line."

"27.5%. Thirty tops."

"Alright." Stephanie glanced at her watch. "Let's get back down below and see if we can make this work. And I don't want you to say a thing. Not a word. You just sit there and look pretty. Got it?"

When *Eliza's Revenge* tied up at its berth in Port Hercule, Sam Leonard escorted his guests onto the quai. Shaking hands, he said, "You've got balls, Mark, I'll give you that. You just make sure you slap them on the table when you're running my business!"

"Sam, in three years you'll be able to buy a *fleet* of these gin palaces," replied Mark.

"That's what I want to hear!" laughed Sam.

Rick was waiting for them at Place Sainte Devote, silent, scanner in hand. Mark and Stephanie kept up a steady conversation while he swiped them. The bug was where Stephanie had said it would be, in the pack of cigarettes in her purse. She fished one out, crumpled the pack and tossed it in a nearby by trash can. They then set off up l'Escalier de la Costa, letting the conversation fade naturally into the distance.

When they were safely out of earshot, she said, "We're clear now. It's was a short-range device. Same one she planted on me last time."

"You must spend a lot of time scanning your wardrobe," said Mark.

Stephanie smiled. "You have no idea."

"So?" asked Rick, the eager puppy.

"We closed the deal."

"No shit! That's fantastic. How much?"

"Five million dollars. The cash will be in the bank Monday morning."

Rick whistled. "How much did you give up? 30%?" It was the cap they had agreed the night before.

Stephanie pretended to wince. "They squeezed us to 27.5%." She chuckled and nodded over her shoulder at Mark. "Mark gave an Oscar-winning performance."

"Stephanie was the star. She played it to a tee. You were so right. When do you think they put the bug in your purse."

"When Cynthia and I were up on the fly bridge. When you were pouting on the bow."

"She's awfully flirty," said Mark. "I think she's got the hots for you."

"Oh my god," said Rick, a grin spreading on his face.

Stephanie cut it short with a withering stare. "Just for once, can you think with something other than your dick?"

Mark laughed at first, then remembered his own circumstances.

"So what now?" asked Rick.

"We celebrate. We just closed five million dollars in first round venture financing for Dynamo. We'll start with happy hour back at my place, then a night out on the town, dinner, a bit of clubbing. Mark's buying."

"Are you sure the cash will be in the bank Monday?"

"It's a done deal. I trust Sam."

Mark laughed.

"What's so funny?"

"It's crazy. You know he's planting bugs on you, yet you still say you trust him."

Stephanie shrugged. "We've been doing business for years. I do trust him. As for the bugs, like I keep trying to tell you, they're par for the course in my world. The stakes are high. Everyone wants an edge when the chips are down. Just part of the game."

"The game ..."

"Yeah, the game. That's all it is. You can't take it personally. It's just business. You accept the rules, get stuck in and win." She wrapped an arm around Mark. "Which we just did."

An afternoon playing boules proved a welcome tonic, especially when liberally mixed with Campari. By the time they were showered, changed, and reassembled in the living room, Mark was noticeably more relaxed. There was a spring in his step every time he thought about Dynamo. Everything was moving ahead. The dark clouds that still loomed over him seemed more abstract, somehow less ominous, with the knowledge that he had just closed first round funding for his fledgling start-up.

"Just a reminder about the ground rules," said Stephanie

as they piled into her Maserati Quattroporte. "We'll be exposed as soon as we leave the house. Assume someone is listening to every word you say, so no talking shop. Give nothing away. And remember, they don't know about our meeting with Sam and I want to keep it that way. Even if Logan does know about Dynamo, he does not need to know that we just closed your funding."

In the rearview mirror, Stephanie saw Rick turn to look at the surveillance van.

"Don't. I've got dark windows, but if they have the right filters they can still see us. I've got them in the mirrors and here ..." She pressed a button on the dashboard. "On video."

"Cool," said Rick and Mark at the same time.

"If they're professionals, which I assume they are, they'll play it by the book." She pointed at the screen. "See, here they come. They were just waiting for us to round the bend."

"Where are your people?" asked Rick.

"They're on it. They know our route and they have access to the GPS on my phone so they will know our location at all times. You'll meet Philippe tomorrow. He's a good guy. A bit scary, but I trust him. Hang on ..." She pressed the button on her Bluetooth headset and spoke in French, a brief exchange. "The bike is moving too. Standard protocol will be for him to take point in the next mile or so. I suspect we'll flush out one, maybe two more vehicles by time we get to Nice."

"How long have you been living like this?"

Stephanie chuckled. "It's not usually like this. Mostly it's electronic surveillance, which is a lot cheaper and easier."

"How many people does it take to follow someone?"

"These guys are pros, probably ex-military. Their hardware's top shelf too. They'll have a minimum of nine people on the ground working in shifts. Maybe more. The size of the operation will tell us a lot. Which is why I want to flush them out tonight."

Twenty minutes later, as they made the final approach to Nice, Stephanie reminded them of the game plan. "Rick, we'll drop you off at the Negresco Hotel. Go shopping, find a nice gift for the lovely Yasmin. And remember, be natural. Don't even try to see who's following you. Let Philippe's people take care of that. Just go about your business like any other tourist, not a care in the world."

"Got it. Then I walk up rue du Congres and catch a cab on Victor Hugo."

Stephanie nodded. "That'll stretch them, making them follow you on foot."

"This must be costing a fortune. For them and Mark."

"It's lucky we closed the funding, then, isn't it?" said Stephanie.

"Sam's going to hit the roof when he sees the first month's management accounts."

"We'll worry about that later. Right now, we need to focus on taking control of this whole situation you've gotten yourself into. You can't get Dynamo up and running until this monkey's off of your back."

CHAPTER 26

Early Saturday morning, Stephanie banged on bedroom doors. "Rise and shine, boys! Busy day ahead!"

"I haven't even had a cup of coffee yet," complained Mark groggily. He checked his watch. 7:30 am. They had been up till 3:00 am the night before.

Stephanie handed him a steaming mug. "There you go. Now, up and showered. Breakfast on the veranda," she said, her voice cheery, no hint of a hangover.

Moments later, Mark heard the muffled sounds of Rick getting the same brusque treatment next door. Shaking off the cobwebs, he climbed out of bed, opened the windows, and closed his eyes, basking in the morning sun, the gentle breeze caressing his skin. He stepped onto the balcony for a moment of solitude with the scent of frangipani and Italian coffee. *I could get used to this,* he thought.

Fifteen minutes later, showered and shaved, he went out to the veranda. Rick was already tucking into a spread of fresh baguettes, croissants, and fruit.

Stephanie swiveled the tablet to share the 4x4 grid of live video feeds, clocks ticking in synch in the top right corners. 7:46:21, 22, 23 ... "Here are our friends." Two cameras showed the now familiar grey van parked outside, front and back elevations. Another camera up the road offered a bird's-eye view of a parked motorcycle. "Poor guy," said Stephanie. "He's been having bike trouble for hours. I offered to help when I took Heathcliff for a walk earlier. He didn't speak French, sounded Eastern European. Definitely not local."

She swiped the screen, switching to a grid of photographs. "Here are the nine we pinged. Philippe's got a contact at the airport. He'll ID them when they fly back to London."

"This guy Philippe …"

"You'll meet him soon enough."

Rick shivered. "This is too weird. It gives me the creeps, all this surveillance."

"I've been telling you for years, you live in a surveillance state. Get used to it. In the UK alone, there are more than six million CCTV cameras. That's one for every 11 people! And that's only the ones that are publicly accounted for. Living as you do in London, you …" Stephanie jabbed a finger at Rick to emphasize her point, repeated, "You are caught on camera more than 300 times a day. So what's more insidious, blanket surveillance by Big Brother or a bit of targeted corporate espionage?"

"Yeah, but at least it's passive. Unless you're a terrorist or something, it doesn't matter. This … this is nine goons parked outside your house, watching us, listening to every word we say."

Stephanie smiled. "And we know who they are."

"What are you saying? Just accept it?"

"Accept the situation, yes. And play it right back at them." Stephanie waved at the tablet. "That's what I do. What *we* are doing right now. *Counter*-surveillance. *Counter*-intelligence. *Counter*-espionage."

"Which is why, Rick old chum, you have to keep shagging the lovely Yasmin," added Mark, trying to laugh off his discomfort.

"Best sex I've had in a long time," said Rick.

"But can you handle it?" asked Stephanie, goading him.

"Of course I can handle it," replied Rick, puffing with indignation.

"Again with the one-track mind," said Stephanie, shaking her head in dismay. "I meant the counter-surveillance."

"Are you kidding? I plan to record it myself," said Rick, laughing, when no one else was.

"This is not some prank like we used to pull at university. This is very serious business. Those nine goons out there ..." She let her words trail off ... "One mistake and we're screwed."

"You make it sound like it's some tactical maneuver."

"That's exactly what it is," replied Stephanie. "Everything is."

"It's still weird."

"No weirder than yesterday. I knew Cynthia would plant a bug on me, so I planned for it. And when she did, we used it, turned it to our advantage. As a result, Dynamo now has $5 million in the bank at a great valuation. I'd call that a success. And, it's how we play *our* game."

"Bond. James, Bond," said Rick, still turning to levity to relieve his discomfort with the situation.

"One big difference," said Stephanie. "In the movies, the bad guys know Bond is a spy. To maintain operational integrity," she hammered out her next words, "They absolutely cannot know their surveillance has been compromised. If they do, we lose our advantage."

"So I keep shagging Mata Hari, pretending I know nothing. I'm beginning to like this."

They all laughed, but talk of the honey trap brought a dark cloud over Mark. Stephanie read his angst, and said, "I spoke to Susan. She'll deal with it. She'll get over the photos. You were set up and she knows it. She just needs time. And she needs you to focus on getting yourself out of this mess."

"Yeah, we talked earlier," said Mark. In a strange way, he was disappointed that she had not been angrier. That would have been easier to understand.

Neither Stephanie nor Susan planned to let him off so easily, but for now, at least, they both needed him to focus on the immediate. "You were an idiot. But it was a set-up, a classic honey trap. Deep down, Susan knows that. When you spoke to her, what'd she tell you to do?"

"Deal with the situation."

"And that's exactly what you're going to do." Stephanie tried to lighten the air by adding, "Even Rick's doing his part by shagging Mata Hari."

"I should just walk away, quit my job, tell Logan to stuff it. I've got my funding. It's over."

"We've already talked about that. It's not over, not yet. It's all still in play, whether you like it or not. Logan's got a lot of resources committed to this operation. He obviously has a lot at stake. He is not just going to roll over. We have no idea what his next move will be, but I guarantee you, there will be one. Besides, we can't just leave Duncan out in the cold."

Mark snorted. He knew it was true. They spent the next few minutes in silence, Stephanie busy at the iPad, Rick eating, Mark going off for a stroll in the lush garden. When he sat back down, Stephanie made meaningful eye contact with both men, a nod of acknowledgement, before turning off the gray noise generator. It was show time. The dulcimer sounds of a sleeping house, birds in the garden were interrupted by her cheery voice, "Good morning, boys! How about some coffee?"

They spent the next ten minutes rustling newspapers and iPads, pretending small talk, idle chit chat. At 8:30 am, Stephanie stood up and said, "Time to go. Shops open at nine. We'll take the Maserati. It's about 30 minutes down the coast road."

Stephanie eased around the corner before stepping on the gas, pushing the Maserati through the hairpin turns as they descended the mountainside, tires just shy of squealing.

"Bike's down," reported Stephanie with a smile. "This

time he really does have mechanical problems."

The rider had been accelerating into a blind turn, intent on catching up, when a delivery van backed out of a driveway. Powerless to avoid a collision, the rider had to dump the bike, skidding along the tarmac into the side of the van.

The van's driver and passenger, dressed in blue work overalls piled out, cursing in French. As the driver attended to the fallen rider, the other man surreptitiously pierced the motorcycle's tank. He yelled that he smelled gas, forcing a hasty retreat to safety, a call to the emergency services.

A few minutes later, Stephanie turned westbound on l'Avenue de Trois Septembre. The twists and turns of the coast road demanded caution from the cumbersome surveillance van but were manna for Stephanie's performance-tuned Maserati. She drove at speed, overtaking traffic, stretching her lead on their pursuers, flushing out the rest of Logan's people.

Twenty minutes later, the Maserati rounded the Parc Municipal de Mont Boron and began its final descent into the Port of Nice. "This is where it gets interesting," she said.

She raced the rest of the way to Rue Rosca, then made a sharp right and another onto Rue Fodere, a left onto Boulevard Stalingrad. Stephanie kept up a running dialogue in French on her Bluetooth headset as her passengers watched and listened in fascinated silence. With a final quick series of maneuvers, she pulled a hard right into a narrow passage that led to a closed courtyard. An iron gate shut behind them. She parked and climbed out.

"Nice driving," said Rick.

Stephanie smiled, flushed with adrenalin.

"Eh, mon amie! Ca va?" Philippe's voice was deep, smoke-cured, resonant. He embraced Stephanie, kissed her on both cheeks, then stepped back to cast his eyes over her friends.

"Philippe Habib. Mark Haddad, Rick Ashton," said Stephanie, making introductions.

Philippe was a lurking 6'4", his solid frame covered in dark, leathery Mediterranean skin. *Habib?* thought Mark, studying the face. One eye was damaged, a long diagonal scar from forehead to cheek, the other intense, penetrating. His smile was crooked but warm, three gold teeth, the rest stained by countless Gauloise.

Mark made an immediate racial profile. Arab. Probably Algerian. Street. Criminal. Probably second generation, raised in the slums of Marseilles. He was a man who lived by a code and it was absolute. Mark immediately felt the privilege of inherited trust. He was glad, because in the depths of Philippe's eyes lurked a fierceness that Mark would never want to see directed at himself.

"Gauloise?" he offered.

"Tekram," said Mark.

"S'hait," replied Philippe, grinning, recognizing Mark's dialect as Lebanese.

The garage quickly filled with the distinctive aroma of the Syrian-Turkish blend. Philippe had a private word with Stephanie then said, "Allez-y." He led them across the courtyard, past a garage, mechanics at work in several bays. Through a door, upstairs, down a hallway.

The office was anonymous, no signage, not even a nameplate on the battered door. The front room had seen better days. A Naugahyde sofa grimy with age, a coffee table, chipped glass and paint. A Pirelli calendar hung above the water dispenser, stuck on February 2006. The walls, once institutional green, were stained with years of tobacco smoke, grease and urban grime. A ceiling fan spun overhead, its ancient motor protesting with a tired wuh, wuh, wuh.

A receptionist sat at the desk, her burning cigarette precariously balanced in an overflowing ashtray to her left. With long red nails, she alternated between dragging on the fag and banging away on an old typewriter. To her right was a dusty relic of a PC that looked like it had never been used.

Philippe led them into the back office. *Coffee?* Nods all

round. *"Giselle! Cafe!"* He closed the door and indicated for Mark to raise his arms, patted him down then turned his palms upward. In each was what looked like a crumb.

"I planted these on you when you arrived," explained Philippe, laughing at Mark's look of shock. "A lesson. To show you how easily your security can be compromised. Stephanie tells me you are now a target."

Mark nodded.

"Then it is lucky you know Stephanie." Philippe's gold teeth flashed in a wide grin. "Very lucky."

Giselle knocked once, then walked in with a tray, four demitasses of strong Italian espresso. Philippe waited for her to leave before taking out a phone and tapping a few buttons. He handed the device to Stephanie and said, "They split up and are now searching the area on foot. My men will stay with them."

Stephanie studied the photos, the same faces they had seen earlier.

"Professional operation. Big team," said Philippe, clearly impressed. "Somebody's spending money." He lit another Gauloise from the butt end, offered the pack around then set it on the table. "Stephanie explained your problem. You have discussed the plan?"

Mark nodded again.

"Parameters still the same?"

This time Stephanie answered. "Nothing's changed."

Philippe nodded. He flipped the latches on a briefcase and spun it around to face the others. "I think maybe a briefcase is not your style."

Mark shrugged and nodded.

"Not a problem. A courier bag, perhaps?"

"New toy?" asked Stephanie, admiring the briefcase.

"Mulberry. Finest craftsmanship. Packed with toys and completely snoop proof. I just field tested it at DefCon. Even dE$0l8 … no one knows her real name … Only 14 years old and already one of the best in the world. Even she could not hack it. The courier bag has the same features. All custom made."

"I'll take the briefcase," announced Stephanie, not even asking the price.

Philippe smiled. It's what he had expected. "Of course." Stephanie was a preferred customer with a penchant for the all the latest toys.

"This is a complete CS package."

"Counter-surveillance." Stephanie helped out with the lingo. She could see Mark and Rick were still in a mild state of shock as they tried to absorb what they were doing, where they were, Philippe.

"My philosophy on CS has been influenced significantly by our mutual friend," continued Philippe. "Most people, they detect and neutralize. Not Stephanie. She likes to turn assets, like a double agent, eh?" His laughter was a deep rolling growl.

Mark nodded. Stephanie had been hammering that message into his brain for the past two days. Obviously she had made a convert of her supplier as well. "Like yesterday, on the yacht."

"Exactly," replied Stephanie with a satisfied smile.

Philippe fired up a calculator app on the smartphone, flashed the screen around for everyone to see. "A calculator. As you say in England, it does what it says on the tin." Philippe laughed again. "But when you hold down SIN and tap MEM+ three times ..." tap, tap, tap ... "then press and hold % ... *Voila!* The interface changes. It is now a control panel for what's inside the briefcase." With a pleased smile, he shared the screen once more.

"Ooh, I like that," exclaimed Stephanie as she leaned in for a closer look.

Philippe walked them through the menus. SCAN. LSTN. VIEW. JAM. RETR. REC. TRANS. Easy enough. Then abbreviations like BLT. WIF. ERT. EMG. RAD. Stuff they would have to learn.

Philippe took items out of the briefcase, describing their hidden capabilities one by one. He leaned back with evident pride in his product. "Usually, this is €20,000. For you, ma cherie, 17.5. 30 for 2."

A few minutes later, there was a knock on the door and a man entered carrying two boutique shopping bags. The Mulberry bag was empty save for a receipt. The Coach bag contained a very expensive looking courier bag, also with a receipt.

"This is Hamid. He will take you in his taxi to Vieux Nice. Your friends have started spreading their search that way. He will drop you where they will find you again. Do some shopping, then enjoy lunch at my cousin Ali's restaurant. He makes the best pizza in Nice."

Philippe nodded at Hamid, who handed him the keys to the Maserati and a parking stub. "Your car is at the Hotel Mercure. You know where it is?"

Stephanie nodded.

"They have searched all the garages around here, where they lost you," he said with a laugh, "but not so far away as the Corniche."

"What about airport security?" asked Mark, examining his new bag. "I'm flying back to London tomorrow."

Philippe laughed with a smuggler's confidence. "This will not be a problem. I guarantee it. Everything has been FSA-tested."

"I always travel with something and I've never been stopped," said Stephanie. "There really is nothing to worry about. If they ask you to turn something on, just do it. You saw. It all does what it says on the tin."

Stephanie slid an envelope across the table. "Keep the rest on account. For manpower, here and in London. Let me know when you need more."

Philippe pocketed the enveloped without counting, almost embarrassed. "Of course, ma cherie."

Hamid took a convoluted route, avoiding the streets where the Ukrainians were searching for them on foot, guided by a steady stream of updates over his Bluetooth headset. He turned onto Rue Sincaire and pulled over halfway down the block. Looking in the rear view mirror, he delivered rapid-fire instructions in French to Stephanie, who took out her phone and dialed a number as instructed. Once the connection was made, she nodded to Hamid and ushered Rick and Mark out of the cab. They doubled back on foot toward Place Garibaldi.

"Two people are approaching from Rue Bonaparte," said Stephanie as they walked. "They'll find us on a park bench, taking a break from our shopping." She hoisted the Mulberry bag as evidence. "Once we've acquired them, we'll head for the old part of town, do some more shopping, then have lunch at Ali's. Philippe's right. He does make the best pizza in town. Oh, and do keep in mind, expect them to plant a bug on you somewhere along the way so be careful what you say. Assume we are being listened to from this point on."

After lunch, they took a stroll through Vieux Nice, cobbled streets winding through a maze of old apartment buildings whose decay was rich with character. Overhead, laundry hung from lines spanning the narrow pedestrian streets, shading the bistros and cafes below from the afternoon sun. They headed westward toward the shopping district, but their progress was aimless and leisurely, their conversation banal and innocuous, as if they had not a care in the world other than enjoying the provincial ambience.

On rue Longchamp, Mark broke away from the group and went into a lingerie boutique, alone. Stephanie and Rick waited outside. It was time for a little scene setting.

"What's wrong with Mark?" asked Stephanie, playing to the mikes she assumed were there. "He seems a bit distracted. Been like that all weekend."

Rick shook his head. "Don't know. I've asked, but he's

not saying. I suppose job hunting's got him stressed out. I know work is tense right now as well. This business with PaySense. You do know about that, don't you? His friend, Duncan, is suing Adware."

"Yes, he told me. I've been following it in the press. It looks like Adware's IPO has stalled. Maybe that's what's eating him, feels it's somehow his fault."

"I think he's involved. He's like … Deep Throat," replied Rick, over-egging the dramatic flair.

Stephanie gave him a sharp look that said, *Tone it down!*

"He did say that he gave Duncan some emails. I told him not to but he wouldn't listen. If it gets out that he's a whistleblower, it's going to make it really hard for me to land him another job. "

"I thought you had a couple of offers lined up?"

"I do. Pretty good ones too. He should be stoked, but he's not. Which is why I think it's got to be the lawsuit. And with the IPO going off the rails … I think he was counting on a windfall from his options."

"Here he comes," said Stephanie, killing the confidential conversation. "Let's work on him tonight."

Mark crossed the street from the lingerie shop, carrying another designer shopping bag. The conversation turned to friendly ribbing.

At Hotel Mercure, they handed the parking ticket to the valet. When the Maserati arrived, they piled in and headed east, back to Monaco.

Body scans and a couple of cocktails later, it was siesta time, everyone yawning, tired from the lazy day. Stephanie flicked on the iPad and hoisted her digital defenses, grey noise making it safe for them to talk. It felt like the room itself exhaled.

"I want one of those briefcases," said Rick, as soon as it was safe to talk.

"Not with Yasmin around. Too risky."

"I'll keep it at the office, scout's honor."

"Alright. Leave it with me," said Stephanie. She had seen the way he had been eyeing them all day, knew him well enough to know he would pout and mope if she said 'no'. "But I have one condition. Until this is over, it stays in your safe. Our whole plan is hinged on them not realizing we are running our own counter-surveillance operation."

Rick nodded, happy as a puppy. "Scout's honor."

"And do us a favor ... tone it down," said Stephanie. "C'mon ... deep throat?"

"But ..."

Stephanie waved away the protest. "You did fine, but you did over-egg it. Just relax, be yourself. Keep it natural."

Rick nodded, suitably rebuked.

"It's a game, but the stakes are very real."

CHAPTER 27

"Daddy's home!" Ben and Layla came running and jumped on Mark as soon as he walked in the door. They competed with rapid-fire descriptions of everything they had done in Wittering over half term.

"Slow down. One at a time," laughed Mark, giving them big hugs. "Ben's youngest. He goes first." He alternated between that and "Layla's oldest. She goes first." Neither child ever argued, somehow subconsciously sensing an intrinsic balance in this parental tactic.

Susan smiled from the kitchen and gave them a few minutes before sending the kids off for their bath. Domestic bliss. When they were finally alone, she gave Mark a deep, silent hug, no kiss, no words.

"What's cooking? Smells great?"

"Cassoulet," replied Susan leading him into the kitchen.

Mark rifled through a drawer for a pen and a notepad. *Remember, the house is bugged. Follow me.* He pointed them out— kitchen, living room (painting above the fireplace), dining room (chandelier), keeping up a steady stream of banal conversation about the Turner's pending visit. Upstairs, he flipped over his desk lamp, pointing out the small oblong device stuck to the base, handed her the magnifying glass from his desk drawer. That was the clincher, actually seeing one close up. The bugs were real, physical, undeniable. "Here it is," he said, rustling papers, cover, talking banalities, a jolt of thrill from the game of deception he was playing.

She grabbed a pen and scribbled. *GET RID OF THEM!* She underlined her words with two bold strokes.

Mark shook his head and held his hand out for the pen. *Then they would know I know. We talked about it.*

Susan searched him, his words.

Mark slashed a finger across his throat, shook his head and wrote *Don't say ANYTHING! Can't talk here. Later. After dinner.*

"So, how about some of that amazing smelling cassoulet?" he pronounced, forcing a return to false normalcy. "I'm starving."

Dinner was a tense affair. The kids laughed and chatted obliviously, but every time Mark looked at Susan, he could see a thousand thoughts firing in her head. In Wittering, it had been abstract, but here, now, seeing the bugs, it all began to take on a much more real tenor. Then, of course, there were the photos, now in Susan's possession.

They cleared the table and loaded the dishwasher, dashes of small talk, domestic chit chat. After tucking the kids in, Mark announced, "I'm taking Patch for a walk." Hearing his name and 'walk' in the same breath, the border collie came skittering in, lead in mouth, and sat, tail beating a tattoo on the floor.

"Good boy," said Mark, patting his head. He turned to Susan. "Beautiful night. Come with me. Kids'll be fine. We can leave the monitor next door."

"Yes, I could do with some fresh air," replied Susan.

"Let's take a bottle of wine," offered Mark, spinning more cover, the reason why he would take a bag.

He remembered Stephanie paraphrasing Churchill— counter-intelligence is letting other people draw your conclusions. He was starting to get the hang of this game.

They crossed the Common to Richmond Park, stopping at an ancient, fallen tree on top of a hill offering a sweeping vista north and west across the city. "Guard!" he commanded Patch as he turned on the signal jammer, choosing a Dylan track to mask their conversation. He dug out a pair of night vision goggles, a Christmas present from Susan's militia-minded stepfather. The novelty had long worn off and they had been gathering dust at the back of a closet for years.

Looking back along the path, he saw two iridescent green forms standing near Bog Gate. Turning his back to the audience, he surreptitiously set the goggles on his shoulder. "Two people following us. They can't hear us. Make it look like you're hugging me, have a look, just inside the treeline."

Susan's reaction was surprisingly low-key. "Two people," she said. "I see them."

"They followed me to Monaco. A team of nine." He let her do the math. "There's so much to fill you in on. Philippe—this guy Stephanie knows in Nice, oh my god! ... it's like a whole other world." Mark drew a deep breath, slowing the rush of words. "They've been tailing me for at least a couple of weeks. And they're not with the fat guy, the one I told you about in Wittering. He probably works for Max. We suspect these guys work for a man called Daniel Logan." His mouth was suddenly pasty dry. "I'm not asking you to forgive me, Susan. Please, please don't take this the wrong way ... but what happened, the photos, aren't important right now. What matters is that I'm in some seriously deep shit ..."

Susan put her hand on his arm, stopping him. She had talked it over for hours with Eric and Stephanie, made her decision. "I understand. We'll deal with 'that' later. Now, fill me in. Sounds like a lot has happened."

Mark dived straight in, the bugs, the bunker, the man, the van, the plan. It was all documented, catalogued and scripted—digitally and in his mind. He recited, visualizing the whiteboard, laid out the players, the people, the companies involved, the battlefield. He showed her his new carrier bag, walked her through its camouflaged electronic wizardry and gave her a primer on counter-surveillance, at least what he had learned so far.

Susan listened, asking only the odd question, letting Mark have his flow. Before motherhood, she had been a marine biologist, and now applied her analytical skills to the sharks her husband had found himself swimming with. What struck her was the magnitude of it, the level of resources being marshaled against Mark.

Patch suddenly started barking. Susan picked up the night vision goggles and watched as he drove the two figures back, keeping the wolves at bay.

"What about Robert?" asked Susan. She had met Durand on numerous occasions, always charming, never trusted.

"What about him?"

"You can be sure he's not standing on the sidelines while this plays out. I guarantee you he's working his own angle."

"Interesting," replied Mark, his mind racing. "You're right, I hadn't thought about him, just Logan. He *is* back in London."

He called Stephanie. "Susan just raised a valid point," he began, no pleasantries. "Robert Durand. What's his game? We can't ignore him."

Susan took the phone from him. As she spoke, Mark raised the night vision goggles and studied his tails, multitasking as he listened to one side of the conversation.

"Can you put a tail on him?" said Susan.

It was a galvanizing moment, hearing Susan playing an active role. Stephanie must have sensed it too. Without hesitation, she said, "Good idea."

When Susan hung up, Mark took her hand, squeezed it. She squeezed back, a thousand words in the silent pressure.

"By the way," said Susan before Mark turned the signal jammer off. "Congrats on the funding. Did you really get $5 million?"

Mark nodded and accepted her hug. She had not been happy with Mark and Peter's failed first effort at fundraising. It had remained a silent topic for the next three years, sometimes an elephant, never addressed. From her hug, the energy that flowed in her touch, he now understood. It had not been the idea she was opposed to, just the half-assed effort.

He remembered a few days earlier in Monaco, cooking up the script he and Stephanie had played out on *Eliza's Revenge*. The storyline, some of the things Stephanie had thrown in. Suddenly it was clear. Susan had been keeping tabs on his progress all along, with Stephanie as her source. He realized, too, that her silent treatment on the subject had given him focus, had been what drove him to do better second time round.

She squeezed tighter. Mark had to believe there was a trace of forgiveness in it. He pulled her closer, urging his deepest love into his embrace.

Susan broke away, put her defenses back up. It was too soon. "We should start heading back."

"Yes, it's getting late."

CHAPTER 28

To any outside observer, it was a normal Monday morning in the Haddad household. It was the little things—the way Susan touched him, the set of her jaw, the way she held his eyes—that spoke volumes.

"Sure you don't want me to do that?" offered Susan, still in her dressing gown. "I can drop it off after I take the kids to school."

"No, I've got it." Mark hefted the bulging duffel bag and slung his courier bag over the other shoulder. He leaned over and gave his wife a kiss, careful not to upset the balance. "Bye kids!" he called as he stepped out the door.

Five minutes later, he dumped the duffel bag on the counter.

"Wednesday okay?" offered the clerk.

"That's fine," said Mark.

He had started the cleanup operation the night before, every step staged and scripted. First, he had scanned his wardrobe, laying on a cover story for his listening audience about a funny smell, maybe a dead mouse in the back of his closet. Stephanie's mantra echoed in his actions, "Everything must be plausible."

The first batch of bugs went in the 'cooker' that evening, a small box that neutralized them to the canned sounds of a washing machine. Then, with a sudden zap—they died, drowned in the rinse cycle.

Now, as the clerk walked away, Mark reached into his bag and activated the cooker once more. This time, it was programmed to slowly drain power from a second batch of bugs to the background noise of dry cleaning machinery. *Everything has to be plausible.* With a satisfied smile, he left the shop and headed for the station, just another commuter on his way to another day at the office.

Mark knew he was being followed but resisted scanning the crowd. Others were doing that for him. With $5 million in the bank, he could afford it. He could also afford the extra security detail he had assigned to Susan. He doubted she was in any real danger, but making the call had been his way of showing that he was protecting her. It had also been empowering, a demonstration of the resources he had at his disposal, the tradecraft he was starting to master.

He flipped through the sports pages before swapping the *Metro* for a Kindle and settling in for the ride, just another routine commute, 22 minutes to Waterloo. From there, he caught the 171 bus to Holborn, climbed the stairs, rode the upper deck.

"Please have a seat. I'll let Lord Barker know you're here. Mr. Levine should be here shortly. May I take your coat? Can I offer you some coffee?"

"Sure," smiled Mark, handing his trench coat to the pretty receptionist. "A latte would be lovely. No sugar."

As she walked away, Mark settled into the settee and flipped through *New Media Age*. The cover story was Webdex.

"Will you be there?" asked Lord Barker, pointing at the magazine.

"Of course," replied Mark, with equal friendliness.

"My sources tell me Adware's the favorite to take top spot. It's why we want you to take the helm at BizTech, Mark.

You have a fantastic track record."

They chatted until Tony Levine arrived, then went into the board room and took their seats around the mahogany conference table, Mark across from the BizTech duo. He put his bag on the table and busied himself fishing out his phone and tablet. He nudged a plain brown envelope halfway out of the bag, visible from across the table. It was exactly like the one he had been sent with the photos of him and Anna.

Levine's eyes were immediately drawn to it. The silent, nervous look he exchanged with Barker removed any last remaining doubts. Mark smiled to himself, relishing the sense of control. It was their play, but he had hijacked the script.

"Mark, I'll be direct. I hope we can agree terms today," said Lord Barker rather pompously. "This is a big opportunity and we want you to lead it." Gesturing at the contract in front of him, he added, "We've made a very generous offer." He turned to Levine and said, "Mark and I were just talking about Webdex. I think that would be an ideal venue to announce his appointment, don't you?"

"Yes, yes," replied Levine as if the thought had not occurred to him.

Mark was conscious of the surveillance, his and theirs, chose his words. "Remind me of the terms. I've been travelling all week and simply haven't had a chance to think about it. Very embarrassing, but I lost the flash drive again." He rummaged in his bag as if searching for it, spilling the manila envelope further out onto the table, leaving it there in plain sight.

"In either case," his eyes flitted to the envelope, "I believe Tony was meant to arrange for your Chairman to join us today."

"Unfortunately, he's been called away," began Lord Barker.

Mark pursed his lips in disappointment then stood. "In which case, gentlemen, I suggest we reschedule. I should add, I do have other offers, so time is of the essence. I suggest your Chairman make himself available sooner rather than later. Then we can discuss all the ... ah ... dimensions face to face. Thank you, gentlemen. I look forward to hearing from you."

He turned and left. Levine and Barker stared after him in stunned silence.

Daniel Logan had been monitoring the meeting from his penthouse. He heard the finality in Mark's words, the non-negotiable demand, the chutzpah. And the way he used the brown envelope. He had been toying with them. Logan mulled this as he watched Mark walk out, his minions scrambling after him.

There was an awkward moment in the lobby as they waited for the receptionist to retrieve Mark's coat. With a curt nod, he stepped into the elevator. "Email me some dates, gentlemen. Today, if you can. My calendar fills up pretty quickly." The doors closed and he disappeared.

"Well that didn't go to plan," said Levine as he glared at his partner.

"No, it didn't," replied Lord Barker.

Out on the street, Mark looked both ways as if deciding, then headed north. He turned left on Theobalds Road then veered into the side streets until he reached a small square. It was nearly empty, just a young mother and toddlers, a couple of pensioners out for a stroll.

He parked himself on a bench, slipped on his headset and started tapping away on the phone's touch screen. To his watchers, he was simply checking in to a hyper-connected world—missed calls from the office, the wife, voicemail, text messages, email, blah, blah, blah.

Hold SIN. MEM+ tap tap tap. Hold %. The calculator morphed into the CS control panel. With a few keystrokes, Mark ended the recording. He quickly checked the audio and video, satisfied that the whole meeting had been recorded. He then encrypted the files and emailed them in for analysis. Next, he shrugged off his coat, folded it and set it on the bench on top of his bag. The scanner flashed positive, a fresh bug, suspicions confirmed. He smiled and dialed Rick's number.

"I just left BizTech. Their Chairman was a no show. Just Tweedle Dee and Tweedle Dum." He laughed, imagining the looks on Levine and Barker's faces when they heard that.

Rick's tone was a little stilted but he stuck to the script. "You really don't like those guys, do you?"

"I'll give them one more chance. Levine's supposed to call me with some dates." Here was the clincher. "But I'm not even going to bother looking at the offer documents until I meet this Chairman. I don't even know who he is. As far as I'm concerned, if he's a no show again, I walk."

"I've been doing some digging," replied Rick. "Lord Barker is listed at Companies House as Chairman *pro tem*. The only shareholder is an offshore company in the Channel Islands."

"Well, I'm rapidly losing interest."

Rick laughed. "Changing the subject, what about the, ah ..."

"The photographs? No, wasn't them. I tried your idea, pulled the envelope out, but got no reaction. I think the timing was just coincidence. I just don't get it. Surely if someone's trying to blackmail me, they want some, they'd make demands. But it's been a week and I've heard nothing."

"Any more thoughts on who else it might be?"

"Other than the cabbie? The only person I can think of would be Max, leverage to keep me from helping Duncan, but that'd be pretty hardcore, even for him. If it is, fine, I'll sign, whatever. I'd hate to do that to Duncan, but ..."

"I hear you," commiserated Rick.

"Anyhow, happier subjects. How are the other prospects looking?"

"Got the latest offer from IBM this morning, but haven't had a chance to look at it yet. Should get two more by midday, one from Accenture, the other from ZapMedia. You liked those guys. Looks like we might have a bidding war."

"Nice, thanks, mate. Don't know what I'd do without you."

Enough for now.

"Anyhow. I gotta run. I've got back-to-back meetings today, not even a break for lunch. Drop me a text. Let's grab a beer later in the week."

"Will do."

Walking back to the office, Mark checked his voicemail, for real this time. Four missed calls, two messages. All Max. He ignored them, would see him soon enough. Besides, they had just pulled off a brilliant performance—two brilliant performances—and he was charged up, wanted to enjoy the moment. They had been smooth, no hamming, seeded all the key messages in natural dialogue, two for two.

When he got back to the office, out of curiosity (and for a bit of practice), he decided to scan his office for listening devices. He was surprised when he got an instant hit. He was under his desk taking a photo of it when Marie Atherton knocked and let herself in.

"Er, just dropped my phone," he explained. "What's up?"

"Max wants to see you in his office. He's with Robert. He's in one of his moods. He's been like this since you left. How was your trip, by the way?"

"It was great. Boys' weekend. Thanks for asking." Mark sighed and put on his game face. "Okay. Let me deal with Max."

"What's going on, Mark? There's a bad vibe, a lot of ugly rumors. Everyone knows it's your friend who's suing Adware. No one's blaming you or anything, at least no one on *our* team, but ..."

"It's complicated," cut in Mark, sensitive to the bug

infestation. He needed to control this conversation. "I've been wanting to have a chat. Are you free for coffee later?"

"Sure," replied Marie. She asked the question that had been preying on the whole team's mind. "Are you job hunting?" There were a thousand subtexts—if so, why bail now, just before the IPO? Why not wait? What was he not telling them?

He gave her a pat on the arm and repeated, "We'll catch up later, promise. Right now, I need a couple of minutes before I go see the green monster."

Marie chuckled. She had coined the term of endearment years ago. Max had been in one of his rants, happened to be wearing a gauche green suit. And it was also the color of his sins. As soon as she whispered it, *green monster* became lodged in their private lexicon.

Mark shut the door, banged off a quick email, attached the photos of the latest bug and hit 'Send'. He tapped a few more keys to activate the voice recorder, drew a deep breath and made his way to Max's office. Was it bugged, too? He patted his pocket, felt the phone, smiled—it would be as soon as he walked in.

The PA's desk was empty, cleared of personal effects. Another pretty young thing used, abused and spat out by the green monster. Annabel, he remembered. Sweet kid. Only lasted a couple of months. It was rumored that the position had been cut. Mark wondered if it was true. He rapped once and let himself in.

Max was stalking the room like a caged animal, barking at the phone. Durand sat watching from the sofa, his face set in an expression of feline conceit. He waved Mark in, eyes shifting to Max, suggesting silence while he finished his call, something about a yacht, big numbers, demands, angry words. Mark had heard rumors about that too. It sounded like Max's world was unraveling. Remembering Susan's words, he studied Durand, wondered about the Cheshire grin.

Max hung up. Mark straight away poked the hornet's nest.

"What happened to Annabel? Sweet kid. I really liked her."

Max glared at Durand, his silence confirmed the rumor Mark had heard—Max's PA had been made redundant, part of the austerity measures Durand was putting in place.

"Where have you been?"

Mark bit back an equally abrasive retort. As Stephanie had put it, "Logan's a predator, you're the prey. You can't walk away." It was harsh, Darwinian, true. He could not play out his own end game until he knew what Logan's was.

"Annual leave."

"You just got back from holiday!" snapped Max.

"That was months ago." Mark look at Durand, shrugged incomprehension. *Is this really necessary?*

"I hope you had a good time," said Durand, casting a look of reproach at Max. "Stressful times. Everyone's a little highly strung. The IPO, the lawsuit, all this cost cutting."

Mark was now sure the rumors were true—a boardroom battle was in full swing.

"Do you know Daniel Logan?"

The question caught Mark off-guard. He furrowed his brow and shook his head. "The name is familiar ..."

"He's the man suing us," explained Durand.

Mark furrowed his brows deeper. "I thought PaySense was suing us."

"They are backed by a VC, Peterman Brown. Daniel Logan is their Chairman."

"Oh, I see," said Mark dragging the words out with wonder, nodding as if just seeing the pieces.

"I know you don't want to get involved, Mark. And I respect that, I really do. And I appreciate your professionalism, always have" said Durand, slathering on the butter. "But you *are* friends with Duncan. I'm not getting anywhere with this Logan character and could really use some help."

"What's the problem?"

"What's the problem!?" echoed Max still rabid.

Durand glared at him. "Why don't you sit down, Max." It was not a question.

He turned back to Mark. "This kind of thing isn't as uncommon as you might think, suing a company as it gears up for an IPO. I call it the Sunnyvale Shakedown. It's all about timing. And these guys got it spot on."

Mark nodded understanding. "They want shares, not cash."

"Exactly. And we want it to go away so we can get on with the IPO."

"They should, too, shouldn't they? I'd imagine the longer it goes on—"

"Yes, the more it devalues the IPO, maybe even kills it altogether."

"The IPO isn't dead, is it?" asked Mark with what he hoped was a genuine look of alarm.

Durand took his time choosing his next words. "I am speaking in absolute confidence here, Mark. Please do not let it leave this room. Do I have your word?"

"Of course."

"The bridge round has been suspended. It's just a temporary measure until we sort this mess out. These media attacks have been ferocious."

"Yeah. A lot of bad blood out there." He glared at Max with these last words.

Durand cracked the slightest of smiles before continuing, his tone reasonable, even, persuasive, and reassuring. "My job is to make this whole thing go away so we can get on with our IPO. That's why I'm here."

Mark nodded, ever the eager team player. "How long are you over for?"

"As long as it takes. I've made them an offer, very generous, considering."

"Considering what?"

"They're bluffing, Mark. We've done nothing wrong, have we?"

When Mark said nothing, they both knew the answer, both knew the other knew. Max was tapping on his phone screen and missed the silent exchange.

"The offer is without prejudice, no admission of wrongdoing."

There was a knock at the door. "There's someone here to see Max," said the nervous messenger, voices rising in the background, a large man bulldozing his way across the office. "He's ... he's demanding a check. Won't leave until he sees you in person." The messenger scurried away hoping his face would be forgotten. Max launched out of the room after him.

Left alone, Durand said, "Mark, I've been hoping for a chance to speak in private. You see how Max is behaving. A bull in a china shop. He's becoming a real liability. I am doing everything I can, but ..." he shrugged his shoulders, "he's not helping. Every time he opens his mouth, he makes it worse. The press are having a field day. Please, Mark, I need your help. Just talk to Duncan. That's all I ask. It's in everyone's interests."

"Robert, like I said, I am very uncomfortable with all this," replied Mark, playing coy. "I told Duncan the same thing. I really don't want to be involved. I have a clear conflict of interest."

"Look at the bigger picture, Mark. Max and Logan are going to blow it for us, for all of us—you, me, your team, the rest of the staff, Duncan. There's a lot at stake. Please, for everyone's sake ..." He let this last plea hang for a moment before adding the sweetener. "I assure you, when this is all over, there will be some changes around here."

Susan's words last night echoed in his ears, *I guarantee he's working his own angle.* And here it was. Machiavellian. Bit of regicide? But before he could continue, Max stormed back in, even angrier. He said nothing about the fracas outside. Mark would harvest that from the grapevine.

"Where were we?" asked Durand.

"Considering ..."

"Considering what's at stake. This whole thing has gotten out of hand. It's in no one's interest for it to drag on."

"I'm not sure what I can do ..."

"All I ask is that you speak to Duncan, as a friend. Let him know *I'm* not bluffing, make sure that message gets back to Logan. We've made a generous offer. The ball's now in their court. They need to accept it so we can move on."

"Okay, Robert. I'll pass on the message," replied Mark.

Max paced in his glass bullpen, visible to all. Real buzz killer. There was a palpable change in the air when he stormed out a half hour later, knives no longer required. Mark worked the room, talking to people, catching up, bit of rah rah, taking measure. Kudzu not grapes, machete required. Morale was down. It was common knowledge the IPO was off, the company was being sued, slagged off in the news every day, layoffs, running out of money. Fear and uncertainty were pervasive.

Rallying the troops was not part of Mark's agenda, he just did not like the negative vibe, nor did the staff deserve it. He called an impromptu team meeting, kept it short, upbeat, lots of positives, at the last a personal request to spread some love, some optimism across the company, unanimous assurances from the team that they would. When they left, Marie remained, shut the door.

"It's serious, isn't it?"

Mark was acutely conscious of the bugs. "Walk with me," he said, grabbing his bag. "Shit. Hang on, I must've left my phone in Max's office. Be right back."

When they were alone in the small, enclosed courtyard, he said, "I need your help with something."

Her face lit up. Finally! "Sure, anything I can do."

"I need to slip out for a couple of hours but I don't want anyone to know. Can you run interference? If anyone calls, just say I'm in a meeting. Don't say where or who with."

"What about Max and Robert?" asked Marie. "Is that what

this is about, the meeting you just had?"

"No, something else," replied Mark, not elaborating. "But if either of them comes looking for me, tell them I'm at a meeting and leave it at that. You don't know anything else."

Marie looked at him curiously, inviting explanation, none forthcoming. "Okay."

Mark scanned the windows overlooking the courtyard, no one watching. He opened the back door and was hit by the waft of garbage from the dingy hallway. "I'll text you when I'm back. If you could let me in ..."

Wrinkling her nose, Marie said, "You owe me. Still on for coffee?"

"Definitely," promised Mark.

He skirted the dumpsters lining the wall, holding his breath, careful not to touch anything. The stench was even stronger when he opened the door to the alley. To his right, he saw a man in a cook's uniform on a smoke break. To his left, the mouth of the alleyway, not so much as a glance from the passersby.

Two minutes later and twenty pounds lighter, Mark stepped out of the restaurant's front doors and onto the main street, turned right and disappeared into the tube station. He was still being followed, but this time it was only his own people, confirmed by a secure message.

Still, he took a round-about route, changing trains and direction three times before exiting at Angel and heading for the pub where he had arranged to meet Peter and Jason. He was early, found a table with a clear view of the door, sat down, ordered a cola and pulled out his phone. The CS app was already loaded. Voice recording was active, had been running since before he went into Max's office. He was about to listen to the recording when Peter arrived.

"How'd it go?"

"Can't complain. How about you?" He slid a note across the table. Don't say anything. Don't react. I'm under surveillance. Take my phone, go to the loo and pass it over your whole body like this ... be thorough. When you come back, stick to small talk. I'll explain later. Got it?

Peter frowned, curious, but played along. By the time he returned, Jason had arrived. He had evidently been given the same routine because he took the phone without asking and went to the loo.

When he returned, Mark reviewed the scanner log, nodded, satisfied, and said, "Okay we can talk. Were either of you followed?"

"What are you talking about?"

"Were you followed? Did you see anyone following you here?"

"What's gotten into you?" Peter was starting to get annoyed.

"You have no idea. But to answer my question, yes, you were followed. Both of you were. I've got a team on each of you."

"What the ...?!"

Mark held up a hand. "I needed to see if anyone else was following you because I am being followed. Not right now," he added, "I lost them on the way over."

"What the hell is going on?" demanded Peter, his raised voice drawing glances from other patrons.

Mark leaned forward and said, "Please, keep it cool and let me explain. I don't have a lot of time. But first, the good news."

"Your trip to Monaco?" asked Jason.

Mark nodded and smiled. He had already use the phone app to log in to Dynamo's bank account, handed it to his partners. It took a moment for the balance to register but when it did, Jason let out a loud whoop, pumping his fist in the air, drawing yet more unwanted attention from the other patrons.

"$5 million!" said Peter. "How much did we give away?"

"Only 27.5% and two board seats."

"That's it? How the hell did you pull that off?"

"We're in business!"

"Absolutely, but don't quit your jobs just yet."

"Why not?"

"That's what I need to explain. And I need to be back before anyone notices I'm gone. But, gentlemen, the cash is in the bank. We can't celebrate yet, but," he raised his glass in a toast, "Dynamo is officially in business."

For the first few minutes, Mark was not sure how much of what he said actually registered, Jason and Peter passing his phone back and forth, expressions of disbelief. Eventually, though, snippets filtered through and they were soon caught up in his monologue, as bewildering as Dynamo's seven-figure bank balance.

When Marked finished, Jason was the first to jump in. "Ivan's come back to me about that second flash drive. He's been studying the virus. It's not the same as the first."

This time it was Mark's turn to listen. What he heard gave him a lot to think about. If Ivan's analysis was right—and there was no reason to think otherwise—the new virus had upped the stakes. The first had targeted his email and PGP key, so they had been working on the premise that it was all linked to PaySense's lawsuit against Adware. But the new target—Adware source code—was a dimension Mark could not explain. That troubled him.

CHAPTER 29

The call came at 7:30pm. "Good evening, Mark. It's Tony Levine. My apologies for calling so late. You did ask me to get back to you today."

Susan made eye contact, mouthed 'Tony Levine?'

Mark nodded, smiled at her intuition, and felt a maudlin moment coming on. He squashed it, focused his attention on the call. "Do you have some dates?" He consulted his diary. They agreed on Wednesday, 3:00 pm. "Whom shall I ask for?"

"Myself or Lord Barker."

"What about your Chairman. He will be there, won't he?"

"Yes, yes, of course ..." stammered Levine.

"Good. And his name is ...?"

"Daniel Logan."

Mark toyed with Levine, made him spell it out. It was what Mark had expected. Still, it was good to hear Levine speak his name.

"Please let me know if Mr. Logan's schedule changes. We would not want a repeat of last week, would we?"

"No, of course not ..."

Mark hung up, abrupt by intent. Playing to the gallery, he said to Susan, "That was BizTech ... that job I've been interviewing for … they want to meet on Wednesday."

They were in the kitchen, cleaning up after dinner.

"That's good, dear. I'm sure you'll do very well in the interview," said the dutiful Stepford wife. It was the persona Susan had adopted since coming back to London to a bug-infested home. At first, it was just a way of taking control, dealing with the invasion of privacy. But as she tuned to its rhythm, she started to draw succor from it, scoring a mental point from every deadpan delivery of glib banality.

A week ago, she could not have pulled it off.

That night down on the coast, in West Wittering, Mark's confession had blindsided her. Everything else—as if it had not been enough—blurred into insignificance as she tried to comprehend what it was she was hearing, the photographs in her hand. "Go," she said

"Su-"

"Just go. Now." Susan walked away into the forest.

Minutes later, she watched the SUV leave, its lights bobbing down the dirt track, disappearing around the bend of the winding country lane.

Eric Turner had gone looking for her when she had not come back with Mark, found her in the woods, sitting on an ancient mound of rocks, her body silhouetted in moon shadow. He knew what had happened, knew not to intrude.

Dawn was early on the horizon, faint tendrils of deepest purple splintering the night sky, cracking daylight. After a while, Susan stood up, walked to the meadow and sat down in the tall grass facing sunrise. Muscle memory guided her body into the familiar Lotus position. Without realizing, her mind tuned to breathing, to the gentle caress of the breeze on her skin, the faint scent of honeysuckle, dew, and wild flowers in the air, cleansing, calming.

Eric watched from just inside the tree line, whispered, "Go girl."

They had met freshman year, hit it off from the start, been best friends ever since. Stephanie had introduced them, roommate to new boyfriend, and within weeks they were all living together in the girls' dorm room. There was none of the friction that so often mars such an arrangement, just an easy, natural flow to their blossoming relationship. It was as if they had known each other all their lives, nothing awkward or embarrassing, no secrets between them.

Stephanie still joked that Eric had landed two soul mates for the price of one, never even a suggestion of discontent in her voice, which made the words ring all the more true. It was a ménage a trois from the start, a three-way love affair, but contrary to rumors, it was not sexual, not with Susan at least. She was the twin sister Eric never had. And he would do everything in his power to protect her.

After a while, Eric went back to camp to brew a pot of coffee, returning to the meadow with two steaming mugs. Susan smiled a silent thank you, her tear-streaked face serene and impassive. They listened to the dawn chorus, the rustle of the rising wind in the trees, as the sun climbed out of the sea behind a billowing bank of clouds, casting a surreal, transcendent orange glow on the day.

Susan broke the silence. "He was set up."

Eric hid his surprise. "I know," he said. "He's still going to have to answer to me when it's all over."

Susan squeezed Eric's hand and did not let go.

Over the next few days, Stephanie was there for her, too, daily calls reminiscent of the year she had led the women's lacrosse team to a record 12-3-0 season. Her game prep and field tactics had been superb, but it was her ability get her players to focus, to keep their problems off the field that gave them their edge. Boys, grades, PMS, bad hair—it did not matter. As their Captain, she had one simple credo: leave it on the sidelines. Until the final whistle, the only thing that mattered was the game. Her gift was helping them find the mental discipline to do that.

Susan had been no exception. Junior year. Build up to the Mid-Atlantic Conference (MAC) Championship game, the pinnacle of her amateur sporting career. She had just started seeing Mark, the first guy who was not thrown by the threesome, the group dynamics with Eric and Stephanie. He slotted in like a fourth wheel. The chemistry was so right, Susan thought they were in a committed relationship. Mark had no clue. So it blew her away the weekend before the big game when she saw him at a party with someone else.

Then, like now, Eric and Stephanie were there for her as rock, coach, counsel, and shoulder. Then, like now, she found her game face. By their last night in West Wittering, she was ready, ready to go back to London, ready to get in the game.

"It's a lovely evening, dear. Why don't you take your wine into the garden? I'll finish up here and join you in a minute. Would you like an after-dinner espresso?" More of the Stepford wife act.

Susan felt Mark's eyes reaching out to her as she washed the dishes, her back to him. She turned, a plastic smile freezing him mid-stride, stopping him from taking it further.

"Yeah, okay." He picked up his tablet and did as he was told.

She knew he did not understand, but that would have to wait. There were times when they could talk freely but they were rare and, by necessity, focused on the business at hand. She had only to look at one of the bugs planted in her house to remind herself of the seriousness of their situation. The outside threat had to take priority, emotions on the sidelines. The Stepford wife routine was part of her game face, and it was not just for the cameras. She needed distance from Mark, as well.

She knew she could forgive, had already started. But she would deal with that when this was over. And she had no intention of letting Mark off lightly. His cock had been in someone else's mouth. That hurt.

Out in the garden, her errant husband was finding Zen in his tablet. She could tell by the look on his face that he was playing with his new app, immersing himself in the web of surveillance that had sprung up around him. Good. It was where she needed him to be, what she needed him to be doing.

He was amazed with the interface. Fluid, intuitive, user friendly, terabytes at his fingertips—bios, dossiers, surveillance logs, video, audio—all tagged, cataloged, and linked, coherent patterns rendered on a multidimensional dashboard. He played for a while, testing his fluency, warming up.

He was thoroughly engrossed by the time Susan brought him an espresso, barely noticed her, only an absent, mumbled thank you. He had that look on his face, the one he got when he was brain deep in a computer. It always felt like he was in another place, Susan, the world around him, blotted out. After 20 years, it was firmly entrenched in their relationship as one of her pet peeves. If she was in a bad mood, seeing it could trigger and argument, a snipe at least. But now, as she watched him concentrate, she was glad to see it. He did not notice her smile as she turned and went back inside.

The nine shadows from Nice had been IDed at the airport, all Ukrainian, all ex-military, all following him back to London, photos, dossiers, surveillance logs. Philippe's people had also tagged a team following Duncan. Again, nine people on a 3x3 rotation. Same background. As far as they could tell, no one else was being followed, not counting Rick, who had Yasmin, also Ukrainian.

The bug he had found under his desk at the office was an older Chinese model. All the others were state-of-the-art, German design, Korean manufacture. Conclusion: different operation. Recommendation: leave *in situ* until they figured out whose they were.

Maybe the fat guy's? He now had a name, Dick Bailey. Lone operator, seedy walk-up and a secretary in Bayswater. Had to be working for Max. Who else? But they needed confirmation on both questions—who he worked for and who owned the cheap Chinese bug. The report proposed two options: 1) follow Bailey, or 2) break in to his office and search his files. Pros and cons were bulleted for each, executive decision requested.

Mark sighed in disbelief. He could be reading any management report, the presentation workaday, almost normal. The products and services were 'different,' but otherwise Philippe's organization operated like any other business, in this case a particularly well-run one. Still, it was strange reading a clinical chronicle of his own day. He knocked off a quick email to close the loop on one open issue, the call from Levine, the positive ID on Logan, and kept reading. Everything was unfolding nicely, deception, disinformation, intelligence gathering. A few minutes later, Stephanie appeared on the secure IM channel. "U there?"

"Yes."

"How do you want to handle Bailey? I have a team on standby, ready to go in tonight."

A break-in was the more expedient and cost-effective option. They were deferring to Mark because it also crossed the line—(counter) surveillance was one thing, breaking and entering another.

"Follow him," replied Mark, erring on the side of probity, although he did wonder exactly where that line was being drawn these days.

"Okay." Stephanie had expected that. "I'm arriving tomorrow. Are you going to seed the Dynamo story tonight?" It was the plan they had agreed, hide in plain sight, script a plausible explanation for the daily meetings that would start tomorrow at Stephanie's office, their new War Room.

"All on schedule. Seen the latest? Levine called. Rescheduled for Weds, confirmed it's Logan."

"Never doubted it."

"True," replied Mark. "Talk tomorrow. Btw, thanks for everything."

☺

Mark put down the tablet and gazed out at the fading sky, dusk, dark clouds on the horizon, maybe rain. How had he gotten himself caught up in all this?

Stephanie was right. Logan was a predator. What he did not know was that his quarry was now taking the game to him and it was essential they kept it that way. Stephanie had anticipated the new bug, taken £20 off Rick on a side bet on it. More to the point, she had told Mark to leave it *in situ,* and they were already using it to feed disinformation to Logan.

Mark shook his head, still stunned by this previously unknown side of Stephanie, someone he had known half his life. He thought back to boot camp, as he had come to think of the weekend in Monaco.

01100101011100110011001011110

For Stephanie, there was no moral ambiguity to her gamesmanship. Her opponents set the rules and she played (by) them. She had explained her code: "If they don't spy on me, I don't spy on them. But if they do ..."

"But you have to spy on them first to know if they're spying on you," Mark had replied.

"Passive detection only. I take a purely defensive posture unless attacked. I never initiate engagement. Ever." Stephanie had been quite adamant about this last point, adding, "All I ask for is a level playing field."

"Never? Really?"

"It's tempting. Look at Logan's setup at Berkeley House. Pure genius. But it's evil genius. Like the man said, 'Do unto others as others do unto you'."

"Isn't it 'do unto others as *you would have* others do unto you'?" asked Mark.

Stephanie just smiled.

"So all you do is level the playing field."

"Stephanie never levels anything. She's always out to win," said Rick.

"Of course I want to win," said Stephanie, "but I play fair. Like I said, they make the rules, I just play by them. And if surveillance is part of the game, I happen to be better at it than most."

"Like with Sam and Cynthia."

"I knew they would try to bug me, so I let them. We scripted for it. And everything worked out." Stephanie's hands framed the scene as she described it. "Tense negotiations. Two sides break for team huddles. Visitors stay in the meeting room. Home side eavesdrops. Big home field advantage."

"Unless the visitors know."

"And if it's not bugged, no harm, no foul."

Mark laughed.

"I'm being serious."

"I don't doubt that. So, anticipating that they would bug you, you used it to feed them 'the best deal'."

"Hey, in the end, everybody got what they wanted."

There was a lull as they pondered this, then Rick asked, "Is it really that common?"

"You saw the bugs I've caught. There's hundreds of them. How much more proof do you need?"

"So what's our game plan?"

0100100110010010010101100

They had set three objectives—extract Mark, protect Duncan, and do right by Mark's team (if possible). Until today, they had assumed it to be a simple case of pre-IPO extortion, common enough, according to Stephanie. That's what Durand had thought, too, when he called it the Sunnyvale Shakedown.

With Ivan's analysis of the second flash drive , that theory had been blown out of the water. The latest virus had also been programmed to target Adware's source code, not just Mark's email and PGP key. Logan did not need that for a simple extortion play. There had to be another motive.

That in itself raised a lot of questions. Was it a new motive? Had the game changed? If so, why?

One thing was certain—the scale of forces being deployed was massive. A £2 million investment in PaySense, two tailored viruses, bugs by the bushel, breaking into Mark and Duncan's houses, a front company complete with offices and a lord on the board, surveillance teams, a honey trap. It was not a low-budget operation. Logan was going to great lengths to get what he wanted. Two big questions remained unanswered—what was he actually after and how far was he willing to go to get it? There did not seem to be any lines he would not cross.

01101100011000010110010 0

Later that evening, Mark watched Susan in the kitchen. Her, the kids ... were they safe? He got up and made his way inside. Time to play to the gallery.

"Babe, I wanted to talk to you about something. You know that idea I had for a start-up? I've decided I'm going to go for it."

That set the stage for an almighty row in the Haddad household.

CHAPTER 30

The next day, Mark went to work as usual. Ordinary, humdrum, routine, no change in patterns. Go to work, attend meetings, go home, sex on Thursdays, youth football on the weekends. Life by rote, predictable patterns played for the cameras.

Last night's row with Susan had set the stage for introducing a new pattern to his life without raising suspicions in his watchers. The next step was to call Stephanie in the morning. He was wearing his bugged overcoat, acted despondent as he confided in Stephanie about the trouble and strife. Did not want to give up on the start-up.

"But there's no way I can work on it at home. She went nuts as soon as I brought it up … and obviously I can't do it at the office, even after hours …"

"Use my office," offered Stephanie. "I'm in town all week and I've got a spare desk. Besides, if you work here, I can help with the plan. Like I said, I think it's a brilliant idea and may even put in some of my own money. Happy to help any way I can."

It mirrored reality. They could not be certain what Logan already knew about Dynamo, so the conversation was intended to achieve several things—provide a believable explanation for the workspace arrangement, cast a protective net of disinformation over Dynamo, and paint a state of mind for Mark.

"It's going to be tough stalling on the job offers I've got."

"Let Rick handle it. Come round this afternoon. Bring him with you. I'm free after half four."

"That's great. Thanks, Stephanie. That really helps."

After he hung up, Mark talked to himself a little, mumbled missives scattered as seeds, careful not to overdo it. Then he set about the day's business as a senior executive at Adware, a pre-IPO company under fire.

The vibe at the office had deteriorated noticeably these past few weeks and had reached an all-time low. Nothing was getting done, everyone was nervous, worrying, gossiping, speculating more wildly by the day.

It did not help that Max was scarce and that Durand had moved into his office, effectively taking it over. He stationed his team from California out front like palace guards. Rumors were rampant and had already started finding their way into the more speculative industry blogs.

Mark intercepted Nigel Thornton on his way back from a meeting with Durand. "He's in there all the time," said some. "Going to take over from Max," said others. Mark played the gossip mill to Thornton's ego. "I hear congratulations are in order."

Thornton's smile said it all. He puffed up with self-importance, tapped his nose and ushered Mark into the privacy of his office, eyes darting this way and that to make sure people were 'watching,' the pretense of 'not' wafer thin.

"What have you heard?" he asked, barely containing his glee.

"Everyone's saying Max has been pushed out and that Robert has asked you to take the helm."

Thornton's smile was munificent. "Well, between you and me, nothing formal yet, but ..." Nudge nudge, wink wink, literally. The man was a walking caricature.

"The reason I'm asking is that Robert asked me to speak with Duncan." Mark saw Thornton's smile fade and adjusted casting himself as a mere errand boy, adding "He asked me to deliver a message to Duncan."

The smile returned, loathsome in its transparency. Mark had never liked Thornton. Now he saw exactly why. "Do as he asks." An instruction. "We have a plan. We're putting this company back on track."

"That's good," replied Mark, sprinkling some more sugar. "I always knew we could be profitable. You just needed a clear mandate."

"Yes. Robert and I think alike. Cutting waste, trimming budgets. We're going to have to raise your sales targets as well, I'm afraid." Exaggerated apology, pausing for the weight of his power be felt. "Max has had to make a lot of concessions, too. Not very happy about that." Thornton made no effort to mask his own glee.

"What sort of concessions?" asked Mark.

Thornton described how he was putting a stop to Max's 'profligate spending'. He leaned forward and dropped his voice portentously. "You know I've been trying to do this for years, but I've never had the authority. Max has run this place like his own little kingdom, spending whatever he wanted, whenever he wanted. But I've put a stop to that now. He now needs my approval for any expenditure over £100."

"Wow. How did you manage that?"

"Terms of the debenture."

Nasty things, debentures, sugar-coated loans, with onerous terms buried in the fine print. Mark knew more than one entrepreneur who had fallen victim to one. Curiosity got the better of him. He had to get his hands on the document, see what Durand's game was, though he could half guess already.

"What's a debenture?" he asked, playing dumb, fishing.

"It's a type of loan. With the bridge round on hold, we've had some short-term cash flow issues. No surprise, with Max's profligate spending," his new pet phrase. "Ignite has extended us a short-term loan. A condition was the appointment of a Finance Committee. Robert and I *are* that committee."

"That's really good news, Nigel," said Mark, fawning some more.

"Well, and please do keep this in confidence, I'm going to need my best people on board."

Mark saw where this was going, pretended he did not, just listened, nodding like a supplicant.

"I've given Robert my plan for taking the company forward. He likes it. I know you may feel, well, you're the only other person who might've been considered, without going outside. What I need to know, Mark, is, are you okay with this?"

Mark choked back a chuckle. Thornton was seeking fealty, affirmation of his presumed crown. "So it is true. You *are* going to be made CEO."

Thornton smiled. He liked the sound of that, especially coming from Mark, his would-be rival. "Yes."

Mark stood up and extended his hand. "Congratulations, Nigel. I'm happy for you. You deserve it." He was tempted to back out of the office bowing, half-certain the irony would be lost on him. He almost felt sorry for the little man. High on his power trip, he was clueless to the ramifications. Max was not someone you wanted as an enemy.

"I owe you a coffee," said Mark appearing behind Marie's desk. He glanced at his watch. "Sorry about yesterday. You know how it is. The day just flew by."

They meandered through Soho and light conversation, catching up on office gossip. It added color, filled in some blanks from his meeting with Max and Durand, the 121, Thornton's loose lips.

"Webdex is coming up," said Mark when the gossip ran dry. "Got your party dress yet?"

"I'm looking forward to it," replied Marie. She sensed that

Mark was stalling, assumed he would turn to the important stuff when they got wherever they were going. "Rumor is we're going to win this year."

Mark nodded and smiled. "So I hear."

"You've had a brilliant run. Five years on the list," laughed Marie.

"*We've* had a brilliant run. I couldn't have done it without you."

"We are a good team, aren't we?"

"Gary Tate calls us the Dream Team," replied Mark.

"You've been talking to Gary?" asked Marie. He had recruited every one of them. If Mark was speaking to him, it was because he was either hiring or job hunting. She knew he was not hiring.

"I need to share something with you. Not a word to anyone, not even Adrian."

A flicker of surprise on Marie's face confirmed what he had suspected for months. He laughed. "I knew it! How long?"

"Six months. I hope ..."

"Of course not," replied Mark. "You're both the better half."

"He proposed last weekend."

"Congratulations! I assume you said 'yes'." He wrapped her in a bear hug. "But tell me, how's he going to like reporting to his wife?"

"You're the boss."

"And you're my deputy. Which is what I wanted to talk to you about."

"You *are* job hunting. I knew it!"

Mark steered them into a cafe. "I am, but I'm also fundraising. I've been working on this idea for a couple of years. And I've decided it's time to go for it." It was a white lie of omission, necessary but also a poignant reminder that he was manipulating Marie along with his broadcast audience.

"Wow, didn't see that one coming," laughed Marie. "But

it's great news. I'm really happy for you. I always figured you'd launch another start-up some time. What is it? Does that mean you've stopped job hunting?"

"I am ... I was ... I mean, I have a couple of offers but I want to see if I can close the funding. Give it a shot."

"After the IPO, you'll probably be able to fund it yourself." Marie rolled her eyes with frustration, "If that *ever* happens ..."

Mark glanced at his coat draped over the back of the chair, folded just right. "Our options are worthless."

"They're talking about a billion dollar valuation ..."

Mark shook his head and put his hand on her arm. "All the money's in preference shares. I've seen the documents."

"Robert Durand!" spat Marie.

Mark nodded. "And Max, the whole board. They've stuffed us."

"I never did trust him!" said Marie. "Said so from the first day he showed up" She had. "Can he really do that?"

"It's already done. I had a lawyer look at the documents. It's rotten to the core, but legally, it's as kosher as halal."

"Is that what yesterday's meeting with Max and Durand was about? Have you handed in your notice?"

"Not yet."

"Wow, lot to think about," said Marie with a heavy sigh.

Mark changed tack. "Webdex is coming up. Look ahead not behind."

"What do you mean?"

"It's a stretch, but if I can close funding by then ..."

"Resign at Webdex?"

Mark smiled.

"Not on stage?" asked Marie with a shocked expression.

"No," laughed Mark, "but that's the point. I *will* be on stage, in the public eye. Great opportunity to get some free publicity. Media, VCs everyone will be there."

"Max will go nuts!"

"Not my problem. They've screwed us. I don't owe them

a thing. Neither do you." Another seed planted. The conversation was going as planned, as if he had written both sides of the script. "I'm staying out of it, but Duncan's lawsuit—between me and you, it's totally justified. And, he's just closed £2 million in funding, so he's got deep pockets. Adware, on the other hand, has pretty serious cash-flow problems."

"I meant to ask ..."

Mark cut her off with a shake of the head. "No, I haven't had a chance," spillage averted. "My point is, Adware's a sinking ship."

"What are you suggesting?"

"The Dream Team. That's what Gary called us."

"Are you making me an offer? If so, the answer is 'yes'," said Marie, an eager smile spreading across her whole face.

"I wish I could. But I can't afford you," replied Mark, smiling back, a little flattery. "But someone else might."

"Anyone in mind?"

Mark smiled his answer, adding, "I want to recommend you for Sales Director."

"Wow, you give a girl a lot to think about," laughed Marie, her words dropping in silence as she searched Mark's eyes, her own thoughts.

"You're a natural leader."

"I hear Nigel's going to be CEO."

"I'm sure he'll make a terrific boss."

Marie laughed at Mark's deadpan sarcasm. "I accept your offer ... is it an offer?"

"Arm's length. Nothing to do with me. Gary Tate will be in touch."

"Webdex is only two weeks away. Sounds like you've been planning this for a while."

"No, I just have a good feeling about the timing. We're not there yet—I don't have investment and the Dream Team doesn't have a contract."

"But if we did, yes, we could all go out with quite a bang,

couldn't we?"

Mark winced. It was a bone of contention, topic of frequent discussion. He saw the arguments—bit of payback, huge PR opportunity, serendipitous, almost fateful timing— but it just did not feel right. He was not out to screw Adware, just make his own exit. So he was thankful when Marie did not pursue it.

"Sales Director," she whispered, trying the title on for size.

"I'd hire you in a heartbeat. You're a natural."

"Max is being pushed?" she asked, abruptly changing subject. It was her way of saying "I'll think about it."

The script was now played, all key messages sprinkled. There was a moment of silence as Mark fiddled with his phone. The next part had to be off air. He hoped he had worked the right buttons on the app.

He leaned in closer and whispered, "I have a massive favor to ask. You're friends with Sally in Accounts? There's a loan document. Do you think you might be able to get your hands on a copy of it?"

Marie wondered what she was not being told. She trusted Mark, but was curious, perhaps a bit wary. "It has to do with this lawsuit, doesn't it?" When he did not answer she said, "Okay, but you owe me. And you never got it from me. When do you need it?"

"ASAP." Debentures, he knew, came with onerous terms. Knowing what these were might shed light on Durand's game plan. Susan was right—Mark did never trust him.

CHAPTER 31

Marie knocked twice and popped her head in. "Your calendar's clear. Team lunch?"

Mark had expected it but not so quickly. Acutely aware of the bug under his desk and the one in his coat pocket, he agreed before more was said. "Let me make arrangements."

She silently dropped a file on his desk. He smiled thank you and stuffed it in his bag.

The team had jumped at the invite. Squalls of uncertainty were buffeting the office, rumors the IPO was dead, creditors banging on the door, cost cutting, the Californians keeping to themselves, no longer standard-bearers of hope. Max had not been in the office in over a week. 'Nigel Thornton as CEO-in-waiting' had gone from rumor to accepted fact, in no small part fed by Thornton himself.

"If anyone should be CEO, it's you," complained Dane, the youngest member of the team, to murmurs of agreement from the others.

"Is it true Nigel nixed our table at Webdex?" asked Nathan.

"Budget cuts," explained Mark, with a cheeky grin. He got a laugh when he explained how Thornton had auctioned the table on eBay, where no one would think to look, no reserve price. Oops. The table was now officially owned by Ashton Tate.

"So what *is* going to happen to Adware?" asked Adrian.

"I honestly don't know," replied Mark, then launched into his pitch.

Dream Team? High-five to that. Marie as the boss? No one blinked. Mark gave her an 'I told you so' smile.

Back at the office, Mark pulled out his phone, ready to set it to record. Then he remembered Monday, how he had forgotten it in Max's office, still recording. He took a minute to email the file to Stephanie before popping his head around Durand's door. "Time for a quick chat?"

"Of course. Come in." Durand dismissed his two staffers and shut the door behind them. "We haven't had a chance to catch up."

"No," replied Mark. "I talked to Duncan like you asked."

"Thank you, I appreciate it," said Durand. "I just want to close the deal and make everyone happy." He paused. "I assume you've noticed Max isn't around."

"Everyone has. All sorts of rumors flying around."

"I won't pretend, Mark. I'm finding a lot wrong here. Nothing with your people ... you guys are rock stars. And your people obviously love you, I could tell, the way you all walked in together just now. Good lunch?"

Mark wondered if Durand was rambling or actually going somewhere with this. "Yes it was."

Durand laughed and changed subject. "Nigel thinks he's being groomed to take over."

"That's the rumor."

"Oh?"

"Everyone's saying it." Mark saw no harm in sharing. He was giving nothing away, the rumor pervasive enough on its own. Besides, he was scoring points by appearing onside. And, there was nothing to be gained by playing dumb. He mulled that logic, not the logic itself but the fact that he was even thinking like this, analyzing every word, every action for hints of conspiracy and subterfuge.

"He actually thinks that!" laughed Durand. "Mark, you simply would not believe some of what's been going on around here." He shook his head in despair. "Nigel's not the solution. He's part of the problem! Has been for years!" His voice dropped to a seething whisper. "No. Nigel will never be CEO. Not at one of my companies."

From years in sales, Mark was comfortable with long pauses. He left this one for Durand.

"I know you're job-hunting, Mark."

It was an abrupt change of topic. Mark held his silence.

"I can tell. And to be frank, I understand why. Right now, it must look like we're a sinking ship. Am I right?"

Mark shrugged.

"Can't blame you. I'd be doing the same if I was in your shoes. But there are things going on that you don't know about. I told you before that I need my best people on board. And by that, Mark, I did not mean Nigel. I also promised there'd be some changes, didn't I? Truth is, for now I'm happy for him to *think* he's heir apparent. He's an idiot! It suits my purposes, *our* purposes. Clean this place up. Start fresh." He leaned forward, elbows on knees and said, "Mark, we're going to be starting a new chapter soon. I'd like you to be my next CEO."

Maybe he was more tuned to it because he had been scripting and staging every second of his own life, but Mark could spot a performance when he saw it. There was nothing sincere in what Durand was saying, wondered if there ever had been. It may be true that he wanted Mark to be CEO, but not for the reason he was voicing.

"Wow, I don't know what to say," replied Mark after due consideration. "Has Max resigned?"

"This company can no longer be run as a personal fiefdom." Earlier, Thornton had called it a kingdom. "When we do go public, our shareholders will demand accountability.

Entrepreneurs are a different breed. They're mavericks. And that's great. That's how great companies get started. But it's not how they succeed. For that, we need steady hands."

"Well, I'm flattered. I'll certainly consider it. And yes, you're right, I have been job hunting. For all the reasons you guessed." *And then some.* "Are you making a formal offer?"

"I'm sure you can appreciate that it's a bit delicate right now. You'll have to trust me until the time is right and, please, keep it to yourself for now. I've always watched your back, haven't I?"

My ass, thought Mark. "Alright. But I will need to see terms before I accept." It was time to draw the meeting to a close. He glanced at his watch. "I'm late across town."

"Not an interview, I hope?" joked Durand. "Please don't turn this into a bidding war."

"Not this time," laughed Mark as he made his escape.

CHAPTER 32

Mark Haddad and Daniel Logan left Mayfair on Wednesday afternoon, around the same time, from different sides of Berkeley Square. Mark traveled by black cab, Logan by Bentley. Both headed to 126 Kingsway, Holborn.

The night before, Mark, Rick and Duncan had met at Stephanie's office in Mayfair. They had to take blackmail off the table. As long it was there, Logan would not come out of the shadows. They also needed Logan to believe Mark no longer suspected BizTech of being behind it.

As they left Stephanie's office, Mark turned to Rick and asked, "Time for a drink? I need some advice." He was wearing his freshly bugged overcoat. He hoped Logan was listening.

"… I don't get it," said Ashton after hearing Mark's story. "If someone's trying to blackmail you, they must want something. There's got to be a reason."

"Yeah, that's what's weird," replied Haddad. "No one's come forward with any demands yet."

They lapsed into a long silence as they nursed their drinks, letting the hidden microphone soak up the angst Mark was projecting.

After a while, he said, "Gotta be the cabbie. I can't think of anyone else. In which case, he's be after money."

"What about Max?"

"Max?" Mark's tone was incredulous.

"Trying to force you to stay at Adware."

"He's a wanker, but I don't think even he'd stoop that low. No, it's gotta be the cabbie. I've heard of this kind of thing before. It's the only thing that makes sense. Easy enough to install a camera in his cab. He's probably just letting me stew before he hits me with his demands."

"So what are you going to do?"

"I won't be blackmailed!" spat Haddad. "I'm have to tell Susan. I've got no other choice. And when the bastard shows his face, I'll turn him in to the police!" He hoped he had not over-played it.

"Susan will kill you."

"No she won't," replied Haddad, his voice brimming with shaky confidence. "I'll tell her the truth. C'mon, dude! I was out cold. And I did stop her. That's the truth. As long as she hears it from me first …"

"I don't know," countered Ashton. "500 quid, a grand? Just pay the man and your troubles go away."

"If I believed that was true, I might. But think about it, once I pay him off, what's to stop him coming back for more? It could go on for years. He'd own me. No. I need to end this now, nip it in the bud, and the only way to do that is to come clean with Susan. She has to believe me. It's the truth."

When Logan heard this, he realized he had misjudged Haddad. Fortunately, the damage could be contained—he would simply let the blackmail attempt wither and die on the vine, let him think it was the cabbie. What angered Logan most was that he had a mistake. He did not make mistakes.

He focused on this as he went to sleep that night. Just like he had done a lifetime ago, he visualized taking his emotions one by one, putting them in a box, closing the lid, locking it. He focused on being cold, calculated, dispassionate, ruthless, destroying Max Greenberg.

The next morning, Logan woke up a restored man. He dressed impeccably, slicked back his hair, put the Queen back in the safe, emotions now safely locked in their box. He sat down at the conference table at 7:30 am sharp, reprimanded Lazarenko for being late, re-establishing the pattern of their relationship.

It was difficult at first, attending to a full agenda when all he cared about was one thing, but the process soon proved cathartic, washing away the last lingering residue of emotional entanglement. He surprised Lazarenko when he instructed him to start a new project. Blackmail. He smiled at the irony.

At 3:00 pm, his limousine pulled out of Berkeley House and set off towards Holborn.

0110010000110010011101101

Mark and Logan shook hands for the longest time, eyes locked.

"I've been looking forward to meeting you, Mark. I hope you don't mind if I call you Mark. And I must offer my sincerest apologies for missing Monday. I was called out of the country unexpectedly."

"A pleasure to finally meet you, too," replied Mark with equal grace. "BizTech's proposition is compelling, but before I make such a significant decision, I do like to know who I'm dealing with, who my partners will be."

Logan smiled broadly. "Well, let's put the past behind us, shall we?"

There were murmurs of approval from Levine and Barker on the sidelines.

"So, please do take a look at the documents on the flash

drive," said Logan, bringing the meeting to a close. "I do hope I've been able to alleviate any concerns you might have had. The business is well funded and, without false modesty, I do have a very strong track record of launching successful start-ups."

"I'll think about it," replied Mark, non-committal to the last.

Logan could not shake the feeling that he was being played.

CHAPTER 33

Robert Durand left the office at 4:00 pm. He was not happy. Mark Haddad was becoming a spanner in the works. He had just had a third interview with a start-up called BizTech. This right after Durand had offered to make him CEO of Adware. To be fair, it had already been arranged, rude not to show up. But 1½ hours? That was more than a courtesy visit. Afterwards, he went straight to his head-hunter, Ashton Tate. It was obvious, he was lining up a bidding war. Durand mused whether it was his offhand joke last time they spoke that had seeded the idea. In either case, Haddad was proving shrewder than expected.

Durand spotted Dick Bailey approaching. The man was repulsive and he wanted the meeting over as fast as possible. Besides, he did not like to be kept waiting.

"You're late," he said.

Bailey smirked, the stink of liquor and stale cigarettes on his breath. "I wanted to make sure the subject was bedded down."

"With his head-hunter."

"Yes." Bailey sensed his client's mood and was glad he had a new twist. He wanted to make the most of it. "There's been a deviation."

"Go on."

"He did go to Monaco. I was able to verify that. Yesterday he and Rick Ashton went to the offices of Pi Capital, it's a venture capital firm. Saw a Ms Stephanie Turner. She's the general partner. I ran a background check. She resides in Monaco."

Dick held a smile. He was good for a few more weeks of cash installments. He produced an envelope, eyes shifty for effect. "Everything's in here. Photos, background on Turner, log of Haddad's activity since last week. There's something else … I don't know if it's significant …" He could tell 'Mr. Smith' was hooked. "Haddad left the office with a woman yesterday. Same today, this time with a few other blokes. Later, she and one of those blokes went for a coffee. More than work colleagues, those two," he chuckled. Mr. Smith did not. "So I caught a bit of their conversation. They mentioned Ashton Tate—Haddad's head-hunter—something about a Dream Team, making their move at Webdex. Their photos are in the reports as well."

'Mr. Smith' reached into his pocket and withdrew a thick envelope. "Watch the woman. Bring in more people if you need. I want daily reports on both of them. You know how to reach me." Without another word, Mr. Smith turned and walked away.

Dick Bailey chuckled behind his back. "Of course, Mr. Durand." With a single, practiced motion, he reached into his coat and swapped the envelope for the hip flask, and took a long drink, pleased with himself.

On arrival at Berkeley House, Durand was immediately escorted to the private lift to the penthouse. The secretary showed him in. There were five men seated around the table, Logan at the head, Lassiter and Edelman, Levine and another man ranged down the right side.

"You have me at a disadvantage. If I would've known this was going to be a full house, I'd have brought my own team," he joked as he worked his way around the table, shaking hands, introducing himself to the stranger, a Lord. "Daniel, I assume with everyone here, you aim to close this matter out today. I'm glad, because I think I've made an extremely generous offer."

Two hours later, Durand left Berkeley House, angry and confused. Logan had upped his demands 10x, from 2% to 20% of Adware's share capital. Durand recalled the shocked looks around the table. Logan's own people had been taken by surprise. Yet he did not strike Durand as the impetuous type. He must have a reason.

Durand wracked his brains, trying to make sense of it, as he made his way back to the hotel. He could only conclude that Haddad had given evidence. That, or it was a really bold bluff. The team assigned to him was professional, switching point every few blocks, a new look every time—change of hat, coat, glasses, bag, walk. Even if he had not been lost in thought, he would never have realized he was being followed.

Back in his hotel suite, Durand was preparing a drink when the phone rang. 5:30 pm sharp. He knew who it was without having to look.

"Hello, Conrad," he answered.

"So where are we? Did you close with Logan?"

Durand's hesitation gave Baine his answer.

"Am I going to have to come over there to sort this out myself?"

"He raised his price. He wants 20% of the company, with a non-dilution clause through the bridge round."

"So, he's not bluffing," said Baine with smug satisfaction that Durand had been wrong. "What's he got? How bad is it?"

"That's just it, he's still holding out. Says he's protecting his sources."

"You still think it's Haddad."

Durand considered his words before replying. "Yes."

"Then we go to Plan B."

"Yes, that's what I decided," replied Durand, rebuffing Baine's attempt to muscle in on the decision. Plan B was his idea. This was his deal, his decision to make.

"If it does cost us 20% to make this go away, we'll still be ahead of the game. Put Plan B into action immediately."

Durand was about to say he already had when he realized the line was dead. He sighed, knocked back the tumbler of single malt and poured another.

CHAPTER 34

"This debenture," said Stephanie putting the papers on the table. "I'm no lawyer, but it looks onerous. Ignite can call their loan any time. If Adware can't pay, they have the right to seize all its assets. Basically, it's a vehicle for a hostile takeover."

"I can't believe Max would expose himself like that. He's got to be part of it. But I still don't get it. Between them, they own most of the company anyway. Do you think it's so they can duck the lawsuit?"

John Harding was sitting on the sofa, listening with one ear, an earphone dangling from the other. "Listen to this." He unplugged and dialed up the laptop volume. It was the conversation between Max Greenberg and Robert Durand which Mark had inadvertently recorded when he left his phone in Max's office.

John handed Mark a marked-up copy of the transcript. "Max is not involved. Durand's after the whole company. He's going to screw Max."

"Why? Because he's pissed off about the lawsuit?" asked Rick.

"That might be what got him thinking, but this is greed, plain and simple."

John smiled and nodded. "Exactly. Drive Adware into the ground, call the debenture, flip the assets into a Newco, and Ignite Capital owns it lock, stock and two."

"Can Durand do that?"

"Sure," said Stephanie tapping the debenture document. "It's all perfectly legal. All the company's assets are collateralized against the loan."

"Read the transcript," said John. He got up, made room for Stephanie. Mark and Rick read over her shoulder as she flipped through the transcript.

"The first part is Max going ballistic because his expense account's been cut," said John. "It's amazing. He's got his wife and nanny on the payroll. Even his Rolls and a new Bentley on order. He expenses everything to the company. But skip ahead to 26:38. That's where it really gets interesting. It's a call between Durand and some guy called Conrad. I think he's in California."

"Conrad Baine. Ignite's Managing Partner," offered Mark.

"Read the first few minutes." John leaned back, put his feet up on the back of the sofa, took a long swig of his beer and waited for their reactions.

"Holy shit!" said Rick. "This is gold dust. Nice move, Mark, forgetting your phone."

Mark shared another bit of news. "I forgot to tell you, Robert Durand just asked me to be CEO." As he recalled the conversation, he remembered something else. "Monday … he said Monday!"

"What?"

"He said he could tell me more on Monday. This must be what he was talking about. Ignite is going to call its note on Monday."

"Flip back to 9:32," said John. Another piece of the puzzle. "Back to the convo between Max and Durand. Max has a £2 million balloon payment due on his yacht on …"

"Monday!" offered Rick.

"No," said John, "Friday."

Stephanie laughed. "Credit to Durand. He's a crafty bastard. He must've been planning this all along, timed it beautifully. He knows Max will be cash-strapped after making the payment on his yacht."

"He also knows Adware's cash position down to the penny, added Mark. "He's been holed up with our Finance Director for the past couple of weeks, practically living in his office."

"So, come Monday, Max and Adware are both out of cash. Neither will be able to pay the note."

"Adware defaults and Ignite takes it over."

The four men looked at each other in stunned silence.

"This guy, Robert Durand, is some piece of work."

"Three guesses who he met with this afternoon," said Stephanie, dangling the latest bit of intelligence.

They all stared at her blankly.

"Dick Bailey."

"You're kidding!" said Mark. "I was sure he was working for Max."

"Evidently not."

CHAPTER 35

Patience is a surveillance team's greatest asset. A week gone and the assignment, Daniel Logan, had only left Berkeley House a few times. Antonio Baroni could not recall a more static subject. His movements were few and the same—chauffeured Bentley there and back, never far. The exception had been Saturday, when he had gone to Battersea Heliport and boarded a private Bell 206L LongRanger. Antonio had radioed in the tail number to Control, wondered if another team would be deployed to meet and greet. Two days later, he felt a tinge of professional pride when his team was dispatched to meet Kilo Charlie Lima Romeo when it landed back at Battersea Heliport at 11:34 pm, the Bentley waiting dutifully in the parking lot.

During the week, Baroni's team stayed sharp by expanding its surveillance to the rest of the building, the private side entrance, tracking all movements in and out, looking for patterns and breaks. Baroni had spotted the most significant of these. Minutes after Logan left Berkeley House, without fail, the same two people left separately via the private, side entrance, a man and a woman. Baroni had followed them to a nearby café, recorded their conversations. Control had fielded another team to keep tabs on them.

Baroni was admiring the red Ferrari pulling out from the underground garage when he recognized the driver. Logan. He radioed in, kicked his bike into gear and set off in pursuit. His team joined in leapfrog formation. Their radio chatter was professional and clipped, but the whole team felt the excitement. In their line of work, a break in pattern usually meant something.

They followed Logan westward then north on the A10, the same route he had taken twice before when he went to Cambridge University. This time though, he passed the M25 junction and stayed on local roads until he reached Waltham Abbey Cemetery on the edge of the Lee Valley Park.

An hour later, as the Ferrari's taillights disappeared over the hill back toward London, Baroni handed it off to and set out across the cemetery on foot. He used surveillance photos to navigate to where Logan had been standing, an area framed by a leafless tree and a small rotunda, presumably a wealthy family's crypt.

Checking the photos once more, he aligned his position exactly and began studying a close row of plain gravestones engraved in Hebrew, some bilingual with a Cyrillic script. A few had small pebbles scattered on them. Antonio examined these closely, all dull, weathered, except one. He knelt down for a closer look. He was sure this was it, the fresh pebble shiny with worry. He double-checked against the photograph of Logan kneeling.

Satisfied, he snapped more photos and hurried back to his Ducati Multistrada 1100S to rejoin his team. Their subject appeared to be returning to Berkeley House.

CHAPTER 36

On the domestic front, Mark and Susan had taken to having long nightly walks in the park, sometimes in silence, good silence, better with each passing day, other times talking logistics, conspiracy drawing them together in common cause.

They never mentioned her, but Anna was always there, like Patch, roaming, sometimes near, sometimes far. In moments, one of them would realize she had slipped from thought altogether, glance at the other and feel their bond heal that little bit more. Occasionally, it happened in tandem, their eyes meeting, the moment awkward, both knowing, neither saying, letting time be a silent healer.

Unlike them, Rick was having a lot of sex, his fantasy ménage a trois in full swing, the chicanery only adding spice. Much to his friends' consternation, he insisted on regaling them with his exploits in graphical detail. He countered their protests by insisting it was in character.

On Friday afternoon, Mark, Rick, John and Duncan were assembled at Stephanie's office for the daily briefing when a name jumped out of the report. Their people had followed two people from Berkeley House to a nearby café. "Adam," he muttered.

"What was that?"

"The guy who works at Berkeley House, the one our people followed. His name is Adam."

"And the relevance of this is …?"

""Jason's mate, Ivan. He's analyzing the virus for us. When he was a Black Hat, his partner was a guy called Adam. Adam Lazarenko. It's who he thinks wrote the virus. Ivan recognized his signature byte pattern. Called it a 'drop loop'. Has to do with the way the virus hides when it detects a packet sniffer. Said it was something they'd written together."

"You think it's the same guy?"

"It could just be a coincidence."

"I don't believe in coincidences," said Stephanie. "Besides, it makes sense. Let's send his photo to Ivan. Anyone want to put a wager on what he'll say?"

A moment later Mark said, "Sent. Now we wait and see."

They were still puzzling over Thursday's strange twist, the visit to the cemetery. Was it relevant? Who was Lev Loginovsky? Why had Logan visited his grave? After two days they still could not find any connection between a long-dead Jewish immigrant buried in East London and an expat public schoolboy raised in Hong Kong.

They had googled 'Jewish cemetery' and 'pebble' and found Yahrtzeit, the annual remembrance of the dead. Ten pebbles, ten years? One fresh, unweathered. But why? What was the connection?

John, who had been engrossed in his tablet, suddenly blurted out, "It's his father." He swiped the tablet screen, projecting its contents onto the whiteboard. "While you boys were chatting, some of us were actually doing some work. Check this out. Lev Loginovsky had a son. Two guesses what his name was..."

"Daniel," said Stephanie catching on. "Logan, Loginovsky." It's not unusual for people to keep some part of who they were, when they change identity."

The word 'why' was just off Rick's lips when John flicked

a 20 year old news clipping onto the screen.

"Wow," was all Mark could say, when he finished reading. He was speaking for them all.

Stephanie typed and email as she talked. "First, we need to establish if Daniel Logan is even his real name. There are usually telltale signs when someone constructs a false identity. We also need to find out everything we can about Loginovsky and this murder." She hit 'Send'.

Moments later, Philippe video conferenced in. "I see we're all present and accounted for," he said by way of greeting. "Your email, Stephanie, we just reached the same conclusion. We've found no other connection. That's when the pebble dropped." He chuckled at his own witticism. "Ten years ago, Lev Loginovsky's body was exhumed and relocated from a pauper's grave to the cemetery we followed Logan to. The timing coincides with Logan's first appearance on the scene in London. You know what I think of coincidences."

"Daniel Loginovsky disappeared 20 years ago. *Wanted for murder.*"

"Yes. It's a cold case. My people are running a full background. What we do know is that he was doing a post-doc at Cambridge. Theoretical Physics. It sounds like he was the next Einstein. He'd already published dozens of papers before he disappeared. The victim, Michelle Faubourg, was his partner. She was also a physicist. Her death was recorded as a domestic dispute.

"New identity, cosmetic surgery, it's not as difficult as one might think. Still, he would have to be very confident in his new identity to come back to England, to London, even after 10 years."

"The scene of the crime," added Stephanie. "Half of Peterman Brown's portfolio is made up of Cambridge spin-outs. He has very close ties with the university. He's gone there a few times since we started following him."

Mark did not like what he was hearing. The connection was circumstantial but he could not argue the logic, particularly in the absence of any other theory. "So what you're saying is that I'm being hunted by a fugitive murderer! Great! What next? Is he going kill me, too?"

"That's not going to happen," reassured Stephanie. "But at least we now know who we're dealing with. At least we think we do. We still need solid proof."

"Why? Are you suggesting we turn him in?"

"Maybe," replied Stephanie. "It's one way to get this monkey off your back. But we need more information before we decide anything."

"Don't worry, Mark, you are safe," reassured Philippe. "In my business I deal with people like this all the time. I'm sending a new team to you, a security detail."

"I can't walk around with bodyguards, Philippe. I'm being watched day and night. They'll know straight away that we're onto them," protested Mark.

"Security can be more invisible than surveillance. Trust me, my people are very good, the best."

"What about my family?"

"And mine?" added Duncan, also not liking the idea of being involved with a killer.

"Leave it with me. Expect an electrician in the morning. I will send you details, a script to follow. Okay?"

Mark and Duncan both muttered, "Okay."

"You saw my email about Lazarenko?" asked Stephanie.

"Yes." Philippe flashed a gold-toothed grin. "I've got someone looking into it."

"So do I," said Stephanie.

Mark found the competitive banter between Stephanie and Philippe amusing, like two kids trying to outdo each other. "The people following me, Lazarenko, they're all Ukrainian." he said.

"Exactly," replied Philippe. "I am working on the assumption that the Logan legend was born in Kiev. That's where we're looking now."

"What about motive? We still don't know why," said

Mark. "Extortion made sense when it was my email he was after. But going after Adware's source code … why escalate? There has to be more to it."

"Max was in Cambridge about the same time as Logan … Loginovsky," said Mark.

"Cold case? Crime of passion?" suggested Rick. "Maybe the girl and Max were having an affair, Logan found out, killed her, ran, and now he wants payback."

"It doesn't explain why he's after Adware's source code. Besides, he's been back in the UK for 10 years, established himself. What's …" Stephanie stopped mid-sentence. "I know what this is about!"

The others stared at her, waiting. "Go on. Spit it out."

"Logan is technical, highly intelligent. Suppose he had developed some software. Max finds out about it, sees dollar signs …"

"… and plots to steal it. The girl finds out so he kills her, torches their flat to cover his tracks."

"Gentlemen, you're getting way too carried away with this," protested Rick.

"I disagree," said John coming off his tablet. "They definitely knew each other … look …" He swiped two bios onto the whiteboard, Max Greenberg's from Who's Who, and Daniel Loginovsky's from the Cambridge Press. "Same age. Same primary school. Same secondary school. Same sixth form college."

Stephanie looked around the room, stopping at Rick, the lone skeptic. "Wow. They go back 30-plus years. No way this is coincidence."

They all nodded in silent, thoughtful agreement.

"Now, work forward. What's ground zero in Daniel Loginovsky's life?"

"The fire. Michelle Faubourg's murder," answered Rick.

"That's right. Regardless of who killed her, it destroyed his life. He became a fugitive. Then his father died. Ten years later he returns to the UK, new identity, plastic surgery, the works. With me so far?"

They nodded and Stephanie continued, "Now, the fire. There are three possibilities. One: It was an accident, pure and simple. Two: Logan set it. Three: Max set it. There *is* a fourth possibility—a random B&E, but let's discount that for now. This is about Daniel Logan and Max. Still with me?"

Rick nodded, the lone skeptic.

"So focus on the three possibilities. There's a 67% probability that either Logan or Max set the fire."

"I'm with you," said Rick.

"Even if it was an accident, Logan could still be after Max. Maybe something he discovers points the finger at him. With me?"

They nodded in unison.

"So if it *was* Logan—at least if he *thought* he had, then spent 20 years on the run ... if he then somehow finds out it was actually Max ..."

"100% Max," whispered, Rick, scratching his head at the logic.

John, who had drifted back into his tablet during the conversation, looked up and said, "Lev Loginovsky died three months after the fire."

"The pieces fit."

"Guys, we need to get to the bottom of this," said Mark, his leg shaking with urgency as he spoke. "Jesus ... We've already set a deadline for this whole thing to play out. Webdex. That's only a few days away."

"We didn't set the deadline, Robert's debenture did."

"You need to need to consider giving Logan what he wants."

All eyes turned to Stephanie.

"If it is about software, if Max did set that fire, then he was willing to kill for it once before. There's a lot more at stake now and we are dealing with a murderer."

"I don't get it. You're saying give the source code to Daniel Logan?"

"Yes. Time to get off the field. You don't want to be caught between them. One is a killer, both are ruthless and there's a lot of bad blood. Give Logan the source code and walk away."

"But then I'd be crossing Max. You just said you think he's the killer."

"Why not just go to the police?"

"All we have is conjecture. The police might re-open the cold case, but it would take time, which we don't have."

"Just jack in the flash drive," offered John. "Let the virus do its work." said John.

"That's an option. We need to think it through." Stephanie walked over to the whiteboard, wiped it clean and began diagramming.

"Add Robert Durand," said John. "He's part of all this too. And two key dates—Webdex, then the following Monday, when Durand plans to call his debenture."

The team settled in for a long night of analysis.

Susan was fast asleep by the time Mark got home. It was unspoken but their evening walks had become habitual, part of their healing process. He hoped she would not be mad at him for missing tonight. He had texted to let her know.

And she was not. She was up before him, which was unusual, brought him a cup of coffee and asked him to come down to the garden.

"I'm going to take the kids out of school next week," she said. "We're going to Monaco to stay with Eric."

Mark searched her face for hidden meaning.

She touched his arm reassuringly. "I just need a few days away. I don't like living with bugs. It's creepy. We're catching a flight this afternoon."

Mark breathed a double sigh of relief.

"Better be good while I'm away." It was said in jest, meant in earnest.

Mark nodded, promised. They would be safer in Monaco,

but he did not want to say that.

They talked a bit more in hurried whispers, catching up. She did not ask where he was last night but he explained anyway, filling her in on the latest developments. He was vague about the Loginovsky connection. It was still conjecture and he did not want to scare her. When he got to the debenture, she smirked.

"I told you Robert had his own game."

When Susan went inside to rouse the kids, Mark banged off a quick email to Philippe with the flight details. He wanted a security detail on them at all times. He was long past worrying about costs. Dynamo had $5 million on deposit so he could afford it. Besides, as Stephanie put it, it was an investment, protecting Dynamo's greatest asset. He could live with that.

With Susan and the kids gone, Mark spent the better part of the weekend out of the house, mostly at John's. He had also grown tired of tiptoeing around bugs.

They were in a holding pattern, the lull before the storm. They had worked into the wee hours Thursday, planning, gaming every possible scenario, shaping an exit strategy. Over the coming days they tweaked and fleshed out their diagrams, had occasional debates but largely it stood the test of time.

An email from Philippe on Sunday afternoon connected the final dots. Daniel Loginovsky had written some software, a fractal search engine. He had published a paper about it, how he was using it to amalgamate and map the world's astronomical data into a single view of the universe.

As soon as Mark heard 'search engine', he knew that was it. There had always been something fuzzy about Adware's search engine. He called Jason.

"Oh, yes," said Jason. "There was always something weird going on there. Real cagey ... here it is ... 'IA'. Max wanted us to purge all references from the code."

"IA?"

"Two letters. India Alpha, all caps, probably an acronym."

"Why?"

"No one knew, but he had all our developers working on it. You know the way he gets—everything else gets dropped when he comes up with a pet project. But we couldn't do it. We could clean up the urls, but that was cosmetic. Couldn't actually edit the source code, not even the comments, because no one had access to it. We did try to decompile it, but it crapped out every time we try to recompile. Max seemed placated with the URL rewrites, so we dropped it and got back to work."

"Here it is?" asked Mark.

"Huh?"

"You said 'here it is'. What are you looking at?" There was a trace of suspicion in Mark's voice. "You have a copy of Adware's source code."

"Uh ..."

"You do!"

"I ... it was ... I installed it at home when I was working at Adware, forgot to delete it ..." stammered Jason.

"Don't worry. I don't care. What matters is that you have it."

"Yes."

"Good. I'm glad. Do us a favor. Back it up off-site. Somewhere safe."

"What's going on, Mark?"

"I can't say right now, but I may need it in the next few days."

"Sure. You know I've written some new libraries for Dynamo. When you come round, I can show you those too."

"Not this week, mate. I've got to sort this out first."

The rest of the crew had been listening to Mark's side of the conversation and looked at him expectantly.

"So, now we know—Max must've built Adware on the back of Logan's—Loginovsky's—search algorithms."

"And we have access to a copy of the source code."

"Which means …"

"We have what Logan wants."

CHAPTER 37

Mark sat in the square staring at the building. He was sitting on the same bench where he had found Anna, been honey-trapped with a faked mugging. He knew he was being watched. His own team, Logan's—all present and accounted for, except Dick Bailey, who he had shaken at Waterloo Station. Cameras too. In addition to the breadboxes mounted outside Berkeley House, Philippe's people had spotted others trained on the square, one now focused on the bench where he was sitting. He had an eerie feeling Daniel Logan was watching him in real time. His hand rose, about to wave to the cameras. He caught himself, morphed into a flicking motion, a bug buzzing his ear.

He made a call. "Good morning, Robert. It's Mark." His tone was bright and cheery, onside.

"Good morning, Mark." Durand was decidedly frosty.

"I was wondering if we could meet today. Are you free?"

"Dinner," said Durand. He was still cold, so it came across as an order rather than an invitation.

"Sure," replied Mark.

"My hotel. 7 o'clock."

The line went dead. Mark stared at his phone for a sec, mild shock. He was about to text 'WTF?!' to Stephanie but changed his mind. Another bug buzzing in his ear reminded him of Stephanie's drawerful, so real—translucent gossamer wings, green exoskeleton, articulated body parts. It made him acutely aware of the surveillance swarming around him. He put his phone away, stood up and walked into Berkeley House. Front door, not side, which he had no reason to know about.

They had analyzed every movement, planned every word, to make sure he did not give the game away. But their battle plan could not fully account for the other side and he was now in enemy territory alone, mired in the fog of war. He would need to think on his feet.

"Mark Haddad to see Daniel Logan," he announced to the concierge. His eyes darted around. Cameras everywhere. In a matter of seconds he counted more than ten, and that was just the visible ones.

"I'm afraid I don't see anything on the system ..."

"I don't have an appointment," explained Mark. "Just tell him I'm here. I'm sure he'll see me. Mark Haddad. H A double D A D."

The concierge stiffened. "Mr. Logan is a very busy man ..."

Mark leaned on the counter. "Just call him. Tell him Mark Haddad is downstairs. Now."

The concierge made the call, hurried, nervous, stumbling over his words. Nods, mumbles, listening, more nodding. His relief was evident when he hung up. "Mr. Logan is in a meeting. He asks that you take a seat ...," he said, waving toward the reception area.

"Tell you what," cut in Mark, ad libbing, "I'll wait upstairs. I can find my own way." He turned and took the marble stairs two at a time, leaving the concierge stuttering after him.

He went into the Africa Room where he had met Rick and Gary for drinks that fateful afternoon, debated sitting at the same table, decided against. All risk, no upside, just pointless bravado. He placed his courier bag on the low coffee table, his faith in Philippe, who had assured him it was top tech, completely undetectable. Still, he was sure he could feel it whirring, tingling electric, every function hot—sniffers, scanners, jammers, recorders, the lot. Could just be nerves.

The waitress took his order and returned shortly with coffee, croissant and fruit. He settled in with the morning paper, relaxed, relaxing. Between the bugs in the park, the CCTV bread boxes outside, the cameras downstairs, his courier bag, the ancient stuffed heads staring down at him (some extinct species), he knew his every move was being watched and analyzed. He noticed his hands shaking as he spread the newspaper. Breathe. Slowly, deeply. *Relax.*

Logan kept Mark waiting for an hour, which turned out to Mark's advantage, giving him time to calm his nerves, put on his game face. When it started to get annoying, he signaled for the waitress, his manner brusque and impatient.

"Please deliver this to Mr. Logan." He handed her a plain manila envelope.

"Of course, Mr. Haddad."

She had a word with the bartender, who took the envelope and made a call. Two minutes later, a burly man in a crew cut and a suit came to collect it.

0110100101111000000110010

The move had taken Logan by complete surprise. When the concierge called, he had immediately called Lazarenko. "Haddad is here. In my club! Why didn't I know?"

Lazarenko had not seen it coming either. He had known Haddad was in the square, seen him on the bench, assumed he was on his way to Ashton Tate, whose offices were on the other side of the square. That's when he had gone for a shit.

Not bothering to wipe, he juggled the phone and his trousers, and hopped out of the bathroom, eyes scanning the bank of screens. "I ... I ... I was just calling. .."

Logan slammed the phone, immediately admonishing himself for it. "Control," he urged, breathing a mantra.

He had spent twenty years controlling his emotions, turning them into nothing more than tools. Max's visit had changed all that. His words, like electric shocks, had rekindled long dead memories of Michelle, his father, the truth, all swirling in the miasma of lies his life had become. He had snapped.

For weeks, he had been consumed by bloodlust, crazed, hungry for revenge, volatile, irrational, blind to everything else. Then, only a week ago, staring into the mirror, he had seen the madness staring back at him. Since then, day by day, he had reined in his emotions, harnessed them, turning back into the cold, heartless predator he had become so long ago.

Deep breaths, control restored, he made an espresso and issued a voice command. "Mark Haddad."

His facial recognition software scanned the data bank of several hundred real time feeds, instantly locating the subject. 'Africa Room, Table Six' appeared in the middle screen then faded, replaced by a bird's-eye view of the table below. One by one, the surrounding screens blossomed to life, giving him a 360° view of the nook where Haddad was sitting.

The two men remained that way for an hour, Haddad reading a newspaper, Logan reading him, both impassive, both sipping coffee, biding their time. Haddad finally broke the impasse when he signaled for the waitress.

Logan's first thought was that the manila envelope contained the photographs of Haddad and Anna, that somehow he had connected the dots. He could not see how, but it was the only rational explanation.

He did not take Haddad for the violent type, but desperate men could resort to desperate measures. He ordered a two-man security detail to be stationed outside his office as a precaution.

So sure was he that he did not open it straight away,

Instead, he studied Haddad on screen, trying to figure out how he had made the connection, his hands absently toying with the envelope, opening it, dumping the contents on the table. When he looked down, his jaw dropped.

00101111001000010011101100

"Mark Haddad. Please do come in. Sorry to have kept you waiting," said a sonorous voice from his left, moving toward him, hand extended, smile cold and calculating.

"Is that really a Pollock?" asked Mark blithely crossing the room.

"Yes," replied Logan. "Number 3. Lost for decades before I unearthed it in 2007. Part of an estate sale. They had no idea what it was. I'd be embarrassed to say how little I paid for it."

Mark made a full show of studying the painting, viewing it from different angles, chit-chatting about the artist, modern art in general. After being kept waiting for so long, he was returning the favor.

Finally, he took a seat in the lounge area. "I didn't come here to talk about art."

"No," replied Logan, eyes casting down at the coffee table, the manila envelope. "No, I suppose not." For the first time in as long as he could remember, Logan could not see a next move. Was it checkmate?

"Now, Mr. Logan…ovksy," said Mark fixing his eyes on Logan. You've not been entirely truthful with me, have you? Before we go any further, I want to make one thing perfectly clear. In one hour, if I do not step out the front door, these photographs—and more—will be delivered to the police and the press. My people are outside right now. Do we understand each other?"

"A little melodramatic, don't you think?"

Mark ignored the comment. "Why don't we start from the beginning? Tell me about you and Max Greenberg."

Logan stared at his adversary for the longest time. He had

underestimated the man. Not for one moment did he doubt that Haddad had the evidence he spoke of. That he did was a testament to his capabilities. In 20 years, no one else had uncovered Logan's true identity.

Yet here he was. Why? Why not take it to the police? What did he want? What else did he know? 'People outside' meant he was not working alone. He had been under surveillance for months yet Logan had seen nothing of this. "He's playing a shrewd game," thought Logan, "Playing me."

Logan knew then that he had met his match. Far from relishing the long-anticipated challenge, he felt only a strange stirring of melancholy, a yearning for something he could not quite understand.

He was at Mark's mercy, a proverbial sword at his throat. Yet Mark's eyes said, "I am not your enemy." *'Compassion?'* mused Logan. The threat was unequivocal, yet it was also without brutality. It simply was, the choice his, thumb up or thumb down.

Logan lowered his head and closed his eyes. It was as if fate had brought him to this moment. He had spent a lifetime exploiting other people's weaknesses, being cold, ruthless, heartless. Ironic, then, that in his moment of defeat, he was being shown compassion, being compelled to search within himself for the strength to accept both. If he had been a religious man, it would have been an epiphany. But he was not. Instead, he put his faith in his own humanity, his trust in another man. It was blind, irrational, but instinct told him it was the right thing to do.

He started talking, did not stop for an hour. From childhood to university, Max to Michelle, Loginovsky to Logan, his story came pouring out. He did not lie, no point—Mark already knew the truth. Nor did he seek forgiveness, only to be heard, to voice what he had kept silent for more than 20 years. He spoke without reservation, hesitation or calculation, putting his trust in his confessor.

He did not think about the consequences. The process

was cathartic, and he gave himself to it. Besides, the cold creature that still lurked within him knew he could always run again.

After an hour, Mark stopped him. "I have to make a call." He dialed a number and spoke into the phone, "Yes, I'm fine … we're still talking … thanks." He hung up and studied Logan. It all fit. He believed him.

There were gaps, inconsistencies, some lies of omission—but the pieces all fit. For his part, Mark had given nothing away, no indication that he knew about the bugs, the surveillance teams, the viruses, the honey trap.

"I did not kill her."

"I believe you."

"Max killed her."

"You're the wanted man." It was Mark's gambit. An eye for an eye, blackmail for blackmail.

"I can prove it." Logan scribbled something on a piece of paper and handed it to Mark. "An Easter Egg hidden in the source code."

Mark remained impassive, put the paper in his pocket. Confession time was over. Logan was now testing him, probing to see if he had access to Adware's source code.

"Why not go to the police?" asked Mark.

"Like you said, I'm a wanted man. Why haven't you gone to the police?"

"You tried to blackmail me."

"A mistake."

Clearly.

Mark left Berkeley House unmolested. He walked to Green Park Station where he caught the Victoria line to Kings Cross, a trail of people in his wake. He had lost Dick Bailey long ago.

He hopped off at Euston Station. Halfway up the stairs, he feigned checking his ticket, realizing he was at the wrong station, and hurried back down to the platform. He brushed past Skinny, the guy he had pinged a couple of weeks ago when all this was starting, made eye contact. Skinny had no choice but to continue toward the exit. One down, two to go.

Kings Cross. "Stop! Thief! That man just stole my purse!" Several good citizens detained the man, who protested his innocence in heavily accented English as he anxiously tried to break free of the growing crowd. "Oh my god, I am sooo sorry," declared the woman apologetically, "This is so embarrassing." Her purse had been in her handbag all along. The man did not wait for the apology, rushing off, cell phone in hand. Too late. He had lost the Subject.

The last tail, farthest back, moved to point position, hurrying to catch up. The crowd was not cooperating. "Pardon, excuse, sorry," The mass of rush hour commuters obstructed his path, each side-step buying Mark precious seconds, distance. The tail dashed round the corner in full stride and ran smack into a hot latte. It went everywhere. He launched into a stream of Ukrainian invective, pointing at his suit, but the woman was having none of it. She began screaming for a guard, drawing a crowd. He never stood a chance.

Outside the station, an elderly gentleman waved his umbrella from the back of a black cab, the door an open invitation. He was dressed in a pinstripe suit, crisp white shirt, school tie, Church's shoes, a Burberry raincoat, the epitome of an old school English banker. The cab pulled away as soon as Mark was on board and quickly disappeared into the London traffic.

The man smiled. He had been in the game long enough to tell fear from thrill. This client was clearly enjoying the operation. A quick learner, too, a natural at tradecraft.

"Well done, Sir," he nodded. "You're clean now."

Mark pulled off his Bluetooth headset. "All three?"

"Yes, sir. No others."

"So now they'll stake out my office and my house, wait for me to show up?"

"Correct, Sir." The man smiled again. "Standard

Operating Procedure. Not to worry. We have eyes on them," he added with a twinkle.

"Thanks, Edwards," replied Mark.

"Of course, sir." Edwards smiled his approval. He had not told the client his name. *Chap does his homework.* He rapped on the window with his umbrella and said, "This will do, Johnnie."

From the familiar way he said it, Mark could tell they had worked together before.

As he climbed out, he turned and said, "Johnnie will take you to where you need to go, Sir."

Mark watched out the back window as Edwards climbed into a waiting Audi and set off in the opposite direction.

"Fife Road, guv?"

"No." Mark gave an address in Soho, leaned back and took a deep breath, his heart rate returning to normal as the adrenaline rush wore off. He was playing a dangerous game, but he could not deny the thrill of it. His mind raced back over the conversation he had just had.

The phone rang, interrupting his thoughts.

"We heard it all. Well done. Beautifully played. The camera was positioned perfectly."

"Good," replied Mark. He did not know what else to say.

"What did he give you?"

"Not sure," replied Mark. "That's what I'm going to find out. Sit tight. I'll be with you shortly."

Mark impatiently pressed the buzzer for the third time. He had called ahead, knew Jason was home, knew too that he was still in bed. The door finally buzzed open and Mark hurried up the stairs two at a time.

Jason was in his underpants, a too-small, dirty t-shirt, and socks. Mark handed him a coffee—a large latte with two extra shots, and breezed into the messy living room.

"I need to see Adware's source code."

"What for?" asked Jason, awake and wary. He had already

gulped down his coffee and was greedily eyeing Mark's.

Mark handed it over, plenty wired already. "Daniel Logan ..."

"That reminds me, there's something I meant to tell you ..."

"Later, I need you to do this first." He handed the slip of paper to him. "Grep the source code for this string." 'Grep' was a Unix command line search utility.

Jason looked at it for a moment. "Do you know what this is?"

"An Easter Egg."

"But do you know what it is? What it means?"

Mark shook his head. "No idea. Does it matter?"

"Bobby Fischer versus Donald Byrne. 1956. The Game of the Century. That is Bobby Fischer's checkmate move." Jason had already fired up a console and typed the instruction, 'grep –i Kc1 Rc2# 0-1 *'.

One file name appeared, a jpeg.

Mark recognized her from the old news clippings. "Michelle Faubourg. Shit, he is telling the truth."

"What are you talking about?"

"I'll explain later. Grab your laptop. I assume it has access."

Jason nodded.

"Good. Get dressed. We gotta go. Good news, though," he shouted at Jason's back as he disappeared into the bedroom. "Looks like we should be all systems go for Dynamo on Monday."

Jason mumbled, "Okay," his mind already somewhere else.

0110111101101111101100100

Logan stood in the window staring out over the London skyline, reflecting, trying to make sense of the meeting. It had been strange hearing his real name spoken for the first time in

289

more than ... That was when it dawned on him.

"Adam. My office. Now!" he barked down the line.

Thirty minutes later, Logan's silver Bentley pulled out from the underground garage. An empty black cab followed at a distance. Behind that, a black BMW. Two more cars and a scooter were stationed en route. Within minutes, Logan had his confirmation—he was being followed.

"Just the cab. Registered to a Reginald Brown," reported Lazarenko. "There's also a listing for Reginald Brown, private investigator, office in Victoria. Small time, lone operator, not even a secretary. Same home address."

Logan took the open invitation. "Send the boys round. I'll keep Mr. Brown occupied for the next hour or so."

"Already on their way," replied Lazarenko, sensing the hunt. His people would find exactly what they were looking for.

"Good." Logan hung up and turned his thoughts back to Mark Haddad. What to do? An hour of solitude touring London in the Bentley was exactly what he needed.

He might have to kill Mark Haddad. He hoped not. He liked him. *Like*. He almost laughed. He had not 'liked' anyone in 20 years. After Michelle died, he had lived on the run, a fugitive, mental isolation a key to his survival. No emotions, no bonds, only purpose, focus, mission.

Another interesting word, *mission*. It dawned on him what his funk was all about. Everything he *did* had a purpose. But what about him, the man? What about Daniel Logan, the life he had created? What was its purpose?

Revenge? That was long overdue. Then what? Who was he? For weeks, he had reveled in visions of Sisyphean torture, knocking Max down, helping him back up, letting him climb ever so tantalizingly close to success, then destroying him all over again and again and again. In moments of rage, he had conjured thousand tortures for Max. Over the past week, he had been make a concerted effort to rein all this in, focus on the task at hand, the objective, the kill.

Still, the question lingered: What next? Everything else had long become bland, tasteless. In an ironic twist, would Max's hell also be the making of his own purgatory? Would he die a bitter old man?

He had searched Mark's face, seen no hint of deceit, no mocking. There was empathy, though its cousin was neither asked for nor offered. He saw fear, enough to sharpen the senses but not drive fight or flight.

Not for the first time, Logan wondered what had compelled him to open up to this man. Was his past finally catching up with him? Hearing his real name spoken after 20 years? What if it had been the Bill, would he have confessed? Was it the olive branch? The craft?

He smiled at that. Check mate by a pawn. Haddad, a rank amateur, had succeeded where the combined forces of Interpol had failed. Logan believed Mark when had said he believed him—that Max had caused the fire, killed Michelle. He had seen it in his face, even before even hearing Logan's story. He had come on trust. *Quid pro quo.* That act had compelled Logan to reciprocate, give Mark the Easter Egg. Logan sincerely hoped he would not have to kill him.

011110010100110101100001

"We have a surprise visitor," said Stephanie letting Mark and Jason in.

"Philippe? Great to see you! What are you doing here?"

"Ca va, my friend," said Philippe, with a warm handshake and a slap on the arm. "This is turning out to be quite interesting, non? All this digging up the past … I'm intrigued."

"They've taken the bait," added Stephanie with a wicked grin. "A team just broke into Reginald Brown's office in Victoria."

The double bluff had been Philippe's idea. "He will realize that someone followed him to the graveyard, so let him find that someone. Then he can stop looking."

"So what's on the piece of paper?"

"That's why I detoured. It's an Easter egg." Mark nodded at Jason, who was deep in his laptop. "Show them." Jason hit Enter.

Stunned silence. They all recognized the girl in the photo.

"You have the source code," noted Philippe with a twinkle in his eye, connecting the dots.

"The Easter Egg is buried in the search libraries, just like he said," explained Jason. "When I was at Adware, one of Max's drop-everything projects was to purge an acronym, 'IA,' from the code."

"Intelligent Agent," said Mark, remembering what Logan had said.

Jason continued, "The weird thing was no one had access to the source code. We tried to decompile it, but it never worked. All we could do was strip it out of the URLs. Which is what got me thinking … Fischer's move isn't just an Easter Egg. It's also the password." He typed, hit Enter. "See? Here it is, the source code to Adware's search engine. It's a bit dated but there's some really clever stuff in there."

"Who's Fischer?"

"Bobby Fischer. Chess Grandmaster."

"You can also call the Easter Egg from a web browser." John turned his own laptop around for the others to see. He had pulled up the homepage of a major high street retailer, an Adware client. He had already typed 'Kc1 Rc2# 0-1' into the search field. When he hit Enter the photograph of Michelle Faubourg appeared. He hovered his mouse over it. "Check out the Alt Text. It's a dedication." He read it out aloud.

"Isn't that proof enough? Why does Logan need the source code?"

"I don't think we can answer that yet," said Mark. He had been moved, a strange feeling since leaving Berkeley House. He felt a bond with Logan, as if he had been his confessor. He was not sure he was comfortable with that. Looking ahead, he said, "I've got dinner with Robert in two hours. He seemed awfully cold on the phone, none of that phony sunny California warmth."

"No, there wasn't," replied Stephanie. She had met enough Robert Durands in her line of work. It was a sign that he was sure of himself. "Now that we know Dick Bailey works for him, we need to go back over everything he's seen and heard. "

"I was so sure he worked for Max," said Mark.

"We all were. No point beating yourself up about it."

"Susan had him pegged."

"Who?"

"Robert. She said he was playing his own game. Now we know what it is."

"Yeah, Monday. Devious bastard."

Durand's plan to take over Adware was forcing Mark's hand. He either had to preempt it or risk getting drawn in deeper. Come Monday, it would be open warfare. Mark had to exit the battlefield before then. The problem was they still did not know Logan's game plan.

"I'm going to have to see him again. Daniel, I mean."

"I agree," said Stephanie. "We need to know why he wants the source. There's still more to it."

"Trophy?" Rick had suggested the same last night but no one agreed then or now—too much trouble for a trinket. There was another motive, probably something darker.

"You guys chew it over while I'm with Robert." Mark checked his watch.

"He could be cold because Dick's reported your daily trips to Stephanie's office. Maybe he thinks you're making your own play for Adware."

"He'd be daft. In either case, we'll find out soon enough."

011100100111100101100001

Max Greenberg was driving to Knightsbridge, a call on

speakerphone. "C'mon mate," he cajoled, "It's just a short-term loan. We're about to close down this lawsuit. Once the IPO's back on track I'll pay you back in full. Plus interest. If it gives you comfort, I'm willing to offer a million of my shares as security. We've been friends for a long time ..."

His face changed as he heard the reply, another 'No'. He hung up, slammed the steering wheel "Fuck!" He was running out of time. He had less than 48 hours to raise £2 million or lose his yacht and the £1m down payment. He was running out of options.

He was rounding Hyde Park Corner when he spotted Mark Haddad climbing out of a taxi. He slammed on the brakes. Ignoring the honking horns, anyone blocking his path, he reversed the Rolls, backing around the corner into Lanesborough Place. He threw the keys to the valet and ran into the lobby of the Lanesborough, Robert Durand's hotel. The staff recognized him, but he ignored their pleasantries and followed Mark to the Garden Room.

"I'm meeting Robert Durand here." It was a guess, but not so wild.

"Yes, of course, M Greenberg. Shall I show you to his table? His other guest has just arrived."

Max held up a finger indicating silence, pretended to take a call. He kept his eye on the maître d', walked out of earshot, and spoke in urgent tones, making it up as he went.

"I'm sorry," he said after hanging up. "A family emergency. I must go. Please don't mention to Mr. Durand that I was here. It would be awfully rude that I didn't even pop in to say hello. But I have to rush to the hospital. My wife ..." He palmed a £50 note to the maître d'. "I appreciate your discretion. I'll call him with my apologies."

The maître d's supercilious smile turned to a sneer as soon as Max's back was turned. He had been sacked from the Connaught because of this man who did not even remember him.

Two hours later, as Durand and Mark left the Garden

Room, Pierre said, "M Greenberg arrived just after M Haddad. Sadly, he was called away on a family emergency. He sends his apologies."

"Thank you, Pierre," said Durand.

A £20 note exchanged hands. Pierre smiled. He would have done it for free.

CHAPTER 38

Friday. Webdex.

Liveried doormen swooped down on two black cabs as they pulled up in front of the Langham Hotel. Mark stepped out of the first, smiling as he watched his team pile out. He winked at Adrian and offered his arm to Marie. The concierge directed them to the Palm Court Lounge, where drinks and canapés were being served to the gathered digerati. Resplendent in an emerald green dress, Marie drew looks, hushed whispers from all corners as soon as she walked in.

There were many familiar faces, veterans like Mark, who had been part of London's boom bust boom dotcom scene since day dot. Webdex was their an annual reunion. It was also rampant with a fresh crop of 20- and 30-somethings riding Web 2.0. Mark and his team spread and mingled with their respective networks.

'I'm back!" thought Mark. It was a long time since he'd been here on his own terms. He looked forward to surprising a few people. $5 million in the bank. He was armed and dangerous. It felt like the old days.

He had resisted the pressure from his friends to use the event to damage Adware. Duncan, especially, had been urging him to hijack the acceptance speech, make it about Dynamo.

As much as Mark wanted to—and saw the all too valid benefits of doing so—it just did not feel right. Besides, by this point, he just wanted closure. He could start the next chapter afterwards. He was thinking about all this when Rick tapped him on the shoulder.

"Someone I want you to meet. How are the new cards?"

He handed one to Rick as they walked.

"I like the logo. Don't look now, but Max just arrived. I assume that's Robert Durand with him."

"It is. I'm surprised to see them together. I wonder if they've seen my resignation letter."

"Letters, plural," corrected Rick with a grin. The entire Adware sales team had also handed in their resignations earlier that afternoon.

Derrick Schmidt was larger than life, 6'6" with a trademark Stetson and Texas swagger. He was a Silicon Valley legend. Over the past 30 years, his image had graced countless magazine covers, from *Forbes* to *Wired*. He had launched dozens of companies, always cutting edge, always big, even when they failed. ABC—Ads By Context—was his latest venture, a next gen digital advertising service, a direct competitor to Adware.

He lived in San Francisco but was a Texan to the core, creased blue jeans, a silk, hand-embroidered shirt with silver collar tips and rhinestone buttons. The Navajo eagle motif of his bolo was mirrored in the silver toecaps of his hand-tooled cowboy boots. Formal wear, Texas style, like a kilt to a Scots.

He placed a massive left hand on Mark's shoulder and drew him into his circle, beaming. "Pleasure to finally meet you," said Schmidt, his drawl a rolling baritone.

Mark could feel the low vibration of gossip mills powering up, camera phones clicking, twits tweeting. He returned Schmidt's powerful grip, locked eyes and smiled back. "Likewise."

Out of the corner of his eye, Mark watched Max closing in

on them, a determined look on his face.

"That's one beautiful filly you had on your arm! Turned every head in the place, boys and girls!"

Mark replied, "Treat her right. She's a star."

Schmidt had been told that he was poaching the team with its leader's blessing, but he had not believed it until now. "I still don't understand why you're willing to let them go." He turned to Rick half in jest, "You sure you haven't sold me a dud, partner?"

"Trust me, they'll be outselling your US team before you know it," replied Mark with a cocksure smile. He had taken an instant liking to Derrick Schmidt, felt he understood him and sensed that a little bravado would not go amiss.

"There's still room for you. Just say the word. I still need a strong CEO here in Europe."

Had it not been for Dynamo, Mark would have jumped at the opportunity. Instead, he fished out a business card and handed it to Schmidt, 'Founder & CEO' the legend below his name. Schmidt smiled and nodded understanding. He pocketed the card before prying eyes caught a glimpse.

"What I would like to discuss is a partnership," said Mark.

Derrick let out a deep, bellowing laugh. "I'm all ears. Dynamo ... Tell you what. How about you come down to Dallas for the Thanksgiving Day game in a couple of weeks? Let me show you some southern hospitality."

"I'm a Redskins fan," replied Mark. Schmidt already knew that.

"You're Derrick Schmidt, aren't you?" said Max, insinuating himself into the conversation.

"That's what my mamma always tells me!" replied Schmidt with a big awe shucks grin. "And you are?" He asked, although he already knew.

"Max Greenberg. Chairman of Adware."

"Pleased to meet you Mr. ... ah ... Greenberg, was it? Let me introduce you around. This here's my good buddy Mark Haddad ..." He pronounced it with a long Texas A.

Max's laugh came out more like a growl. "Mark works for me."

"Does he, now?" replied Schmidt, a glint in his eye. "Well ain't it a small world?" Schmidt continued the introductions keeping them short, perfunctory, before resuming his conversation with Mark.

"Like I was saying, Cowboys are looking real good for the Super Bowl this year. It's been a while. Lotta folk, me included, figure they'll finally bring the trophy back home this year. Jerry—Jerry Jones, that is—tells me that's gonna happen. Hell, I've been in San Francisco as long as I can remember but I'm no 49er. Seen Montana put four rings on his fingers. Helluva quarterback."

He spoke with his whole body, holding up four fingers, pausing at each for emphasis. "But I ain't never been and never will be a 49er. No sir! Born and bred a Cowboy, ever since I was knee-high to a grasshopper."

He let rip a roaring laugh before patting Mark on the shoulder in mock commiseration. "Not like the old days, eh, good buddy? Redskins been bottom of the East ever since Gibbs left. What's it been? Ten years if a day since you last made the playoffs."

Mark parried smoothly. He kept up with the NFL through a fantasy league he and some friends had kept going since university. "As I recall, we beat you a couple of weeks back. I sure would have liked to have been there." Mark's accent had slipped to Dixie, though north of Atlanta.

Schmidt laughed. "Hell, I gotta fly half way around the world, for you to remind me! 17-14. A field goal with three seconds on the clock." He shook his head with an exaggerated sigh. "Tell you what. I'll send my jet. Bring the wife and kids. Betty Sue would sure love to have your brood join us for Thanksgiving. After lunch, you and I can take the chopper over to Texas Stadium. Got a private box."

"I'd like that," replied Mark with a smile. It was clear Max was going nowhere as long as he was talking to Derrick

Schmidt. It was also clear he was on the verge of exploding. Mark took his leave, holding his hand out, "I'd best mix. Lot of people here I haven't caught up with in a while. Good to see you, Derrick."

"Alright, son. We'll talk later," replied Schmidt with a wink and another gripping (though thankfully brief) handshake. "And don't forget about Turkey Day!"

Mark headed to the bar, Max hot on his heels.

"You know him." An accusation not a question.

Mark plucked a glass of champagne from the tray of a passing waiter and led Max out to the verandah.

"Didn't know you'd taken up smoking again."

"Bad habit," replied Mark.

Max lit a cigar. "What's going on, Mark?"

Mark shrugged, raised his eyebrows. *You tell me.*

"First, I see you going to the Lanesborough to meet Robert on Wednesday night. Now I find you talking to Derrick Schmidt …"

"Yes, I had dinner with Robert," said Mark. "I half-expected you to be there."

"But I wasn't."

"No, you weren't."

"Am I being pushed, Mark?"

"I handed in my notice two hours ago, Max. It's on your desk."

"Is that why you met Robert? Why you were just talking to Derrick Schmidt. Are you joining ABC? You prick! After everything I've done for you …"

Mark cut him off. "No, I am not joining ABC." He did not add that his team was. "As for Robert, *he* invited *me* to dinner. Like I already said, I assumed you'd be there."

"What'd you talk about? Does he know you've resigned?"

"I don't know. I made my decision this morning, left my letter on your desk."

"Why? We're about to IPO … I've always been generous

300

with you, haven't I? You've got millions of stock options."

Mark almost felt sorry for Max. Almost. Despite all his faults, there was still some part of him Mark liked, even admired. And he had no idea what was coming.

Any misplaced sympathy vanished when Max snapped at him, "You sonofabitch! This is all about leverage isn't it? Think I don't see what's going on? Think I don't know Robert is trying to force me out of my own company. You little shit! You made a deal with him, didn't you? Help push me out, so you can take over." Max hunched his shoulders and took a menacing step forward, like a boxer closing on his opponent.

Mark stepped back. The sound of a door opening, three people spilling out, laughing and chatting, breaking the tension of isolation. "You don't get it, do you Max? I'm out! No subterfuge, no games. I handed in my notice. I quit. That's it. If you really want to know, I'm starting up my own company. I could have made a big deal about tonight but I chose not to. So, you're welcome." He started to walk away, then turned after a few steps. "You know, Max, bad deeds have a way of catching up with you."

"What the hell does that mean?" spat Max, his voice drawing looks from the three other people on the verandah.

Mark shook his head and shrugged an apology to the threesome. As soon as he stepped inside, he was accosted by Marie.

"I saw Max follow you out. He looked pretty aggressive."

Mark nodded. "He saw me talking to Derrick Schmidt."

Marie smiled. "I can't believe it's all happening."

Nor could Mark. For weeks, he had been caught in a whirlwind of surveillance and counter-intelligence. It was now end game, an exit in sight. "Derrick will be tough, but he strikes me as honest, a salt of the earth type."

"On a first name basis, already," laughed Marie. "By the way, how's your funding coming along? Since you resigned, I assume ..."

Mark was glad to end this particular deceit. Necessary at the time, but he had never enjoyed lying to Marie. "I closed $5 million from an Angel."

With a shriek of glee, Marie threw her arms around his neck, drawing glances from around the room. He hushed her, explaining that it was not public knowledge yet.

"There's a lot more to it, isn't there?"

Mark nodded. "Yes, it's complicated."

"And it's not over yet."

"Nearly," replied Mark. "Nearly."

"If there's anything I can do to help ..."

"You've already done more than you realize. But thanks."

"Thank you. I can't believe I'm now EMEA Sales Director for ABC," A broad grin stretched across Marie's face. "The one downside is that I'm going to miss working with you."

Mark choked back the lump in his throat and said, "You're going to be great. And I'll always be there for you, though I doubt you'll need my advice on managing those miscreants."

Marie laughed and gave him a hug. "I really am going to miss you."

Mark felt an arm around his shoulder. "We need to talk." It was Durand.

Mark turned to Marie and said, "Why don't you round up the team. They'll be seating us for dinner soon."

Marie nodded and left.

"I refuse to accept your resignation. You really should have talked to me first, Mark. I told you there'd be big changes on Monday. You're an important part of that." He reached into his breast pocket, fished out an envelope. "I'm going to tear it up right now, pretend it never happened."

"Don't," said Mark, suddenly feeling very tired. After weeks of living under surveillance, meting out words and deeds to appease and deceive the cameras, seeing sides of people—of himself—he knew were there but had never really looked at, all he wanted was for it to end so he could get on with his life.

"Whatever they're offering, I'll add 20%."

"This isn't a bidding war," replied Mark. As soon as he said this, he realized that is exactly what Durand thought. "I'm sorry, but I've made my decision."

It dawned on Mark that Durand had not mentioned his team, their resignations. He must not have seen them yet. Out of the corner of his eye, he saw Logan coming toward them. It gave him a brief flutter of silent panic as he muddled facts, forgot the script, who knew who or what.

Logan helped him out. "Robert. So good to see you." He shook his hand warmly and turned to Mark. "You must be Mark Haddad." He smiled as if his 'guess' was right. "I've heard good things."

"All lies," joked Mark, returning the handshake, pocketing the piece of paper Logan pressed in his palm.

"You have a lot of friends here. Everyone says you're going to win tonight. It's almost a foregone conclusion."

"Well, we'll see." Mark already knew it for fact. "Max!" he yelled over Logan's shoulder. "Max!"

Max turned, caught his eye, saw Durand and came over. Logan's back was turned to him, so he did not recognize him until it was too late.

"Max, I'd like to introduce you to Daniel Logan."

"We've met," said Max.

There was a long awkward silence. Mark watched the other three men, felt the note burning a hole in his pocket.

"Excuse me, gentlemen. I expect you have some business to discuss amongst yourselves."

He found Rick, exchanged a quick word then made his way outside. A few minutes later, Rick joined him.

"Logan slipped me a note," he said. "All it says is 'Table 39'."

"I guess he wants to talk. Think he knows?"

"At this point I have no idea who knows what," joked Mark, although there was a serious edge to his words. "I was with Robert when Logan came over, couldn't remember whether Robert knew I knew him, Logan, I mean."

"He doesn't, at least he didn't. Does now. Either case, you're doing fine."

"Yeah, just a panic moment."

"Almost there. What do you think Logan wants?"

"Dunno. But I'll stop by his table and find out. The way Robert was acting, I don't think he's seen the other resignations."

"They must've handed them in after he left the office."

The lights dimmed, signaling dinner. Inside, the digerati were slowly making their way to the Grand Ballroom.

Table 39 was in the farthest, darkest corner of the room. It was occupied by a shaggy, bearded Cambridge professor and his four spotty-faced, post-grad acolytes. The founders of Digivet looked uncomfortable in their tailored tuxedos, in awe of their surroundings.

Logan had laid on the full Monty—his personal tailor (please, keep the DJs and accoutrements, you'll need them, hahaha), a limo (stocked bar, pampering, fawning executive assistant), a rare private audience in Logan's penthouse residence (benevolence and fealty reaffirmed), guest suites at Berkeley House (Rohypnol, Natasha's girls and boys for fun and insurance). A little attention, a few baubles, and they were putty in his hands.

"Is this Daniel Logan's table?" asked Mark.

"Yes, yes," said the older chap with an apologetic air. "I'm Professor Edward Rasmussen."

Mark shook his hand, which was shaking, nervous, fingers long, dry, bony, almost like a chicken foot but without the claws. "Do you mind if I wait? He asked me to come over."

"Of course not. Please do sit down. Would you like some wine?"

"I'm fine, thank you," replied Mark. No one at the table was socially adept. He had seen that as he approached. "So what is Digivet? What's your connection to Daniel?" he asked, making small talk.

"Oh yes, Digivet, well, these are four of my post-grads from Cambridge," said the Professor. They acknowledged without acknowledging, noses buried in handhelds, more comfortable in the digital world than the analog one. "It's an app for veterinarians. Today, most pets are chipped, but that's only used to identify them. It can be so much more …"

Mark could see that he had given the man an opening to a topic he was comfortable with and he was fast getting into the flow. What he was more curious about, though, was his relationship with Logan. He recalled that Philippe's people had followed Logan to Cambridge a few times.

"Is Digivet something Daniel's funded?"

"Well, Mr. Logan is the Chairman of Peterman Brown," replied Prof Rasmussen. "Stuart Lassiter, the Managing Partner is also here this evening. Do you know him as well?"

Mark shook his head.

"The University has a 10-year agreement with Peterman Brown to create commercial spin-outs from our research."

"That's great," replied Mark. "Are you involved in every project?"

"Goodness gracious, no, that would be impossible," replied Prof Rasmussen, with a modest chuckle, "Though I do Chair the Advisory Board."

Professor Rasmussen liked titles, capitalized his words. Mark nodded, looking suitably impressed. He reminded him of Nigel Thornton.

"So how does it work?"

"Well, Mr. Logan, or should I say, Peterman Brown, have been very generous. They endowed a Chair to fund projects in areas of special interest. I work with Peterman Brown to define those each year. Of course, some spin-outs become successful, others fail. Digivet is one of the successful ones."

"I see," said Mark.

He was about to ask another question when Professor Rasmussen said, "Here comes Mr. Logan now."

Mark stood up to shake hands.

"Please, do sit down," said Logan, gesturing toward two empty seats at the far end of the table. "I see you've met Professor Rasmussen." It was perfunctory, his body language making it clear that the rest of the conversation was to be private. "Professor, if you don't mind, I would like a moment alone with Mr. Haddad."

"Yes, yes, of course," bumbled Rasmussen, nudging his acolytes, shepherding them away.

When they were alone, Mark took the initiative. "I have a proposition."

Logan nodded.

"There are two things you need to know. One, I've resigned from Adware. I handed in my notice and my laptop this afternoon. Two, Ignite Capital is planning to put Adware into pre-pack administration on Monday morning." That last bit came as a surprise to Logan. Mark explained, "They have a debenture and are calling the note. Adware doesn't have the cash to pay it."

He paused to let Logan digest this. It was, in effect, a hostile takeover, the debenture a trap waiting to be sprung. It would be a lightning strike, the whole thing done by lunch. Less than 72 hours from now.

"What is your proposal?"

"First, my conditions. One. I want my life back. I'll set up this deal but otherwise I want no part of it. Two, PaySense You've sunk £2 million into it. Duncan Brown is a good man and he knows what he's doing. It's a wise investment. Let him run it, without interference. I promise, he will make you a good return."

"What else?" asked Logan.

"That's it. Those are my conditions. Do you accept?"

Logan was perplexed. What Mark was asking for was trivial. Then it dawned on him. *'I want my life back.'* Mark had used those words once before. He cherished his 'life' above all else—family, friends, relationships, all the things that made him human. He was a survivor but unlike Daniel Logan, he was not a predator. Nor, as it turned out, was he easy prey. His fight instinct had proven strong.

Daniel Loginovsky's natural instinct had been flight, his youth spent cowering in fear on the playground, hiding in his lab, running away from Michelle's murder. In Daniel Logan, he had nurtured a brutal fight instinct, a ruthless predator on a relentless climb to the top of the food chain. When he looked at Mark he saw a man at peace with himself and his world, a man without want or need of predation, the elephant to his lion.

"I accept," said Daniel offering his hand.

Mark's face did not betray the slightest hint of duplicity. A man of his word. At that moment, Logan needed more than anything for Mark to see the same in him. For that, he first had to believe it of himself.

It seemed an eternity before Mark nodded.

Logan could see his guard was still up—he was sincere, not stupid. He would put his faith in Logan, but trust had to be earned. Logan felt honored, indebted, foreign sensations, vital emotions percolating in his dead black heart. He did not know why, but it was suddenly important that he earn that trust, prove himself worthy of it. It was as if his very humanity was at stake. For a brief moment, it even dampened his desire for revenge.

He listened as Mark laid out his proposition.

Robert Durand had laid out his own end game over dinner at the Lanesborough Hotel. Mark had not let on that he had already figured it out. Nor did he act surprised when Durand reiterated his offer of the CEO role. Mark had always figured he was just being played. There were other surprises, too. Mark gave nothing back, said he would think it over.

That night, back at John's house, they had burned the midnight oil, gamed out all possible permutations and end games. The team was at full strength, their battlefield a workflow diagram projected onto a whiteboard. Mark's exit strategy was already secured—Dynamo had $5 million in the bank. But he was standing in the middle of a minefield. He needed a clear route to the exit. Which is what he had just proposed to Logan.

"What happens after that is between you and Robert Durand," said Mark, wrapping up the pitch.

"And me and Max."

"And you and Max," conceded Mark. His tone said he did not want to hear more.

Logan also detected a hint of disappointment. Food for thought.

Mark stood up and held out his hand. "Now, I need to return to my guests. Dinner is being served."

Mark felt eyes boring into him as he made his way across the grand ballroom. It felt like the whole room was watching him.

Max intercepted him midway. "I saw you talking to Daniel Logan." His voice was seething. "If you even think about helping him with his lawsuit, I'll bury you!"

The words came out louder than intended drawing nervous stares from nearby tables. In the past, Mark had always seen Max as a posturing bully, ultimately harmless if you called him on it. Now, though, the crazed look on his face was truly frightening, made more so by the secret knowledge that he was looking into the eyes of a murderer.

Mark jerked his arm away and continued to his table.

"What was that about?" asked Marie as he sat down.

"You don't want to know. Just be glad we won't have to deal with him anymore. Now, time to celebrate!" He raised his glass, toasting the table. To the Dream Team!"

The entire room was seated, waiters making their way between tables, arms laden with dishes, when the last three guests walked in. Derrick Schmidt was impossible to miss, standing 6'6". His presence at Webdex had already caused a stir. ABC, was moving into Europe. This was big news. The rumor mills had been buzzing since he was seen talking to Mark. Now, all eyes followed him as he joined the Ashton Tate table, 22. Whispers spread around him like wildfire.

Mark avoided eye contact with Table 18. Max and Durand glared back, a sea of gossip between them.

"And now, the moment we've all been waiting for, the fastest growing technology company in the UK in 2009." Silence spread, lights dimmed. Spotlights began roaming the tables, mounting the tension. The MC continued. "Our winner is no stranger to these events, having graced our list for the past four years." Pause for the audience to look around, puzzled. "A record, I believe, in itself a remarkable accomplishment. To sustain double- even triple-digit growth year on year. Overall, we've not seen the growth rates this year that we've come to expect. The recession has had an impact, but I think it's fair to say that many here today have turned adversity to advantage. I congratulate you all. And now, ladies and gentlemen, it is my pleasure to present the UK's fastest growing web company ... Adware!"

There was a round of applause as the spotlights settled out tables 18 and 22 to canned fanfare. Durand, Max and Mark all got up and made their way to the stage. Mark stood to the MC's left facing the crowd, Max and Durand to his right. Few people other than Gary would have noticed the MC, Lee Atwood, shift the microphone from right to left. He smiled to himself, silently thanking Lee. He owed him one.

"Max Greenberg is a legend in his own right." Titters rippled through the audience. "Last year Adware reported remarkable growth, 106% year on year." A round of polite applause. "With him is Robert Durand from Ignite Capital in San Francisco. Robert, welcome to London." A more subdued round of applause.

"And on my left I have Mark Haddad." A loud cheer went

up, led by Table 22. "Mark joined Adware as Sales Director five years ago. It's made the Webdex 100 every year since. That, my friends, is no coincidence. Mark Haddad, congratulations on making the Number One spot this year." There was another loud round of applause.

As the assistant approached with the glass trophy, Lee Atwood announced, "Ladies and Gentlemen. I give you the leader of this year's Webdex ... Adware!"

Max grinned and hoisted the trophy in the air. His acceptance speech was prepared. But Lee had handed the microphone to Mark instead.

"Thank you, Lee. It's an honor and a testament to all the people at Adware who have worked so hard this year. My team ..." He pointed out across the darkened room, the spotlights sweeping dramatically over Table 22. Another round of applause. Short speech, Mark thanking his team by name then handing the mike back to the MC.

As the trio made to leave the stage, Lee Atwood spoke into the microphone, "Mark, can you stay behind please?" Max turned too, but the ushers guided him and Durand gracefully but firmly back to their table.

"This year, the judging committee has introduced a special award, an individual award." A murmur went through the crowd, the sound of rustling paper.

"Sorry," laughed Lee, "You won't find it in the program." He paused for a moment to let the murmur die down. "Especially in these difficult times, consistency is an essential ingredient for long-term success. Since joining Adware, Mark and his sales team have posted astonishing results—120, 92, 63, 131 percent—and this year 106 percent annual growth. Tremendous. Mark, it is my pleasure to present you with the inaugural Webdex Individual Achievement Award."

The audience gave Mark a standing ovation as he accepted the award. He hoped sufficient surprise showed on his face.

"Wow. This is a real honor," said Mark, taking the microphone. "I've been a part of London's tech scene since the early 90s. We've had our ups and downs …" pause for a chuckle from the crowd "… When the bubble burst, I guess it was Y2K …" a few more titters "… everyone wrote us off. *All of us.*" His arm swept across the audience. "But we've proved them wrong, haven't we?" The crowd roared approval.

"We've proven that London has what it takes to be a world leader in technology!" There was more cheering as Mark dropped his tone, "I look around this room and I see a lot of familiar faces. The same people, but not necessarily the same companies … More than a few of us have been to the wall, me included. Rags to riches to rags." Subdued laughter. "But we're back, and we're stronger than ever. I salute each and every one of you." A cheer went up as Mark hoisted the trophy.

"I just want to add that I could not have achieved this on my own. I'd like to invite my sales team to join me here on the stage …" Mark paused to make sure they were all getting up. "Nearly five years ago, when I told my close friend Rick Ashton, from Ashton Tate over there at Table 22 … I hope you don't mind a shameless plug, but I wholeheartedly recommend them …" Mark let the murmur die down. "Ashton Tate has placed each one of these amazing people with me." Mark slung his arm over Marie's shoulder, the action cascading down the line, the five of them standing in solidarity. "Lee, on behalf of myself, Adware and most importantly, my team, I'd like to thank you and the Webdex committee for this honor. And especially, I'd like to thank my team for making me look so good." There was a roar of approval as the room jumped to its feet, clapping, whistling, catcalling.

There were lots of handshakes and backslaps as the Adware sales team made their way back to their table. Taking the stage had come as a surprise, and they had clearly enjoyed their moment. It was also not without purpose.

"Ladies and Gentlemen," announced the MC, "If you can

finish your drinks and make your way back to the Palm Court. We'll be clearing out the tables shortly. Dancing starts at 9:30." The ceremony was over.

Back in the Palm Court bar, the party got underway, the DJ's sound system booming as the bar shifted from champagne to cocktails. Some people left, including Max, Durand, and Logan, but most stayed. It was not the same as the champagne and cocaine-fueled days of the late 90s, but then again, neither were they. Eager 20- and 30-somethings had matured into seasoned 30- and 40-somethings.

"Great speech," said Rick.

Mark laughed. "Thanks."

"Seriously. And thanks for the plug. I've already run out of business cards."

"I'm nearly out, too. Just a few left."

"Definitely created a buzz. First, everyone was convinced you were joining ABC, seeing you talking to Derrick, then him joining us at our table. Must've taken them by surprise when you started handing out your Dynamo cards."

"Yeah," smiled Mark. "I'm just glad it's over."

CHAPTER 39

Monday morning, Mark was enjoying the solitude, letting it all sink in. He had woken early out of habit and had to remind himself over coffee that he did not need to rush. It was over.

He had spent the morning doing nothing, just lounging and reading the morning papers. More than a few journos had got it wrong, run stories about him being appointed CEO of Adware. He assumed Durand's PR machine had issued the press release before the weekend, before he had handed in his notice. A couple of articles even carried quotes attributed to him.

The doorbell rang. Mark got up from the sofa and went to the door, still reading an article as he flipped the latch. The door burst open and Max came charging in, wild, crazed, fists flying. Mark almost tripped as he backpedalled, reeling as much from bewilderment as from the first blow, which caught the side of his head. Adrenaline kicked, time slowed and he reacted, dodging, arm absorbing blows to protect his head as he backed down the hallway.

Max was screaming incoherent expletives and accusations punctuating his punches. Mark yanked open the closet door handle as he passed it, a temporary barrier, enough time to reach the kitchen and slam the door shut behind him. His left arm hung limply, numb from the battering it had taken. The door shuddered as Max battered it with his shoulder.

The doorknob turned but there was nothing he could do. His left arm was hanging numb and useless. Trying to use his right would have meant shifting his weight off the door. He kicked off his slippers. Bare feet would have better traction on the wood floor. He braced for impact. When it came, it was harder than he had imagined, driving him backward. But it was a hammer blow, not a sustained push and his weight slammed the door shut again.

Feeling was returning to Mark's left arm. He gave it a shake, flexed his fingers. The door knob turned and he braced for another assault. "What the fuck are you doing, Max?" he yelled.

Max replied with another stream of invective, enough for Mark to begin making sense of it, Max's insane behavior.

"It's bullshit! The papers got it wrong! I quit on Friday. You have my letter. If you want to blame someone, blame Robert." He did not add, 'and yourself,' because it would just have riled Max further. "Are you listening to me?"

Max responded with another litany of curses and accusations, another shoulder battering. The door jarred with the impact but Mark's counter-weight slammed it shut again.

Mark flexed his left hand, testing its returning strength. He gripped the doorknob and waited. Max twisted it back and forth with increasing force but it did not turn, not enough to release the latch. The twisting stopped, footsteps receding. Mark breathed a sigh of relief. "Max, you need to calm down. Whatever Robert told you, I had nothing to do with it."

"Bullshit! It's in the newspapers!" Then silence, eye of the hurricane.

The impact came with a loud crack. The doorframe splintered, the latch rendered useless. Max was coming through next time.

Mark scanned the kitchen, assessing his options, not panicking. Back door locked. Knife block by the window.

Phone on counter. Neither in reach. In a fluid motion, he eased himself off the door, one hand reaching for the phone, feet pivoting, backing up to the counter, then reaching for a knife. He hefted it, readied his stance and waited.

Seconds ticked by, time catching up as the adrenaline ebbed and the silence grew. Mark thumbed the phone without taking his eyes off the kitchen door. He considered calling the police. It would take them too long. This would be over in a matter of minutes. He launched the calculator app instead, breathing steady his breathing as he thumbed in the complicated code. He hit the PANIC button. It activated all surveillance functions and sent out an SOS SMS.

More seconds ticked by, the silence growing eerie with every tick of the kitchen clock. Maybe Max had come to his senses. Maybe he was gone. Mark picked up the keys to the garden door, and edged his way toward it.

A polite knock on the kitchen door startled him.

"Mr. Haddad. Is Okay. I open door now." The voice was deep, Eastern European. Mark tensed, gripped the knife harder, positioned himself best he knew how.

Skinny, the guy he had pinged weeks ago, opened the door. Max lay in an inert heap on the floor behind him, a pair of wires running from his back to a Taser in the hands of another 'Polish builder' dressed in paint-streaked jeans and boots.

"Premises secured," said the man. He spoke neither to Mark nor in English.

Then Mark's phone rang.

"Please don't say my name. These gentlemen work for me but they do not know who I am."

"Like Charlie's Angels."

Logan laughed. "You're welcome."

"Thanks. Why? ... How? ... If anything happens to me ..."

"Come now, Mark, if I wanted you dead, I would not have stopped Max."

"Why are they here? Have you been following me?" Mark

hoped his tone expressed sufficient shock.

"Not you. Max. Have you seen the morning papers?"

"No," lied Mark though he did not know why.

"You've been appointed CEO of Adware. It's in all the papers, mostly the Business section. There's even a nice quote from you in the Telegraph, how pleased you are, etc."

"Don't believe everything you read. I told you Friday that I resigned. Why would I lie?"

"More to the point, why would Robert lie?" countered Logan. "Surely you don't believe this story was released by accident."

Of course! Durand had done it on purpose, set him up, dangled him, red rag to Max's raging bull. The prick!

"I dare say, Max might have killed you if my men had not been there."

"I had it covered."

"I am not a bad man, Mark. You said yourself that you do not believe I killed Michelle. I loved her with all my heart. She was my life. Max killed her. I think you know that. And he just tried to kill you."

Logan played his words deliberately, teeing up one emotion at a time—anger with Durand, fear of Max, gratitude to Logan, compassion for loss and injustice, closing with a reminder of debt.

"What do you want?"

"The flash drive Tony Levine gave you …"

"Which one? The eight gigabit one?"

Logan chuckled. "Yes, the eight gigabit one. All I ask is that you plug it in and log on to Adware's VPN. Then give both drives to my men."

"Why? What's on it?"

Mark's question was met with silence.

"It'll do you no good. I resigned on Friday. They'll have closed my account by now."

"Humor me. I would not be so sure Durand has locked you out of the network yet."

316

"And if I don't?"

"My men will leave. They will take Max with them. And they will take that knife you are holding." Logan enunciated his words, the threat unspoken yet unequivocal.

Mark's mind was racing, trying to understand. It did not make sense. The deal he had brokered gave Logan direct, legal access to the source code. He had his revenge. What more did he want?

011011100111100101101111

Mark had arranged the summit meeting between Daniel Logan and Ignite Capital for the previous Saturday, immediately after Webdex. It took place on neutral ground, at the offices of Pi Capital.

Logan had anticipated a negative reaction from Durand, prepared for it by conferencing in Conrad Baine. He had been teeing off from the 6th hole at the Palo Alto Hills golf course at the time. Conveniently, he was with his old friend, Jim Bradley, CEO of American Mutual Bank.

Logan had reiterated his proposal. AMB would match Peterman Brown's £2 million stake in PaySense, taking an equal 10% shareholding. PaySense in turn would drop its lawsuit against AMB. When Baine had mouthed the figure, Jim Bradley had nodded without hesitation. It was cheaper than he had expected. He would have an even bigger smile after the call was over, when Baine filled him in on the rest.

Next came Adware. Mark had proposed that Ignite call in its debenture on Monday as planned and put the company into pre-pack administration. Peterman Brown would participate as an equal shareholder in the restructured company. Baine had been about to protest the inequity when Logan had added, "Of course, Peterman Brown will pay for its stake in the business, injecting $31 million, to match Ignite's investment to date. Baine had smiled and nodded approval as he heard this.

Logan continued. PaySense would drop the lawsuit against Adware, leaving it free to get the IPO back on track. Ignite would net around a half a billion dollars on exit—not the whole pie, but a much bigger slice than it had started with.

"If we are in agreement, gentlemen, then I propose we now discuss the future. There is a natural synergy between our three companies. I propose we sign a tripartite agreement so that Adware transactions flow through PaySense's gateway and get cleared by American Mutual Bank. Everyone touches the money along the way." No one needed to calculate how much would stick to their fingers. They all knew it would be substantial.

Even Durand had had to admit—though he did not say it—that there was an uncanny symmetry to it. The deal was agreed, papers signed. Everyone would come out ahead. Everyone except Max Greenberg.

011011100110010100111111

"And if I do as you ask, you leave Max here? That's the part I don't get."

"My men will secure him until the police arrive. Good Samaritans, passersby who intervened. He will be arrested for aggravated assault and breaking and entering. With no priors, I doubt he'll be sentenced to anything more than community service."

"Then what?"

"Then our business is concluded."

"Then what?" Both knew what he was asking but neither wanted to speak it openly.

"I gave you my word." Mark heard the subtext, *and I honored it.* "Now you must trust me."

Mark now saw the flaw in his plan. For all his carefully considered diagrams and what-if scenarios, the end game had always focused on his own exit strategy. He had not seen past that, not factored in an aftermath.

318

Robert Durand had. *Mr. Distress.* In his tenure on Sand Hill Road, he had led enough hostile takeovers to know that founders and CEOs rarely walked away quietly when their babies were snatched from them. He could not predict *how* Max would react, but he had known that he would, planned accordingly. The stories in the papers had been intentional, designed to deflect Max's wrath toward Mark.

Logan had seen it coming, anticipated Max's reaction. His intervention had not been by accident. And now he had repaid a debt.

Mark realized all this in a flash as he stared at Max's inert body lying on his hallway floor, Taser wires dangling from his back.

It was still not over. Logan's threat left him no choice, yet in a strange way Mark could forgive him that. He was what he was. It was all he knew. But he had also just saved Mark's life.

Mark still did not understand why Logan wanted him to plug in the flash drive and release the virus. He already had access to the source code by virtue of owning 40% of Adware. Yet he was still trying to steal it. It did not make sense. Still, for Mark, with a word it could finally, truly be over.

"Okay."

"You and Daniel Loginovsky might have been friends."

"Perhaps," replied Mark.

CHAPTER 40

A light rain shimmered red, white and blue in the flashing lights of the emergency services, whorling with the smoke and steam rising from the burned out mansion. A small crowd was gathered just beyond the police cordon, attention fixed on the blackened windows, a fine mist settling on upturned faces.

"They found a body ..." said one bystander. "Murdered," said another. "Arson ... police asking questions."

A well-dressed man hung back from the crowd, the collar of his tailored trench coat turned up, obscuring his face. In his right hand, he held a black umbrella, to protect him from the elements. He watched, as a man in handcuffs was led from the back of an ambulance to a waiting police car.

Daniel Logan shot his cuff and checked the time, his cufflinks glistening in the rain, two White Queens. He ran his fingers through his thinning blond hair. It was getting late. He had seen enough.

As he started to climb into the back of the Bentley, there was a commotion. He turned to look. Max Greenberg, never one to shy away from a camera, was facing the reporters as if at a press conference, protesting his innocence. Disheveled, face rain-streaked with soot, he was still a commanding presence.

The police woman gave him rope. He had already been read his rights to silence. And, as she knew from experience, bulls like him took careful handling. Then, of course, there was the press. Fire on The Bishop's Avenue, London's famed Millionaire's Row, enough to attract a handful of them. The story would be on the evening news. She had to be on best behavior.

Daniel Logan caught the odd word but did not stay to listen. He would see it in the news. He handed the umbrella to his driver and climbed into the Bentley, luxuriating in the smell of hand-tooled leather, only the faintest scent of cinder trailing in behind him. The driver pulled away from the curb, heading south, to Berkeley Square.

CHAPTER 41

Mark sat on the veranda gazing out over sparkling azure waters, enjoying the crisp warmth of the morning sun, the scent of orange blossom and frangipani, a hint of summer on the warm breeze blowing in from Africa. He was alone, late morning, the Sunday papers scattered on the over-sized divan. Two stories had gripped his attention. He had been following one for months. The other was breaking news. Only a few people knew there was a connection.

First the trial. The verdict was in. Guilty. Manslaughter, arson, and multiple counts of insurance fraud. Max Greenberg had been given a 24-year sentence.

Ever one for the headlines, he had outdone himself this time. His photo stared back at Mark from the front pages and business sections of all the major British broadsheets. Even *Le Monde* and *Figaro* had run the story, their French readership always happy to lap up a good scandal, especially a British one.

It was the story of a desperate man. Facing financial ruin, M. Greenberg had torched his mansion home on the famously nicknamed Millionaire's Row. An insurance scam, a last bid, desperate attempt to save a crumbling empire. There had been an overwhelming preponderance of evidence, the guilty verdict inevitable—arrest at the scene of the crime, traces of petrol in the boot of his car, his fingerprints on a jerry can in the back garden, no sign of forced entry, his code the last one entered to turn off the alarm system.

In the months following the fire, speculation had never been rife over the death of Jo Greenberg. Accident or murder? She had been insured.

She wasn't supposed to be here. Max's declaration to the media on the night of the fire had spurred endless analysis that in the end both condemned him to and saved him from prosecution—arson, fraud, manslaughter. Not first degree murder.

Mark was not so sure.

The second story, not sensationalist like the trial, still had broad coverage on the inside sections of the major dailies— business, education, science, technology. Depending on the context, it was run as a story of lost genius, lost love, human tragedy, an unsolved crime, scientific discovery and commercial opportunity.

The Times led with the headline, 'Intelligent Agent Discovered at Cambridge University,' an article about an early search engine recently discovered in the dusty digital archives of Cambridge University's famed Cavendish Laboratory. "Daniel Loginovsky was one of my students ... I remember him well ... a brilliant physicist ... a tragic story," said Professor Edward Rasmussen, whose team had found it. The article went on to describe the Loginovsky Algorithms as being ahead of their time, using fractal dimensions to map data relationships with incredible speed, accuracy and insight.

The Observer ran its piece on page 3 of the Business section. Again quoting Professor Rasmussen, "The IA algorithms represent a radical departure from traditional search methods. We already have keen interest from several parties." He deferred all further enquiries to Stuart Lassiter of Peterman Brown, the London-based venture capital firm with which the university enjoyed a long-standing and fruitful relationship.

Mark's thoughts drifted back to London. That morning. Max's inert body in the hallway, zapped senseless with 1,200 volts of Taser. Daniel's last words, *Trust me*. For months, Mark had puzzled over why Daniel had wanted to steal something he already owned. He now had his answer.

Two more articles in the Life & Arts section of *The Financial Times Weekend*. The first was a human interest piece, a tragic story of two young lovers, the loss to the scientific community, a presumed suicide. It included a picture of a young Daniel Loginovsky, the quintessential geek, looked nothing like Daniel Logan.

The second was headlined 'Foundation Established to Advance Research in Theoretical Physics'. Mark read on with growing interest as Stuart Lassiter spoke of how his venture capital firm had been moved by the tragic story of Daniel Loginovsky and Michelle Faubourg. After discussion with the university, they had agreed that the intellectual property rights for Loginovsky's research, including the IA search engine, would be vested in the newly formed Loginovsky-Faubourg Trust to fund scholarships and post-doctoral research in the sciences. When asked about the moral implications of naming a trust at the world's leading academic institution after a murderer, Lassiter had replied, "It was a tragedy. We will probably never know what really happened. By all accounts, Daniel Loginovsky was a gentle, peaceful academic. He was not the kind of man to murder his fiancé. Michelle's tragic death was the result of a botched robbery."

He went inside to make a fresh espresso. Waiting for the Moka pot to boil, he idly flipped through a stack of mail, the usual, mostly bills and junk mail. One envelope, though, grabbed his attention, the contents stiff as if on card stock. He opened it and began laughing. It was a personal invitation from Daniel Logan to join the Board of Directors of the Loginovsky-Faubourg Trust.

Yes, Daniel," he said aloud, "Perhaps we could have been friends."